"I absolutely loved this super fun, believably romantic, and emotionally thoughtful novel. In fact, I can't remember the last time I smiled so much while reading a book. Carlie Walker will be an auto-buy author for me."

—Annabel Monaghan, author of
Nora Goes Off Script and *Summer Romance*

"Steamy, swoony, and laugh-out-loud funny, *The Takedown* is part Finlay Donovan mystery, part Emily Henry rom-com—and 100 percent perfect. The clever dialogue! The hot bodyguard! The twists I didn't see coming! I couldn't turn the pages fast enough and can't wait to see what Carlie Walker writes next."

—Colleen Oakley, *USA Today* bestselling author of
The Mostly True Story of Tanner & Louise

"Carlie Walker's debut novel is an absolute knockout! Her sparkling wit and keep-'em-guessing plot had me totally smitten and also dreaming of a new career as a spy. One minute I was laughing, the next I was swooning, the next I was gasping in shock at the brilliant plot twists. This book is for everyone who (correctly) insists that *Speed* is a romance!"

—Falon Ballard, author of *Just My Type*

"Riotously fun and perfectly swoony, *The Takedown* is the spy rom-com you didn't know you needed. I loved every page."

—Allison Winn Scotch, bestselling author of *The Rewind*

"*The Takedown* by Carlie Walker is hands down a master class in romantic comedy writing. The plot is original and thrilling and the heat between Sydney and Nick is a literal inferno right off the bat. Carlie has taken the genre to a new level with her razor-sharp prose, quick wit, and genuinely hilarious dialogue. I love everything about this book. I'm a Carlie Walker fan for life. The easiest five stars ever."　　　　—Lizzy Dent, author of *The Summer Job*

"Sizzling with romantic tension, *The Takedown* effortlessly blends romance, action, and shifting sibling dynamics into one firecracker of a story—you won't want to put this one down!"
　　　　　　　—Kayla Olson, author of *The Reunion*

"Walker makes her adult debut with this might-be-mob caper that is both a romantic comedy and a holiday mystery, complete with snow, carols, and gorgeous bodyguards wrapped in a bow."
　　　　　　　—*Library Journal* (starred review)

Also by Carlie Walker

The Takedown

CODE WORD
Romance

Carlie Walker

BERKLEY ROMANCE
NEW YORK

BERKLEY ROMANCE
Published by Berkley
An imprint of Penguin Random House LLC
penguinrandomhouse.com

Book design by Jenni Surasky

Library of Congress Cataloging-in-Publication Data

Names: Walker, Carlie, author.
Title: Code word romance / Carlie Walker.
Description: First edition. | New York: Berkley Romance, 2025.
Identifiers: LCCN 2024024325 (print) | LCCN 2024024326 (ebook) |
ISBN 9780593640418 (trade paperback) | ISBN 9780593640425 (ebook)
Subjects: LCGFT: Romance fiction. | Novels.
Classification: LCC PS3623.A35884 C63 2025 (print) |
LCC PS3623.A35884 (ebook) | DDC 813/.6—dc23/eng/20240604
LC record available at https://lccn.loc.gov/2024024325
LC ebook record available at https://lccn.loc.gov/2024024326

First Edition: March 2025

Printed in the United States of America
1st Printing

To everyone who supported me during my pregnancy, as I tried my best to write this book; Leo and I are forever grateful.

And to my parents, for everything, always.

CODE WORD
Romance

PROLOGUE

ROME, ITALY

Night air slaps my face. We're speeding faster on the motorcycle, swerving around a restaurant with patio tables, and I accidently clip one, rattling several plates full of antipasti. A glass of Aperol spritz topples. Blood-orange liquid stains the napkins, and—"Sorry! *Scusi!*" I say, both words emerging with a wheeze. No time to stop, though. I'm too focused, too rattled, too aware of Flynn's fingers, which are digging—harder now—into the curve above my hip bones.

"This may be a bad time to tell you!" I shout over my shoulder, unable to stem the terror in my voice. "But I've never driven a motorcycle before!"

"You *think*?" Flynn bleats out, and immediately I picture his face, how his pupils must be dilating with every dangerous zip of acceleration. "Make a left! Left, Max!"

"I'm trying!" I fire back, easing up on the throttle for a second, and . . . where's the turn signal on this thing? *Don't be stupid, Max.* They shouldn't know I'm turning! Makes it more difficult to follow me. Before the traffic light flashes green, I bite the inside of my cheek and just go, blasting across the intersection to a symphony of horns. A man stops short in his Fiat, yelling out the window, *"Muoia, signora!"*

I don't speak much Italian, but I know that one. *Die, lady.*

Unfortunately, Fiat man isn't the only one who wishes me dead.

My grip tightens on the motorcycle handlebars. "Are they still following us?"

Flynn checks, the hard plane of his stomach pressed against my back. He's warm, like Italian summer, and I feel the way his body moves: a sharp head-flick, a quick glance at the trailing cars. "Three of them now."

Three? A peek at my mirrors reveals—Flynn's right. Two black cars, probably bulletproof, and someone following them on a Vespa. Which almost makes me laugh. Driving a Vespa to an assassination is like bringing a loofah stick to a sword fight.

At least no one is shooting at us.

"Any second," Flynn shouts over the traffic, "they're going to start shooting at us."

"Well . . . *shit!*" I say, because it's the only thing I can get out. I'm usually more articulate than this. More composed than this. To be fair, though, it's only seven o'clock at night—the summer sky has just turned a dusky pink; I haven't even had my evening gelato—and two separate people have already tried to kill me.

Or rather, two people have tried to kill *Sofia*.

Flynn slips his hands tighter around my waist, gripping me closer, almost cradling me—and I'm not thinking about it. Not thinking about the heat of him; the crisp, clean scent of him; the look on his face two nights ago when he slowly unbuttoned his shirt, letting the fabric pool in a puddle on the floor—or the way my cheek brushed against the bare skin of his chest as he held me. At this moment, I know that Flynn is just holding on for the ride. Just praying that I don't end the assignment this way. *This can't be how it ends.* The two of us, crashing into a porchetta stand by the Campo de' Fiori, or losing control outside of the Piazza del Paradiso, toppling into a group of tourists who'll *click, click, click* their cameras. Then, front-page news. International news. **PRIME MINISTER OF SUMMERLAND VICTIM OF TRAGIC ACCIDENT BEFORE EVEN MORE TRAGIC ASSASSINATION**. Or something snappier than that. That's a terribly uncreative headline.

"Take the Via dei Baullari." Flynn's breath caresses my ear, words almost eaten by the hum of the motorcycle.

"You say that like I know where that is!"

"On your right!"

"*When* on my right?" I bat back, weaving past a Lamborghini and a jewelry store, shiny gold rings winking at us in the windows.

Flynn's chin is almost resting on my shoulder. "Now! Now!"

We make a hard turn, tires gripping the ancient road, and I have a flash of how others are seeing us—a woman in a bright cream pantsuit and heels, a man in a dashing beige jacket, and a busted-up bike that looks newly rescued from a second-rate junkyard. Cars and a Vespa chasing after them. Bullets soon to fly through the air. This isn't how my Italian getaway was supposed to go, is it?

No. No, it isn't.

It will be easy, they said. *Straightforward*, they said. Just sit there, and look polished, and don't open your mouth. Shake hands with the right people. Smile politely but not like an American; not too wide, not with too many teeth. Do what you're told, and it'll feel like a vacation. *Don't you want a vacation, Max? A simple job in beautiful Italy?*

That was before the disastrous TV broadcast. Before the incident at the museum gala. Before I met Flynn again, and my whole world turned upside down.

"They're gaining on us," he says, once again into my ear. It's obvious; Flynn is trying hard to steady his voice, trying to be the cool and calm one in this scenario. Despite this, something in his throat gutters. "Our best chance is to make a sharp turn some-where, pull off where they can't see. Confuse them. Let them pass us . . ."

"Where are the *police*?" I gasp out. "Where's the armed escort? They should be—"

"*There*," Flynn says, but he's talking about a gap between build-ings. A little nook by a flower shop, barely large enough for a motor-cycle. I take the chance, jamming on the brakes, back tire skidding to the left. My pulse hammers in my ears, climbs higher as we slip into the alleyway. I cut the engine. Thick stone walls bear down on us, and the air smells like . . . focaccia. Flowers and focaccia, yeasty and sweet, but I hold my breath. As if our hunters can hear me. As if one tiny sniffle will give me up.

Luckily, it's a Saturday night in Rome. The streets are stuffed with distractions. Above the sound of tourists laughing, horns beeping, gallery doors squeaking open and closed, there's the dis-tinct noise of two armored cars rattling by the alleyway, fast. Fol-lowed by a Vespa, *zzzz-zip*, even faster.

Behind me, Flynn also seems to be holding his breath. His stillness is palpable, not a muscle moving. As soon as the vehicles pass, he loosens a little, whispering, "Close call."

I swallow, gathering myself, feeling blood return to the tips of my fingers. I unclench my fists from the handlebars. "What now?"

I'm asking Flynn, although my body already knows. I'm al-ready swinging my leg off the bike, stamping the ground, travel-ing forward on foot. We can't stay here long. We can't wait for them to reach the main road again, figure out what we've done, and throw their cars in reverse . . .

I shrug off the cream blazer, about to ditch it in the street, when—at the other end of the alleyway, no less than thirty feet ahead—someone appears. A shadowy silhouette in the dying sun, moving to block the exit.

My heart claws at my throat.

This person . . . there's a knife in their hand.

And I *know* them.

1

KENNEBUNKPORT, MAINE
Six Days Earlier

Food has always been my life. The rush of the kitchen, browned butter sizzling in a cast-iron pan, the hard *crack* of a lobster claw. I've never wanted to be anything other than a chef. My dad bought me my first chef's coat when I was ten years old, and I wore that thing everywhere—until the starch white took on this Dijon mustard hue, and Mom insisted that maybe the other kids at school would pick on me a little less if I wore, say, overalls.

Come to think of it, she had a point, but I had a wildly optimistic dream. I'd open a restaurant by the water, serve hot cups of chowder on snowy days. I'd spend late nights in the kitchen, batch-testing new recipes, and in the morning, I'd whip up potato doughnuts with fresh, local ingredients.

In short, I'd be happy.

"You don't look so good," my boss observes. He's giving me the once-over from across the rough-cut lawn, face a mask of sympathy, and I wonder what he's referring to specifically: the holey Boston Terriers sweatshirt I've had since college, the thick sheen of sweat on my forehead, or the general vibe I've been giving off lately, that I may or may not scream into my throw pillows at night. I'm almost thirty years old, so far in debt that it makes my eyes water, and I've spent the last hour lugging cheap boxed wine from the catering van.

Peeling off the sweatshirt, sticky in the heat, I readjust my tee and give him what I hope is a reassuring smile. "Just got a little warm."

"You sure that's all?" he asks. "You really look terrible."

"Yeah, thanks, Andy," I say, puffing my bangs from my eyes. I'm gentle about it, because I'm always gentle—and honestly, after the year I've had, I'd be concerned for me, too.

The breeze cools me off a little as I zigzag around the outdoor bar, pour a glass of ice water from a pitcher, and take a swig.

This is my twenty-seventh wedding of the summer, and it's only June. Each one goes something like this: beautiful couple, ceremony on the waterfront, reception on the lawn outside the picture-perfect inn. Charcuterie boards, glasses clinking, the flash of a hundred photographs. And me, rushing around, making sure that everyone's having a good time. I'm front of house now, a task rabbit, the person who freshens your drink, asks if you'd like cocktail sauce with that shrimp, and occasionally breaks up fights between groomsmen when they've had too much champagne. (*Excuse me, can you guys hug it out?*)

Don't get me wrong, I'm incredibly grateful for this job. I'm also incredibly aware that it's the only work I could find—at a second-rate catering company, for an hourly wage that hasn't chipped away a dollar of my debt. For the past three months, I've been living off discount macaroni, expired blueberry pancake mix, and whatever's left over on the catering trays at the end of the night.

Gary, the inn's resident goose, starts squawking by the waterfront, and it reminds me to check my watch. I'll have to shoo him back to hell before the guests arrive in an hour. Gary is what you might call an instrument of chaos (during two of our May weddings, he bit the brides), and these seaside weddings are already chaotic enough. Something about the salt air, I think? During my last shift, the maid of honor gave a heartfelt speech about how she once made out with Nicolas Cage at a bat mitzvah, before ramming her Kia Soul straight into the side of the inn.

When I clunk down my water glass, I notice that one of the guests has already arrived. *Way* early. She's hovering several yards from the bar, by the empty cake table, and she is full-out staring at me. I corral a few strawberry blonde strands into a bun on the top of my head, adding a polka-dotted headband that I keep behind the bar. Do I really look *that* bad today? Do I have something on my face?

Or does she know me from somewhere?

She's in her early forties, with short chestnut hair, and has a gaze that could crack eggs. No one else is around—everyone's disappeared inside the inn, prepping for the reception—so it's just me and her on the sun-drenched lawn, like two cowboys facing off at daybreak.

"Can I . . . help you?" I ask, a tingle running down my neck.

The soft grass bends under her footsteps. "Are you aware," she asks, making up the distance between us, hands in the pockets of her trench coat, "that you look exactly like Sofia Christiansen?"

Ah, okay, so that's what this is about. The tiny fist in my stomach unclenches.

I get this question a lot. Sofia and I have the same body shape—moderately tall, rounded hips. Our faces are essentially identical: square jaw, light brown eyes, with a look that sometimes says, *I'm more powerful than you give me credit for.* The only *minor* difference is, at thirty, Sofia Christiansen is the youngest female prime minister in history. Magazine spreads across Europe herald how glam, assertive, and competent she is at leading a country. I'm, as has been established, ferrying two-dollar boxed wine across a lawn that gives me ankle hives, after my life exploded into flames. Right now, I'm also wearing frayed jean shorts and a Maine State Fair T-shirt with a talking raccoon on it. World-leader material? Perhaps not.

I offer a polite nod and a muted shrug. "So they tell me."

"It's uncanny," the woman says, stepping closer. Too close. "You're like twins. Are you related?"

"Nope, it's just one of those random look-alike things . . ." My shoulders scrunch together as I scooch around the bar, then past her, hoping to leave it there. I need to change into my catering uniform, set out the lobster roll trays, and deal with Gary before he starts pooping all over the lawn chairs.

Unfortunately, trench-coat woman doesn't get the hint. "We're rather low on time, so I think it's best if I speak for a short while, and you don't speak, and then we can move on from there. We've established that you're familiar with Sofia Christiansen, prime minister of Summerland. What you might not know is someone would very much like to assassinate her."

My chest starts to prickle with heat, little pops of red under the collar of my tee. I half spin around in my Birkenstocks, thinking *What kind of conversation is* this? Summerland, I do know. It's a small island nation off the coast of Norway: rocky cliffs, slate blue sea, puffins. That's where my grandmother was from. Those are the pictures I grew up with, black-and-white snaps of the ocean, a coast I'd visited only in my imagination. But everything else—the prime minister bit, the assassination bit—makes me wonder if this woman's dipped into something a little harder than the boxed wine.

"I say someone," she continues, "although we've narrowed down the suspects, logically, to a Summerlandian crime family. Imagine the Hells Angels but more Scandinavian; they ride actual bicycles. The first attempted hit came directly after the prime minister cracked down on their illegal gambling and weapons trafficking networks in April. Did you catch the hospital incident on the news?"

I blink, long and slow, eyelashes flicking in the sunlight. Who *didn't* see that news story? It was everywhere, a constant video loop of the prime minister ducking and covering outside of a children's hospital, a bullet lodged in her bodyguard's arm; after a moment, she ran over to put pressure on the wound, shielding *him*. The footage gave me a lump in my throat, all of those kids peeking out of their windows, checking if the prime minister was all right—if she was still coming inside to read them a book.

My mom even texted me about one of the news clips: **Can't believe how much she looks like you. Scary to watch as your mother!**

"You're probably wondering what this has to do with you," the stranger says, over the sound of Gary, honking. "Normally we'd spend months cultivating an asset, but with the time constraint, I have no choice but to be blunt. We'd like to hire you as a decoy. To make sure the assassination doesn't happen."

I'm sorry. What?

The drum in my chest starts pounding in an unsteady beat.

When I take a sideways step, she matches me. "I know it's not an easy pill to swallow, but—by some miraculous trick of genetics—you and the prime minister look remarkably alike. Minus the blondish hair color, of course, which we'll change. But your bone structure is identical. Eyes, height, body shape, indistinguishable. No one could possibly spot the difference. So you'll come with us to Italy, where the prime minister is set to go on her yearly vacation. You'll play an easy role in a difficult-to-secure—"

"Who is *us*?" I hiss out, a sound like fuzzy, far-off waves crashing in my ears. I understand the words that are coming out of her mouth, but they don't . . . make any *sense*. Italy? She wants me to pretend I'm a *prime minister* in *Italy*?

"You can call me Gail," the woman says, pointedly dodging my question.

Gail. No one intimidating is called Gail. There's also something about the way she says it. *You can call me.* Not *My name is.* Why does that make the breath catch in my throat?

I've left my phone in the catering van. Should I call 911, just in case this person is as dangerous as she is misinformed?

"And *your* name is Margaux Adams," Gail says, following me down the wedding aisle. She's walking fast enough that the tie of her trench coat *flap-flap*s like a beached squid, and I'm secretly hoping that Gary will attack it. "Shortened inexplicably to 'Max.' Decent grades in college before dropping out to test your luck in the restaurant industry. Used to hostess during the summers at a place called Lobster in the Rough, but your first real job was . . . Robbie's Clam Hut, if I'm not mistaken? Worked your way up. From Robbie's to LaRocca to Pierre's by the Sea to a restaurant of your very own. Charming place. Frida's, wasn't it?"

It's like the blood stops moving in my body. Frida's, named after my grandmother. Frida's, with her white-brick façade and sweeping back porch and windows that let in all the winter sun. My dream. I remember every dish I ever served—every fish I ever filleted, every oyster I ever shucked. I remember standing in the kitchen for the last time, flicking off the lights, and crying so hard I retched.

That was four months ago. My restaurant didn't survive the pandemic. We were open for two and a half glorious years before the crash hit, before I blew through my governmental loans, before I accepted money from family and friends to keep Frida's afloat. She sank anyway.

I force myself to turn and look at Gail by the edge of the parking lot, the corners of my eyes threatening tears. "Honestly, why would you bring up my restaurant? That's cruel."

She takes another step gingerly toward me, eyes sharp. "No, Max. That's the CIA. This is how we make the world a safer place. I'm showing you there's something you've lost, and there's something I need, and we can meet each other in the middle."

CIA. She said *CIA.* The knot in my stomach tightens into a fist again, because it feels . . . *true.*

"You work for the CIA," I repeat slowly, tasting the words. Bitter.

"Mmm." Gail nods before reaching into her jacket pocket, pulling out a security badge that reads (helpfully) *Central Intelligence Agency.* "You could work for the CIA, too, as an asset. While I might be new to the CIA, I come with twenty years' experience at the FBI, and—"

"Stop." I hold up my hands, pockets of stars bursting around my eyes. I'm dizzy, like I've been on my feet in the kitchen for two shifts too long. *"Not now, Gary!"*

The goose, who's come over to investigate—nipping the backs of my knees—toddles off into the parking lot.

"If you're worried about the precedent," Gail plods on, "body doubles are common. Many notable figures have one. There was a British general, Bernard Montgomery, who spent most of World War II in hiding. His body double commanded troops in his absence. And you're lucky. You look so much like Sofia, you won't need any plastic surgery. No—" In the air between us, Gail does the universal motion for scissors, snipping.

"What are you snipping?" I half shriek, waving my hands at her. "What was that supposed to be snipping?"

"Forget I mentioned it! As I was saying, the CIA brought me in because of my extended experience with crime families. Did you hear about the Jones takedown over Christmas last year? That was me. That was my agent. Anyway, we've picked up chatter that this family—the one who's targeting the prime minister—will attempt to finish the job on her upcoming trip to Italy. By stepping in, you'll buy us time to gather enough evidence to bring them down, while keeping the prime minister safe in the process . . . So, what are your thoughts?"

Thoughts? What are my *thoughts*? "I think you should get the hell away from me."

Gail tuts. "Max, just consider the—"

But I'm already storming off, at a walk and then a brisk jog, every instinct in my body telling me *run*.

2

rarely drink. But late that night, when I get back to my apartment, I pour myself another glass of tap water and add a shot of
whiskey. It's cinnamon flavored and objectively disgusting, the
only liquor in the cupboard, left over from my ex-best-friend's
bachelorette party almost two years earlier; even with the water,
it burns going down my throat. I don't stop chugging until the
glass is empty, until I'm wiping my mouth with the back of my
hand.

"Calvin?" I gasp. "Are you in here?"

In here sounds better than *home.* I wouldn't use that word to
describe our apartment. My old loft was two blocks away from
Frida's. Every window on the south side had a view of the bay, and
in the mornings before kitchen prep, I'd sit in my grandmother's hand-me-down armchair with a mug of chamomile tea and
watch the boats come in, not fully realizing just how blissful my
life was.

I miss those mornings. I miss everything about that time in
my life.

From somewhere in the (albeit small) depths of our apartment,
I hear a muted *Sup. Sup,* for my roommate, Calvin, is still very

much in today's vernacular. He did not leave it in 1992. When I first met him, he reminded me of that strange roommate in *Notting Hill*, the one who hotboxes in his scuba suit. Only, Calvin has exceptional hair. He briefly moonlighted as a hair model before finding his calling as an employee of the York County tax bureau—and, like *Notting Hill* man, is also perpetually high.

Tumbling out of his bedroom in a gray sweatsuit ensemble, he offers me a glazed blink. "What happened tonight?" This is Calvin's favorite question. It's like he's very gently interrogating me, not asking if I had a good evening.

"Not much," I say, shrugging, although the shrug comes out too fidgety. My shoulders jump, jive, and suddenly I'm looking for something to do with my hands. Eating. I could eat something. Riffling through our cabinets, I try to process everything that's just happened, but how is that *possible*? How does a person even begin to process a CIA solicitation before a wedding, or—

Bingo! The third cabinet reveals a semi-stale bag of Humpty Dumpty sour cream and clam potato chips. I shove a fistful in my mouth as Calvin cocks his head in my direction, curly black hair springing over his ears. After observing me for a second, he circles his pointer finger around my face, finally landing in a gentle nose-boop, like I'm a golden retriever. "Something's *different* about you."

"Couldn't tell you what that is," I say. Really, I can't. I'd sound like I'd hit my head on the bar and hallucinated Gail's body-double request. "Hey, do me a favor? If anyone comes to the door for me, can you not answer it?"

"What if it's a pizza?"

I speak around potato chips, pushing my bangs back with the polka-dotted headband. "I'm not going to order any pizza."

"What if you change your mind?"

"I won't."

"Right," Calvin says. "You want to rewatch that Australian show we like, about those farmers who're looking for wives?"

"As tempting as that is," I reply, "I'm . . . I think I'm going to hit the hay. Maybe another time."

He wishes me good night and hands me the potato chip bag to take with me. I like Calvin. It was a random roommate situation. He had an ultracheap spare room; I needed somewhere to live. That's it. Well, that, and I was fairly confident that if this did turn out to be a serial killer situation, I could take him. He may or may not have a turtle living in his bathroom. Not a pet turtle. Like, one he rescued and is rehabilitating in the bathtub. Say what you want about him, but the man is wonderfully soft.

In my room, I wrench open the window and let the night air wash over my skin. I feel shaky, sick. The breeze helps; soap scent from the laundromat downstairs hits my nose as I cocoon myself under my Nana's summer quilt, mentally replaying Gail's speech. *Assassin. Prime minister. Vacation. Easy role!* The more I think about it, the more batshit it sounds. If the CIA thing is true, if someone *is* trying to kill Sofia Christiansen in Italy, wouldn't the smart plan be just to cancel the damn vacation?

Polishing off the rest of the potato chips, I whip out my phone, tapping the cracked screen to wake it up, and google the prime minister of Summerland. I've done this before. Never so intently, with my heart jumping in my throat. Like before, though, all the images that pop up are sparkly. Clean-cut shots of a clean-cut person. In one, she's commanding parliament with a pensive expression, dark brown hair pulled into a low bun. In another, she's sporting a black-sequined blazer and tailored shorts, heels sky-high, using a small handbag to shield her face from paparazzi. **PRIME MINISTER OR PARTY PRINCESS?** That's what the headline reads, and it strikes me as dramatically unfair. Surely the woman's allowed to have a life? She takes only one vacation a year—an annual trip to Rome and the beaches of Positano, just like she did when she was a kid.

We're not related somehow, are we? Somewhere down the line? That's crossed my mind before. We're definitely not first cousins or second cousins, or anything super close—but Nana Frida *was* from Summerland. Everyone on the island has a hint of similarity.

I click on another article. According to British *Vogue*, Sofia has reframed her platform to lobby even harder for women's access to education around the world; she's single, loving it; she's a mental health advocate, with a heart that's equal parts gold and steel. There's a picture of her opening a shelter for homeless cats, another of her supporting a martial arts class for survivors of domestic assault. She's put a near-total end to weapons trafficking in Summerland. It's hard not to like her, and *really* hard not to see the glaring similarities between us: the roundness of our ears, the freckles by our noses, the way she cocks her head when she's thinking, the way *I'm* doing that, right now, at the screen.

"If I'm too forceful," Sofia says in a YouTube video clip, "too powerful, speak my mind too clearly, I'm labeled words that I won't repeat here. If I'm quieter, gentler, then I'm meek. I'm not powerful *enough* to lead my nation. And there is no in between. There is no middle ground for women. In some people's eyes, we are always one or the other, aren't we?"

By three in the morning, I've gone so far down the Sofia rabbit hole, I'm unconsciously whispering at the video, at all of her videos, wondering if I can get my vowels to sound like hers.

Body double. Could I actually pull that off? I mean, seriously, could I? How hard would it be to play a prime minister on vacation? If anyone did try to come after me . . . I *am* fit. After months of manual labor, hauling everything from kegs to banquet tables,

I'm in the best shape of my life. I feel like I could run pretty darn fast, if I tried, and dodge just about anything that's thrown at me. Plus, goose shooing aside, it's not like I'd miss much back home, and wouldn't this give me a purpose? Who deserves protection more than a woman spearheading all these international causes, who's fearlessly leading her country and—

For crying out loud, Max. Do you even hear *yourself?*

I chuck my phone across the room, yank my quilt over my head, and force myself to sleep.

The next morning, someone is pounding at my door.

My eyes spring open, the heels of my hands swiping at my face. Outside is the muted pink of sunrise, and it takes only a second before everything from yesterday comes flashing back. I know exactly who's at my door—and exactly what she wants. Calvin isn't answering. *Good! Good, Calvin.* Cautiously, I slip out of bed, black-and-white catering uniform half-unbuttoned, bangs plastered across my forehead. Through the front door peephole, I spy Gail's distorted frame, haunting my hallway.

Not today, Satan! The *last* thing I should do is open the door. Only, after the sixtieth knock, each one growing increasingly louder, the neighbors start banging on the walls. If we get another noise complaint, if I get kicked out of this apartment and can't afford rent anywhere else . . .

"We started off on the wrong foot," Gail says, thrusting a white paper bag through the newly opened doorway. "I brought bagels. You don't look like you slept well."

"Thank you," I say through gritted teeth.

She clearly thinks I mean about the bagels, not the insult. "Poppy seed," she says, waggling the bag. *Dammit.* Poppy seed is my favorite. Brushing past my shoulder, Gail cranes her neck into my apartment. "Perhaps this conversation might be better suited for inside your home. Is that charming roommate of yours about?"

My head's starting to throb. "I . . . I don't know. Probably?"

"Mmm," Gail says, pulling out her phone and shooting off a quick text. Asking for surveillance on Calvin's whereabouts? Less than three seconds later, her inbox pings. "Ah, he's gone out to purchase some coffee and what looks to be about two hundred grams of marijuana. A little much for a Monday morning, but to each their own, I suppose."

"Look." I rub my thumb, hard, between my eyebrows. "I said no. I said no to what you're asking. So, if you don't mind—"

"Oh, but I do mind," Gail says, fully pushing past me now. "You didn't say no about the *bagels*. The bagels really are crucial to this part of the operation."

I snatch the bag from her hand, just to get her to shut up about them. "They're not drugged, are they? I'm not going to bite into one and wake up on a plane to Positano?" Gail pauses at my hunter green sofa, swiping off a few crumbs before smoothing the back of her coat and sitting down. This only adds to my snippiness. "I thought people like you wouldn't wear trench coats."

She cocks her head. "People like me?"

"Spies. It just seems a little obvious."

Gail crosses her legs, folding both hands on top of her knees. "Well, Max, I wouldn't call myself a spy." She glances around the apartment, at the stacks of used coupon booklets and a full bin of empty ranch dressing bottles. "I would call myself your best option to get out of this hellhole."

"Hey!" I'm genuinely offended. "We have a microwave."

"I am absolutely sure, Max, that hell has microwaves." Gail is the type of person who says your name a lot in conversation—and not in the friendly way. In the condescending way. As if she's speaking to a disobedient six-year-old. "May I ask what is with the ranch dressing? Surely one can't need that much. That's nearly . . . fifteen bottles."

At least I can answer that one. "My roommate gets stoned a lot. He puts ranch on everything." Tired and frustrated, I plop down in the opposing fold-out chair. "Even if you are who you say you are, you've made a mistake, okay? You don't want a washed-up chef. My main skill used to be making really, really good clam chowder, which isn't—"

"Did you know," Gail says, cutting me off, "that Julia Child was an asset for the CIA? Chef, too, wasn't she? You'd be just like her, in a foreign country, carrying out clandestine duties. Who doesn't want to be like Julia Child?" Gail perks up even more. "Think of this as a getaway for *you*. Don't you want a nice vacation, Max? What we're asking, it isn't hard. Mostly, you'll just sit in a beach chair, read a book. It's a simple job in beautiful Italy. The food will be exquisite. Eating with the season. Fresh pancetta and buttered noodles. Lemon gnocchi . . ."

"And all for the low, low price of . . . possible death!" I say, like I'm a game show host.

"Max," Gail reasons, "we all trick ourselves into believing that we're safe. The truth is that every time we step out our doors, we're in danger. Every time we drive our cars, we're in danger. Every time we step in our showers, *danger*. Eating, danger. Sleeping, danger. Do you know how many people accidentally strangle themselves in their bedsheets every year?"

I stare at her, unimpressed and vaguely horrified. "Hallmark would not hire you."

"Fine," Gail says, clapping her knees and rising to a stand. "I thought that some shut-eye might help you think clearly about all of this. Five million dollars is a lot of money."

The living room tilts sideways. The ringing returns to my ears. "What did you just say?"

"Five million dollars. The five million dollars we're offering you, if you complete the assignment to our specifications."

"You never mentioned five million dollars." I'm standing now, too. All the blood is rushing to my face. "If you were going to offer five million dollars, you should've led with five million dollars."

"I'll note that for next time," Gail says, infuriatingly. "Although, it could have been that I purposefully withheld that information, knowing that you'd say no at the first approach, and this is all part of the gentle process of acceptance. I should also mention that I know about your financial situation."

Memories flash through my brain, ones that always come when I'm low—of my mom, stopping by my apartment with a few groceries when she noticed the barren state of my fridge; of my dad, selling his Chris-Craft for cash and draping his arm around my shoulder. *It's just a boat, Max-a-million.* But that boat was his whole damn life. "It's bad."

"Yes, it's horrendous."

Actually, it's worse than horrendous. Horrendous would *just* be losing my restaurant. Horrendous would *just* be an insurmountable mountain of debt. Here's what I'm looking at: the dissolution of every relationship I valued. I borrowed money from *everyone.*

And I lost every penny.

"It's not often, Max, that one gets the opportunity to completely turn their life around within a matter of days. Think of your parents. Think of what they could do with a share of that money. Retire, perhaps? And your friend Jules. Your relationship's a bit strained, isn't it? Wouldn't you like to mend that in seven simple days? Just a quick trip to Rome and the Amalfi Coast, then back again. You can return to your . . ." She gazes around at a stack of moldy pizza boxes. "Your home. Move on with your life. Maybe even open a new restaurant. This isn't just an opportunity; it's a time machine. Turn back the clock. Right your wrongs. Reclaim your—"

"Hello, hello!" Calvin has wandered through the door, plastic grocery bag stuffed with coffee beans and weed. "Who's our new friend?"

"I'm from the Maine State Lottery," Gail says automatically, turning to Calvin. "Your roommate has won one of our secret cash prizes. An all-expenses-paid European getaway."

Calvin's already-dilated pupils widen at me. "Dude, *really*?"

Intrinsically, I know I have seconds. I know that the deal's on the table, and something tells me if I don't take it now, I'll regret it for the rest of my life. My family deserves this chance . . . and honestly, if I need another reason, Sofia deserves it, too. Protecting her would be, by far, the noblest thing I've ever done.

Swallowing the gigantic lump in my throat, I do my best to smile like I *have* just won the lottery. "Yes. I'm going on vacation."

3

Gail isn't kidding about the time constraint. We leave within the hour. At the very last second, a tremble starting in my hand, I scribble a note (pathetically, on a bright yellow Post-it) for my parents to find if anything does happen to me—*I'm in Italy. I love you both more than words. I'm sorry*—and shove it under my pillow. Then, it's quick into a black van, Gail chattering while I mostly stare out the window, trying to keep my breathing steady. The bay flashes by. Little peeks at the ocean between concrete buildings. When the city center fades away, colonial houses pop up to take the place of businesses. Swing sets and aboveground pools. Kids running through sprinklers on sparkling, green lawns. Happiness, summer, life.

By the time the driver drops us off at Portland International Jetport, my left eyelid is twitching. "So . . . what are the odds of me actually getting murdered here?"

"You want me to give you a distinct percentage?" Gail tilts her head from side to side. "Thirty-six percent?"

My throat hitches. "Jesus *Christ*. It's that high?"

"I really have no idea. I pulled that number clear out of the air. I thought it would soothe you to have something concrete."

"It did not soothe me."

"Oh. My mistake, then. Seven percent."

Needless to say, I don't sleep on the chartered flight to Italy. I spend most of the time stress-munching mini pretzels, watching preloaded videos of Sofia's speeches, and whenever I even *think* about closing my eyes, I picture myself biting into a poisoned *cannolo*. Cream squirts from the crunchy shell as I swiftly keel over in the street . . . before, to add insult to injury, getting run over by a Vespa. Why my brain has settled on this very specific method of assassination, I can't say, but by the time we land at Rome-Ciampino International Airport, I'm paranoid; if you tapped me on the shoulder with a feather, I'd swear it was Big Bird come to murder me.

"You're pale," Gail says to me, gripping the steering wheel of a BMW sedan. We've picked it up from the airport parking garage. Who left it there? Someone from the CIA? The interior smells of high-end perfume and those tiny, thin cigarettes. "Are you not holding up well?"

"No, I'm just—" We swerve around a Fiat 500, whose driver has the audacity to obey the speed limit. Gail drives like she's fleeing the scene of a crime, paying very little attention to trivial things like stoplights, stop signs, or traffic laws. In the passenger's seat, I thread my fingers through the grab handle, holding tight. "Just thinking. Overthinking."

"Don't do that."

"Sorry."

"Also, don't apologize," Gail chides. "Prime ministers never apologize."

"Seems like maybe they should," I mutter, considering one or two in particular. Then, a little louder: "Are we headed to the hotel now? Didn't you say we're going to Positano first?" The small digital clock on the BMW's dashboard reads a staggering 4:28 a.m. Outside the windows is a sleepy Rome, the outskirts lined with spindly trees, stonework walls, and posters for big-budget American films. It feels impossible to take it all in, to process that I'm in *Rome*—that any moment, we could turn off the highway and come face-to-face with famous cathedrals, art museums, the Spanish Steps.

"We have a few items to tick before that," Gail says, only half answering my question. "You'll meet with your handler—"

"Hold on. I thought that *you* were my handler."

"No. As I was saying, we'll do something about your hair. Catalog the rest of your visible appearance, see if there are any scars to cover up, or any freckles we need to add. Then we'll dive into your prep work: how to present yourself as Sofia. But don't worry. It won't be too extensive, considering we're time-pressed, and you'll mostly just be sitting there."

Sitting duck, my brain whispers. I ignore it.

"Your handler will take care of the bulk of your training," Gail continues. "You two are going to be like peas in a pod by the end."

By the end. Not ominous at all! I nod tightly, adjusting the neckline of my faded white tee, pretending this conversation is very normal. "Okay. What're they like?"

"Competent," Gail says.

"And?"

"Tall," she says, leaving it at that.

A dozen follow-up questions spring to mind (*What's their name? How long have they been with the CIA? Have they trained people to walk into positions of power before?*), but Gail jerks the car to the left, narrowly missing an early-morning pedestrian—and I spot a flash of the Roman aqueducts by the side of the road, arches glowing in the moonlight. An exhalation of breath leaves me in a small, awed gasp. They're magnificent. They're something I never, *ever* thought I'd see.

The only stamps in my passport are Canadian. After months

of working at Lobster in the Rough, a local seafood joint, I'd cross the border with my family at the end of each summer, holing up in a pine cabin with bunk beds. Bear repellent was involved. We'd start with washing all the sheets and wiping away dust from the windowsills. There'd be packed lunches—sandwiches, mostly, with Hannaford deli meat and sliced cheese—and hiking would be the only activity on the agenda. Sometimes, hammock swinging. Sometimes, a freezing dip in the local lake.

This is not that. This city, even in the half-dark, even on the outskirts, is still so elegantly alive. When Gail takes the next exit, the architecture changes. Limestone churches bloom from the ground. Terra-cotta-colored apartment complexes give way to community gardens. A few people are lingering, zipping around on scooters, smoking outside of shuttered newspaper stands, and I'm . . . feeling incredibly guilty, honestly. Who am I to deserve any semblance of a vacation?

Beyond that, this city is *romantic.* Perfect for couples. In an ideal world, I'd be here with someone other than trench-coat Gail. *That would require an actual relationship, Max.* Fast-paced restaurant work and romance don't mix well. The last guy I dated (Damien, fellow chef, with a sleeve of tattoos and a penchant for baking soufflés at three o'clock in the morning) told me that I always seemed too busy, *too casual about us.* Maybe that's true. Casual doesn't hurt.

The car turns again, residential streets giving way to even more glamorous surroundings. Here are the polished hotels and the columned cathedrals, the flower shops and gelaterias with sparkly glass windows. Brilliant little cafés with rolled-up awnings wait for their early-morning visitors. You can almost smell the espresso beans, lingering from late-night drinkers, and I *love* it. I am so instantaneously in love, it makes me feel sick. *You don't get to enjoy this. This isn't supposed to be fun.*

Gail throws the BMW into park outside of an eight-story apartment building. I peek out the window, neck craning up at the layers of wrought iron balconies, potted vines hanging over the edges. The building looks stately enough for a prime minister. "Is this where I'm staying?"

"Not quite. Get your bag." Gail fishes a rattling set of keys out of her coat pocket; it's a lighter coat for the weather. In Maine, there's always an under-chill, like winter is never more than a few footsteps away, but here, the early-summer morning is already washing over my skin. I step out into a flower-petal-blown street, wondering what the sunrise looks like over these buildings. I'm imagining orange. I'm imagining sherbet in neat glass bowls. "Hurry, Max."

"Yeah, sorry—" I catch myself. "Not sorry."

"Better."

Unlatching a delicate gate, Gail takes the marble steps two at a time, and I more than keep up with her, floor after floor. It's a small reminder that I'm capable. I really am fitter than I've ever been. My kind of restaurant work takes a while to leave you; you spend hours and hours on your feet, rushing between stations, barely pausing for water or food. Add that to the intense physicality of the last three months, and it's easy to trick myself into believing—just for a second—that my body's strong enough to dodge whatever might come my way.

You think you can outrun an assassin because you climbed some stairs?

Get a grip.

We stop at apartment 4B, with its lion-headed door knocker and less-than-conspicuous keypad. Gail types in a long code, shoves a key into the lock, and we're in. First impression? I'm shocked by how nice it is. Movies tell you that everything in the CIA is stiff: concrete walls, hard-looking chairs, underground bunkers with flickering yellow lights. Off to the side, maybe, a stressed-out guy is vigorously blacking out files, or leaning nervously over a computer. But *this*? This apartment is luscious. Gold-tasseled pillows sit plumply on velvet furniture. Sage green walls show off a variety of botanical prints. Above my head, a low chandelier dangles with delicate crystals, and I reach up to tip-tap one.

"Don't do that," Gail says.

"Right." I hold in the *sorry*.

"Hello?" Gail calls into the living room, stripping off her coat and hanging it on a standing rack carved into the shape of an olive tree. Underneath she's wearing a nondescript white button-up, and I wish I'd done the same. Something classy. I've settled for travel wear: black jeans and a comfy cotton shirt, with room to wiggle my toes in my Birkenstocks. "Come say hello to Max, please!"

There's commotion around the corner—and my stomach tells me with a little swoop that I'm nervous to meet this person. My handler? Who I'll be joined at the hip with for the next five days. In my mind, my handler looks identical to Sandra Bullock: sleek and agile, with a long brown ponytail and a face that says, *Let's get down to business*.

My assumptions are . . . off.

"Ah, there you are," Gail says to the man in the hallway. "Now that you're here, I'm going to pop back down to the car to make a few phone calls and maybe pick up some pastries around the corner. Anyone want anything from the shop? It opens in fifteen minutes. Yogurt? *Cornetto?* Max, he has my number. I'll leave you two to get reacquainted."

And then she does leave, swiftly, closing the door like she's shoving me off a cliff. I take one good look at my handler, at his tall frame and sea blue eyes, the undeniable coolness of his posture—effortlessly laid-back—and instantly, blood rushes to my ears. He winces with the tiniest hint of crow's-feet, the corner of his pretty mouth turned up, and the way his forehead creases triggers some long-buried memory, tugging at the core of me.

"Hi, Max," he says, silky smooth, voice like spearmint gum tastes.

I might black out for a second. Because it's impossible. Totally, absolutely impossible.

Standing there in the safe house foyer is the first and only man I've ever loved.

4

Flynn?" I manage with a gasp, my tongue starting to swell in my mouth. It *is* him, isn't it? The foyer might be spinning a little, but he's perfectly in focus. Unmistakable, even after all these years. I know him like the lyrics of the Johnny Cash songs we used to play on our Sunday road trips. I remember every note, every chord, every—

"It's okay," Flynn says, quickly stepping forward. The word *suave*, it was invented for this new version of him. Even in his plain black T-shirt and well-tailored khaki pants, beard short and freshly trimmed, he has an air of old Hollywood glamour, as if he's playing a CIA agent in a movie. "Max, it's okay."

Like hell it is!

"How—" I stammer. "How are you—?"

He holds up his hands, like he's about to subdue a bear. "Just take a deep breath."

"What the *fuck*, Flynn?" I burst out, definitely not leaning into that advice. The problem is, my head's swimming with memories. All at once, he's there. Eighteen years old, sun-kissed, on the beach. Dropping a steady stream of sand on my toes as I belly-laugh, clutching my knees on the beach towel. He's there in the restaurant where I was a hostess and he was a busboy, and we'd spend our breaks sneaking fried oysters from the kitchen, talking about sailing and school friends and everything in between. Flynn Forester. The first person I told: *I want to open my own restaurant.* The second guy I ever kissed, his lips brushing mine under midsummer fireworks, fingertips tracing the side of my cheek, and—

"I'm going to tell you this fast," Flynn says, keeping those hands up as I circle around him and he circles around me. We're our own miniature whirlpool, and it's pulling me under. "We have a lounge room in the station house where I was working. This was a couple weeks ago. Prime Minister Christiansen came on TV, and I made this offhand remark—that I knew someone, way back when, who looked like her. Next thing I know, I'm here, and you're here."

"No," I still say, the only thing I can *think* to say. His eyes are tracking circles around my face; he's obviously waiting for me to shout or scream or sock him in the abdomen. Each option has its merits, honestly, although I suspect that touching his abs would be like petting a block of wood. He's so *tall* now. So toned. "I don't get it. I don't understand this. You're . . ." I wave a hand at him, up and down, from the tips of his boots to his perfectly chiseled jawline, half-hidden under that tidy, tidy beard.

"I'm . . . ?" he says, raising a thick eyebrow, and there are too many ways to finish that sentence. *You're a fully adult man, Flynn; You're working for the CIA? You're* here?

In all the scenarios I'd imagined, all the ways I thought we might meet again, this wasn't in the cards. This wasn't even in the same hemisphere as those cards. We were supposed to just bump into each other, at the Creamery, say, waiting in line for cones. Or buying toothpaste at the supermarket. Or we were *never* going to see each other again. Half of me believed that Flynn existed only in that strip of summer, eleven years ago, almost like I made him up.

"You're CIA," I finish, electricity racing up and down my spine.

"Eight years now," he says, so smooth, like maybe this outrageous scenario—him, me, Italy—isn't affecting him at all. Just a normal day at the office! I'm just another asset. An asset that he's currently trying to contain, because I haven't stopped moving. Flynn's hands are still up in the air, palms flat, as if he's trying to coax me not to slap him. "I get it. The odds of this scenario occurring are astronomically small. A zillion to one. Normally, if the CIA wants to find a decoy, they use facial recognition software. Driver's license photos."

I cringe harder than I want to. "Did you see my driver's license photo?"

"No," he says. "Okay, yes. And I thought it was damn cute, actually, even with the—" He makes a choppy, swiping motion across his forehead. I'd cut my own bangs, on a whim, with kitchen scissors. The raccoon on my state fair T-shirt would've done a better job, and I—

I'm more exasperated than I've been in years. My breath's coming out in puffs.

How can he be so *calm* in this scenario? Seeing me again, for this?

Unless our time together never meant a thing. Unless I was the only one in love.

"What I'm saying is," he continues, visibly unaffected, "we almost never recruit decoys for foreign nations, but the US and Summerland are close allies. They came to us. Their entire population wouldn't even fill a city in Texas, so they couldn't identify anyone in their country who'd be a passable decoy for the prime minister; the CIA started looking."

"So . . ." I swallow, throat burning, taking all this in. "*You're* the reason why I'm here."

Okay, now it does look like I've slapped him. Only for a split second, though, before the hint of a grimace disappears. "I need you to know, I didn't request to be your handler, or ask to be put on this job. The higher-ups just thought that since we share some history together . . ."

Some history. Some. Is he joking?

A bitter laugh threatens to spill out of me.

Because no, nope, he isn't joking. He's giving me a straight look, less than four feet away, his chest barely rising with a measured breath, and he's dropped his hands, hooking his thumbs in his pockets. The brownish-blond strands of his hair practically twinkle under the chandelier light. I can't decide if this version of Flynn—this older, CIA Flynn—is more rugged or pretty, and why both of those options piss me off so much.

"Okay," I say, face prickling. "Thank you so much for that information."

He squeezes his eyes shut for a blink, and when he opens them again, he says, "I'd get it if you hate me. In your shoes, I'd hate me, too."

Hate would certainly be easier. And there is, admittedly, a flicker of it—a deep-down anger that fizzes at my fingertips. The last time I heard from Flynn was in an email, over a decade ago, and it shattered me; I couldn't even bring myself to reply. Now he's just ambushed me, half a world away—and the way I'm remembering our relationship is *definitely* different from the way Flynn is. Otherwise, he wouldn't be this devil-may-care.

"No one else can be my handler?" I ask, finding my voice again.

He doesn't even have the decency to look wounded. He just folds his arms tight across his chest, and man, I wish he wouldn't. The dark cotton of his T-shirt hugs every muscular curve. I am intensely physically aware of him, in a way that almost shocks me. "You really want that?"

"Oh, I really, *really* do."

He looks pensive for a moment before placing his hands on his hips. "Well, that's a shame, Starfish, because you're stuck with me."

Starfish. He did not just call me Starfish.

I drop my bag and hear it clatter against the floor; I hadn't entirely realized that I was still holding it. "Is there a bathroom I could use?"

"Sure thing," Flynn says, infuriatingly nonchalant. "Down the hall."

I quick-foot it inside, clicking the door shut and throwing my back against it, hands flat, willing myself to calm down. *Just calm down. Just think.* What are my options here?

Don't have many, do I?

He's my handler. He's going to handle me. God, the more I say it, the dirtier it sounds. Which is how I know, intrinsically, that if this mission is going to work, if I'm going to bank the money, get my life back, and protect Sofia in the process, then I'll need to shove down every memory of me and Flynn. No thinking about us perched on a picnic table, Flynn leaning over to tuck a stray hair behind my ear. No remembering that delicate sweep of his finger, cicadas buzzing in the background, the salty scent of his beach-drunk skin. *Definitely* no nicknames. I'll have to bury everything with a shovel, under the sand, back on the Maine shores. Like my seventh-grade hamster, Sir Nicholas. May he rest in peace.

Splashing cool water on my neck, I jump around a little, shaking out my shoulders and my hands. *Pull it together, pull it together.* I'll be . . . professional. Aloof, slightly distant, but professional. That's the only way I'll be able to pull this off.

"We're going to have to set some ground rules," I tell Flynn, emerging from the bathroom when my heart rate is no longer in stroke range.

"Absolutely," Flynn says, nodding. "Absolutely. But first . . . I might've gotten you something, to set us off on a different foot."

One of my eyebrows quirks at him, wondering what angle *he's* playing.

He holds up a finger, disappearing around the corner for a second before returning with an honest-to-god wicker gift basket, the kind you'd pick up for a sick relative at the airport. *Oh . . . kay?* Inside, I'm expecting soaps, potpourri, maybe some Italian-made socks, but when he holds it out for me, I notice the compact orange boxes of—

"Macaroni and cheese," he says, finishing my thought. "Gourmet. All made right here in Rome. One's four cheese and truffle, another's with sun-dried tomatoes, and there's two boxes of the dehydrated langoustine one. It's good. Made one last night. A little soft if you cook it for the full time on the instructions, so I'd drop a minute." He cocks his head back and forth. "Maybe a minute and a half."

He's still extending the basket toward me, a peace offering, which I take. At least physically.

"Thank you," I say slowly, trying to figure him out. Is this part of the CIA handler manual? Manipulate your assets with custom gift baskets? Or is this a weak attempt to say *I remember your favorite comfort food, even though I broke your heart, then inadvertently threw your name into the pot for a CIA mission*? That's a lot of miles to cover in a gift basket.

"You didn't have to do this," I say, firmly.

"I did," he says, firmer.

"Well, okay." Basket cradled in my arms like a newborn, I stand there uncomfortably for a second before tipping my head to see farther into the apartment.

"Be my guest," Flynn says, stepping aside, and I think I'm

untangling the dynamic here. If I'm aiming for neutral profession-
ality (think Switzerland, in the dead of winter), then he's approaching this with the easygoing friendliness of a golden retriever.
"Take a look around. Nice, isn't it?"

I nod, eyes traveling over the botanical prints: olive branches,
oleander, Aleppo pine. Anything to divert my mind away from
Flynn, Flynn, that is Flynn. "Does someone live here?"

"You," he says, joining me by the prints, so we're almost shoulder to (much taller) shoulder. He smells like a crisp linen shirt, before you even cut off the tags. It is, unfortunately, invigorating.
"For the next couple of hours, at least. The CIA uses it as a safe
house for higher-profile assets. We wanted you to start feeling like
a prime minister, even before you stepped into the role. The last
safe house I was in? Rural *Iowa*. I can tell you, it did not feel like
this."

"So you did get to travel," I say, already slipping up. *No jokes,
remember? No memories?* At one point, Flynn's dream was to solo-
sail the world.

"There's that sense of humor," he says out of the side of his
mouth. We lapse into a horrifically uncomfortable silence before
he fills it again. "Hey, you hungry?"

I lift my gift basket a little higher. "Think I'm all set."

"Nah, that isn't breakfast."

At the mention of breakfast, *I'm* the one who finds the kitchen.
Breakfast is the most underrated meal. We never had the budget
to serve it at Frida's, but that didn't stop me from dreaming up
new hollandaise recipes and perfecting my salt bagels—extra-
crunchy rock salt on the top. I can almost smell them, the yeast,
the fresh plume of steam when I pulled out the roasting pan.

Yeast is bread perfume, my grandmother used to say. I've always
loved that.

The safe house kitchen, unlike the rest of the apartment, isn't as much to look at. It's simple, utilitarian, stainless steel pots hanging from a ceiling rack. Already on the stove is a small moka pot, almost bubbling over with coffee. On instinct, I set down the gift basket and switch off the burner.

"Have a cup," Flynn urges. "Hell, have two. I put it on for you. What do you normally eat for breakfast nowadays? Toast? Eggs? Name it, I'll cook it."

I hit back with a plain, "I can manage. You don't have to—"

"Again, I do." Sweepingly, he gestures to a chair at the edge of the kitchen island, by a bowl of overripe plums. "You must be used to making food for other people all the time. My mom"—he says, like I do not remember his mom ultraclearly, her crocheted sweaters and dangly cat earrings, reading in the corner booth at Lobster in the Rough—"she was a chef before she retired. Well, a cook, technically. Worked in kitchens for thirty years. She always used to tell me, 'Flynn, when you work in food, no one ever cooks for *you*.' So . . . eggs? I would offer something else, but that's all I know how to make."

I settle stiffly into the chair, thinking, *I'm not a chef anymore.* Also, *How is any of this real? How is Flynn here right now, in Rome, asking to cook me breakfast?* "Eggs are fine."

"I can't guarantee that they'll be *good* eggs," he says, picking up a spatula and waggling it in my direction. He was always great at bussing tables but never could cook. "Poached, I don't do. Omelets, I'm testing my limits. Scrambled? We're in the right territory . . . I think I spotted some sun-dried tomatoes in one of the cabinets. Maybe, if you're lucky, some *salt*."

"Salt?" I deadpan. "Never heard of it."

This, regrettably, makes him smile. His mouth lifts up a little higher on one side, exposing straight, white teeth and deep-set dimples—a grin that, in any scenario, will always look a tiny bit mischievous. He moves through the kitchen, humming, before reaching for a pan above my head, the soft skin of his arm almost glancing my cheek. I notice that the inch-long scar on the palm of his hand—the one he got from a shard of beach glass—hasn't faded. It's the only non-smooth thing about him.

Growing up, my dad always told me to look at a person's hands—that's how you can tell if they've had a hard life. People hold tension in their hands. *History in their hands.* My dad's? He has one finger that's crooked at the tip (boating accident) and scars that crisscross his palms like hiking trails; they're tanned brown, even in December, from the winter sun cracking off the water. He's soaked up every bit of dirt and sea that life has offered him. My hands are starting to look like this—wrists, too. A burn from yanking a tray of popovers out of the oven. Speckled splashes of grease.

Sofia won't have those. Will I have to cover mine? How does that work?

Gail's words come back to nip at me. About my handler, how he'll catalog the rest of my appearance, see if there are any freckles we need to add.

Like Flynn doesn't already know every freckle on my body.

Jesus Christ, Max. Bury thoughts like that.

"So you're training me," I say, not a question, swiftly moving on.

Flynn nods, setting the pan on the stove with a gentle *clang.* "Mmm-hmm, I am. I know Gail got started with some of the prime minister's speeches on the plane. We'll keep going after breakfast, begin with some gestures, some expressions, the way she walks, the way she lifts a wineglass, how she waves. You've already got the face, though, and most of her mannerisms. That's ninety-eight percent of the battle."

I'm unconvinced. "I'm guessing you've trained people to do this before?"

"Impersonate world leaders?" Flynn asks, pouring a short cup of espresso and sliding it toward me. "No."

"But you've helped people thwart assassination attempts before," I say, again not a question.

Flynn takes a sip from his own tiny cup, leaning back on his heels like *That's good stuff.* "You could say that."

I almost roll my eyes. "Such a CIA answer."

"As in, it's not a full answer?"

"It's an answer in a trench coat," I say, matching the strength of his sea blue gaze. "It's hiding something."

Flynn sniffs out a laugh. "That's a good way to put it. I like that." From the refrigerator, he extracts a cardboard carton of speckled eggs—some copper-colored, some seafoam green. "So here's the thing. You're not alone in this. I'll do everything in my power to make sure this is a smooth, laid-back operation. You'll check into two five-star hotels, go to the beach, eat some nice dinners—five days split between Rome and Positano, in and out."

"*Wow*, that's delicious," I say, setting down my cup. I've just tasted the strongest, richest espresso of my life: nutty, with a hint of vanilla, the perfect balance of bitter and sweet. "How in the loop do I need to be?"

He palms one of the eggs, rolls it gently between his nimble fingers. "What do you mean?"

"You know, keeping me up to speed with the operation. Like . . . how do we know it's this crime family who're after her?" I pause, grinding my molars for a second. "After *me*."

Beneath Flynn's short beard, I see a muscle tic in his jaw, but it's gone as soon as he blinks. "The first assassination attempt came less than twenty-four hours after the PM's gambling ring crackdown. The Halverson family looks like they were the most affected. Add in some dodgy phone calls to a number in the Czech Republic, where the CIA located a known assassin . . ."

Goose bumps popping all over my arms, I shiver in the warmth of the kitchen. "We know which assassin tried to kill Sofia?"

"Allegedly. A guy we're calling 'the Producer.' He has about a hundred aliases, used to produce results but now his work's gotten a little shoddy. We don't know his real name. Or what his face looks like." Flynn tips his head to the side. "*And* we also lost track of him in a railway station outside of Prague. You'll keep up appearances while the CIA re-pinpoints his location and brings him in for interrogation. Summerland's prepared to throw a boatload of money at him for a confession. He'll give up the family. Then, it's over."

"What if he doesn't confess?" A lump's growing in my throat again. "What if you can't even find him?"

"We will."

"But what if you don't?" I press, knee starting to bounce up and down. "Gail said there was 'chatter' that someone was going to finish the job. What if 'the Producer' shows up in Italy?"

"Then we take him down in Italy." A lock of Flynn's hair tumbles over his forehead, and with a breezy hand, he swipes it away. "Look, it's true that vacation spots on foreign soil are more difficult to lock down than, say, the Villa Madama, where dignitaries usually stay in Rome. Almost anyone can enter a hotel, a beach, a gift shop. But we've got you."

"Says the guy who lost track of an assassin," I mumble.

Flynn catches his bottom lip with his teeth, almost smiling at my snark. "Hey, when I say *we* lost track of an assassin, I meant agents on the ground in the Czech Republic plus some guys in a bunker in rural Missouri. Let me rephrase. *I've* got you."

He says the last part in this confident, velvety way, his eyes tracing the lines of my face, and everything in the kitchen suddenly narrows. In my mind, I start assembling that list of ground rules, if I want to make it out alive. "Why not just cancel the trip, then?" I add. "Skip the vacation this year?"

Flynn cracks four eggs into a blue ceramic bowl, and gives me a look like *That's what I asked, too.* "Three reasons. One, canceling an annual trip—that the prime minister makes religiously, every year—might tip off the family. Two, since we picked up that chatter—from a cousin of a cousin of the Halverson brothers, that something might be going down in Italy—it sets the stage to draw out the Producer; we need to give him a reason to come out of the woodwork. And three, the PM's drawn a hard line. She's scheduled several can't-miss events during her trip. A museum gala, a luncheon, a brief appearance on Italian TV . . . Don't worry, the real PM will be tackling the more secured events, the ones where she'll need to liaise with diplomats. You take the vacation stuff; she tackles the state affairs." He forks the eggs, whipping air into them, giving me that almost-mischievous half smile again. Warmth runs through his blue eyes. "You're just the same, you know. You haven't changed a bit."

So I've always looked this sad? "Let's not go there."

"What about me?" he asks, coy. "Am I the same?"

I bring the espresso cup to my lips, prepared for the kick this time. "You're taller. More CIA-y."

"CIA-y?" he repeats with a smirk.

"You know exactly what I mean."

Flynn nods, slow and then quick. Pouring the eggs into the heated pan, he runs a thumb slowly along the crease of his lips, not looking at me when he asks, "You sure you want to do this?"

"Eat your eggs? Fifty-fifty."

"Be a body double," he clarifies, still not meeting my eye, stirring the eggs with a casual flick of his wrist. "All this is moving fast, fast, fast, but if you want to back out at any point in this operation, just give me the word. No matter what Gail's told you, no one's trapping you here."

My forehead creases into a frown. "You're my handler. Aren't you supposed to be convincing me to stick with it?" When he doesn't answer that, just keeps cooking, I tuck a stray piece of blonde hair behind my ear. "Even if I did want to back out, I can't. I don't really have a choice."

Flynn tips the scrambled eggs out onto a plain, white plate, sliding the meal in front of me, and starts wiping up the kitchen, soapy water on the countertop. His back's to me, but after a moment, he turns and says, "You always have a choice with me, Max. Always."

There's something about his expression that's so painfully earnest, I have to look away.

First rule, I tell myself. *Never, ever fall for him again.*

5

My past life is full of bright images: A white-brick building by the edge of the bay. Glistening picnic tables on the patio. Big blue-and-white umbrellas and chilled glasses of chardonnay, guests sipping and laughing. Those summer sounds. The almost-unbearable heat inside the kitchen. Throwing open all the doors and all the windows, and cooking my heart out.

In the early days of my restaurant, I was always in a flow. Creating something beautiful, something that was mine. Hours passed like minutes, and suddenly I'd find myself standing in the kitchen at midnight, shaky on my feet and vaguely out of breath, wondering where the light went outside the windows. The kitchen is its own time zone, its own ecosystem. I was happiest there, even when I was miserable. My grandmother Frida never got to open her own restaurant, under her own name. So when it came time to name my little place by the sea, the choice was obvious.

Opening night, I shucked over two hundred oysters, baked dozens of miniature blueberry pies, and prepared the lobsters for bisque. I'd settled on a simple menu of coastal favorites. Nothing's better than letting local ingredients speak for themselves. Nothing's better than the smooth crunch of a home-brined pickle, or the way a lump of fresh crabmeat melts in your mouth.

After the first service, my friends and family came into the kitchen, clapping. Guests I'd never met stayed until the wee hours, asking to meet the chef and say *Welcome to the neighborhood.*

I was so damn proud of that place. It felt like my grandmother was there, by my side, beaming. The kitchen, it *was* me. And in the dark weeks that followed Frida's closure, I often found myself wondering, *Who am I now? Who am I without it?*

Funny.

Turns out, the answer is someone else entirely.

"Colored contacts," Flynn says after breakfast, passing me a tiny white box. "Sofia's eyes have a few more flecks in them; these'll fix that. You ever put on contact lenses before?"

I grab the box, careful not to let our fingers brush. "No, never."

"They'll feel weird at first, when you're putting them in, but you'll get used to them." Furrowing his brow, he surveys my face and reaches out a finger, hovering about an inch from my cheek without touching my skin. "You'll need a freckle, here. Gail's going to take care of the other cosmetics. Now show me how you'd wave to a crowd."

It feels silly—walking back and forth in an empty room, waving to invisible people, as Flynn points out the inaccuracies in my posture, how Sofia would stroll instead of slink—but after close to six hours of picking up dinner forks like Sofia, and tying my hair back like Sofia, and sitting in a chair like Sofia, something shifts. Flynn's no longer correcting my gestures. My movements are fluidly, naturally hers. Then again, outwardly we're so similar anyway—it wasn't a huge jump.

"What about speaking?" I ask, after a brief water break. Training is a distraction that I'd like to lose myself in as deeply as possible. "The accent."

"Mmm," Flynn says, swallowing a gulp himself, a bead of water trickling down the line of his throat. "You won't speak in public. The PM's press team has told everyone she has an extreme case of noninfectious laryngitis."

Involuntarily, I massage the base of my own throat. "Painful."

"Right, so you're conserving your voice. Most people in Summerland speak either Norwegian or English. Out of an abundance of precaution, I'll teach you a few Norwegian words. *Hello, goodbye, toilet*, that sort of thing."

The corners of my eyes crinkle at him. *Since when do you speak Norwegian?* "Sure, comes in handy if you ever want to say goodbye to the toilet," I bat back. "Or hello to the toilet, for that matter . . . What're you doing?"

It's almost seven o'clock at night, tangerine sunset filtering through the blinds, and Flynn's pushing the living room sofa against the wall, all the cords and tendons in his forearms flexing. I tear my gaze away as he grabs both sides of the nearest armchair and lifts it effortlessly. "Just making room. You're going to fight me."

I let out a snort before realizing—"Oh god, you're serious."

"It's highly unusual for an assassin to make an attempt at close range," Flynn says, scooting a coffee table out of the way with the tip of his boot, then lowering himself to his knees to roll up the sheepskin rug. "No one's going to touch you. We'll stop anyone before they get close, and you'll have security with you at all times. But I always teach my assets a few self-defense moves. Helps boost confidence." He dusts his hands emphatically, unfolding to a stand as I pace in a tight line, knowing that I shouldn't run away from his offer—but also unprepared to practice any "moves" with Flynn.

"If it's not necessary," I say, "I'll pass."

"Oh, come on. Humor me. Please?"

I press my lips together. "Okay, fine, let's do it," I say before I lose my nerve.

In the center of the room, Flynn explains what's about to happen: He'll reach out, as if he's going to wrap his hands around my neck, and I'll twist to the side, raise both my arms, then chop down on his elbows. "After that," Flynn says, "we'll see how you react on instinct. You ready?"

No, I'm not ready. His hands are about to graze my pulse; he'll know exactly how fast my heart is beating. Steeling myself, I take a few deep breaths and step forward, nodding, the smooth skin of his fingers glancing my jaw as he slides his hands toward my ears, and I don't hesitate. Don't let this moment drag on. I'm twisting like he taught me, arms raised before letting them down, and he's—

"What?" I press, stepping back.

He runs his thumb over his mouth. "No, nothing."

"It's obviously not nothing. You looked like you were about to laugh."

"I wasn't going to *laugh*," he says. "It's just—"

I twirl my hand at him, urging him to spit it out.

"All right, if you really want to know, we need less kitten, more tiger."

"I thought this was supposed to *build* my confidence," I say.

"It will," he assures me. "Run it again."

This time, annoyed, I slam down my arms, Flynn mumbling something like "*Yes*, Max." Then I give myself space—as much space as the room allows—before he's advancing a second time, and my reflexes take over, thrusting the heel of my hand toward his nose. Flynn ducks with a lazy smile, driving his shoulder forward like he's about to lift me off the ground, but my knee rockets up to clip his chin.

That tigerish enough for you?

He steps back, massaging his jawline. The look of pride on his face is unmistakable, and even though I'll never use this lesson, dammit if confidence doesn't zip through me like electricity.

"Better," he says, then refines my approach, teaching me a few more moves—how to deal with a rear-facing attacker, how to do a single-finger strike. "Now, put it all together. You counter-attack."

We circle each other, hardwood creaking under our feet; I'm wondering what the neighbors are thinking as I fly at him with a grunt, and Flynn slides elegantly back, dodging me. It's like a dance. We're like partners. Sure, one of those partners is pretending like they're trying to kill the other with their bare hands—but it's still skin glancing skin. Close range. The heat of him pouring through his T-shirt, my pulse running higher and higher.

"If there's a threat in the area," Flynn says, footsteps light, "your best bet is to cover or conceal. Run behind the nearest wall; place as much distance as possible between yourself and your attacker." He swoops forward, and I duck left. "It's harder to hit a moving target. Cover's only good for about seven seconds. Don't zigzag, but get yourself from place to place."

I nod, telling myself it's just the movement, just the physical activity; that's the only reason I'm breathing harder. When he wraps his arms around my shoulders, though, the solid plane of his chest pressing against my back, his breath tangled in the wisps of my hair, I—

I practice what he taught me.

"Sweet baby Jesus," Flynn groans, falling back, pinching his nose. The nose that I've just rammed my fist into with a crackling crunch.

Panic flits through me, all the way to my Birkenstocks. "Oooh, I'm sorry."

"Don't apologize," Flynn says, nasally, bent over at the waist.

"I went too hard."

"I *told* you to go hard." Eyes watering, he half stumbles over to the living room mirror, checking the angle of his nose in the fading light. Is it my imagination, or is it tilting slightly more to the side?

"I can try to snap it back in place?" I offer.

He laughs before he realizes I'm not kidding. "No way!"

"Why not?"

"'Snap' does not imply that whatever's about to happen is going to go well," he says, another dry chuckle in his throat. Unpinching the bridge of his nose, he moves his mouth around, testing the tenderness. "It's fine. No real damage."

"Well . . . good," I say, hands on my hips.

He readies himself again, squaring his shoulders, facing me. There's a devilish twinkle in his eye. "Next time, Max? Harder."

I give him harder, solidifying the ground rules in my head. *Rule number two?* After this little lesson, *no touching*—unless my life literally depends on it.

"Milk," Gail says, plopping a carton on the countertop an hour later, back from the longest shopping trip in human history. Sweaty, running the collar of his tee over his face, Flynn starts putting away the rest of the groceries—a pack of tortellini, some olives—as Gail beckons me into the primary bathroom, where bottles of brown goop linger on the countertop. Gail, it turns out, is a master of disguise; she tells me that she used to change the appearances of mob-boss wives before they entered witness protection. "I don't know what I'm handier with, a weapon or an applicator brush," she says, hovering over me as I perch on the edge of the tub. "Either way, a salon is a no-go. Anyone who sees you actually transforming into a prime minister is a liability."

"This will look . . . professional?" I ask, swiping a drip of brown goop from my temple. I'm just glad that Flynn isn't the one massaging my scalp.

"I took an in-depth cosmetology course for the mob wives," Gail says, dabbing more color onto my roots. "So yes. Anyway, we couldn't bring in an outside stylist. Too risky. Now, tilt your head to the left. Less to the left. Okay, *more* to the left."

When all of my natural blonde is covered in a thick coat of chestnut, Gail snaps a translucent shower cap over my head to let the dye sit.

My phone must've auto-connected to the nearest Wi-Fi, because in that time, it buzzes. A text from Dad that says, **He's back!!** Attached is a photo of the world's pudgiest squirrel, the one that snatches all the birdseed in my parents' backyard. Dad pretends like he's at war (*The darn thing's a menace!*), but then chuckles and leaves out extra seed for gobbling.

Looks like my mom's texted me, too: three new pictures of the hats she's knitted. Every week, she drops by the local hospital, meeting her friends to make beanies for newborn babies, so their tiny heads don't get cold.

I stare at the pictures, guilt battering me—for letting my gentle, gentle parents down so fully, and for everything I'm about to do to make up for it.

Without a word, I re-pocket the phone, stress building. I may've gotten a kick of self-assurance from the defense lessons, but alone in the harsh light of the bathroom, the paranoia from the plane reemerges. Every creak in the pipes, every little street noise outside—newspaper stands shuttering, car exhausts backfiring—heats up my skin. Grabbing a washcloth from the pretty marble rack, I shove it under the tap, hands shaking, and wrench on the cold water—colder, colder, letting it pool in the sink—then flop the cloth on the back of my neck. It makes a wet *splat*, excess water trailing down my back. This is the part where I should be looking in the mirror and asking myself: *Shouldn't you run?* But I can't seem to meet my reflection.

I'm not sure who'd be staring back. Me or Sofia?

"Hey, look at you," Flynn says when he sees me late that night, dropping his sponge as I shuffle into the kitchen. The area around his nose is, in the right lighting, a little purple. He's stopped cleaning up from a quick spaghetti dinner, his eyes tracking over the curves of my new brown hair, which Gail has washed, blow-dried, and trimmed. Chestnut locks unfold over my shoulders, falling in the exact same way as the prime minister's. Gail's also polished my nails, added a prosthetic beauty mark by my ear, and scrubbed my face with this slightly stinging exfoliant that's given me extra shine. Rome wasn't built in a day; my new and "improved" appearance, on the other hand, took under two hours.

"It's almost creepy, isn't it?" says Gail.

I thumb one of the strands, massaging it between my fingers. "Gee, thank you."

Gail shrugs. "We were both thinking it."

"For the record," Flynn says, pointing a suds-covered finger between us, "that is not what I was thinking." It makes me wonder what he *was* thinking, especially when a dimple pops under the tidy stubble of his beard.

Twisting my hair into a bun, as I've seen Sofia do in videos, I aggressively change tacks. "When do I switch with the prime minister?"

"On the way to the hotel tomorrow," Flynn says, drying his hands on a dish towel before bracing his fingers on the countertop, explaining the switch like you'd illustrate a football play. "When her motorcade comes through the tunnel, you and I'll be waiting in the middle. The PM will get out of her car, you'll get out of *our* car, and we'll make the swap. That'll be brief. No more than fifteen seconds. You won't see her except for the initial switch, and during one face-to-face meeting in Positano."

"I'll follow by train," Gail says, brushing a few pastry crumbs off her lapel. "It'll draw suspicion if we're clumped together. Plus, that'll give you two extra prep time on the way down—one-on-one. I'll call once you're settled into the hotel."

From the depths of my jeans, I pull out my cell phone again, Dad's text unanswered; the battery is over half-drained, and we didn't exactly have time to stop for an Italian SIM card at the airport. "You have my phone number, right?" Even as the words leave my mouth, they feel idiotic. Gail is CIA; not only does she have my phone number, she probably knows which bunk I stayed in at Millinocket Lake Summer Camp, over two decades ago.

"Here you go," Flynn says, pulling a jet-black brick of a phone from his back pocket. He gives it a little flip between his fingers before handing it to me. "Encrypted, top of the line."

I take the phone, turning it over in my palms, wondering if I should send a text to my family now. *It's Max, new phone. In Europe, won the lottery, LOL, isn't that weird?*

When I'm silent for a moment, when Gail leaves the room for the night, Flynn adds, "If you're having second thoughts . . ."

"I'm not," I lie.

"Okay, but if you ever do," he says, words soft at my back.

I decide not to answer, just wave a hand *good night*, slipping into one of the cool, dark bedrooms and telling myself that maybe—*maybe*—the shock of seeing him will have worn off by morning.

6

My sleep isn't long, and it isn't great.

"How are you feeling?" Flynn asks in the kitchen, early the next day.

"Fine," I say, like I'm shutting a door. "You?"

"Fine," he says, refusing to get the hint. "Did you . . . uh . . . did you know that you snore?"

I scrunch up my face, grabbing another cup of espresso. "No, I don't."

"Yes. Yes, you do. I heard you through the wall. I almost woke you up to see if you were okay."

"That's . . . thoughtful," I say, noting that it's morning—and the shock hasn't gone away.

The sun's rising over Rome as I strip off my tee, leaving the shirt in a tidy pile before changing into the outfit that Flynn's laid out on the bed. I can hear him pacing in the other room, speaking to someone in hushed tones on his phone, as I slip into the sky-blue linen dress; it reminds me of summertime and those haughty European cruise commercials, where people laugh over their salads. *Who picked out this dress? Gail? Flynn?*

The dress fabric is weightless against my skin. Bending over,

I do a little hoppity-hop, strapping on my new sandals—which are probably, *oh*, 2,000 percent more expensive than my Birkenstocks—and this time, actually do glance at myself in the mirror above the dresser. I startle, doing a double take. A chill sweeps down my spine, because I see it. I see it completely. The bangs are still mine. The nose and the lips are still mine. But the brunette woman in the mirror, the one with the posh sandals and resort-style dress, she isn't a washed-up chef. She isn't the girl who grew up in Maine, who shucked all those oysters, who made a series of bad decisions and ripped her whole life apart.

I lean in, hands gripping the edge of the dresser. My fingertips are turning numb. I tilt my head, examining my sharp jawbone (like hers), the small splatter of freckles under my left eye (like hers), our cheekbones like tiny, rosy apples. Add the gold-flecked contact lenses and the beauty mark, the polished skin and the flawless nails—

Holy. Shit.

On the other side of the door, Flynn gently raps his knuckles. "You ready to rock and roll?"

I clear my throat. "Yeah. Coming."

In the foyer, Flynn appraises my full transformation with a quick sweep. "Ten out of ten," he says, although I can't quite make out his expression behind his round, trendy sunglasses. "No one's going to be able to tell you apart, even if they get close. Which they won't, physically. *Especially* not with your moves."

"Yeah, yeah," I say, trying not to smile.

"No, I mean it. I had worse sparring partners at the Farm—you know, the CIA training camp—and they went on to become field agents." He tosses me the small metal compact in his hand; it's makeup, shaded to my exact skin color. "That's to cover up those little scars. The burn mark near your wrist? Just in case anyone zooms in with a camera."

I clench the compact between my fingers, tucking it into my dress pocket—and ignoring the fact that this man knows my skin. "How's your nose?"

"Never better," he says, chipper, even though—if you look closely—the area under his left eye is mildly bruised.

Gail's left her trench coat, a sun hat, and a pair of glasses by the front door, and I slip them on at Flynn's instruction, shielding my face as I slide into the back seat of yet another vehicle. It's beginning to feel like musical chairs, transport edition. This one's a Range Rover with fully tinted windows, and Flynn's at the wheel, pulling away from the curb and into already-building traffic.

"The hair suits you," he says when I yank off the sun hat. "Not that the blonde didn't, of course, but you can pull off both." It sounds a hell of a lot like a genuine compliment, but isn't that what he's supposed to do, as my handler, to establish trust?

Like me, Flynn's also changed outfits. No more Mr. Tight Black Shirt. He's wearing a tailored linen suit, cream-colored, like he's off to a high-society wedding. He doesn't look bad. In fact, I wish he looked much, much worse.

One hand on the wheel, he reaches into the passenger's seat, picking up an iPad and handing it back to me. "Code's 1-2-3-4."

"No, it isn't."

"It actually is. It's so obvious, no one will guess it. Top folder on the right, you'll find a condensed list of facts about the prime minister, her policies, and people she comes into contact with on a monthly basis—friends, special advisors, parliamentarians. She comes from this big political family; everyone's wrapped up in the government somehow. Next folder, I've put together a video compilation for you to watch. Press conferences, speeches, interactions with the public, campaign materials. It'll help you cement her mannerisms."

"And this folder?" I ask, after typing in the code on the tablet. "The one labeled *A*?"

"All the hit men working in the area," Flynn clarifies, sliding off his sunglasses. "*A* for *assassin*."

"So the darker cousin of *A is for aardvark*."

Flynn chuffs. In the rearview mirror, I can see the reflection of his mouth, quirking up.

"Are you making fun of my elaborate filing system, Max?" He strokes his chin for a moment, a different kind of look passing over his face, before coming out with, "God, this is surreal. You and me."

I swallow in a way that I hope is unnoticeable. "I think the word 'surreal' was invented for this exact scenario."

"Look," Flynn says, folding his sunglasses and hooking them in the V of his shirt, "before we dive into all this, I think it would be a lot better if we could figure out a way to be friends."

"Friends," I repeat, dubious.

"Yeah."

"Friends don't throw your name in the pot for potential death missions," I say, keeping my voice jokey, "then show up unexpectedly in a foreign country. A mac and cheese gift basket doesn't fix that, even if one of the boxes is truffle flavored."

"You are absolutely right," Flynn says, matching my tone.

"Don't *agree* with me," I say, choking on a laugh.

He's the one to laugh now, although it's strained. "I'm not allowed to agree with you?"

"You are, but I'm just . . . honestly not sure if you mean it."

He exhales slowly. "I do mean it, Max. Lying to people on the job is shit, and I feel like shit when I do it. And I know I shouldn't correct you right now, but—this is *absolutely* not a death mission."

"I have a folder in my lap," I say, pointing to the iPad, "of literal assassins."

Flynn looks like he's about to refute this but can't, so he stops, glancing between the back seat and the road. On all sides of us, taxis weave across twisted streets. Bundles of fresh parsley and rutabaga spill out of corner shops, and chalkboard signs advertise the daily specials in swirly, white cursive—BOTTARGA, OSSO BUCO ALLA MILANESE, RISOTTO DI SEPPIE ALLA VENEZIANA. The language tastes as good as the food.

"Just tell me how this can work," Flynn presses. "Please. Tell me, and I'll do it."

"Okay . . ." I begin, heart rate ticking up. "Here's the thing. I think it'd be best if we had a few set-in-stone rules. Like, we probably shouldn't talk about the past. No reminiscing. Pretend that I'm just a regular asset, and we don't have any history together." *Should be easy for you, as you've mostly been doing that anyway.*

Flynn snags my eye in the mirror. "You sure?"

I think about the last time we saw each other in person, at the end of summer, how he kissed my open palms and said we'd meet again for Thanksgiving. He left me with the fleece sweater he wore for sailing, and for a week, I clutched it as I slept, the scent of him making its way into my dreams. I literally counted down the days until we saw each other again, scratching them off on my wall calendar.

Right before Thanksgiving, though, he called and said he wasn't going to be able to make it. That ticket he thought he'd be able to afford, he couldn't. Soon after, the email arrived. *Please believe me when I say that was the best summer of my life, but this is going to be really hard if we can't see each other. I just want you to be happy, Max. I truly just want you to be happy.* I'd stared at Flynn's letter, unblinking in the darkness of my childhood bedroom, and thought that breaking someone's heart seemed pretty damn antithetical to bringing them happiness. Maybe I should've replied, but what was there to say? It was so clear that he'd already made up his mind.

"Very sure," I say to him now. "So no nicknames. No *Starfish*."

He started calling me Starfish halfway through the summer, when we found one on a beach walk. *Just like you. Happiest in the water.* I told him I was happiest in the kitchen—the ocean was a close second—but the nickname stuck.

"Okay." Flynn presses his lips together. "Okay, I hear you."

"And no physical contact," I manage.

"Can't say I'm going to stick to that if I have to pull you away from any threats," he says, rolling down his window a sliver, summer breeze in his hair. "Otherwise, understood."

The warm air makes its way to the back, tickling my face. I try not to dwell on what those threats might be. "We should also have a code word for uncomfortable situations. If one of us is breaking the rules, or—I don't know. If we need a reset."

"Did you know," Flynn says, weaving around a tourist bus on the narrow road, "the CIA hasn't used code words since the 1960s?"

"Well, we're bringing them back! How about—?"

Flynn snaps his fingers. "*Pesto.*"

"Are you suggesting a code word or thinking about lunch?"

"Both, now that you mention it. *Trenette al pesto* was on the board we just passed. Why, do you have something against pesto?"

"As a sauce and as a code word, they're just fine."

Now that I've laid some easy ground rules, best not to linger there; instead, I refocus on the tablet in my lap, clicking on the *A* folder. Inside are pictures, profiles, data. "Michelangelo DiNicco," I read, selecting the first black-and-white photo. My stomach lurches at the image: a white guy with unfriendly eyes and a semi-vacant smile. He looks like a late-night TV wrestler, crossed with a bulldog. Or a plunger. Not an appealing combo, especially in a man who might try to kill me.

Now that I'm actually here, with this folder, my argument to myself—that I've never been fitter in my life—seems paper thin.

In retrospect, it's like saying I've taken a few Pilates sessions at the local YMCA, and now I'm ready to summit Everest. (No offense to the Pilates people; they have killer thighs.)

"I thought you said it was only one assassin?" I ask. "'The Producer'?"

"That's who the Halverson family used on the first go-around," Flynn clarifies. "Allegedly. But we want to cover all of our bases, on the off chance they hire someone different for a second attempt."

"*Super*," I say. "One assassin wasn't enough. Okay, tell me about Michelangelo."

"Thirty-seven years old," Flynn says, switching into more of a robotic mode. "Notice the scar. Over his lip on the right side? It's from a botched job in Brussels. Tried to take down a UN ambassador's aide after some fight over hot dogs on social media."

"I don't even want to know," I mutter.

"You're right. You don't. You'd be surprised how quickly things can devolve from GIFs of the Oscar Mayer Wienermobile. Anyway, DiNicco's much more accurate when it's a contract kill and he isn't emotionally invested. The ambassador's aide, he tried to do 'for fun.'"

"He should try Scrabble. Seems healthier."

"Or pickleball," Flynn suggests with a slow blink. "People get so into that. It's like a cult. Did you know it's the fastest growing sport in America?"

"I actually did. My parents play."

"Richard and Denise?" Flynn says, not missing a beat, shocking me. Does he remember them from before, or from my CIA file? "They should join my team."

"You play?"

"Religiously."

"So that's what CIA officers do on the weekends," I say, cautious, censoring my emotions. I wonder how the hell he even ended up in intelligence services. Last time we spoke, he was mapping his solo journey around the Horn of Africa and planning his future as a sailing instructor, literally teaching kids the ropes.

We go over six more names, six more profiles, from an elderly Lithuanian duo to a former orthodontist from Latvia, before I notice, "There are no women in this file."

Flynn flicks on his blinker. "Correct. Generally speaking, women aren't assassins."

"What about *Killing Eve*? Villanelle?"

"One in maybe a hundred assassins are women, but only six are actively working in Europe at the moment. Another option," he says, literally switching gears, his hand gripping the shift, "is that someone from the Halverson crime family might accept the job. Keep it close. It's personal with them." At the next stop, Flynn reaches back to enlarge a black-and-white group photo, the scent of his cologne hitting me: spice, bourbon, woods. Not a trace of the sea, of the salt that used to cling to him. "If anyone's going to do it themselves, my bet's on him. The youngest Halverson brother, Aksel. Good news is, he's tall. Almost six-six. Easy to spot in a crowd."

"It says here that he"—I squint, wondering if I'm interpreting this right—"*only* eats meat?"

"Yep. He's on something called 'the lion diet.' Beef tartare, rib eye steaks, pork chops. No vegetables, no fruit, no bread."

That legitimately makes me shudder. "I'm not sure I could live without bread."

"I know you couldn't," he says as we burst onto the highway, picking up speed, sun streaming in through the bulletproof glass. Flynn closes his window and turns up the blowers, cool air blasting against my skin. "Memorize their photos the best you can. The hotel and the surrounding area will be crawling with the PM's security, Italian police, and CIA, but you'll have an earpiece and a small microphone by your neckline. If you see anyone who even slightly resembles them, tell me immediately."

I fidget in my seat. I didn't know that Flynn would literally be in my ear.

It's fine. That's fine. Purely professional, remember?

"It's weird to think that some of them probably go home to their families at night," I say, clicking back through the photos. "Or is it more of a lone wolf sort of thing? I know I shouldn't be, but I'm kind of fascinated. Aren't you? About what kind of person would sign up for something like this?"

"Oh, absolutely," Flynn says, rearing his head back a little. "The psychology of it. I'm also curious about what kind of person would do something like *this*." He tips his head at me, the body double.

"The broke kind?" I say flatly. *The desperate kind?*

"And no part of you thinks this is a bad idea?" he presses.

"It's not the worst idea," I volley back. "It's not—I don't know— sleepy chicken."

He throws me a confused look. "What's sleepy chicken?"

"Know what? Forget I mentioned it."

"Max," he says, deadly serious, "you *have* to tell me what sleepy chicken is."

"*Pesto.*"

"Nuh-uh," Flynn says. "You don't get to code word this. This is not code word territory."

I blow out a breath that fans out my bangs. This whole conversation, we've been treading too close to friendship. "It's one of those social media cooking trends from way back. You marinate chicken cutlets in NyQuil and then bake them in the oven."

Flynn's face reveals the appropriate level of disgust. "No. No, that isn't a thing."

"It is if you want to poison yourself, trip out, and get two servings of protein at the same time . . . Seriously, though, we should get back to work."

"We should," Flynn says, clearing his throat. Something about the way he's pressing his tongue against his cheek tells me he wants to add more, go back to *This is a bad idea, Starfish*. Instead, he twirls his finger in the air. "Turn up the volume on that video compilation. We've got two hours to Positano."

7

It's an intense two hours. Flynn underlines crucial members of the prime minister's family-and-friends tree, delineating her most frequent known associates, and I do my best to memorize the fifty-page fact sheet about her, reading it aloud. (She was born on the southern coast of Summerland; likes show horses; is allergic to cucumbers; graduated third in her class at law school. Politics is a family business; her mother was a lobbyist, her father was finance officer for the Council of State, and her brother's the special advisor to the deputy prime minister.) From the driver's seat, Flynn colors in more detail as we hug the coastline, all the way down to Positano.

The sea is a different blue than Maine's, brighter and more inviting than the waters I'm used to swimming in, and every time I look up, the gorgeous vistas make the breath catch in my throat: multicolored houses perched on craggy rocks, lush gardens and sailboats tucked into half-hidden coves. Roadside flowers burst in plumes of orange, and we pass several lemon groves, fruit ripe and ready for picking. We're buoyed by the sweet sounds of—

"I'm sorry, but what is this?" I ask, pointing to the stereo.

"Summerlandian polka!" he shouts over the song. "I thought it might help put you in the right frame of mind. What, you don't like it? No sexier instruments than an accordion and the arctic flute!"

"You know those middle school dances?" I half yell over the sound. "Where chaperones come around with flashlights and tell you to make room for Jesus?"

"I'm familiar!"

"Well, they wouldn't have to do that if they just played this music! No one would go near each other."

He laughs again, boyish, waiting until the song finishes before shutting it off.

Near the end of the journey, after I've covered up the small cooking scars on my hands with makeup, we resettle into our roles—him, the friendly and upbeat handler; me, the mildly aloof asset—and he goes over the switch one more time: The prime minister's Range Rover will pull up right alongside ours for the swap. When we trade places, it's also a test—a vetting process, to make sure there are no leaks in the security personnel. "We need to trust her people," Flynn says. "Confirm that they won't talk to the press—or, worse, enemies of the state. There's a plan every step of the way. You'll be driving with Lars. He's part of Prime Minister Christiansen's special protection group, Summerland's equivalent of the Secret Service. He'll take you straight to the hotel. He's in on it—knows that you're the body double—but even with him, never break character."

I swallow heavily. I wish I had some water. Or some lemonade. Or honestly, some of that whiskey-water from back home. Yes, it's nine thirty in the morning; no, I'm not a big drinker. But even with the upbeat polka break, reality is crashing in with the force of a boot-kick.

We're approaching the tunnel.

Jesus Christ, we're approaching the tunnel.

"Max?" Flynn asks. In my peripheral vision, I catch his head swiveling, the concerned look on his face. "Max, hey-hey-hey, breathe."

His voice is coming from a far-off place. I've managed to stave off a good chunk of the paranoia, the anxiety, the all-consuming *what-the-fuck*-ness, because up until now, this experience has felt like a dream. A nightmarish dream, yes—the kind where I may or may not end up running down the street, screaming—but now that we're so close, now that this is *happening* . . .

I'm vaguely aware that my face is heating. My chest feels like a firework, fizzing, exploding. I can't get enough air, even though I'm gulping it. Big, gasping gulps.

"Okay, it's okay, just try to keep on breathing," I hear Flynn say, too far away from me. Darkness almost consumes us as we plunge into the tunnel, the eggshell blue sky disappearing. "I'm going to pull over. Max, I'm pulling over, all right? You just hang in there." The tone he's giving me, it's quiet and calm. Soothing, but not *nearly* soothing enough. How am I supposed to be a fake prime minister in a matter of *minutes*? Or is it seconds? Minutes or seconds, ticking down, like a bomb.

When we're tucked into the edge of the tunnel's curve, Flynn does not tell me to calm down. Thankfully. No one in the history of panic has ever un-panicked thanks to a *calm down*. Instead, he pulls up the emergency brake, exits the vehicle, climbs swiftly into the back seat, and—

"Max, look at me."

I don't. Can't.

"Max, *look* at me."

One of my hands is death-gripping the center armrest, and he covers my fingers with the weight of his, squeezing gently, until my brain finally decides to let him in. When I turn my head, he's there, repeating the words *it's okay, it's all right*, like a heartbeat. Like something I can feel above the fizzing in my chest.

"I can still get you out of this," he half whispers. "Say the word, and I'll—"

"Damn it, Flynn!" I'm firm, the response bursting from me in a heady gulp. I shake my head feverishly. My bangs tangle with my eyelashes. "You're supposed to say something supportive! If you're my handler. That's how this works, right? I worry, you give me a reason not to worry. Don't just tell me to quit. You know that I can't quit."

"Well, you actually can if—"

"I *can't*," I repeat, almost a shout. The shock of tension bubbles in my chest. "You don't understand. I really, really can't. It's not just about protecting Sofia. I owe close to two million dollars in loans, and I've . . . I've borrowed over half of that from my friends and family. Maybe you know all that already from Gail, but short of actually winning the lottery, this is the only way—literally the only way to make things right with everyone I care about. So if you actually want to help me, you won't just sit there and tell me 'You can't do this' or 'You shouldn't do this.' You'll give me a god-damn pep talk."

To Flynn's credit, he doesn't shrink away from my anger. He scratches the short whiskers on his chin, nodding a little to him-self, before smoothing his hands together. "All right. Let's see . . . I've worked with dozens of assets." Not a bad start, even though he's delivering it like an Oscar speech at knifepoint. "You're right, when I become someone's handler, I learn as much as I can about them. In this case, I had a bit of a head start. Believe it or not, none of my past assets were as inherently capable as you."

"That's not—"

"It *is* true," he says, cutting me off. It seems like he's forcing the spark back into his eyes, but I don't care. This is what I need.

"No reason to lie to you, Max. Not about this. Now, you're probably going to sit here and tell me you haven't worked in politics, you haven't trained at law school or in the halls of parliament, so what've you got? Well, you've run a complex operation before. The kitchen. You've gotten timings right. You've commanded a large room. The girl I knew was also *incredibly* smart. Fast-thinking, quick on her feet. And yeah, I know what you're going to say to that—your restaurant failed, so you're not any of those things, but that's bullshit. *Bull-shit.* From what I've read, what happened with Frida's wasn't even your fault. Just bad timing. Hell, I'm not sure there's ever been a body double more innately prepared than you."

He's wrong. He's wrong in so many ways. It embarrasses me that he knows about Frida's, how epically and deeply I've failed. But also . . . my breath is coming a bit easier. The snake of tension is uncoiling in my chest.

"How was that?" Flynn asks, closing one eye like he's unsure. "Pretty good?"

I blow out a long breath through my nose. "Pretty good."

"Yeah?"

"Seven out of ten."

"Well, I'll try for the extra points next time." He glances down at the center armrest, where I'm gripping *his* hand. Cutting off his circulation, probably.

I release it wordlessly before rubbing the corners of my eyelids, hoping I don't smear any mascara. *Fantastic.* The mission hasn't even really started yet—and I've already broken our *no touching* rule. "How much time do we have?"

"We got here early, so . . ." He checks the sleek black watch on his wrist. "Four minutes and forty-eight seconds."

Shit. Sweat beads at the base of my neck. I readjust the collar of my linen dress, so it no longer feels like it's choking me.

Flynn examines my face in the half-dark of the tunnel. The

collar of his linen shirt's slightly rumpled, his hair a bit less coifed than it was before, but he still has that confident, well-rested look of someone who's just come back from a nice vacation. The Italian summer is already agreeing with him. A hint of a suntan dusts the edges of his beard, and I can't help but notice how *strong* he looks, crunched there in the back seat, his suit stretching over his shoulders. "You really can do this," he says, with such authority, sea blue eyes boring into mine, that—for a second—I believe him.

"Okay." I breathe out. "Okay, I'm good. I'll be fine."

Flynn nods, clearly questioning that but hiding it better. He doesn't dare ask *Are you sure?* "In that case, we need to go over your gear." Reaching between us, he retrieves the tech from the center console, fishing out an earpiece and a necklace with gold and silver crosses, a duplicate of the one I've seen Sofia wear in pictures. Only this one . . . "Has a microphone on the back. Just keep the necklace facing this way."

Gingerly, I take both from him, clipping the jewelry around my neck; it's weighted, heavy, real silver and gold. Next, I try to slip the little bud into my ear, but my traitorous fingertips are shaking. No matter which way I twist it, the darn thing won't seat properly. It keeps popping out or jutting into my cartilage.

"May I?" Flynn asks, almost back to his full, breezy self. "Those things are finicky."

"Oh yeah. Sure." I swallow again, my throat tightening anew, but maybe . . . not for the same reason as before. Flynn cups the piece between his fingers, rotating it before leaning over and smoothing a chunk of my hair behind my ear. It's such a delicate movement, such a tender brush, that a few goose bumps pop on the back of my neck. Something in the dead center of my belly flip-flops as he slips in the earpiece, adjusting it so that the plastic seats perfectly, no wiggling, no jutting, his fingers warm against my skin.

"That better?" he asks, repositioning the hair in front of my ear, just as delicately as the first time.

I clear the knot that's suddenly lodged in my throat. "Much. Thank you." My index finger presses against the device, making sure it's entirely secure; at the same time, I wonder what it'll be like to hear him this close—like he's whispering into my ear. "You'll be walking me through everything, right?"

"When I'm not physically in earshot," he says with a dip of his chin, checking his watch again. Less than a minute to go. "We'll meet in your room at the hotel. Wait for the knock. Although, if you see me before then—in the lobby, out in public—remember that we don't know each other. Try your best to ignore me."

"Okay, I can do that." I unbuckle my seat belt, prepping. "You won't even exist."

"Don't *completely* ignore me," he adds with a winsome smile. "That would also look suspicious."

"Fine. I'll give you a diplomatic and very polite nod."

He salutes me with one finger, tapping it to his forehead. "Good thinking." He moves to exit the car, his head angling back at me, just as I hear a parade of sirens in the background. Lights flash. Flags fly. "Let's do this."

It's humid in the tunnel, the air hanging thick like sea clouds. When I step out of the SUV, sandal soles hitting concrete, adrenaline bursts in my veins. I feel like I've had at least eight—maybe eighty—of Flynn's tiny espressos. But I can't spend the next five days swaddled in an abject, mind-bending panic. If I'm going to complete the assignment perfectly, if no one is going to clock me as the decoy, I'll have to wear confidence like a perfume. Prime Minister Christiansen is sharp. She's assertive. She takes shit from nobody. *And you can fake that, Max,* I tell myself, straightening my back and shoulders. *For five million dollars, for Sofia, you can pretend.*

I sniff in one last big breath, ducking behind Flynn's Range Rover—like I've been instructed—as a rumble of cars bursts through the darkness. Sofia's motorcade arrives in a haze of heat, shimmering. Five cars, all black SUVs, with bright flashing lights and flags soaring over the headlights: big, yellow-trimmed streamers with tassels on the edges. Crouched, I stiffen. Between the lights and the fabric fanfare, announcing HERE IS THE PRIME MINISTER, HERE SHE IS, I'm wondering if they could've made Sofia—could've made *me*—into any bigger a target. Why not just paint my skin orange and place a bull's-eye on my forehead? Or I could walk around with bells on, like a cat.

The middle SUV slows to a halt.

"*Go,*" I hear Flynn say directly into my earpiece, his voice urgent but controlled, and I rocket forward, around the car, keeping low. The prime minister's Range Rover is only a few feet away, parked close, the door already opening, and—

We come face-to-face.

Sofia and I.

I could say *It's like looking in a mirror,* but that would simplify it. Trivialize it. This is not an out-of-body experience. It's an out-of-universe experience. It makes me believe in the impossible. I *am* this woman. This woman *is* me—or rather, a sharper, more leonine version of me. She has such an intimidating energy that it walks out in front of her, a physical presence, like an extra bodyguard. I'm in awe of her, instantly. And she . . .

She's brushing past me, wearing the same sky-blue linen dress that I am, staring at me with quick flicks of her lashes. It's the type of look that could dissuade treatymakers, that could end—or start—wars.

Honestly? She looks like she absolutely hates my guts.

Which can't be right, can it? *Can it?*

At the last millisecond, I feel her slap something papery into the palm of my hand, and then we're out of time. It's done. I'm climbing into her Range Rover, and she's climbing into Flynn's. My heart is pounding so hard in my stomach, I almost double over in the back seat, door slamming, as the SUV rushes forward again.

In the driver's seat is . . . Lars. This must be Lars, a member of Sofia's special protection group. Like the Secret Service, Flynn said. I recognize Lars from his pictures.

"Prime Minister," he says with a slow nod of his bald head.

Prime Minister. Directed at me. Doesn't *that* sound bizarre.

Both of Lars's hands are clasped tightly on the wheel. He's so tall and muscular, it's like he's been animated from an ancient Roman sculpture. I tip my head back at him, authoritatively, as I keep a close eye on my pulse. I find it's somewhere between *I'm about to drop over the hill on this amusement park roller coaster* and *I've been stabbed in the leg and need immediate medical assistance.*

One thing that helps my nerves is the music trilling in the background. When Lars turns it up, I realize it's the *same* song. The polka! The terrible Summerlandian polka with the accordion and the arctic flute. What's funny is, the song is so clearly Lars's favorite. His bald head's bobbing to the beat in a way that indicates it's his *jam.*

I do not jam. I do not bob. Yes, the beat is kind of catchy—if you are at a wedding, and everyone's on the dance floor, and you've had six more drinks than you should've—but I'm still clutching Sofia's note. It's on stiff paper, the same cream color as Flynn's suit, folded into a tiny, firm square. Do I open it now? Here?

In my lap, away from Lars's eyeshot, I peel open the note. So-fia's handwriting stares back at me in rushed, bleeding ink.

We must speak privately when we meet tonight. Tell them you have to use the powder room. I'll follow you inside. I don't know why you would accept this position, but I urge you, carefully consider your role. You're in more danger than you were told. Destroy this note.

Well, that's . . . nice. My hands shake as I tear the cardstock into miniature, unreadable pieces.

8

We arrive at Hotel Giorgio, on the Amalfi Coast, approximately six minutes after the switch. Back molars clamped together, I brace myself for the sea of paparazzi. The motorcade pushes through them slowly, armed guards and Italian *polizia* standing at metal barriers. *All this for someone going on vacation?* Makes partial sense. Sofia's a world leader, but she's also the kind of celebrity who regularly appears in the tabloids. I remember that sequined blazer of hers, the sky-high heels, the **PRIME MINISTER OR PARTY PRINCESS?** headline. Candid pictures of her must fetch a steep price, which—right now—isn't good. I'm the type of person who would eat a slice of tiramisu too enthusiastically (eyes lolling, moans emerging) and end up making international news.

An unflattering photo, though, is the least of my worries. I'm clutching Sofia's ripped letter, fisted in my hand, unsure of what to do with it. *Danger. Destroy this note.* Through the tinted, bullet-proof windows, I scan the crowd, dozens of people milling outside the hotel gates. Any one of them might be just posing as paparazzi, hired to shoot something other than a photo, something like—

"You breathing?" Flynn reminds me, his voice sudden and soft in my ear. A rush of electricity runs down my back at the sound

of him. *Don't think about it, don't think about it,* but there it is—
Flynn's fingertip, smoothing my hair, tracing the curve of my ear.
There's his reassuring tone, steady and insistent that I'm okay.
Back then. Moments ago. Time, bleeding together.

"You should teach yoga," I rasp into the microphone, then
wince. It's slipped my mind for a second: I'm not supposed to respond in cases like this, where there's no visible threat. Not with
my "laryngitis." And certainly not with my American accent.

Of course, Lars doesn't hear Flynn in my ear, so he picks up
the compliment, turning down the Summerlandian polka. "I took
a course at an ashram once, ma'am," he says, starkly serious, as the
hotel gates click shut behind us. "I'm not as flexible as I'd like to
be, ma'am."

"Mmm," I hum, the image of Lars in yoga pants now singed
into my mind, burning right alongside Sofia's note. I shove the letter scraps into my dress pocket, vowing to unpack her warning
later. *One thing at a time.* Worry about surviving this before surviving that.

The Range Rover slows as Flynn wishes me a "good luck, doing great." By that he means, I don't trip on my way out of the
vehicle. Despite my pounding pulse, I hold my head high and walk
with a briskness in my step, like Flynn and I practiced yesterday,
saying a silent thank-you to whoever chose my flat sandals. The
pavement's uneven, and everyone from the motorcade is strolling
up, flanking me. It's already more attention than I've ever received
in my life.

First impression? Hate it.

Hate the chatter and the flashing lights and the police on
walkie-talkies, speaking in a language I barely understand. My
relationship with Italian is almost entirely confined to late-night
food-blog scrolling, and one Frommer's guidebook that's gathering dust in my parents' garage. I know the words for sixteen

different types of pasta, but that's not going to help me in an emergency, is it?

Unless it's a pasta-based emergency.

My guess is that, worldwide, there are very few of those.

Naturally, I don't check in like a normal person. There is no waiting in line before a front desk, no presenting my debit card and a form of ID. Half of the staff greets me at the front of the hotel, hands clasped at their waists, with polite smiles and crisp white uniforms. Their calm demeanors contrast with the chaos outside the gates. Some of them look genuinely excited to meet me, eager faces waiting for a nod—or any type of recognition, really.

But Flynn's in my ear. "Don't shake any hands," he reminds me, all business, a change from how easygoing he is when we're alone. I realize, in those four brief words, that there are two Flynns: behind-closed-doors Flynn, and an out-and-about agent of the CIA. Right now, this feels formulaic. How he's handling me is simple, ritualistic. "Don't get too close to anyone."

The rest of his sentence goes unsaid. *Don't get too close to anyone who could stab you.*

No handshakes, then! Instead, I wave. Does it look as if I'm saying *heeeeeey* to a friend across a crowded restaurant? Actually, no! I nail the gesture. Palm at my back, Lars saves me from any further interaction with maybe–secret assassins, escorting me in the direction of the main entrance. We sail past the German shepherds in their police vests, their noses sniffing around the perimeter, as I'm doing everything I can to channel Sofia's poise, her presence, the way she'd effortlessly glide into the hotel, just like she glides into trade negotiations.

She would not stop to pet the police dogs. I do not stop to pet the police dogs.

"You want to pet those police dogs, don't you?" Flynn says, a chuckle in his throat.

Ignoring him, I keep walking.

In case it needed to be said, this is an incredibly nice hotel: a terra-cotta-colored mansion that rises up from the water, tiered like a wedding cake. Freshly painted white balconies overlook a sapphire-blue sea. A concrete statue of a mermaid winks at me from behind bundles of ferns. Everything is purposefully overgrown—controlled chaos in plant form. It's lush and brilliantly green, shrubbery overflowing from clay pots. A thin skim of algae glitters on top of a pond that looks deep enough to swim in, next to a line of brand-new Vespas, waiting for guests to climb aboard.

Climb aboard and run you over, my inner voice warns.

I tell it, *Oh, stop it with the Vespa thing, will you?*

"Signora Prime Minister! Signora!" In the tiled entryway, a man in his seventies rushes toward us. White puffs of hair foam out of his head like sea froth. "Welcome, welcome, *welcome* to Hotel Giorgio! I am Giorgio. My father was Giorgio. My grandfather, *he* was Giorgio. They are dead. But we are so honored for you to stay at our resort. This hotel, it's all about family. You're here, you are now family. My grandfather, he started this resort after the war, as a place to relax, for everyone to relax, so whatever you need to relax, I will help you relax."

Instantly, I love him. He's so insistent, like he's about to shove cucumber slices over my eyeballs. In another life, if I came to this resort on an actual vacation, I'm sure I would want to lounge around in a plush white bathrobe, eat canapés, and backstroke in the pool. Just not now. When Giorgio offers me his warmest smile, clasping a hand over his heart, all I can think is, *Oh god, I hope nothing happens to me in this man's hotel. It would* kill *him.*

"The prime minister is conserving her voice," Lars tells Giorgio as the whole entourage moves briskly forward. "Laryngitis."

Desperate to add something, I tap the base of my throat for

emphasis, and wince (the colored contacts are irritating my eye-balls).

"Oh, signora." Before the security team can stop him, Giorgio moves his hand to rest on my shoulder. I don't even flinch—Giorgio is about as scary as a starfish—but I swear I hear a hiss of breath from Flynn, echoing through the earpiece. "Signora, I know exactly how you feel. Last summer, a bee—I was gardening, and a bee flew *right* into my mouth, *right* down my throat. Stung me. Swelled up. My whole throat, poof!" He mimes this, as if his jugular flat-out exploded. "Couldn't speak for three weeks. My mama, she will be ninety-*six* this month, she makes me tea with honey, but I couldn't even look at the honey! Reminded me too much of the bee!"

My face is sympathetic, with a hint of horror. Both reactions come naturally.

"May I just say, anything you like, Signora Prime Minister, I bring it to you. Anything! You want the paper? I give. You want limoncello? Straightaway." He claps his hands in front of my face to demonstrate the quickness of his future action.

"Will you please show the prime minister to her room?" Lars says, urging us continually along.

"Yes!" Giorgio bleats. "Yes! It would be my great privilege." He pats his breast pockets—once, twice. "I . . . *Mi scusi*, Signora Prime Minister, *un minuto.*"

While Giorgio fumbles to find the misplaced key, my gaze slides anxiously around the lobby: white marble desks, blue-tiled floors, and a flowing fountain in the middle. It spurts water from—*what* is *that?* Discreetly, in a Sofia-like way, I lean forward to confirm my suspicions. The fountain piece is a stone man-angel, having an extended pee.

"Found it!" Giorgio says a fraction of a second later, blue-tasseled key emerging. It dangles from his trembling hand as he

leads me—plus Lars and five other black-suited security officers—
down the first hall and into a cramped elevator, rocketing us up
to the top floor.

"*Magnifico*," Giorgio says on the landing. "This, Signora Prime
Minister, will be where you stay. Anything you need. More soap?
We have goats. We have goats that make the soap, just down the
road." He's become so nervous, so fumbling, that he almost takes
away *my* nerves. "Not to suggest that you need more soap. You
look very clean. Very clean."

When Giorgio throws open the doors to room 6C like *ta-da*,
Lars stalks in first, prepared to side-tackle anyone waiting to
strangle me. I stand back as he reinspects the flowers on the circular foyer table: a bouquet of white lilies and summer greenery.
He's checking them for . . . what? Explosives?

Best not to think about it too much.

The rest of my security team congregates in the hallway, looking busy and important.

"You like the suite?" Giorgio asks me, so hopeful that it cracks
my heart. I recognize parts of myself in him—a passion for his
trade, a business he's proud of. I nod three times, just to reassure
him. "Oh, good. Good. When they say you were staying here, that
you chose my hotel this year, I—" He claps his chest. "I don't think
I've ever been so nervous in my life. This is going to be some vacation, no? Well, again, if there's anything you need . . ."

He backs out with a bow as Lars arranges my suitcases by the
bed—and makes his exit, too. The front door clicks shut, and then
I'm alone, with luggage I've never seen in my life, in a hotel room
that feels like a movie set. Half the surfaces are glittering, mir-
rored, or brilliantly white. Everything about this suite is built for
relaxation. The leather armchairs look like they'd support your
body perfectly. High-backed dining chairs surround a long table,
fit for luxurious dinners. A plush beige rug, delicately age-worn,

leads to the world's most sumptuous bathroom: marble, huge shower, tile cool under my toes. Even the air is thick with lavender, and I . . . don't deserve any of this. Not a drop of this. None of this should be for me.

How long until Flynn arrives?

I'll just . . . unpack. Kill time.

Unzipping the first suitcase, I bristle; I cannot tell you how strange it is to open a bag, *your* bag, and find someone else's stuff. Someone else's books, summer scarves, and high heels. My fingers run over the linen and light cashmere, trousers in creams and earth tones, a bottle of fruity yet stately perfume. I give myself a spritz, rubbing the scent on my wrists, which makes the cover-up run in thin beige streaks.

"*Crap,*" I say out loud.

"What is it?" comes Flynn's immediate response, a tad less breezy than before.

"Nothing, I'm . . ." I tiptoe over to the bathroom, blotting the makeup with a towelette. It stains in a peachy burst. "I'm alone in the suite. Just spilled something, that's all. Have you checked in yet?"

"Just did," he says, half under his breath, like he's disguising the fact that we're speaking. "Turns out, there's a big commotion because a *prime minister* has also just checked in."

"Another one?" I say, going with the bit. Familiarity chafes at me. "What are the odds?"

Flynn gives a slight chuckle. "I'll be up in three."

When the knock comes, though, I glance out the front-door peephole—and Flynn isn't there. Only Lars, a series of security officers, and two Italian policemen line the hall.

"It's me," Flynn says through the earpiece. "Go ahead and answer it."

"Yeah, but where are you?"

He knocks again, and this time I realize it's coming from a door *inside* my room, the one I thought led to a rather grandiose closet. A painted-white lock blends seamlessly into the wood; I unlatch it, swinging open the door to find Flynn, a sheen of sweat glistening near his temples, almost as if he's been out surfing and he's just stepped off the beach. His hair is gently tousled, his collar limp from the humidity, and it shouldn't strike me *every time* I see him: how I wish that my handler wasn't so unexpectedly good-looking.

Behind him is a brightly lit corridor leading to a second elevator. "Private entrance," he explains, strolling inside my room. A worn leather suitcase dangles from one of his hands. "Also, an emergency exit. The hotel had it built for VIP guests, so they'd have exclusive access to the wine cellar and some of the other amenities. CIA came in yesterday and changed the keypad and the code, and there's additional security downstairs on this end."

Carefully, he sets the suitcase next to the others.

I point to it. "That mine, too? How much luggage does a person need for a few days?"

"Oh, we . . ." Flynn pauses, a look of uncertainty crossing his face. It involves a dent in his brow, a tic of his jaw. Two very un-Flynn-like motions. "Gail didn't tell you, did she?"

A flicker of panic settles in my gut. "Tell me what?"

He runs a smooth hand through his hair, tousling it further. "Shit."

"What?"

"You really don't know?"

"I *really* don't know."

"Okay, uh . . ." Flynn clicks his tongue. "I didn't know that you didn't know, but . . . here's the deal. I'm supposed to be staying with you."

Panic sparks down my neck as I clock his meaning. "Staying with me, like . . ."

"In your suite. On the couch."

"Ha! No way. We don't—" I gesture between us with a floppy hand, unsure how to finish that sentence. *We don't know each other anymore?* "We don't need that."

Flynn's hands migrate to his hips as he scrunches up his mouth. "Gail was supposed to go over the arrangement on the flight over. She distinctly said that she told you."

"Well, she did not. She started training me, gave me an unnecessarily long lecture on Northern European agriculture, then played some farming game on her phone while I learned the Summerlandian national anthem. This suite is too . . ." I glance around, a little frantic. "It's too . . ."

"Too what?" Flynn prompts, eyelashes like crescent moons on his face.

Romantic, I think, teeth gritting around the word. It couldn't be any more romantic if there was a saxophonist spread out on the bed playing "I Will Always Love You," if there were rose petals in the bathtub and champagne in the— Okay, there actually is champagne, chilling in an ice bucket near the bed. "It's too small for both of us," I finish nonsensically. This suite is twice the size of my living space back in Maine, with way fewer clipped coupons and no ancient microwave (or Calvin) in sight.

When Flynn speaks again, his voice brushes against my skin and the inside of my ear simultaneously. I rip out the earbud as he tries for reason. "I'm sorry, the agency thought it'd be safer to condense roles, so I'm your handler and your in-room bodyguard. There's no way I can let you sleep alone." He reconsiders his phrasing with a small, awkward tilt of his head and a cough into his fist. "Alone in your suite, I mean. Not . . ."

"*Obviously* not that," I say, my eyes jolting over to the full-size bed before I can tell myself *Danger, danger, don't go there.* Heat rushes to my face until I'm approaching the terra-cotta color of the hotel. It's just . . . hard to wrap my mind around. Flynn, in my suite. Flynn in my suite when I'm falling asleep at night. When I'm wearing (someone else's) pajamas. When I'm shuffling out of bed in the morning and my hair's a crown of tangled knots. This arrangement makes sense logically. As the double, I have a body. He is bodyguarding. Therefore, he must be *close* to my body. But the couch is maybe six feet from the bed, and the thought of Flynn, with his biceps and his back muscles, lounging next to me at night is—

Know what? It's fine. It's totally fine.

Once again, I have bigger things to worry about. Assassins masquerading as paparazzi. Claiming the five million dollars, paying back my family and friends, and honoring my grandmother's love for her home country. How I'm going to maintain my role perfectly, do a leader like Sofia justice, and not out myself as the double. Flynn sleeping two yards from my face? No biggie.

"Actually, I understand," I tell him with a half-forced shrug. "Go ahead. Stay."

His blue eyes sweep across my face, trying to pick up a lie.

"We're all good," I tell him.

"Good," he parrots back.

"Good," I say again, wishing I hadn't. We're going to need a whole new set of rules.

9

No changing your clothes with the other person in view. No speaking once our heads hit the pillows. No Do you mind rubbing sunscreen on my back? before we head down to the beach. Absolutely no walking around in just a towel. Never—

"You look like you're in your head," Flynn says. He's neatly placed his shirts and shorts into the corner armoire and is now lounging on the couch, hands interlaced behind his neck. The movement accentuates the tone of his arms, the broad swath of his palms. He's tall enough that he has to kick his feet up on the armrest.

"Can you blame me?" I ask, shoving Sofia's expensive pantsuits into the closet.

"Let's get you out of it, then. Tell me what's new with you."

I throw him a look. "You mean, in the last forty-eight hours? Nothing notable."

He throws me back the same look. "I'm just wondering what you've been up to all these years."

It takes effort to withhold the skepticism from my glance. "I'm sure you know. If I'm in this position, the CIA must have a file on me that's a mile long."

"Oh, they absolutely do," Flynn admits without pause. "Still not enough to know someone. The CIA organizes people's lives into neat boxes. Work history, family history, any special skills . . ."

"For me, it's—what?" I question. "Egg-poaching skills? Soup-making skills? That the kind of stuff you mean? I can chop those mini carrots *super* thin."

Flynn considers this with a tip of his head against the pillow, blondish hair fanning against the fabric. "Usually it's more like 'asset speaks fluent Swahili,' or 'asset knows how to pilot small aircraft.'"

I shut the closet door and zip up the final suitcase. "Yeah, I can see how those would be more strategically useful."

Unlocking his hands, Flynn swings his legs to face me, elbows on his knees. Even hunched over like this, he seems impossibly huge. "Come on, give me something, Max. Anything. Maybe *I'm* a little nervous about sharing my room with someone I haven't seen in ages."

An actual snort comes out of me. "Good. Very believable."

He's still gazing my way, leaning forward with one eyebrow raised. "Random fact about yourself. As random as you'd like."

This is so silly. And frustrating. At one point, after a summer of car trips and conversation, we knew almost everything about each other—like, how Flynn's grandparents owned a garden center back in Texas, how his dog Ted died two summers prior and he wasn't over it, and how (sometimes) he'd skip school and kayak down the Colorado River with Pierce and Alejandro, his two best friends. My friend Julia (aka Jules) even met him, way back when, on one of our Sunday-morning potato doughnut runs. *I like him, Maxie*, she whispered conspiratorially over the picnic table. *I think we should keep him.*

I sigh, giving in, just so we can get this over with. "Fine, okay, uh . . . a couple years ago, I finally tried a peanut butter and Fluff sandwich, and despite the fact that the culinary gods were rolling over in their graves, I liked it. Actually, it was borderline magical. Will that work?"

"See?" He opens up the palms of his hands. "Completely comfortable now. I'm a peanut butter and banana guy, myself. Although, one of my CIA colleagues told me about the deep-South alternative."

"Which is?"

"Banana and mayonnaise."

Horror flickers across my face. "Why would you tell me that?"

"Hey, I had to hear about your sleepy chicken."

"It isn't *my* sleepy chicken," I argue, choking on a laugh. "I'm not just running around with bottles of NyQuil and chicken cutlets in my purse."

"If you were, I think that would've automatically disqualified you from CIA selection. And you would've had a hard time explaining that at the airport . . . In all seriousness, while we're here, in the suite, I'll give you your space. I know the Italians don't have a word for privacy—not in their native language; they just say it in English, with an accent—but I respect your boundaries." He pauses expectantly. "Don't you want to ask me a question?"

I know he means about himself, about what he's been up to the last ten years. I *am* curious—of course I am—but this conversation's already getting a little too friendly. Given our new temporary sleeping arrangement, it's even more important to keep our dynamic steady. Neutral. Emotionless.

"Yeah," I fire back, one hand on my hip, "why does Sofia hate me?"

Standing up, Flynn smooths out his pant legs until they're completely crease-free. "What do you mean?"

For some reason, I don't tell him about the note, tiny pieces stuffed in my pocket, just—"She gave me this look when we switched places. It was very . . . penetrating."

Flynn frowns. "You know I drove her to a safe house when we swapped in the tunnel? She didn't say anything about you. Kept quiet and answered messages on her phone." Waltzing over to the bar, he pours himself a glass of seltzer water and tips it at me. "Listen, let's just focus on your first outing as the PM. Get that out of the way before we worry about anything else. The schedule from the PM's comms team says you're due at the beach in fifteen minutes."

"And you'll follow me," I supply, glad that we're back to just business. "What's your cover story, then?"

"Simple, another guest at the hotel." As he speaks, he's stripping off his linen jacket and hanging it on the back of the sofa, careful and slow. A bead of sweat trickles down the hard line of his throat; the white cotton of his shirt sticks to his chest muscles in a borderline obscene way. Can someone get this man some air-conditioning? It seems like there's a laissez-faire attitude about the weather here: *It's hot, it's Positano, so what?* "Did you hear me?"

I blink at him. "No, sorry."

"Don't apologize. I was talking about my alias. I'm a restaurateur, scouting the area for real estate. Thought you'd like that. You can give me some recipe tips, beef up my backstory."

"Oh yeah. Fine."

"You just missed one hell of a pun there. Beef up?"

Distracted, I open the dresser drawer and yank out the blue-and-white one-piece swimsuit that I've just folded away. That's when the hotel phone rings on the nightstand, a sharp and insistent trill. "Who's that?"

"Don't know," Flynn says with the touch of a frown, strolling over to answer it. He cradles the receiver like he's in an old detective movie, shoulder holding the phone to his ear. "Hello, yes?"

A pause.

"Mm-hmm," he says. "Mm-hmm. That won't be necessary. No. Don't worry about it, I'll tell her . . . Really, I can tell her . . . Mm-hmm, she's— Okay, hold on. One second." He lowers the handset, palm over the bottom so the caller can't hear. "It's Giorgio."

Ah. "Okay, what does he want?"

"To speak with you about the soap."

"All . . . right."

"He's insistent. Would you mind just hearing him out for a minute? I kind of like the guy."

"Yeah, me, too," I say.

"Giorgio?" Flynn says into the phone. "I'm passing you over."

Gingerly, I take the phone, pressing the receiver to my ear, as Giorgio begins without preamble. "I feel I have made such a fool of myself, Signora Prime Minister, I am so sorry! All the talk about the soap! The soap and the goats! I have been playing it in my head, over and over and over and over, and in my head, I say, *Giorgio, shhhh. Shhhh. Do not say it.* And yet, I say it! My mouth, it just blub-blub-blub." He makes a sound like his mouth is a burbling brook. "So please accept my apologies. Also, I have your brother on the line."

I blanch. *My brother?*

"I will transfer you now," Giorgio says dutifully, like it's his great honor, and of course, I can't *say* anything. Short of hanging up, all I can do is stand frozen in the suite, heart jumping, waiting for another voice down the line.

"Sofia?" The new caller's tone is nasally, clipped, annoyed. His Scandinavian accent bursts into my ear. "Sofia, I have been trying to reach you all day, but no one would patch me through. The fact that I had to ask your communications director for the name of your hotel and dial it up like you don't have a *cell phone* is *embarrassing*. Fillip is asking about the joint-party resolution and I need to know your answer by *Monday*. Monday at the *latest*. Can you really not speak? For Christ's sake, Sofia, eat a lozenge. Drink some herbal tea. All right, goodbye for now."

My palms grow clammy in the short time it takes me to hang up. "I got transferred to her brother."

Flynn's gaze snaps to look at me. "Jakob?"

"I forgot his name."

"That's fine. That's fine. What did he say?"

"Something about a joint-party resolution." I run my hand down my neck. "Are you sure that *he* doesn't want to kill her?"

"Why would you think that?" Flynn asks, confused.

"Because it sounds like he wants to kill her."

"I think we can very safely chalk that one up to sibling rivalry. They might not get along, but Jakob's not a bad guy. A little high-strung, maybe, but—shake it off." He actually shakes his shoulders in demonstration. "No unexpected phone calls or visitors from now on."

I nod, breathing through my nose, hands on my hips. "What about the other people in and around the hotel? The ones who aren't security?"

Flynn catches my drift. "The resort will keep the area as locked down for you as possible when it comes to paparazzi. Italian police, the CIA, and the PM's intelligence service have all pulled the guest lists, and they're clean. What we're trying to ensure is that none of *those* guests bring a guest, someone who pays them to tag along for the day, maybe under the guise of using the pool. But 'using the pool' is actually code for—"

"Shanking me at the buffet table," I finish for him, stomach a bit watery.

The corners of Flynn's eyes crease. "Wouldn't put it that way. That's not going to happen." His cell phone gives an aggravated little buzz, and he checks it, scrolling. "See? Just what I was saying. Summerland hacked the last Halverson brother's phone fifteen minutes ago, so we'll be able to monitor any and all communications coming out of their compound. And the CIA just got a lead about the Producer's identity—some recent footage at a convenience store in Prague. I'll be surprised if we even need the whole five days." He shoves a stack of brand-new books and a bottle of sunscreen into my beach bag before grabbing a pair of baby blue swim trunks from his own luggage. "I'll just let you . . ."

I clear my throat. "Yeah, I'll get changed in the bathroom and head right down."

"Don't forget to keep your necklace on," he says, tapping the base of his own throat. He has a few freckles there, at the edge of his tidy beard. "Earpiece, too."

One thing I don't keep on me? Sofia's message. In the bathroom, I shove my hand into my pocket, where bits of paper rest like shrapnel. The prime minister's words swim around my brain. *Danger*, she'd written. *Destroy this note*, she'd written. To be extra safe, I scatter the pieces into the toilet, watching them swirl—with a violent flush—down the drain.

10

Summer might be my favorite season. That has a lot to do with my family. Dad likes to instruct guests on how to crack a hard-shell lobster, how to extract every ounce of meat from the spindly little legs, and Mom is always up for bike riding—especially down by the coast, on this perfect trail by the cedar beach houses. I love summer foods, too. Huge cones of moose-tracks ice cream by the lighthouse. Fresh-chopped coleslaw, with its deep purple cabbage; corn smoked on the backyard grill; and perfect, cold egg salad sandwiches. Eating on the back deck with my parents.

I wonder if we'll ever have those carefree summers again. Mom and Dad don't do guilt trips, but *I* feel it. The crushing disappointment. How they wanted so much more for me than chasing a goose around a lawn at someone else's wedding.

When the pandemic hit, and Frida's hit her first rough patch along with it, I didn't tell my parents. But they knew. They could see the stress lines on my face, especially after I blew through my governmental loans. Without telling me, they sold their rental property on Long Sands Beach, the one with the bright blue porch swing and the backyard hammock. *What do we need some beach property for?* my dad countered when I said, *No, tell me you didn't.* He thought his money was safe with me. Months later, he was refusing coffee at his favorite shop. I think about the fishing trips he'll never take. The retirement he'll never have. Because of me. All for my dreams.

On my way out the door, as Flynn dips into the bathroom to change, I consider dashing off a text to my parents with my non-CIA phone. That's allowed, right? No one warned me against it. My phone's on 12 percent battery and takes a few beats to connect to the hotel's Wi-Fi. When it does, another text from Dad pops up: a message reminding me about Mom's fifty-eighth birthday party next month. He's wondering if I can make the cake, **carrot cake with the walnuts**—but **no rush in answering, Max-a-million. Call when you can**.

My fingers just hover over the keyboard. If I text him back, he'll call immediately, then worry when I don't pick up. If *I* call, he'll hear the tension in my voice. No way I'll be able to keep up the charade—not with him. Instead, I shove the phone into the mahogany buffet table, hating myself, and take one last glance in the entryway mirror. Sofia's wearing—*I'm* wearing—a long cotton cover-up over my one-piece, my hair pulled back into her trademark bun. Classy, refined, not showing too much skin. Ready for the sand and the sea. Quick as a reflex, Gail's words pop back into my head: *Mostly, you'll just sit in a beach chair, read a book. It's a simple job in beautiful Italy.*

Let's put that theory to the test.

Puffing out a hard breath, I readjust the microphone-laced necklace and secure my earpiece once again, drawing a lock of hair from the bun to hide it. *That'll do.* Exactly on schedule, outside in the hall, Lars greets me with another stiff nod; he's a good actor. Even though he's in on the decoy plot, he's making me feel as if I really am the prime minister. Together, along with seven of Sofia's closest members of security, we slip into the elevator, trail past the dining room and the back terrace, and head down to the sea, following the rocky stairway carved into the cliff. *Rocky. Cliff.* Nothing worrisome about this.

People are staring. Are they plainclothes security? Guests at the hotel?

Assassins?

Nope, Max, don't go there.

Once the sea air tickles my face, it's easier to pretend this *is* a normal vacation. Never mind the bomb-sniffing doggies and the paparazzi looming behind the gate; the sea is still the sea. The sun is still the sun. Automatically, at the bottom of the stairs, I strip off my sandals, tiptoeing over the hottest part of the shore before settling by the water. Someone's set up a blue-and-white-striped beach chair with a matching umbrella, almost like the ones on my old restaurant patio.

"Here we are, Prime Minister," says Lars, pretending to swipe sand from the chair, his palm coasting over the fabric—but I hold in a flinch when I realize what he's actually doing. Double-checking the seat for . . . well, just about anything you *definitely* wouldn't want to sit on.

Once again, I channel Sofia—her unflappableness. This is a woman who once went head-to-head with alleged war criminals at a summit in Budapest. When there was a security breach at a conference in Berlin, and someone rushed her during a speech about every woman's right to education, she calmly reached down and fisted one of her high heels, prepared to take him on with the business end of a stiletto. I think I can plop my ass into a sun lounger. How brave.

"Thank you," I mouth to Lars as he steps to the side, joining the rest of my security, and I settle, kicking my legs out on the chair, listening to the soothing pulse of the waves—and the not-so-soothing sound of other guests on the beach. From yards away, I catch a snippet of a conversation. Wild, wild whispers to the tune of: *Is that really her?*

Yep. Really! For real! Just don't look at my face too carefully, or judge my mannerisms too closely, or ask me to speak.

"Take out a book," Flynn's voice says, out of nowhere, into the earpiece. A hot prickle goes up my spine. "I've run all the titles past the PM's team. She said she's on board with anything recommended by the Obamas."

Bending to the side, I fish out the first novel I find, Hilary Mantel's *Wolf Hall*, and crack open the spine. Just a bit of light beach reading at 560 pages. Good news is, if anyone does try to shoot me, this would definitely stop a bullet. And then I could chuck it at them, like a brick.

"Nice choice," Flynn says about the book, and where *is* he?

Ah. Right. My head swivels as he passes. Flynn is distinctly less clothed than a few minutes ago, popping down to the shoreline in those baby blue trunks. The hem is European short, grazing halfway up his significant thigh muscle, and the buttons of his white linen shirt are mostly undone, a long V of bronzed skin open to the breeze. Without giving me a second glance, he settles directly in my vision—unfolding his beach towel on a lounger before tackling the rest of his buttons, stripping the shirt slowly off his back. A sun-kissed trail of hair descends below his waistline, the smooth ridges of his tendons popping in his forearms. Even if I didn't know that Flynn was a handler for the CIA, I'd assume he had a job that required regularly flipping people over his shoulders. A job that also required crunches. Just . . . daily, or hourly, crunches. Over the top of *Wolf Hall*, I try not to look as Flynn slinks into the water, soft spray on his bathing suit shorts.

"I was thinking," he says into my earpiece, voice jolting straight to my core. He's no longer facing my direction, his toned back to the beach, but with the high sound quality, it's like he's sitting smack-dab next to me on a lounge chair. His microphone used to be tucked underneath his shirt. My guess, it's now hidden in the case of his sports watch. "You never asked me a personal question, back there, in the hotel room. What I've been up to, what I like now. I'm going to choose not to be offended by that."

I can almost see the confident curve of his smile, working its way up his face. Of course, he knows I can't actually *respond*; otherwise, it'd look like the prime minister's mumbling to herself, or trying to sound out the words in her big-girl book. Like it or not, Flynn has my undivided attention. Seems like he's going to milk it for all it's worth.

"Let's get to the serious stuff first," he says pointedly. "Peanut butter and marshmallow sandwiches are delicious. I agree with you on that one. However, I am now a bigger fan of banana bread than I've ever been before. Banana bread surpasses all other foods, no question. Sweet potato fries, on the other hand, are an abomination. Fries aren't supposed to be healthy; they're supposed to be from Idaho, and they're supposed to be thin and crispy."

Well, he's got me there. Crispy fries are superior. On the other hand, this isn't exactly vital information passed between handler and asset. I start to read the first line of *Wolf Hall*, assuming he's finished. He isn't finished.

"I had a growth spurt," he says. "When I was seventeen and a half. Right after summer ended. By then, though, everyone at school had already given me the nickname 'Pony,' and I thought it was because I was fast and agile. A friend of mine later told me that it came from My Little Pony, because I was short for my age."

Fighting a smile with all my facial muscles, I shake my head imperceptibly. *Why is he telling me all this stuff about—*

"Action films. I like them now. But only the terrible low-budget ones, with the unrealistic stunts. They actually filmed one near my parents' place, in the mountains. They moved there a while back. Sold the Texas house and opened a bed-and-breakfast in New Hampshire. They made their own jam. Strawberry-rhubarb preserves. My mom's name is Barbara, so they put rhu-BARB on all the labels, with her face on it, and barely anyone got the joke, but it was a big seller at the local farmers' market."

Despite my efforts, the very corner of my mouth turns up. I'd buy that jam.

At the same time, it makes me a little sad—that I didn't know any of this. That he doesn't remember that *I* remember Barbara. Flynn got his travel bug from her. Every summer, she'd take their family somewhere new, somewhere by the water—Nags Head, Cape May, Ogunquit, and then, one summer, my little town.

Flynn keeps chatting through the earpiece, seawater on his skin, and while I refuse to drop my guard with him, my jaw does untense. My pulse treads into neutral territory. Right now, I'm relieved not to be obsessing about Sofia's ominously ambiguous note, floating somewhere in the Positano sewer system, or the crush of photographers outside, or those profiles in the folder marked *A* for *assassin*.

That's the point, isn't it? Why Flynn's going on and on.

Or adult Flynn just likes to hear himself talk, I think, as he finishes a soliloquy about the importance of farmers' markets that is only slightly shorter than the book in my lap. When he's done, he turns around in the water, sunlight threading through his hair, and it strikes me with renewed intensity that, in a short number of hours, we're going to be trapped together—all night—in my suite.

Luckily, the novel's another distraction. It's exceptional. Sweeping and sumptuous and surprisingly easy to get into, even if you're the type of person who normally reads cookbooks. I used to have a whole stack of cookbooks by my bed at home: *Ottolenghi Flavor*,

La Grotta: Ice Creams and Sorbets, The Art of Simple Food. I like reading the stories behind the recipes, the way chefs develop a dish, from conception to table.

After the first chapter, the heat has soaked so thoroughly into my skin, my cheeks have turned pink—and the sea starts calling my name. Would it hurt to take a quick dip? Just wade in up to my knees? Slowly, I make my way to the shoreline, wondering if anyone's going to stop me; it's bathwater warm but still so refreshing, the quick crash over my feet, my ankles, my thighs. The edges of my cover-up are going to be tinged with salt.

Flynn's a couple yards away, and I can feel his eyes grazing over me as I tread a bit deeper, the ocean floor cool under my toes.

"See?" he tells me quietly into the microphone. "Nice, easy vacation."

"Sorry that you don't get more danger, Secret Agent Man," I volley back just as covertly, facing away from the hotel.

"Hey, there could be a rip current," he says, checking behind me to ensure that no one can see us talking. Satisfied, he relaxes. "In all honesty, I will take a low-key mission any day."

"What, do things get hot and heavy out in Iowa?" I ask.

He chuckles softly. "You did not just say 'hot and heavy.'"

"Seriously," I press, "is your job mostly this chill? Like . . . your last assignment, whatever it was. Did it feel like a vacation, or an easy work trip?"

Flynn wades a little farther into the sea, and so do I, until both of us are almost floating—separate but together. He doesn't meet my eyes.

I frown, keeping my back to the beach. "You're going quiet on me now?"

A long, weighted pause tells me that he's debating something, his hands swishing through the sea. When he finally speaks again, a bit of the lightness is gone. "I can't actually tell you much about my last assignment. One, because it's classified. And two, because I woke up in the hospital a week later."

The thought of Flynn lying in the hospital—and me not even knowing about it—twists my stomach. I'm actually dumbstruck, the water suddenly cold around me. "What happened?"

"It was a very different assignment than this," he says, back-tracking a step, his voice warm and reassuring once again. He scoops up a palmful of seawater, running his fingers through his hair—and tries to cover up the confession with humor. "'Course, I did learn a lot about myself. That whole your-life-flashes-before-your-eyes-right-before-you-die thing? Total bullshit. Do you know what my last thought was before everything went black? 'God, I really want a sandwich.'"

A stiff little laugh comes out of me. It's pretend; all I'm thinking is, *Wait, dying? You almost died?* "What kind of sandwich?"

"Pastrami. Sauerkraut. Swiss cheese."

I nod, a lump in my throat. "That's a good one."

He pauses. "I shouldn't have told you that."

"Your death-sandwich order?"

"I'm sorry," he says, skipping over my attempt at humor.

"Don't apologize," I say, mirroring him. Against the horizon, I spin to look in his direction, but he's already heading to the shore, water beading along the golden plane of his back, implicitly telling me to follow.

It's harder to focus on my book after that.

I'm relieved when, two hours later, Lars crouches under my umbrella and tells me that it's time to head up to the room. I snap *Wolf Hall* shut. First outing as a fake prime minister, done. Maybe it shouldn't, but a swell of satisfaction rises in my chest; I did it, I made it, without even getting a bad sunburn. No embarrassing mishaps, either; no way that anyone could look at me and say, *Are you sure she runs an actual country?*

Is it possible that Flynn's right—in one way, at least? Is this getaway, for all intents and purposes, just a glamorous, free vacation? Brushing a smidge of sand from my cover-up, I tell myself to *be grateful, Max. Be thankful for this opportunity that's fallen into your lap—and don't try to pick it apart, or tell yourself that you should have to suffer through it.*

As soon as I stand up, though, I notice the man behind me. Not Flynn, not Lars, not anyone from my security team—this tall, lurking man, with dark brown hair and sun-drenched skin, a tennis bag slung over his shoulder. He's approaching me in all white, a smile on his face like he's just won Wimbledon, and immediately I think, *What the hell is in that bag?*

And security isn't . . . reacting as strongly as they could be.

They're surrounding him, sure, but they're just vaguely patting him down—from his thigh-hugging white shorts to his ample shoulders—before he's swaggering my way. His hip swing is so exaggerated, I'm half-convinced there's a rock in his tennis shoe. Or some small crustacean, biting him in the pants. "Sofia, Sofia, Sofia," he says to me, almost teasing, and I stand stock-still as he plants two gentle hands on my shoulder blades, kissing my cheeks—once, twice, three times.

He smells of citrusy cologne, like he's bathed in a bucket of orange juice, and a corner of my brain says, *You remember him.* From the files. From *one* of the files. But it's kind of important to remember which one! The friends-and-family tree? Or the known-assassins folder?

First Sofia's brother, now this. *No unexpected visitors, huh, Flynn?*

"I know this is last minute," the man says in a vaguely Scandinavian accent, not bothering to introduce himself. "I'm sorry, I should've warned you."

At the same time, microphone feedback crackles in my ear, and Flynn says, "His name's Roderick Flaa. He wasn't on the registry this morning—but the prime minister knows him. Summerlandian businessman-meets-diplomat. Just smile and nod."

I smile and sweat. My underarms are starting to chafe in the linen cover-up.

"I heard that you'd checked in this morning," Roderick continues, throwing me a smile that could be charming. He's unquestionably gorgeous, in an effortful way—and obviously comfortable with Sofia. Maybe he's the same with everybody? Everything from his swept-back hair to his confident posture screams ladies' man. "I was in the area, and you know that Hotel Giorgio has some of the best courts—I heard you were here and was wondering if you'd like to join me. Say, twenty minutes?"

No. No, Roderick, I would not like to join you. I will join you in hell.

But, of course, *speaking* is forbidden. Instead, I'm a mime. I need one of those black-and-white-striped T-shirts and the sad-face paint with the vaguely gang-like teardrop. When I try to wave him off (*No, thank you, go away*), he completely misinterprets the gesture. A wave, in his language, is a tennis swing. It doesn't help that I've given him a smile and a nod, as Flynn explicitly told me to do.

I'll see Roderick on the courts in twenty.

11

ou don't have to go," Flynn hurls at me, back in the suite. He's planted by my empty suitcase tower, one hand on his hip, the other running through his hair. "In fact, you *shouldn't* go. The CIA doesn't always . . . they don't always get things right. Under these conditions, Roderick Flaa shouldn't have even been let through security."

"A little too late for that now," I say, frantically searching for a tennis outfit. I definitely unpacked one: breathable top and a white skirt that hits just above the knee. For this vacation, security's ditched the staff that normally helps with the PM's wardrobe; I'm on my own. "Would it be uncharacteristic of Sofia to back out of a match?"

Flynn rubs his eyebrows. "Probably. But we can easily make up an excuse."

"What's on the schedule for the rest of the afternoon?"

"Late lunch, tour of the grounds, piano bar, dinner, meeting the real PM tonight."

"Okay, so I'm touring the grounds, with an emphasis on the tennis courts." My eyes sweep around the suite. "Did you see a pair of tennis shoes anywhere?"

"Closet to the left," he says, those blue swim trunks clinging to his thighs. His shirt's half-unbuttoned, like he hastily did it up, racing back upstairs to conference with me, and I have a flash of him in the water, telling me about his last mission. *What the hell happened, Flynn?* "Max, hold up a second. This is a step above sitting on the beach. Most of the guests here have never met the prime minister face-to-face, and you've managed to stumble on the one that has. It's low risk. He doesn't know her extremely well; they're just acquaintances, political allies, but . . . Are you positive you're up for this?"

"No," I tell him honestly, grabbing the sneakers and tying them tight. The laces do not shake in my hands as I bunny-loop. "But I don't want to feel like I'm failing at the first hurdle. How hard can it be, if they're not that close? I have laryngitis; we won't talk. I can play half an hour of tennis, if it keeps my cover."

I'm acting more confident than I feel.

Maybe Flynn sees through it. After the tunnel, though, after my demand for a pep talk, he has no choice but to build me up. "Fine. All right, fine. It'll be a good practice run for the back half of the holiday, if you happen to bump into any diplomats in Rome. The prime minister has a wicked backhand, and I remember that you do, too, so . . ." He blows out a breath. "Give 'em hell, kid."

In that blown-out breath, I hear everything Flynn isn't saying: that it's a smidge suspicious for Roderick to show up, unannounced, in the middle of a potential assassination plot. Definitely thought about that myself. "Do we trust him?" I pry.

Flynn runs his tongue over his teeth. "He's been vetted by Sofia's offices."

"Not what I asked."

"I trust him enough to be on the opposite side of a tennis court with you, in broad daylight, thirty feet from my face," Flynn finishes, and that's closer to an answer. "If anything happens, which

I highly doubt it will, I'll be right there. It's a bigger worry that you'll out yourself as the double."

"Which I won't," I add, again. If I underline my confidence enough, maybe it'll carry me through the rest of the trip. "I've been thinking . . . Should I at least practice her accent, just in case I really need to speak, in an emergency? That way, I can protect myself, but not out myself."

"Have you ever tried to do a Summerlandian accent?" Flynn asks.

I think back to the first evening after my recruitment, where I stayed up late watching the prime minister on YouTube, my lips curling over the vowels in the dark. "Not in any serious way. But it's basically Norwegian, isn't it?"

Flynn's eyes light up, golden flecks around his pupils. "And you can do a Norwegian accent?"

"Oh, I didn't say that."

"Then just . . . just give it a try. Hit me with it. Tell me, in Sofia's voice, that you . . . are very pleased to meet me."

I clear my throat, feeling like I'm about to give a speech in class. "*I am . . .*" I say, trying to wrap my tongue around the accent: melodic and pitchy, just like Sofia's. "*I am very pleased to meet you.*"

Flynn's face drops. Which is understandable. I've heard it, too.

"Oh my god," I breathe out.

"It wasn't—it wasn't terrible."

"Flynn! I sound like a bad impression of the guy from *Frozen*! The one who owns that ski lodge slash sauna. I should be riding on the back of a reindeer."

He pats my shoulder in a way that's meant to be reassuring. "We can practice, if you want."

"Good, because if I use that accent, I won't have to be assassinated. They'll throw me out of the hotel and onto the next plane back to America."

Flynn tells me to brush it off. And mostly, I do.

"You caught the sun a little," he says, pointing to the pink on the back of my shoulders. "Do you want me to aloe that?"

Do I want Flynn rubbing gel onto my bare skin with his bare hands?

Best not.

"I'm good," I say.

"I know, I know, the rules," he says, grabbing a bottle of aloe from the bathroom countertop and tossing it, underhand, my way. Luckily, my reflexes don't fail me; I catch the bottle midair. "No touching. You can't look like a lobster, though. Ruins the ministerial image."

Annoyed but taking his point, I squirt some of the green gel into my palm, lathering my shoulders and a stretch of my back.

"You missed a spot."

"Where?"

"Midback," he says.

"I got there."

"No, you didn't."

I try again, contorting my arms.

"Still missed it," Flynn says. I throw him a pointed glare before he holds up his hands, the picture of innocence. "Hey, I'm just trying to keep you from peeling like an iguana."

I actually do believe him. "Lobster, iguana, I'm a carousel of animals today, aren't I?" Half under my breath, I mutter, "Okay, fine, we're wasting time. Just do it."

Taking the bottle, he spills a dollop of aloe into his own palm, positioning himself behind me. With one long, delicate finger, he strokes away a piece of hair from the back of my neck. A shiver— not necessarily the bad kind—zips down my spine.

"Sorry, must be cold," he comments, noticing my goose bumps, as if the aloe has already touched my skin. I suppress a gasp when his palm meets my midback, working a light circle beneath my shoulder blades. It isn't overtly sexual; I can tell that's not his intention. But the slick feel of his hand, grazing gently over me; the cold sting of the aloe under the heat of him; the way I could back up a few inches and nestle myself between his hips—it's enough to make my nipples pinch. A part of me wants to linger here for a second longer.

And I wonder if he feels the same, if that little hitch in his throat is because of me.

"There," he says. "You're good."

"Good," I say, forcing out the word.

"Good," he says, like this has become a game of ours, our own private tennis match, except neither of us can quite look each other in the eye.

Moving on!

I drag myself into the bathroom. Shoes on, skirt on, Nike shirt and matching tennis hat on, I spring into the entryway, waiting for my handler to change into tennis gear as well. (In the bathroom, too, obviously. Not in front of me.) Maintaining his I'm-merely-a-guest façade, he throws on a lightweight shirt that waterfalls over his torso, and follows me from forty to fifty feet behind, all the way down to the courts. I'll admit, having Flynn at my back—all muscle and suaveness and speed—makes me feel a bit invincible. As he laced up his shoes, he also gave me the lowdown on Roderick—the PM's known him tangentially for five years, they run in the same Summerlandian circles, and he has a Chihuahua named Boudicca, after the British warrior queen.

The last bit of intelligence proves to be especially useful.

Boudicca—or "Boudie," as she's called—is present at the tennis courts, scuttling around Roderick's feet. Her ears perk when she sees me, and I wonder if the one who's most apt to clock me as the double is actually an eight-pound ball of buttercream fur. That tiny, twitching nose *knows* something's different. When she prances up to me, yapping across the court, my throat clenches. Luckily, after the first sniff, she melts against my shoes, practically cooing.

Another test, passed.

Once again, Roderick swaggers up to me, Flynn pretending to stretch his hamstrings next to the opposing court. We're around the backside of Hotel Giorgio, a stone's throw from the infinity pool, where two clay courts cut into the cliff. "I'm ready for a rematch," Roderick says, pausing at the net. I'm on one side; he's on the other. Covertly—or what *feels* like covertly—I reposition my necklace so Flynn can hear, just in time for Roderick to add, in a dipped-down voice: "Otherwise, I can think of other activities."

Come again, buddy?

"Remember when we played that match in London?" he adds, not just bordering on flirtatious. He's full-out scaled the wall. One of his dark eyebrows is sky-high, and he's dragging his thumb across his bottom lip in a way that looks, quite frankly, like he wants to rip off my tennis outfit and lick my naked body. "And . . . afterward?"

I most certainly do not remember that.

The corners of Roderick's eyes crinkle, approaching a double wink. In his courtside-green tennis outfit, disturbingly snug across his pectoral muscles, he is halfway between a catalog model and an advertisement for lawn restoration services. "You're conserving your voice, but we've never needed words, have we, Sofia?"

I blink at him, from his tight-tight shirt to his sparkling white sneakers, holding in an almost-guttural reaction. Schooling my face into a neutral expression takes *work*. Flynn was wrong. This isn't a low-risk, one-on-one interaction. Sofia doesn't just know this man tangentially. She *knows* this man, in a biblical sense.

That's suddenly painfully obvious as Roderick gazes at her—gazes at *me*—with virtually unrestrained lust in his eyes.

"Oh . . . kay," Flynn says slowly and quietly into the earpiece. By the second court, he's recalculating, pretending to focus on toe-touch stretches as light reflects off his tennis whites. "We can either get you out of here on urgent business—cough for option one—or you can back away from the net with a noncommittal smile and play the game."

He's leaving it up to me? Why would he leave it up to me? That confidence I was feeling earlier doesn't have nearly as much float as a tennis ball.

Roderick's waiting for my response. So is Flynn.

Sunshine beats down on my bangs as I wonder—darkly, in the back of my mind—if Roderick is the one Sofia was trying to warn me about in her note. The reason this mission is more dangerous than I presumed. Is her secret lover a secret assassin?

I back away, more out of fear than commitment to the game. Fear of Roderick, but also fear that—if I leave—I'll break my cover. On the first day. In the first couple of hours. Five million dollars and my chance at a better life, down the drain, in one abandoned tennis match.

Across the net, Roderick whispers something to me in what sounds like Norwegian. Or Swedish. Or possibly Danish. Hard to tell when you speak literally none of those languages.

"Try to remember what he's saying," Flynn prompts, hovering close by. He doesn't sound that worried, so . . . I shouldn't be worried? "We'll debrief later."

The dog wants to debrief *now*.

She's weaving between my ankles like there's a treat stuffed in my socks, and Roderick chuckles, jogging around the net with his hair flip-flopping, scooping up the Chihuahua—who immediately starts biting him. I'm talking full-out munching on his

palms, nibbling with loud gremlin noises. *Grrr-aarr-aaaa!*
Graaaa-rraaaaaa! I'm flinching, from the visual, the sound, and
the closeness of a maybe-assassin.

Roderick isn't flinching. Boudie must be a bit gummy, no teeth.

"She's always like this!" Roderick says to me, thankfully in English this time. "Still! When she came up to you so calmly, I'll be
honest, I was surprised. Maybe this holiday has changed something about you already, Sofia. You must be more relaxed."

At this, I nod and press my lips together, picking up a racket
and a ball from one of my security team members. For this time,
and this time only, I'm grateful I can't say anything. Let's not
question the Chihuahua's observations (although, Roderick really
should. Who doesn't notice that the woman they're lusting after
is a completely different person?).

I wonder how much Sofia actually likes him—if she ever did.

Understandably, she's verbally evasive when it comes to relationships. People are always asking her—and she manages to spin
their questions into conversations about feminism in the twenty-
first century, or how the press unfairly targets women. In all her
years in politics, she's given only one quote about her romantic
history, in that British *Vogue* article I read before Gail dropped by
with bagels: "Dating in politics is a minefield. I always feel like a
spy. Never going anywhere a camera could reach, every meeting
behind locked doors. It may seem like a good way to get to know
someone, but I could never . . . walk with them in Sommerang
park. Get a coffee, browse a bookstore. Normal Sundays. Normal
couple things. That sort of isolation, it distorts your impressions.
You think you love someone—when actually, they're the only one
there."

Anyway, it's my serve.

It occurs to me, as I toss the ball up into the air—half-blinded
by the Italian sun—that I might've exaggerated my readiness to

Flynn. I might've considered, a touch more deeply, the last time I played tennis. Which was approximately a decade ago, in a recreational league near my grandmother's retirement home. Hazily, in the background, I hear the metal gate to the court squeak open— all the way on Roderick's side of the net—and I take in a deep breath as I swing. My racket cuts through the heat, a quick swipe. The movement feels *good*. Natural. Muscle memory. Flynn and I, sometimes that summer, would play after our shifts, squeezing out that last bit of post-dinner-rush energy before bed.

The ball rockets forward, a yellow missile.

I think I've crushed it.

But really, Giorgio's entered at the side of the court. To watch us play? To cheer us on? To receive a tennis ball in the jugular?

That's what happens.

My serve is more than a little off.

I watch with unrestrained horror as the ball crashes into his throat, knocking him back, and he staggers around the court like he's had twelve limoncellos too many, pawing at the water table, gasping. Flynn hisses into my earpiece.

Shit! Shit, shit, shit.

Rushing up to Giorgio, the world's biggest apology on the tip of my tongue, I help stabilize him as he insists—absolutely *insists*, in a raspy voice—that he's fine. Perfectly fine. *Completely* fine! It's no worse than the bee! He has braved extreme throat pain before! *Go back to your game, Signora Prime Minister, go back to your game. I have just come to tell you your brother called again. I take a message. Don't worry about Giorgio.*

It's all going very well.

After checking on Giorgio as well, Flynn decides (apparently) that the best way to keep me calm is to crack a joke. "At least we know how you might take down any assassins now," he says, speaking into cupped hands on the other court. "Tennis ball, straight to the jugular."

I sniff out a laugh, able to breathe again.

I couldn't repeat that shot if I tried.

The rest of the match unfolds much less violently. We volley back and forth as I find my swing. Boudie rushes the court like a streaker, yapping at Roderick's heels, and we pause the play until she's safely on the sidelines again. "Your serve!" Roderick yells, right before he dives after the ball—and misses dramatically, racket swinging into empty air. "It's getting better! Bravo, Sofia! Bravo."

This, I can do. Move confidently on the court, like Sofia. Glide and swing and sweat. Be the active decoy. Unless Roderick is the greatest actor this side of Kenneth Branagh (doubtful), he's fooled by my performance. What I'm less sure about—much, much less sure—is the chitchat afterward. Roderick wipes his brow with the back of his hand, pausing play after half an hour (we aren't actually keeping score), and asks if I'd like to grab lunch with him. It's a suggestive invitation. "Get lunch," from Roderick's mouth, sounds an awful lot like "get laid."

Mmmm, Roderick, no.

I gesture vaguely toward my security team, hoping this says, *I have other plans, my schedule is full of . . . things.* Prime minister things. Important, vacation things. Roderick doesn't quite grasp the message; his eyebrows quirk in a lost-puppy way, his head tilting to the side. Fortunately, his cell phone rings—I wonder, somehow, if Flynn orchestrated that—and he's called away to another lunch, promising that he'll be back at the hotel late in the afternoon.

Goody. I'll be looking forward to that!

Boudicca trails by his heels, doggy paws padding up the stairs.

I hear her, around the corner, trying to tussle with the bomb-sniffing German shepherds.

I'm left on the courts, cocooned in Sofia's security team, chugging water from a glass bottle. It's sweating just as much as I am. Condensation dribbles down my neck, the sun even higher in the sky than it was a few minutes ago. We're "isolated," up a hill and behind a gate, but the sounds of distant Vespas sweep on the streets. Layered on top of that is the slap of the sea, and the shuffle of Flynn's footsteps in my direction. He jerks his head toward the small, covered cabana by the courts—the one that houses fresh towels and extra tennis balls.

Catching his drift, excusing myself, I meet him briefly inside, away from any prying eyes. "Sofia *really* knows that guy," I say immediately, taking another quick swig of water. It's hotter in here than on the courts, and I want ice cubes, a cold bath, a dip in the sea. "He doesn't seem like her type. At all. Not that I'm an expert on her personal life."

Flynn fans the neckline of his shirt, skin glistening, and the already-cramped vestibule starts to feel . . . tighter. Warmer. He glances at my water, and without even thinking, I offer him some; he grabs the bottle, taking his own swig, and it's so unexpectedly intimate. His mouth on the same glass. Casually sharing a drink. "This'll look suspicious, fast," Flynn tells me between gulps, "so before you forget, what did Roderick say to you, exactly, when he was whispering? The Norwegian? Can you remember?"

"Uh . . ." I scrounge for the words, doing my absolute best to replicate his verbiage. "It was something like . . . *Du sah-ret meg . . . some . . . en vakker vannmelon?*"

Flynn pinches his lips together. "I don't think that's right."

"Why, what's it mean?"

"'You hurt me like a beautiful watermelon.'"

"Okay, fair enough." Pushing my bangs back from my eyes, I

catch Flynn's forearm before he turns to leave—and then immediately drop my hand, remembering the rules I set out. "Hey, how
was I?"

"As the double?" Flynn asks, his eyes flicking down—just for
a second—to where I touched him. "Believable. There was only
that slight mishap with Giorgio."

"Oh god." My stomach gutters. "We owe him a gift basket. Get
him that . . . macaroni and cheese one. Maybe with socks." We
should swing on by the lobby, right now, to check on him. See if
he needs some ice, or some goat soap added to his apology basket.

"Giorgio asked me for your full schedule, by the way. Earlier."
Flynn grinds his molars for a second. "I'm not sure how I feel
about that."

"He's just being accommodating."

"Probably. But there's always a chance he could be coordinat-
ing with the enemy. Narrowing down your whereabouts. Times,
activities, locations."

"No," I say, unwilling to believe it. "Not Giorgio. He's too . . ."

"Giorgio?"

"Exactly."

Flynn says, "Just keep your guard up. Anyway, we should go."

I puff out a breath. Is anything else going to get thrown at me
today? An impromptu tennis match with Sofia's maybe–secret
lover was already more than enough. Statistically speaking, the
afternoon has to run smoothly, right?

Back inside, Flynn's walking a respectable distance behind me,
and I'm enveloped inside my security team, strolling toward the
elevator, tennis shoes pounding the tile. From outside the dining
room, white-wine glasses and sparkling dinner plates already set
for the next meal, I have a clear shot of the lobby. Hotel staff push
glimmering gold suitcase trolleys. The fountain's spurting out a
steady stream of water. Giorgio looks okay! He's puttering around

like a peacock, welcoming several new guests in a non-raspy voice—a woman in elegant, wide-legged trousers, an elderly couple with more luggage than the prime minister, and . . . someone on the fringes. Someone who, even at this distance, looks familiar.

"Max!"

My neck stiffens, ears ringing, like I've just heard an explosion.

"Max!" the voice calls again from the lobby.

No. That's all I can think as my pulse skyrockets. *Absolutely no way. Nothing else can possibly go wrong today.* There must be another Max in this hotel. A French tourist called "Maxime," or a member of the PM's security team, or someone in the dining room. A waiter! The piano guy. The Italian greyhound in the miniature hat, sniffing his owner's shoes by the bar.

"Margaux *Adams*!" the voice shouts for a third time, and that's . . . my name. That is my first name and my last name, assembled in the correct order, and I should keep in character, keep striding toward my suite with brisk efficiency—but it's instinct. *Hear full name, freeze.* When I stop on the fancy white tile, right as the elevator doors ding open, I see him bobbing toward me. A crown of black curls, flashing through the hotel lobby.

My throat constricts, as if I'm being strangled.

As if he's strangling me.

Calvin. Against all odds, against all reason, the man hurtling in my direction is none other than my roommate.

12

t's your roommate, Calvin!" he adds for extra clarity, waving his hand like he's trying to hail Positano's very last taxicab. I don't know what's more striking: his bright yellow board shorts, his Hawaiian shirt, or the way his American accent cuts through all the melodic Italian like a machete through butter.

How . . . How is he . . . ?

In a split second, we catch each other's eyes, the wave of his hand growing impossibly larger as his flip-flops flap against the tile. The only way he could be more conspicuous is if he were shooting off fireworks from his ears.

My face goes almost completely numb.

How did Calvin know I was here? How'd he slip past the hotel gates? How'd he afford airfare to Italy, if he won't even splurge for name-brand ranch dressing?

Those aren't the questions I should be asking. I should be asking how to stop him from getting all-out dropkicked by half of the PM's security team, who're rushing with such speed, they make their own breeze. Thanks to pre-vetting, Roderick and his dog cruised past the guards. That isn't going to be Calvin's fate, is it? The ringing in my ears turns to a full-out alarm as, from over a dozen yards away, Calvin's eyebrows crunch together in an inquis-itive zigzag, like *Oh, damn, maybe I should've texted first?* I don't see much else. Just a glimpse of it: guests scattering in the lobby as two officers charge, each man grabbing one of Calvin's shoulders before slamming him to the ground. His back hits the tile in an almost cartoonish *thud.* I would say that Calvin goes down like a sack of potatoes. But really, he goes down like a flailing toddler wrangled into a car seat, and it's all *fast.*

Chaos erupting, fast.

Sofia's security pushing me into the elevator, fast, yelling, "Down, down, down!"

The last flash of an image I get is Calvin staring up at Lars with the wide eyes of an abandoned possum, as if to say: *Dude, why? So not cool.*

Then, Flynn's at my side so quickly I didn't even see him com-ing. The top of his shirt is haphazardly buttoned, a lock of his hair dangling over his forehead. He's messy, sun-kissed, a tennis towel slung around his neck. Automatically, his hand is at my elbow, pulling me even farther into the corner of the elevator, shielding me as the doors start to ping closed. Flynn's acting as if I actually am the prime minister, like protecting me is the most important thing in the world—and I am startlingly aware of his closeness, his power, the strength radiating from every muscle in his body. He has me securely pinned, all of him pressing against all of me. If we were lying down, he'd cover me completely.

I don't want the touch of his hand, the press of his body, to send an electric current across my skin, but *dammit,* there it is. An un-deniable, dangerous spark. From less than two inches away, I watch the steady pulse near the freckles at the base of his throat, and have to admit to myself that—in this little protective pocket— I have never felt safer in my life.

Having a bodyguard is one thing.

It's another thing because it's *him*.

The jolt of the elevator, starting its ascent, snaps me out of it. I cough, wiggle my shoulders a bit, implicitly signaling, *I'm fine, honest.* It's just the two of us in this cramped space—much smaller than the tennis court cabana—and Flynn can take only a half step back, soft elevator music punctuating our jagged breaths, the warmth of his fingers protectively wrapped around my elbow, like he's forgotten to let it drop. His skin is exactly as I remember. His scent is exactly as I remember, salted with the sea, and he's—

He's punched the emergency stop button with the palm of his hand.

The elevator screeches to a halt.

"Why'd you do that?" I say, voice coming out a little hoarse.

"Security needs time to reach the sixth floor," he says, tone deeper than normal. His hand finally drops from my elbow, the absence of his touch making me cold. "And to contain the threat."

"Calvin is not an assassin!" I whisper-shout, well aware that someone might be listening between the second and third floors, where we've stopped. I shouldn't let anyone know that *I* know who Calvin is. "In case you've forgotten, he's my roommate. He recently rescued a turtle. He cries during rose ceremonies on *The Bachelor*."

"Mind telling me what he's doing in Italy, then?" Flynn asks, thumbing the space between his eyebrows. Calvin, on top of Roderick, back-to-back, is probably a lot for any handler. Flynn hasn't lost his cool, but I notice a hairline crack in his demeanor. The smallest touch of worry, slipping in. "Because it looks a little goddamn suspicious that he shows up, for no plausible reason whatsoever, on the same day that you show up, at the same *hotel* that you've just checked into, only to rush the prime minister's body double, mimicking an assassin, in the middle of an assassination plot."

"That is obviously not ideal."

"How did he even know you were going to be in Italy?"

The question hits me like a dart in the ass.

The note. I remember the note. The one I scribbled for my parents and tucked under my pillow, right before I left my apartment: *I love you both. I'm sorry.* A knowing tingle works its way up my spine. Well shit, Calvin! No one was supposed to find that note until later. Actually, I'd hoped—nay, expected—that no one would find it at all. Is it possible that Calvin traipsed into my room immediately after I was gone?

Why would he?

"He might've . . ." I begin, wondering how to make this sound anything other than bad. "He might've read the note I left?"

Flynn's eyelashes flick. "What note, Max?"

"Okay, listen, all I thought was if anything happens to me, I want my parents to know I love them. I didn't give any specific details, besides that I was in Italy, and that was only so they'd know where to collect the body. Which I know doesn't make much sense, but . . . the note wasn't for Calvin! I figured someone else, someone official, would search my room, just not two seconds after I left."

Flynn pokes his tongue into the side of his cheek, clearly digesting this, his hands now firmly on his hips. He still has a clear aura of calm, despite the absolute clusterfuck of this situation. "But how'd he know where you were staying? Which part of Italy, precisely, and which hotel? Kind of a big country, Max, and Gail turned off the geolocational services on your cell phone. Not to mention, we've triple-checked the guest list. Unless he booked under another name, and unless he's good for three thousand dollars a night, which is the minimum spend here, up front, this is unexplainable."

"Maybe he . . ." I begin, but I've got nothing. Literally nothing. I'm half expecting to hear him shout through the elevator doors, telling anyone who'll listen that the woman in the tennis clothes isn't the prime minister of a small island nation off the coast of Norway—she's his roommate from Maine, the same one who makes electric-orange mac and cheese at two in the morning. And then what? Then where would we be? "I need to talk to him."

"Absolutely not," Flynn says with the ghost of a laugh. He tucks a longer chunk of hair halfway behind his ear. "Calvin's a suspect, and this is different than with Roderick. Roderick thinks you *are* Sofia. Which is a little ridiculous, that someone who knows her intimately can't tell the difference immediately, but . . . Calvin can blow up this whole operation. We need to contain this. Assure him he's got the wrong person. Tell everyone from the lobby staff to the security team that the 'Max' thing was a mix-up. He was high, confused."

My teeth worry over my bottom lip. "Do you know where they'll take him?"

"There's a conference room downstairs," Flynn says. "Giorgio offered it in advance, as a holding station in case there was a perimeter breach."

"I still think I should talk to Calvin," I insist, stomach roiling as I remember the sound of him hitting the floor with an inelegant *whack*. "Flynn, he knows it's me. He clearly knows it's me. It would be much better to just tell him the truth and beg him to keep quiet, rather than try to gaslight him into—"

I've made a mistake. In the heat of my argument, I've leaned forward—at the same time that Flynn's re-angled his body, reaching to un-press the emergency stop. We collide in a delicate brush, his beard grazing my forehead, my hand against the ridges of his stomach, and both of us just sort of . . . freeze. It's like puzzle pieces snapping together.

Is he going to *pesto* this, or should I?

Flynn tsks. "We're not great at following these rules, Starfish," he says, right by my ear, voice husky and teasing. "Is there some sort of punishment for breaking them?"

I swallow hard, struggling to maintain my professionalism. "Why, Flynn?" I bat back, breath on his neck. "Do you want there to be?"

He chuckles at that, palming the button, like I've won this round for now, and once again we're speeding along.

Back in the room, security swarming outside, the door shuts with an agitated *click*, and my CIA phone buzzes on the coffee table. Flynn and I reach for it at the same time, but I'm closer and just a hair faster. I answer, knowing it's Gail. No one else has this number, right? "Hello?"

"I'm getting word that there was an assassin in the lobby?" Gail says, as if someone's just forwarded her a picture of a flailing Calvin, half-knocked-out by the peeing-angel statue.

"He's not an assassin," I supply.

"Then why did he have a knife?"

"Jesus, *what*?"

She's quick after that. "He didn't. I was just testing your reaction. Seeing how much you actually trust this man."

A knot tangles even more tightly in my throat. "Is that standard protocol for the CIA? *Hello, your roommate just tried to kill you, how does that make you feel?*"

"Not usually," she says as Flynn whispers in front of me, twirling his finger to say *Volume up, put Gail on speakerphone*. I do, just in time for her to add, "We have a minor problem."

"I'll tell him to forget everything he saw," I assure her. "To stay quiet and go back—"

Gail cuts in. "We're on different pages here. Calvin is a pressing issue, so is the Roderick man—I got the security footage from this morning, from the tennis courts—but I've just received something else, a picture, in the seconds we've been speaking. I'm now talking about Agent Forester."

Crowded against my side, Flynn jerks his head back like *Me?*

My left eyelid twitches for the first time since the flight to Rome. "What about Agent Forester?"

"He's supposed to act as your bodyguard *in your room.*"

"And?"

"He was not in your room," Gail says flatly, like I'm an idiot. "He was very much on full display, in the lobby, sweaty, tennis shirt unbuttoned like a pirate on the cover of a romance novel."

"Hey-hey, I wouldn't say *that,*" Flynn interjects as I jump in to question the existence of Tennis Pirates, but Gail is far from done.

In fact, she's picking up speed. "The paparazzi have obviously paid off someone from the hotel lobby. They have a shot of you and Flynn exchanging a weighted look, both of you glistening with sweat, before getting cozy in the elevator. We're going to have to get ahead of the story—tell everyone that the prime minister has a new head bodyguard. Otherwise, the press will latch on to another narrative."

"Which is?" I grimace, already half knowing the answer.

"That the prime minister has a new gentleman suitor."

Flynn chokes out a laugh. "That's ridiculous."

His words shouldn't sting. Objectively, I know he means that the press are ridiculous, that the situation is ridiculous, even the term *gentleman suitor*—especially in relation to a world leader—is ridiculous, but a vicious part of my brain hears: *What, me and Max? Never. No way.*

"That's *juicy,*" Gail corrects, even though I wouldn't peg her— by any stretch of the imagination—as a person who'd use *juicy* in a sentence. I'm also now imagining her in pink velour sweatpants with the word *JUICY* bedazzled on the bum, and that could not be further from her vibe. "A woman in power—much less a single woman, leading on her own—always makes men itch. Speaking of, we have an update on 'the Producer.' The footage from the convenience store was too grainy to tell anything other than the fact that he's around five foot ten, but Interpol flagged one of his aliases at a bus station outside Vienna. Two hours too late to catch him, I might add, but we're on the trail."

"Vienna." The hairs prick on the back of my neck. "Austria. So he *is* on his way to Italy. What do I do?"

"Sit tight for the next four and a half days," Gail says, "while we keep drawing him out of the woodwork. And try not to look like you're about to have international relations with your bodyguard."

The line disconnects. She's gone.

13

The twitch has traveled to both eyelids. Flynn convinces me that a prime minister wouldn't confront her potential attacker in a hotel wine cellar (*fair enough*), so I'm perched in the next room with a pair of headphones and a video monitor, trying to focus on an image of my American roommate—and forget that an international assassin might be buying currywurst in Austria right now, fueling up to kill me.

Easier said than done.

The monitor shows an expensive-looking conference room with plush green dining chairs—and Calvin, handcuffed to one of them. He looks a bit like Houdini, pre-escape from a water tank, wrists bound behind his back. Is it just me, or does he also look . . . unfazed? So perfectly at ease in this utterly bizarre situation. In the middle of the room, flaky pastries and already-drunk espresso cups rest on what can be described only as an interrogation table. Flynn dismisses the Italian police before stalking forward, repositioning a chair, and situating himself intimidatingly in front of Calvin, who isn't a big guy. The height difference is striking.

"What do you think is going on here?" Flynn asks calmly, like he's done this before. Maybe not this *exact* scenario—body double, Hawaiian-shirted roommate, conference room on the coast of Italy—but close enough that he's played the part. He knows to clasp his hands together and make just enough eye contact with the guy strapped to a chair.

I increase the brightness on the monitor. Calvin's considering Flynn's question with a pensive glance. He's more sober than I've ever seen him—which, honestly, isn't saying much. His pupils still have the half-glazed look of a Krispy Kreme doughnut. "I think . . ." he says, closing one eye a smidge, "that I saw Max. In fact, I know that I saw Max. But everyone's saying that wasn't Max, which is weird, because that *was* Max."

Oh, he absolutely knows.

Flynn switches tactics, approaching him like a kindergarten teacher might speak to a student accused of eating Play-Doh. "Calvin, do you think you can tell us why you are here?"

"I needed to be here," Calvin says, dead serious, one black curl springing across his forehead. "This hotel is also *much* nicer than my and Max's apartment. Did you see that fountain in the lobby? Solid marble. I bet this is the type of place where they give you those tiny pillow mints and the chocolates with the—"

"Calvin," Flynn says, cutting him off, as I wonder if the take-down gave him a concussion. Or is he being purposefully evasive? "Start at the beginning. Can you please explain why you thought 'your roommate' would be at this hotel?"

"Sure thing," Calvin says, jumping into story mode. "Picture this: a normal morning. I go out, grab some bean juice, pick up some weed—" He pauses briefly, like maybe he shouldn't have mentioned this particular detail in front of a federal official, but, oh well, cat's out of the bag now! "When I come back, who do I find? Someone wearing a trench coat, who says she's from the Maine State Lottery." He taps the side of his temple. "But I used my noggin, and I thought to myself, 'Calvin, when you won the lottery, no one came straight to your door.'"

My eyelashes flit at the monitor. *I'm sorry, what?*

Flynn, rightfully, questions this. "You mean like a scratch-off ticket?"

"No, I won megabucks, the lottery-lottery," Calvin says, without so much as a flinch. "Four point two million dollars. Well, just about half of that after taxes, because I opted for the cash payout. That's what my certified public accountant advised me. He's my desk-buddy at the tax bureau."

On-screen, I glimpse Flynn's dubious expression, which must match my own.

"He's kidding," I say to myself, flat.

"You won megabucks," Flynn says, just as flat.

Calvin's eyebrows squiggle. "I think I've told Max that before."

This is where I slide off my headphones and stand up, giving a *one second* gesture to the security behind me. *I'll be right back.* Two of the black-suited officers try to stop me, reason with me, but I absolutely insist. It's ridiculous for me to just sit here and listen; I could get to the bottom of this so much faster.

When I pass through the connecting door between rooms, Flynn doesn't look surprised to see me—and neither does Calvin. "Heeey, Max," he says, slowly tipping his chin in my direction.

This familiar movement, the friendly smile he's giving me, sends a pang of affection straight into my chest. Calvin's well-meaning, isn't he? Even if he can't read the room.

I pull up a chair. "I know I've been a little bit out of it lately," I say, "but I think I would've remembered you telling me that you won over four million dollars. Why do you . . . only buy bargain-brand salad dressing, then? And eat so much cheap frozen pizza?"

Calvin shrugs, unperturbed. "I like cheap frozen pizza. Everyone likes cheap frozen pizza. It's got the extra crunch from the freezer burn, and you can buy a lot of it with coupons. I have money, but I'm not *made* of money. I've invested a lot of it in Bitcoin."

Flynn nudges the conversation back into a reasonable direction, clearing his throat. "So you saw the woman in the trench coat and you . . ."

"Oh, right," Calvin says. "I decided to noodle that one for a while, when I went to feed my . . ." He trails off for a second, like he's said too much and he's covering his tracks. "My pet."

"His turtle," I clarify to Flynn.

Alarm flares on Calvin's face. "How do you know about Kevin?" Of course the turtle's name is Kevin. Kevin and Calvin, an iconic duo. Guiltily, he continues, "Our lease doesn't allow reptiles. Anyway, when I opened the terrarium that morning, I couldn't find him. Thought he'd escaped. I checked in Max's room and found the note."

"I just want to make sure I'm getting this straight," Flynn says, rubbing his forehead. "You thought your turtle, who probably walks at a pace of a mile every six years, somehow—in the course of a single morning—unlatched the door to Max's bedroom, either jumped or crawled at a *one hundred percent vertical angle* onto her mattress, and burrowed underneath her pillow?"

Once again, Calvin shrugs, as if this might be a likely scenario.

The terrible thing is, I believe him. My gut believes him.

Flynn is visibly less sure, especially when Calvin explains the rest—how he traced my phone to the airport before Gail turned off my navigational services. How he *knows a guy who knows a guy*, made some calls, and paid an undisclosed sum to track me down. Apparently, Calvin thought I'd been *taken*, kidnapped by *the woman with the bagels*, and he came here to rescue me like Liam Neeson in *that movie*.

"We're going to need a moment," Flynn says, holding up a long finger, and Calvin's like *Yeah, sure, take your time*. In the corner of the conference room, Flynn closes the gap between us and whispers to me, "This is the biggest load of bullshit I've ever heard."

"It could be true," I hiss back, neck craning up to look at Flynn. "Can't you just verify his story?"

"Which part? The lottery winning, the illegal reptile, or the privately commissioned black ops mission on foreign soil?"

"I realize it sounds a little far-fetched." I run my tongue along my teeth. "Did you background-check him?"

"'Course. Thoroughly."

"And there was nothing about the lottery?"

"No. To be fair, the state doesn't have to disclose the winners." Flynn wipes a hand down his face. "Okay, here's what we're going to do. You tell him to stay silent while I secure a noncommercial jet to send him discreetly home. On that journey, he won't speak to anyone—not security, not press, not his seatmate on the airplane. Not even about his turtle."

Over the next three and a half minutes, I manage to convince him that mum's the word. Does he fully grasp that I'm pretending to be a prime minister and he's just crashed the party? Doubt it. He accepts the terms anyway. As long as I haven't been abducted, he's cool. Which sincerely makes my heart swell. Add Calvin to the long list of people I owe.

"I can't believe my roommate traveled halfway around the world to Liam Neeson me," I tell Flynn back in the suite.

Flynn's quiet for a moment. "You just used Liam Neeson as a verb."

"I did."

"I like that." Opening the balcony doors, he steps outside. It's just shy of three o'clock, the midday sun golden on his skin, as he shoves his hands in his pockets and takes in a view of the sea. He doesn't turn around when he says, "For what it's worth, even though I don't believe a word of what he's just said—I don't blame him."

14

On the outside, the rest of the first day is the "simple vacation" I've been promised. Anyone watching would see a young prime minister, touring the grounds with Giorgio, sipping an Aperol spritz at the piano bar with a book in her hand, and dining on her balcony, security on all sides. Dinner's placed in front of me on white ceramic plates. The creamy scent of mushroom sauce hits my nose first, followed by the fresh tang of vinegar. The side salad is half burrata, a giant lump of cheese in the middle of a spring-lettuce crown; when I poke at it with my fork, the center splits in a delicious flow. I remove a few chunks of cucumber, remembering that Sofia's allergic. Pistachio gelato's next; the color of seafoam, it stares back at me from a cool, silver bowl.

I wish I felt like eating.

To keep myself distracted, any spare moment I get, I'm practicing Sofia's accent, listening to her voice over audio recordings and trying to make mine match. "I'm just going to grab a shower," I tell Flynn, sounding a *bit* more like her. Tonight, in an hour, I'm supposed to meet the real Sofia Christiansen, before slipping away with her into the powder room. The burning ashes of her note flicker in a dark corner of my brain, and I think, once again, that maybe I should bring it up to Flynn. But if Sofia wanted the CIA to pass me a message, wouldn't she have given it directly to them?

Snatching one of her pantsuits from the closet (cream linen, gold buttons), I slip into the bathroom and close the door behind me, trying to recenter myself. Trying to focus only on the pleasant scent of goat soap that Giorgio's staff have pyramid-stacked in the shower, on the cool water coursing down my body in the Italian heat. Not on Calvin, currently being escorted to the airport by Italian police; or on the Producer, somewhere outside of Vienna; or the fact that—

There isn't a towel.

There isn't a towel in here.

There are towels out there, by the sink. A whole stack of them. Fluffy ones. Luxurious ones. In here, there's a three-thousand-euro suit that'll wrinkle with water damage, a rubber-bottomed bath mat, and a loofah stick that'll barely cover my upper thighs. *Perfect. Today keeps getting better.* Washing the suds from my skin, I shut off the water with a groan, suck up my pride, and peek out the bathroom door. "Flynn?"

He's shirtless, changing into a fresh suit for the meeting. "Max?"

"Towel?" I ask, maintaining a neutral voice. No desperation.

To his credit, he's quick about it. Respectful about it. He shields his eyes as he passes the towel to me through the door crack, and I tell him *Thanks*, ignoring the leap in my heart rate.

"Anytime," he says as I shut the door and let out a breath in the fog, drying my hair and toweling off my arms, Flynn's words from the elevator washing over me like water: *For what it's worth . . . I don't blame him.*

Within half an hour, we're moving. It's the reverse of this morning, the opposite of our arrival. I'm shoved into a shiny black Range Rover, Giorgio waving goodbye from the steps of his hotel.

Instead of meeting Sofia in a tunnel, we'll see her at a restaurant on the outskirts of Positano, a quiet neighborhood spot that's closed for a private meeting. She'll filter in the back, disguised, alongside the head of her special protection group and two officers recruited from the Summerlandian military (since her private security force is currently protecting me); I'll saunter in the front of the restaurant, pretending to be Sofia.

This time, though, there's less fanfare to our journey. Fewer flags flying. No flashing lights and no police escort. We aren't drawing attention to the meeting. Flynn's driving instead of Lars, schooling me on select Norwegian words. *Hello, goodbye, yes, no.* I learn how to say *excuse me, good,* and—at Flynn's insistence—*Where is the library?*

"Always important to know," he says, brightly colored houses flickering past the bulletproof glass, "even for security reasons. Libraries are safe zones. Though, the press would follow her in there."

"It sucks that the press are after her," I say, thinking back to Gail's scolding over the phone.

"Of course they are," Flynn reasons, just as annoyed as I am. "The press are awful, and she's one of the most beautiful women on the planet."

I stop dead, the hint of a smile—despite everything—working its way into the corner of my mouth. "You think she's one of the most beautiful women on the planet?"

Flynn pops his lips. He's going to try and backtrack. Big-time. "What I meant was—"

"Because logic would dictate," I argue, arching an eyebrow at him in the mirror, "that if you think *she's* extremely beautiful, and I happen to look just like her—"

Flynn raises a finger, but no words come out of his mouth.

"Boy," I say, "for someone who claims to be all cool in a conversation, you sure walked right into that one."

Flynn snorts. "You're going to be cocky about this for the rest of the night, aren't you?"

"Could be," I say, dropping it before I have the chance to think about it too much. I go back to practicing Sofia's accent, quietly mumbling to myself until the Range Rover slows, pulling up to the restaurant. No one's tipped off the press, so when I step into the street—surrounded by the PM's security team, wobbling a touch in Sofia's stilettos—no cameras flash. It's an uneventful stroll into the building, past outdoor tables with lemon-colored cloths, purple flowers brimming from terra-cotta pots. Inside, the restaurant should be bustling, diners chatting loudly over their risotto, but all the tables stand empty.

"Go to the back," Flynn instructs, keeping pace at my side, and my neck cranes, glancing up at the ceiling, where those same purple flowers burst on vines, elegantly tangled like a jungle canopy. Everything's soft, light-filled, airy.

Except me. I'm sweating already, again, and it's not just the summer heat or the thickness of my suit. I jump when Flynn's phone rings, and he takes the call with his finger pressed to his ear, muttering, "Mmm-hmm, mmm-hmm, all right." And then to me: "They're late."

I scratch the space under my ear, uncomfortable. "Okay, do we wait back in the car?"

Flynn shakes his head. "No, kitchen. It's been cleared. We'll go upstairs when they get here."

The kitchen's at a standstill, too. Clean pots and pans, shimmering in the light. Gas cooktops, un-ablaze. I drum my fingers against the countertop, feeling—at once—at home and out of place. "How long until they get here?"

"Maybe an hour."

I blow out a long breath, taking a seat on a swivel chair. "All right."

Flynn peruses a few mason jars next to one of the stoves, glancing at the labels, and tip-taps his fingers on the countertop. "I know we have this asset-handler dynamic right now, but I was thinking—just a thought—that we could just be Flynn and Max for an hour. Just two people, hanging out. And then, if you want, shields right back up."

This sounds like a dangerous plan. I fidget in my seat. "What did you have in mind?"

"We could talk."

"About . . . ?"

"Whatever you want, I don't know." He shrugs, suddenly boyish, dragging a hand over the back of his neck.

Maybe it's the semidesperate look on his face or the eerie quiet of the restaurant, but the idea of sitting in silence for the next hour isn't appealing. "Okay," I begin cautiously, "why don't you tell me a story about your work."

This makes him smile. "CIA story time?"

"Yeah, everyone has work stories. Like, Gary the Goose."

Flynn raises an eyebrow. "Come again?"

"Never mind. Just—there must be something. One story that isn't classified."

"There is . . . a case that comes to mind," Flynn says, a bit hesitant. "One Gail told me about. From her FBI days . . . Oh, fuck it. Are you familiar with Nextdoor.com?"

I cross my legs in the swivel chair, settling in as best I can. "It's like Facebook for neighbors, right?"

"Yeah. Lots of recommendations for gardening companies and pictures of backyard snakes. 'Found this by my mailbox, what kind is it, is it poisonous,' that type of thing. And then fifty people in a row commenting that it's a harmless king snake, followed by some spam advertising for dishwasher detergent. Anyway, there's an eighty-two-year-old woman. Let's call her Sally."

"Her name really was Sally, wasn't it."

Flynn sucks his teeth. "Yeah, it was."

"Go on."

"So Sally posts a picture of her tulips, accusing someone in her neighborhood of clipping them. All the heads are gone. It's a tulip massacre."

"Tulip decapitation," I say, tutting. "Very serious."

"Only, her actual next-door neighbor, Mike, takes a zoomed-in screenshot of the tulips, pointing out that there are bite marks. The deer got them."

"Tough blow for Sally."

"Well," Flynn says, stroking his beard, "Sally isn't happy about it. She's unconvinced, and now thinks Mike is the culprit. Maybe he didn't bite them with his teeth, but he definitely clipped them somehow. So, in retaliation, she steals his cat."

"Oh, okay, that escalated quickly."

"He's an outdoor cat, so by steal, I mean she invites Marshmallow inside and gives him some trout-flavored Whiskas while they watch *Murder, She Wrote* together. Soon, Mike's posting pictures all over Nextdoor.com, asking if anyone's seen Marshmallow, because he has kidney disease and needs his medicine."

"The cat has kidney disease."

"Yes."

"Just making sure I'm keeping things straight. Okay." I urge him on with a twirl of my hand.

"Well, *another* neighbor, the one from across the street, who apparently spends most of his day peering out of his curtains to spy on the neighbors, *he* suggests, in the Nextdoor.com comments section on the original tulip post, that Mike might want to check at Sally's house, because the third neighbor may or may not have seen Marshmallow baited into Sally's foyer with a line of strategically placed cat treats."

"I literally have no idea how this is going to end," I say, leaning forward again, on edge. "Please tell me that Marshmallow's okay."

"Oh, cat's fine. *Mike* isn't fine. He climbed through the window of Sally's laundry room while she was sleeping, reverse-kidnapped Marshmallow, and went back to bed at his own house. With his cat. When Sally wakes up to find Marshmallow gone and a box of her Tide pods spilled on the laundry room floor, she's out for blood. She goes to the yellow pages to find a hit man."

My brows furrow. "Can you find a hit man in the yellow pages?"

"No. Which is why she then goes to Nextdoor.com."

"Nooooo, she doesn't."

"Oh yes. Oh yes, she does. She sets the post to 'private'—not sure what she thinks that's going to do—and that little blue button where you can 'request professional services'? She requests the speedy assistance of a trained assassin."

I bury my face in my hands. "Oh, Sally, no."

"Everyone thinks she's joking. Except for the people who think she has dementia, who refer her to a local assisted-living community with memory care. Well, at least one person doesn't think she's joking—the wannabe hit man who DMs Sally with his price, which is a hundred and twenty thousand dollars."

"Is that steep?"

"Meh. But Sally doesn't have her glasses on, thinks it's *a hundred and twenty* dollars followed by zero cents, and hires him on the spot. Gives him Mike's address. Turns out, the hit man was a federal agent in disguise, and now Sally's spending some of her golden years in a penitentiary in upstate New York. Marshmallow's living it up with Mike."

"Wow. That was . . ." I puff out my lips. "That was an exceptional story."

"Thank you," Flynn says, fingers dancing along the countertop, and it strikes me that work Flynn and *this* Flynn, behind closed doors, couldn't be more different. To the outside world, on duty, he's stoic and sleek; here, with me, he's chuckling through a story that features a cat named Marshmallow. "What about you? Any work stories? Tell me about this Gary."

I shrug. "There's nothing really to tell. He's just the embodiment of a troubled Victorian ghost in goose form."

Flynn laughs. "Okay, fair enough. What about stories from your restaurant?"

"I try not to think about my restaurant, honestly."

His shoulders tighten. "Why not?"

"I don't know, because it was a total failure?"

This actually appears to piss him off. "Jesus Christ, Max, don't sell yourself short like that. Do you know how many exceptional restaurants folded during the pandemic? Half the state of Maine folded. It didn't matter how good your restaurant was—how good you were."

I swallow, barely getting out words. "How do you know it was good? What if my food was terrible?"

"I'm sure it wasn't."

"Yeah, but how do you know? I could oversalt everything. I could be one of those people who puts cilantro on fish."

"Not a cilantro fan?"

"Do *you* want the taste of dirty dishwater on your tacos?" I ask.

"Guess not," he says, suppressing a smile. "For what it's worth, though, I'm proud of you. You said you were going to open a restaurant, and you did. You did the thing. Not many people can say that. I'm sure your parents were proud of you, too."

Can't argue with that. They always supported my dream of becoming a professional chef. When I was a kid, my mom used to sneak secret tastes of my recipes, dipping a sly spoon into the soups and casseroles before exploding with, *Oh! Maximillian! You've outdone yourself this time. Needs more salt, though.* (My mom had an undiagnosed iodine deficiency until I was eighteen. Everything, to her, needed more salt. I could provide her with *just* salt—and she'd say, *More salt.*)

What're they up to, right this second? Is it board game night? Bingo night? They're always going on these dates around town, laughing together in a way only two people who've known each other a long time laugh: heads fully back, voices to the ceiling.

All through my twenties, I kind of wondered if I'd ever have that—what they have. A relationship that lasts more than six months and doesn't culminate in a breakup box dropped unceremoniously at your door. (*Here is your Neato Burrito T-shirt and the novelty waffle iron you left at my house, good luck, goodbye.*) As I finally flicked off the lights at Frida's, I couldn't help but question if the pandemic wasn't to blame—if *I'd* screwed up my restaurant, just like I'd never managed to find the right person. If there was something about me, at the core, that wasn't assembled properly, and I'd forever be off-kilter, like one of those wonky tables that people keep shoving wads of napkins under, trying to balance out the legs, but your margarita is always, perpetually, just a little tilted.

My throat is starting to feel uncomfortably tight. "Thank you," I tell Flynn.

"You're welcome," he says, with enough good sense to move on. He pauses by one of the mason jars, an idea practically lighting over his head like a bulb. "I think I know something that can keep us entertained for the rest of the hour. Well, ten minutes, tops, plus recovery time."

"'Recovery time' doesn't sound promising." I sidle up next to him, glad about the change in topic. The labels on the jars are all, obviously, in Italian—but the clear glass shows a series of bright red chilis, suspended in liquid. "Every single one of those is hot."

"They won't miss a couple." His dimple pops, the temperature in the kitchen rising several notches. "I think we should eat one each, and see who breaks first."

What a terrible but intriguing idea. "How do you know I haven't developed a superhuman spice tolerance?"

"Oh, I'm counting on that, because I've already run out of un-classified stories—so we've got to make this activity last. Come on." Ushering me to one of the untouched countertops, he plunks six jars of peppers onto the stainless steel, arranging them in in-creasing spice level.

"So you know your peppers," I tell him, a little impressed.

"Are you impressed?"

"Didn't say that." I run my tongue along my teeth. "How do I know that *you* haven't developed a superhuman spice tolerance?"

"You don't," Flynn says. He unscrews the lid on the thickest peppers, fat red plump ones suspended in vinegar. An acidic plume hits the air, stinging the corners of my eyes. I grab one with pinched fingers. "Shall we?" he asks, his pepper kissing mine— like we're clinking *cheers*—and then it's bottoms up.

My teeth nip at the tip. "Do we have to bite it all in one go? How many times do we have to chew?"

"No real rules. Just chew it up and get it down."

I do that. "It's not . . . so bad."

"It's fine," he says.

"It's not even that spicy."

Then it hits.

"Holy *fuck*," Flynn says, immediately doubling over and laughing. Laughing so hard—*burning* so hard—that tears are streaming down his cheeks. "Gives a new meaning to 'I burn for you,' doesn't it?"

I cough, straining. "Are you the assassin? Is this how you kill me? Because it kind of—" *Hack, hack, cough.* "It kind of feels like I'm dying."

His forehead wrinkles with concern. "Should we stop?"

"No! We're only one in." Painful little bumps are starting to form on the tip of my tongue. "Remind me why we're doing this?"

"Fun distraction."

"Oh, right," I say, as Flynn passes me the second pepper.

He chews, coughing even harder. "I think I hate this."

"Hate in a fun way?" I'm chewing, too, waving a hand over my mouth. "It feels . . . It feels like the devil is tap dancing on my tongue with thorny red boots."

By the fourth pepper, we mutually decide to stop, raiding the fridge. Milk dribbles a thin line down the skin of Flynn's throat as I smear Greek yogurt over my tongue with a spoon.

"Flynn, you're supposed to swish!" I tell him, mouth half-full. "Swish and spit the milk into the sink, not swallow it!"

"Woooo," he says, dancing around with a little one-two step, like the fire has reached his feet. "I really wish you would've told me that about ten seconds ago."

"Everything okay in here?" Lars says, popping his head in.

And Flynn has to wave him off with a thumbs-up.

After Lars leaves, Flynn and I catch each other's eye—and absolutely burst out laughing. Because this is ridiculous. This whole thing is ridiculous. The peppers, the milk, the two of us, in Italy, waiting on a prime minister. I'm half-hysterical. I'm uninhibited.

It just comes out. "Did you ever look me up?"

Before the mission, I mean. Before the CIA tracked me down.

Flynn stills, hand on his stomach, but his face is soft. "Of course I looked you up," he says quietly. His Adam's apple bobs in a way that tells me, just maybe, he's nervous. "Did you look me up?"

Yes. Too many times. I even thought about getting back in touch, but there's a noticeable lack of information about Flynn online. Makes sense now. He doesn't even have any photos tagged on Instagram; his profile picture is a husky in a Christmas sweater.

I wonder if this is the time to break out the *pesto*. Instead, I say, just as quiet, "Once or twice."

The room's getting warmer. We're not quite as close together as we were in the elevator, but if he reached out, he could run his thumb over the seam of my mouth. He's gearing up to say something. I can feel it. The weight of his words building between us.

Then his phone buzzes, agitated, on the countertop.

"Flynn here," he says, clearing his throat, and we're snapped back into the mission. Thank goodness . . . right? Did I even want to go wherever he was about to take me?

Flynn hangs up the call with a deep breath, motioning me to follow him upstairs. "The PM beat traffic. Let's go."

15

chew the inside of my cheek all the way to the second floor. We pass a sign that proclaims CHIUSO PER UNA FESTA PRIVATA. *Closed for a private party?* I'm guessing.

"Just be yourself," Flynn tells me out of the side of his mouth. "But also, you know, be her."

"Very helpful, thank you," I bat back.

Leaving the security team outside, Flynn and I enter through a set of ornate wooden doors, and I clock Sofia right away: back turned, arms crossed, hair in a low chestnut bun. She spins at the sound of heel-steps, and once again, the sight of her—this close, this *similar*—is enough to snatch my breath.

If I didn't know better, I'd think we were twins, separated at birth.

"Prime Minister Christiansen," Flynn says, greeting her with a dip of his head, and he is like the mirror between us. We pass our stares through him, looking back at our reflections, and part of me thinks this is about to be a lovely, *Parent Trap*–style moment. Alone in this empty restaurant, with curtains yanked over the windows, we can laugh, finally, about the strangeness of our similarities. Have a good chuckle about the randomness of genetics, and how the hell we ended up here.

Instead, Sofia's lips thin to a solid line. "And what will my people think, mmm? If this ever gets out?" She's speaking in my direction, but mostly—it seems—to the man several feet behind her. A middle-aged guy in a beige suit, the head of her special protection group, is quietly assessing the situation with intelligent blue eyes. "That Sofia Christiansen is a coward. That she'd let a civilian—an innocent and a foreigner—step into her shoes and die for her? No. No, absolutely not. If I die, then I die on my feet. *My* feet." She punches two fingers into her chest before snagging my eye. "And *you*. Why would you agree to this?"

I'm so caught up in her gaze—her quiet, quiet wrath—that my first instinct is to defuse the tension with a joke. Like, *I'm here for the free tagliatelle at the fancy hotel.*

"Don't do this," Sofia says, shaking her head. "Please don't do this."

I genuinely can't fathom what to say, standing there, sweating through the silk lining of her designer pantsuit. Isn't it already done? Haven't I already committed, partially out of my respect for *her*? Flynn, to my shock, looks mildly flabbergasted; he isn't even trying to hide it. "Forgive me, Prime Minister," he says to Sofia, perfectly composed, even after all those peppers, "but the CIA was under the impression that *you* requested the body double."

Sofia laughs in a completely unfunny way, neck whipping to glare at the man behind her. "This is what you told them?"

"We want to see you safe, ma'am," says the man behind her. He's calm, his accent even thicker than Sofia's. "Ma'am, if I may speak plainly, you can be a bit bullheaded sometimes."

"Bullheaded," she sniffs. "Perhaps you've been listening to Jakob too much. You're starting to pick up his verbiage."

Here's where I chime in, "Jakob. Your brother. He keeps calling Hotel Giorgio."

Sofia eyes me. "How did he sound?"

"He mentioned something about a joint-party resolution?"

"No, how did he *sound*?" she repeats, like I'm an idiot. "Angry? Perturbed? Insolent?"

"Oh. All of the above."

The man behind her picks up where he left off. "The rest of the security team and I, we floated the idea of a decoy with a few strategic members of intelligence services. They're the only ones who know, ma'am. Our country can't—"

"You think that this woman's life is any less valuable than mine?" Sofia says, pointing at me. She lays into her head of security like he's an opposing politician, blocking her in the halls of parliament. "Intrinsically less valuable? You let our team and the United States think that of me? That I requested for someone else to lead our country, our people?"

Whoa, whoa. I want to interject that I'm not leading a damn thing. I'm reading a book on a beach. I'm eating some cheese in a hotel room. "That's not really—"

But she doesn't leave a moment to spare. "I suppose you want me to cut my hair to look like her? Bangs? Tell me, what world leader has ever had bangs?"

"Boris Johnson," Flynn supplies, then holds up a palm, backing down with a "Sorry, sorry."

More words arrive in my mouth, and I push them out fast enough this time. "I promise you that I'm taking this very seriously. I might be a 'foreigner,' but my grandmother was from Summerland, and I truly respect your policies." Tentatively, I step toward Sofia, chestnut hair sweeping across my shoulders in the exact same way hers does. "I'd never do anything that would put your reputation in jeopardy."

"You wouldn't?" Her lips purse. "Then what's this I'm hearing about someone calling out your name, *your* name, Max, in the hotel lobby? Or—wait a moment. *Et minutt.*" She turns on her heels, digging into a bucket-size leather bag before extracting a fresh newspaper. Swishing over to me, she slams the paper onto the nearest table, flat-palmed, with a jolting *thud*. "Care to explain?"

Inhaling sharply through my nose, I scan Positano's local paper. Tomorrow's date stares back at me. She must've gotten an early copy. Above the fold, two men pedal happily on a tandem bicycle. "They're . . . enjoying a nice ride by the sea?" I venture, knowing this can't be what she's talking about.

Sofia gives a tidy scoff before flipping the paper below the fold—and there she is. There *I* am. In the lobby this morning, right after Calvin rushed across the tile, my face outlined in newspaper ink. Beside me, Flynn lingers, his hand resting tenderly on my elbow, and we're exceedingly close. I could lean forward and tuck my head into the crook of his neck. His shirt's half-unbuttoned, his hair wild. Both of us are glistening, like we've just had a nice roll across the tennis courts, in the euphemistic sense. No one else from the security team is present; the angle is *just* right.

I get it. It's suggestive.

If you're a particularly gullible person, you might misread our body language, believe that Flynn and I are going back up to my suite to, as Gail put it, *have international relations.* The Italian photo caption is gibberish to me, but the whole package is clear: This isn't a piece about Sofia's foreign policy. This is a gossip article speculating about her sex life.

"See the way he's looking at you?" Sofia says, tapping Flynn's eyes in the photo. "He must never look at you like that in front of the camera again, do you understand? When you look like you're in love, *I* look like I'm in love."

Flynn moves to interject, but I get there first, agitated, ready to brush this under the rug. "I don't look like I'm in love." Really, I don't. In the photo, my teeth are mildly gritted, my eyebrows gently creased together. "If anything, I look constipated."

Sofia does not laugh. Neither does her head of security, standing stoically in the background. "And you, Agent Forester?" she asks. "Would you say the same thing?"

Would he say that I look constipated?

"You know this photo was the result of a once-in-a-lifetime security breach," Flynn offers, examining the paper. "It's not repeatable. It won't happen again. And if I may add, Prime Minister, Max's part in this is already a fifth over, at least. I have every confidence that, between the CIA and your intelligence services, we'll find the original assassin and neutralize the threat."

"What about your smiling?" Sofia asks, turning back to me.

"My . . . smiling?"

"In the other photos," she clarifies. "From when you arrived at the hotel and you were waving. You smile too American."

I study her face, which is my face. "How do you smile like a nationality?"

She does it, wide and big, like she's just caught a fly ball at a summer game, a box of nachos in her other hand.

"Okay, yeah," I say. "That's fair."

"Every move you make," she adds, "it's captured, even at the beach. For me, perhaps especially at the beach. Then the newspapers will pick apart my physical appearance, and that will be the narrative for months. Not my work with advancing educational opportunities, not my crackdown on Summerland's crime families. Funny how that never happens to male presidents or prime ministers on holiday. 'Has Emmanuel Macron gotten pectoral implants?' No."

I almost smile at this, at her sharpness, the cool way she delivers a line. It's like watching a bolder version of myself.

"Sofia, we don't have much time," says her head of security, glancing at his watch. "We need to—"

"Go to the bathroom," I interject, my pulse pounding thickly as I put our meeting into motion. "I need to go to the bathroom. Is there a powder room nearby?"

Sofia glances at me like, *American woman, is that the smoothest segue you can offer?* And yes, honestly, right now it is. I'm not a spy. I'm not a politician. Clandestine meetings with world leaders in Italian toilets aren't something I've practiced.

Sofia sucks her teeth. "I'll escort you."

Her head of security puffs out a breath like *Women! Always going to the bathroom together!* But Flynn isn't buying it. He passes me an odd look (*Was it the peppers? Or are you lying?*) before smothering the expression, leading us out another set of double doors, down the back stairwell. Side by side, matching Sofia's steps, I feel an immense pressure to break out my small talk before diving into a few questions about Roderick. *Are you two currently together? In your mind, would he ever accept money to kill you?*

At the bottom of the stairs, Sofia pauses for a fraction of a second, as if deciding something. "I apologize if I was harsh with you back there. No, not *if.* I was, and I'm sorry."

"I thought prime ministers weren't supposed to apologize," I say gently.

"Only when we're wrong," she says with a slow blink. "My annoyance was misplaced. I'm angry at a system that bestows certain value on people. I am no more inherently valuable than you are, Max. To be honest, you remind me of that cat that the French shot into space."

She's lost me with the last part.

"In the 1960s," she clarifies. "Space race. The Russians sent a dog, the US sent a chimp, the French sent a stray cat. They're always strays. Do you have much family?"

A cord tightens in my throat. "My parents."

"Relationship with them?"

I think about versions of the message I've yet to send: *Hey, it's Max, I've won the lottery. Hey, it's Max, I'm in Europe for you.* "Strained."

"Family is tricky." Sofia nods, then glances back at Flynn. "Do you mind?" We've reached the powder room door, and she's asking for space; Flynn obliges, stepping farther away. I shake out the tension from my fingers. Once I'm alone with the prime minister, who knows what she'll tell me? Who knows how I'll react?

Her hand barely grazes the handle, brushing the door open half an inch, when Flynn shouts behind us, *"No, wait!"* It's an urgent plea. A throaty, strained yell.

His voice is the last thing I hear before the *boom*.

16

"Max! *Max!*"

Someone is yelling through the ringing in my ears. Vision blurry, temples pounding, it's like I've dunked my head in a bucket of seawater, and all I can think is *I can't believe it, it's happening, this is really happening but I can't believe it.* Wooden shrapnel tangles in my hair, ashy smoke burns my lungs, and I'm spreading out my fingertips, reaching, reaching for anything stable. A wall. A chair. What I find is someone's hand, someone's fingers wrapping tight around mine—gripping, tugging, and now I know it's Flynn shouting, close enough to my ear that his words break through. "Get—*out*—of here." His arm loops around my midsection, helping me stand upright; I feel the frantic energy of him, the solidness of him, the way his pulse becomes my pulse as we shuffle together, darting through the smoke. He is all muscle and movement, the only thing holding me together besides the pounding in my head that's telling me *Run, run.*

I tell myself to focus on Flynn and only Flynn. *That's all you need to do, Max.* Just the sound of his voice. Just the press of his hand, the brush of his beard against my cheek. How he's protecting me with his entire body, tucking me into the familiar nook of his chest. Where I've always felt safe. Where he's always held me.

Am I *bleeding*? I feel that now, alongside the ear-ringing and the heat of his core, a slow trickle down the side of my neck, and—

Sofia.

Where's *Sofia*?

I must be yelling her name. Must be screaming. In my throat is the startled throb of my heartbeat, and her name, burning, and I'm just . . . closing my fingers around Flynn's hand, putting one foot in front of the other, staggering into the main dining room, a few of the vines hanging down from the ceiling, broken wine-glasses under my feet and dishes cracked. More sounds: the crunch beneath my shoe soles, Flynn's breath against my ear, the panicked bleat of a growing alarm. The restaurant's fire alarm?

In the chaos, I glance behind me, hoping to spot Sofia, and I do see her, the hazy outline of her, coughing, her head of security throwing a protective arm over her shoulders and leading her, along with another officer, out the back way. Two chunks of hair sweep from her bun, and—that's all I catch before she disappears. That's all I'm processing, except the grip of Flynn's hand and the strength of Flynn's arms as we lead each other—me just as much as him—out into the street. We burst with the smoke through the door, patrons from distant restaurants already clamoring toward the scene. Neighbors are fleeing their houses, rushing to help, rushing to see the cause of the blast, but I'm being swallowed by security. Shielded by security. Shoved into the passenger's seat of the Range Rover as Flynn takes the wheel, speeding us away with a surge of motion, foot flat on the gas pedal. "Just listen to my voice," he says, quiet. So quiet. Is he speaking that low, or are my ears that bad? "Max, can you hear me? It's okay, you're going to be okay."

"Are *you* okay?" I manage, throat dry, half-choked with fumes. Eyes unglazing a touch, I blink over at him—and he doesn't *look* okay. His blondish hair is black in places, covered in debris and soot. The linen of his suit is singed, ripped at the collarbone, exposing a thick slice of skin. He doesn't seem to be bleeding, but—

I take that back.

He swipes at a cut above his eyebrow, wincing. "Don't worry about me."

Too late. I'm already scanning his whole body, up and down, before settling once again on his eyebrow. Some guys *say* they have your back, but this . . . "Flynn, you're—you're going to need stitches."

"It'll be fine. Just worry about you. Where does it hurt?"

Sort of everywhere, I think, not daring to say it aloud. Not wanting to worry him when he probably looks worse than I do. There's something else, too. Something bubbling up. The realization that Flynn read me completely right. He knew exactly what I needed in that moment. He knew how my body would react, how I'd reach out, how we could escape the threat together by moving as one.

"How'd you know about the bomb?" I ask, head pounding. "Or whatever the hell that was? I heard you yell, and I just . . ."

"Trip wire," Flynn says, gritting his teeth. His jaw must be killing him. The outline of a swiftly purpling bruise is popping along his bone. "Little hint of it, top corner of the door. Probably the equivalent of a grenade. The blast wasn't as powerful as it could've been—maybe it was old explosive material, denatured— but someone clearly knew the prime minister would be there. I just don't know how we fucking missed it." That veneer of calm is shredding. His irises are darkening, almost matching his pupils. "How did we *miss* it?"

"Her head of security," I say, swallowing, tasting ash on my tongue. "He isn't involved, is he?"

Flynn grimaces. "He's been with her for years, no issues. Not to mention, he's the one who just got her out of there. Every single member of her team has been vetted to the max, but that doesn't mean we should rule them out. Sometimes intelligence services don't know what the hell they're talking about. I'm starting to think . . ."

"Starting to think what?"

"That maybe this isn't so simple. Maybe we've gotten it wrong."

Chills rush down my arms. "You mean, like . . . the crime family paid off someone from her team?" I grip the grab rail tight as we swerve. "Or they hired a different assassin to— Wait, where are we going?"

"Hospital," Flynn says, cutting to the left, curving around a series of parked Fiats.

"What? For me? No." I shake my head, even as my neck throbs. "We can't—we can't drop the ruse. What if Sofia and I end up at the same hospital? How would we explain that? I'm fine."

"Your ear's bleeding."

"I'm *fine*," I tell him, wiping away the blood with the edge of my sleeve, and—

"Jesus *Christ*, Max," he almost shouts, finally losing his cool. Broken syllables. Hands gesticulating off the wheel. I've never seen him like this before, heard him like this before, his voice as ragged as the tattered jacket on his back. "You just lived through an explosion, your head's probably killing you, and I, I'm trying to do my job. I'm trying to keep you alive. I don't want to see you— fucking—beat up like this, okay? Beyond the fact that we're trying to avoid an international scandal, and we might have to explain why we let an assassin into an Italian restaurant and why the prime minister has a body double in the first place . . . You're not the type of person I'd want to see dead. Not that I want to see anyone dead, I just—" He blows out a quick breath. "I need you to get on the first flight out tonight."

Part of me expected this, but it still knocks me back. "Drive to the hotel."

"Hospital first, then embassy, then—"

"*Hotel* first," I grit out, blinking away the chemical sting from my eyelashes. "If you care about my safety, I'm safest there. Half of Sofia's security is at Hotel Giorgio and I'm guessing the nearest American embassy is in Rome? I'm sure you have some sort of first aid training. You can bandage me up in the suite, but I am *not* backing down from this."

Now that the initial shock is wearing off, now that cool air from the blowers is streaming into my face, I'm *angry*. Someone thinks they can try to kill the world's youngest female prime minister in a restaurant toilet? They think *that's* going to be the end of her historic career? Maybe I should listen to Flynn, look up flights on my CIA phone right now, find the fastest way out of Italy.

But honestly? Screw that. Screw whoever just tried to assassinate her.

I'm not abandoning this mission. There're only four days left. I can survive for four days. Now that I've seen firsthand—*felt* firsthand—that someone wants Sofia dead, there's no way in hell that I'm walking away.

Flynn swallows, hard, and I follow the movement all the way down his throat. He doesn't look like he's given up trying to convince me to leave, but—"There's an extra jacket in the back," he says, jerking his head toward the rear seats. "Change before the hotel."

"Can't we sneak in through the private entrance?" I ask, shedding the marred jacket and throwing on a fresh one. It smells of lavender, like the hotel room, and that softness—that bit of comfort—throws me even more. It doesn't fit with the rest of the night.

"We will," he says, changing his own shirt and jacket—fast—at a stoplight. There's a flash of tan skin, a trail of cologne unleashed: sandalwood, sea. He's biting back pain in the hard set of his jaw, and I fight every instinct I have to place my hand on his shoulder. "The private entrance goes through the kitchen."

Flynn can barely look at me as he pulls up to the hotel, past the gates, where some of the paparazzi have waned. A camera flashes along the side of the Range Rover, and I flinch, schooling my face back to neutral as we stalk out of the car, my security shielding me on all sides, even thicker now. At least six bomb-sniffing dogs are patrolling the grounds. Police are doing loops through the garden, speedy Italian flying through their walkie-talkies.

And I think I've had enough for a single day.

CIA safe house in the morning; random Roderick and random roommate surprises by midday; assassination attempt by dark. The sky is purpling like the bruise on Flynn's jawline.

Security clears the hotel staff from the kitchen, and we pass by empty workstations, knives at a standstill, microgreens waiting to be plated and cut, and this should be my happy place. My soothing place. The kitchen, with its stainless steel and bright surfaces, its cooking smells baked deep, deep in, but I'm already shivering, the whole night hitting me in waves. Goose bumps prickle along my arms, rush up the backs of my thighs. I just want to get back up to the room, check on Calvin's status, and then slip under the duvet. Under the duvet, no one can hurt you. No monsters, no assassins. That's a fact.

Flynn's right, though. How did someone know that Sofia was going to be there, at the restaurant? Did her head of security tip them off? Is he capable of that? How did her special protection group miss the equivalent of a *grenade*?

It's a solemn elevator ride to the top floor, calm music chiming through the speakers, and then Flynn and I are bursting into the suite. "On the dining room table," he tells me, pointing toward the center of the room, and at first, I don't catch his drift. I think there are Band-Aids on the dining room table, gauze on the table, but he gives me another verbal nudge. "*Max*, get on the table."

He's in triage mode, his voice throaty and rough. For the moment, all the breeziness has left him, like he's taking on my pain. Because I *am* in pain, now that I'm safe and allowed to feel it. My face is tender; the side of my neck aches piercingly; and my shoulder blade is definitely throbbing more than a shoulder blade should. Aftershocks of adrenaline coursing through me, I scoot backward onto the table, shrugging off my jacket by the bouquet of still-blooming flowers, and Flynn strides forward, first aid kit in his hands. Where'd he get that from? His suitcase? He sets it down by my thigh, riffling through it; I can feel the tension wafting off him like cologne.

"Flynn," I say, throat tight, unsure how to finish. Do I tell him it'll be all right? Will it? My mind flashes to Sofia, stumbling from the smoke, and the image makes my throat clamp down even more.

"Here," he says, gazing at my neck through hooded eyes. "Sorry if this hurts for a second." He presses a cotton pad, full of something sharp and stinging, against the space under my ear—and *Yep, yep, that is excruciating.* On instinct, one of my hands reaches out to steady myself, grabbing on to the hard plane of Flynn's shoulder. Like mine, the tempo of his heart is fast, fast, fast; it's pulsing through his whole body. He grunts a little when I touch him, but when I start to pull back, my touch lightening, he says, "No, it's okay. Keep your hand there if you need it."

I do need it. That is what I need.

He makes quick work of my neck, wiping it clean, and despite the fact that this is *awful*—truly, terrifyingly awful—a part of me leans even farther into him. I wouldn't mind if he placed a supportive hand on my knee, if his hands glided over the curve of my collarbone, just to check if I'm all right.

"Your turn," I say when he's finished, glancing at the nick in his eyebrow.

"It'll heal on its own," he says, almost back to calm again. "I told you not to worry about—"

I grab him lightly by the hips and drag him forward, between my knees. "Hold still." Tenderly, I press a finger to his eyebrow, around where the gash is, assessing just how deep it goes. It isn't as bad as it looks, but it'll need a butterfly suture. I've bandaged myself up in the kitchen enough times to know.

After a moment of surprise, Flynn accepts my touch, angling forward and pressing his palms flat against the table, on opposite sides of me. The heat from his fingertips brushes against my thighs.

"Almost done," I say, fighting the thrum in my ears. One of them is much worse than the other, like I've just swum in Sebago Lake and everything's muffled. I comb through the kit, finding the antibiotic ointment. Flynn barely winces as I apply a bit of Neosporin, blowing on the cut like my grandmother used to do with me, and—yes, I did just blow on my CIA handler's face. Shouldn't have done that. Wasn't medically necessary.

My lips hover over the crest of his head, his hands on either side of me, and it would be so *easy*. Bridging the rest of the space between us. Despite all the chaos, in the quiet moments, when I listen, there's that old energy. The hum and the spark. I'm not the only one who's feeling it, am I?

Am I?

Flynn's tense—because of course he is—but in the last few seconds, it's become a new kind of tension. He's holding back like he wants to spring forward. Both of us are practically motionless, just breathing, linking our breath, and I don't want to break it. Don't want to snap away from this brief period in time, where I'm safe and thrumming and alive, with him.

When the pressure becomes so great, my body can't take it anymore, I give in a little, closing the gap and pressing my lips, featherlight, against his forehead. It's barely even a touch, so soft that I wonder if he even feels it. My hand travels to the sides of his face, the tips of my knuckles grazing the stubble of his jaw, like running my fingers over sand, and he responds with the gentlest touch of his own, a single finger tracing the outer length of my thigh. It's too light, too good, and the urge is strong enough that I finally let myself admit it: I want to kiss my handler. Not just on the forehead, not like I'm saying good night, tucking him in after he's fallen asleep on the couch. I want to thread my hands through the silk of his hair; I want to tip his chin up as he traces the edges of me, let his lips capture mine, feel the weight of his tongue in my mouth.

The problem is, that's *so* dangerous. That's the last thing I should be looking for, the opportunity for him to hurt me again. Especially tonight, when so much else is on the line.

I wait to see if he'll say something. Anything else. A window into what he's thinking. "You aren't trained for this level of action," he finally whispers, which isn't what I expected. He's almost shivering as he says it.

And I'm torn, suddenly, my own voice just as shivery. "You don't think I can do this?"

"I think you can do anything," he says, staying put, inches from my face. "But it's not about you. I mean, it is, just not in that way. I undersold this mission. To myself and to you. You're not just lounging on the beach. We're past that. We were past that by noon. Which means you should have a choice, again. Five million dollars is a shit ton of money, I get that, it's life-changing. But that only matters if you *have* a life, Max."

The sadness in his gaze is palpable. It carves into me. I'm not sure how it's possible to maintain eye contact with someone this close, for this long, and not burst into flames.

"Hold still," I tell him again, so quiet that the words almost dissolve in the air. When I stick on the butterfly bandage, he looks good as new. Well, almost good as new. His hair's ruffled, his beard scruffier than even this morning. My teeth skim over my bottom lip. "Don't you do this all the time?"

His words are like a caress on my cheekbone. "Do what all the time?"

"Dangerous missions." If he's experienced enough to work on an assignment like this, then he's trained for unexpected attacks, tricky interchanges, and assets who might not always be 100 percent up to the job. "I'm guessing I'm not your first asset who's found themselves in a tough spot."

He sighs, like he can see where I'm going with this. "No, you're not."

"And I'm guessing that you didn't urge them to walk away. So what's different here?"

The question hangs heavy in the air.

Am I *what's different here, Flynn?*

When he takes too long to answer, when the silence grows too weighted between us, I press him further. "Talk to me."

"I *can't*," he chokes out, finally taking a small step back. "That's the thing, I can't. I'm terrified to say the wrong thing. I've been walking this . . . this *line*. Trying to make things comfortable for you, while also trying to make you reconsider the role you're playing here. If I don't walk it just right, if someone from the agency

thinks I'm no longer the right fit for this mission, they'll send another handler, maybe someone who's not as good at their job—and
I won't be able to protect you. To get you home safely."

I blink at him in the half-dark of the suite, processing. My
chest is rising up and down in a trembling beat. "I thought you
said that you didn't request to be my handler? That the CIA basically threw us together because we had 'some history'?"

Flynn wipes a hand over the back of his neck. "The truth
is, they wanted me to recruit you because of our history together. They wanted me to show up at your work instead of Gail
and give you that pitch before the wedding. I absolutely fucking
refused. When you formally attached yourself to the mission,
that's when I stepped in. Put in the request to handle you. It had
to be me. It couldn't be anyone else but me, and I—"

The ringing of his phone cuts him off. Terrible, terrible timing. A hard lump lodges in my throat. *And you what?* The sexual
tension between us is so pressurized, you could burst it with a pin.

"I have to take this," he says roughly, like he's dragging his
voice through gravel. I notice another small cut on his hand when
he steps even farther back, reaching into his pocket for his cell
phone.

My throat burns as I swallow. "Okay, yeah, of course."

I slip down from the table, wringing my hands, and wander
around the hotel room. Back and forth. Zigzagging nervously. Is
he getting an update on Sofia? Has anyone from her family been
notified? Her brother? Who would've notified *my* family, if tonight
had turned out differently?

I stumble toward my own cell phone—my American one,
which has been powering up for hours, after Flynn offered a
charger—and press the cracked screen. Curved bars at the top tell
me that it's still connected to the hotel Wi-Fi, and the screen
shows two new text messages from my dad: One's about making

a big pot of summer-bean chili for supper, and the other's a blurry photo of my mom holding up a handmade cardigan. She's probably crocheted it herself with all her leftover yarn. It's bright yellow, objectively hideous, and—I'm not sure how this is possible—it makes me love her even more.

If I'd been inside that powder room, all my parents would've had left of me is that under-the-pillow note (if a turtle hasn't munched on it by now).

I'm so sorry we haven't talked in a while, I finally text my dad. **It's a long story, but I'm traveling for a little bit, and I'll be back next week. Hope you and mom are doing okay. That sweater's a pretty color. Love you.**

Falling back on the bed with a wrecked sigh, I let my body sink into the mattress, mind churning. Is it possible that the Producer made it to Italy, that he orchestrated the explosion tonight? Then again, if he *used to produce results*, is it likely that he's missed twice in a row? Flynn keeps saying that the CIA doesn't always get it right. I'm thinking he's speaking from experience?

"That's right," Flynn says, seriously, on the phone. "Correct."

I'm catching only snippets, but the breather is giving me space to think. Process how much things have shifted. How much *I've* shifted. Can't I be more than just a sitting duck? I know the key players of this operation, and I'm motivated. Why can't I help take down the people who did this to us, to Sofia, in whatever way I can?

I start running through everyone who was there tonight. Her head of security, Lars, other security personnel. Who did the original sweep of the premises?

"We're pulling footage from in and around the restaurant," Flynn tells me between calls, pacing by the couch. He explains how the CIA will contain the news—how they'll say it was a gas explosion, and that I was never there. Sofia was never there.

Anyone who saw differently is mistaken. There's no update on her yet, but the footage should help narrow down the culprit. Someone must've slipped in—somehow—after security swept the place. "My gut's telling me that the Halverson family didn't pay off anyone from Sofia's side. We've pulled all the incoming financial transactions, from every member of her team—nothing. Hold on, got another call coming in."

My American phone beeps, too, and I shoot up in bed, thinking it's my dad.

It's not. It's Calvin. His messages are dated up to forty-eight hours ago, only trickling in now. Why? Did he cheap out on his phone service like he economizes on pizza?

Do you want a slice of pizza?

U R not in your room.

I'm leaving the pizza outside your door.

U didn't eat the pizza outside your door.

The pizza outside your door is getting stale.

When Flynn gets off his final call, *his* phone starts pinging with texts, and he takes a second to read the messages, hand over his mouth.

Automatically, adrenaline floods me again. "What's wrong?"

Flynn gazes at me with profound disbelief, then lets out a strained, singular chuckle. "Calvin. It's all true. He really did win the Maine State Lottery, and he really did come to Liam Neeson you."

My body can't seem to decide if I want to smile, laugh, or cry a little. It settles on a fun mixture of all three. "At least that's something."

"I don't want to know why he had eight bottles of ranch dressing in his suitcase, or how he thought that was going to help his rescue mission, but he's on a chartered flight out of Rome in less than two hours."

"He can pick up a souvenir at the airport," I add, patently avoiding the ranch dressing, fighting to tamp down the post-panic rush. "'I traveled all the way to Italy to rescue my roommate from an abduction scheme, then got trapped in a hotel conference room, and all I got was this T-shirt.'"

Flynn plops down on the couch, his whole body sagging into the cushions. He looks impossibly awake and exhausted at the same time, and honestly? I just want to give him a hug. "It's going to have to be *extremely* small print. That's a lot to fit on your standard-size tee."

"Maybe it's shorter in Italian," I say with a wince, reaching over to see if my phone will dial out. FaceTime works over the Wi-Fi, but no luck, Calvin isn't answering. I dash off a text, wondering if he'll receive it: **I know we have tons to talk about when we get home, but . . . thank you.** "I'm not imagining it, right? This day was weird and horrific even by CIA standards?"

"Definitely one for the books." Flynn shrugs off his second jacket of the day, hanging it over the armrest on the couch, and his words echo alongside the ringing in my ears. *It couldn't be anyone else but me, and I—* "I really could get you out of Italy tonight."

"Let's wait for the footage from the restaurant," I say, stalling. This could almost be over. I have a purpose, after months of feeling so, so lost, and I'm not abandoning my post until it's done. "Things could look different in the morning."

Readjusting his position, Flynn, with a muffled groan, lies back on the couch. He grabs his ribs in a way that makes *mine* ache. "Max, will you just consider—"

"*Pesto*," I say, firm, wishing we'd picked a more serious-sounding code word. "I'm staying." No way am I running back to America with my tail between my legs at the first sign of trouble. Yeah, it was a big sign of trouble—explosive, you might call it—but I haven't felt like a survivor in a long time. I do now, a little. I am.

Cutting off any further opportunity for argument, avoiding Flynn's glance, I get out of bed and thumb through the dresser for a pair of satin pajamas. In the bathroom, I change quickly out of the pantsuit, noting the bruise on my cheek in the mirror, before brushing my teeth as gently as I can, practicing Sofia's accent under my breath. Flicking off the light on my nightstand, I climb under the sheets.

That's it. End of the night.

Only, an hour later, I'm still wide awake. Part of it's the stress of the last forty-eight hours, the smell of smoke tangled in my hair, the weight of Flynn's fingers as he bandaged me up, but it's also the atmosphere. Summers in Maine, whenever I lie awake at night, the loudest sound is my own breath—maybe the trill of cicadas, maybe the bay. Here, it's a restless kind of quiet. This seaside city is only ever half-asleep.

Don't say anything to him. Just lie here. Just keep your mouth shut.

"Flynn?" I whisper into the almost-dark.

"Yeah?" comes his voice immediately.

"Can't sleep?"

"You *pesto*-ed me." Flynn lets out a slow breath. "I can't believe you *pesto*-ed me."

"We need a new code word," I tell him. "That just makes it sound like I covered you in basil sauce."

Flynn snorts.

I fiddle with the sheets under my fingers. "I'm tired, but . . . I always open the windows at home. I like falling asleep to the sound of the water." Why'd I just tell him that? Why am I breaking my own rules? *No talking after your head hits the pillow.*

"Me, too," he admits. "Best way to drift off. Maine ruined me for city noises. I don't think this counts as reminiscing, but— Lobster in the Rough? Still the best job I've ever had."

I ask the first question that comes to mind. "How'd you end up working at the CIA, anyway?"

"I went to Boston College because of their sailing team," he says, quiet. "Got a scholarship. A recruiter contacted me during my junior year."

"Park bench?"

"Job fair," he says.

"Ah, so a little less James Bond than I'm imagining."

"Just a little. Basically, the recruiter said that I could 'see the world' with the CIA, and I was an idiot kid who didn't realize how much they tailored their pitch to exactly what I wanted to hear. They must've read me from a mile away. I wanted to travel; they told me I could travel."

A hint of discontent bleeds through his voice. Does Flynn even like this job? "And have you? Seen the world?"

"I spent half of last year riding a desk in Milwaukee."

"The Paris of the Midwest," I say. "City of lights."

"City of lights, parking tickets, and the world's largest dinosaur head. Big draw for the tourists." The moon glows silver through tiny gaps in the curtains. I see Flynn half-heartedly plump the stiff little pillow under his head, roll over onto his side, and gaze at me from across the room. His phone's clutched in the palm of his hand, ready for any updates. "I have been to some cool places. Parts of the Middle East and Africa. All across Europe. Never been to Summerland, though."

"I'd really like to visit one day. See where my family's from."

"Then you should." When he falls silent for a second, I know he's revving up again. *Go back to America, Max. Forget about the money, forget about Sofia, save yourself.*

I swerve in another direction. "What's your dream vacation?"

He shifts his head against the pillow. "You first. What's *your* dream vacation?"

"Oh, this," I deadpan, pulling the sheets to my chin. "If anything, I wish there were *more* assassins."

Flynn snorts again. "You better give me a straight answer. Otherwise . . ." He pauses, and I can almost see the (semipainful) arch of his eyebrows. "Otherwise, I'll tell Giorgio that you hate gelato. No more gelato will be brought to this suite."

My mouth drops open in a faux gape. That pistachio gelato from earlier? I wasn't even hungry and I had three scoops. "You wouldn't."

"These are my negotiating tactics, honed from years of service."

"Wow, the CIA knows how to go for the jugular." I run my teeth over my bottom lip, thinking. Although, to be honest, I don't have to think about it too hard—the answer's already there. "My parents and I, with my nana Frida, we took a road trip when I was a kid. All the way down the coast, from Maine to Florida and back up again, stopping at as many pie places as Nana could find."

"Sweet or savory?" he asks, undoing the top two buttons of his shirt. He says it with such a serious tone that—despite this historically shit day, and the ache in my entire body—my chest feels a touch lighter.

"Nana Frida was a wild-blueberry pie aficionado. So, mostly sweet. Some savory. Actually, her favorite from the trip was crawfish pie, in South Carolina. She found it at this gas station, and every one of us was like *Absolutely do not eat that pie.* She didn't even have a fork. But she was so stubborn that she ate it with her hands, in the back seat of my parents' station wagon. And that's my dream vacation."

"Eating fish pie with your hands in a station wagon," Flynn repeats, nonjudgmental.

"Being spontaneous," I say to the ceiling. "Searching for good food in unlikely places. Just . . . being with my family."

I really, really miss my family. Maybe, especially, Nana Frida. Breast cancer got her when I was fourteen, a long time ago, but the loss still feels fresh. When I had my restaurant, people assumed that my authority over a room came from the cooking world. Actually, it came from Nana. My grandmother wielded her wit like a rolling pin; she could flatten just about anybody with it. She was no more than five foot three, standing on a step stool, but in pictures your eyes go right to her. She could command a photo like she commanded a kitchen. Most of the time, I think about how disappointed she'd be—that I turned out to be her heir. I tried to elevate her legacy, her memory, and instead took it right down to the ground.

I kind of had this dream of passing my restaurant down to my future kids. Keeping it in the family and having all of us work there together one day. In my mind, I was seeing all of these family dinners, sitting down with everyone who worked at the restaurant, becoming this big, unbreakable unit. It was about the food, but it was also about building community.

I pause before I tell Flynn too much. "You answer now. Ideal vacation?"

"This is awkward," he says, "but mine *is* eating fish pie in the back of a station wagon."

I want to fully shove him off the couch, in a nonaggressive way. "*Flynn.* Don't be an asshole."

His quiet laugh filters into the air before he's pensive again.

"Seriously, though, mine is similar to yours. My dad and I took this vacation right before he passed. Road trip."

He . . . passed away? When? How? "I'm sorry," I say, almost whispering, remembering what Flynn said about the farmers' market and the rhu-BARB preserves. Remembering how his dad gently teased us as we held hands in the back seat of his car. "I didn't know."

"How would you?" he says quickly, like he's fighting an emotion in his throat. "But thanks. We went from New Hampshire all the way to the *other* coast—California. He wanted to see the sequoias. Said he could die happy if he saw them." By the end, his voice has trailed off, but he picks it up again. "I didn't take any pictures. That's a big regret of mine. I didn't want to take any pictures, because I didn't want to remember him sick. But now, I think I'd give just about anything for a photo of him staring up at those trees."

It is so unexpectedly tender that my eyes mist, and it's not just an aftereffect of the smoke from the blast. It isn't the pain in my shoulder or the way my ears are throbbing. I get ahold of myself before I'm way too vulnerable with him. "I was thinking you were going to say Las Vegas or something."

He chuckles dryly under his breath. "What about me screams Las Vegas to you?"

"Everyone likes a good magic show, with the . . . hoops and the . . . sparklers, and the . . ."

"You've never actually seen a magic show, have you?"

"No, never."

"One day, then, Max, I hope you get your station-wagon-fish-pie-magic trip."

"That sounds like I would have to be *incredibly* high. Calvin-level high." I pause, admitting, "I've only been high once in my life. I might've . . . I might've told you this, but my dad kind of put the fear of god into me about substance abuse—lots of fishermen are part of the opioid crisis—anyway, it was a pot brownie and I ended up glued to a twelve-hour marathon of *I Love Lucy*, thinking that Lucy was going to pop out of the TV and try to kill me."

"Loo-cy," he says in Ricky's voice. "Loo-cy, no!"

"I would describe it as traumatizing," I say, curving my hand under my cheek and scrunching up further into a ball. I trace his outline across the room, long frame scrunched onto the couch. Maybe it's the Italian influence, but the first thought I have is: He reminds me of a tipped-over Michelangelo sculpture, perfectly carved. I'm still not sure if I can close my eyes again. I'm not sure what'll happen if I stop talking to him, if I roll over again, if I don't hold on to Flynn's voice in the dark.

"Good night, Max," he says after I'm silent long enough, his voice like a kiss on the forehead.

"Good night, Flynn."

I drift off to the sound of his breathing, steady in the warmth of the room, and hope that tomorrow, no one tries to kill me.

17

'm dreaming about gelato. We're on an Italian side street, Flynn and I, dipping into the nearest shop, above-the-door bell tinkling. Inside, it's all white marble and cool surfaces, with giant tubs of gelato in shiny glass cases. *Stracciatella. Cioccolato con Peperoncino. Lampone.* Flynn translates, pointing to the labels. "That one's vanilla with shaved chocolate; that one's chocolate with spicy pepper; and, bingo, this is my flavor. Raspberry gelato."

I want twelve of them. I want all of them.

"I think if I died," I say, cone suddenly appearing in my hand, "this gelato could literally bring me back to life." Fresh whipped cream fluffs the top. At the bottom is a pool of dark melted chocolate, smooth as silk. Each bite gets better and better as we stroll under the moonlight, winding our way through late-night Positano, restaurant windows lit up with diners savoring their food. Last bites of risotto, shrimp, *spaghetti alle vongole.*

"You make a face," dream-Flynn says, "when you're eating something you like."

"What do you mean? What face?"

His eyes half roll back in his head.

"Oh," I say, chocolate on the seam of my lips, "that is not a good-looking face."

He chews on the side of his smile. "No, actually, it's a pretty good face . . . You want a lick?" He offers me his raspberry cone, so innocently, and suddenly the image snaps.

I'm no longer with Flynn, no longer sharing gelato on a close-to-midnight walk. I'm in an unfamiliar restaurant, scraping charred bits off a pewter pan, and chaos is erupting. Glass shatters in a tremendous *boom*, rattling the cutlery, knocking plates from shelves and—

I jerk awake to the sound of a phone buzzing, sweat beading down my neck, visions of last night popping behind my eyes. I can't tell you how strange it is to wake up in a room that isn't your own, in pajamas that aren't your own, with hair a different color than it was two days ago. It fans out on the pillow in thick brown strands, almost like a stranger's lying in bed next to me.

A glass of water rests on top of my bedside table. I did not put it there.

Did Flynn, after I fell asleep?

Rolling over fully, I catch a glimpse of him, white cotton T-shirt falling over his torso, a tan sliver of skin flashing me as he stretches in sleep. Long, lean lines and taut muscle. His hair is mildly disheveled, a few pieces sticking up at the back, jostled by the pillow. He's going to be incredibly stiff when he wakes up—from the couch, but also, wow, from last night. My own body's suffering, my collarbone much more tender than I thought it'd be, even though this bed is sensationally comfortable. Angels have blessed this mattress. And the linens smell amazing. I want to full-on sniff the sheets.

Tentatively, I lean in, burying my nose in the lavender, and of course, it's at this moment that Flynn chooses to open his eyes. "Whatcha doin'?" he says slowly.

I startle. My voice is croaky as I answer him. "Sniffing the sheets."

"For . . ."

"I lost a cookie in here earlier," I deadpan. "No, it's the lavender. Does your couch smell this good?"

"I don't know, Max, do you want to come over here and give it a sniff?"

I roll my eyes, trying to shuck away the residual adrenaline from the dream. From last night. Flinging back the covers, I swing my legs out of bed. "Now you went and made it weird."

He huffs out a laugh, voice almost as strained as mine. The butterfly suture has held on overnight. "Oh, *I* made it weird? Okay . . ." Clearing his throat, he fixes the flyaways on the side of his head. "You hungry?"

The phone buzzes again, and this time, Flynn bolts up to answer it. An imprint from the pillow slashes across his cheek. I heard him up at odd points throughout the night, checking his email, shooting off messages. Were there any updates overnight? Is Sofia okay? Has Calvin made it back to the States? Do we know who tried to assassinate the prime minister?

"Firstly," Gail says over speakerphone, her voice filtering into the summer heat of the room, "how are you both feeling this morning? Max?" It's the most concern I've ever heard in her voice. Which, I know, isn't saying much; she isn't exactly the touchy-feely type.

"Yeah, I'm fine," I half lie, out of bed now, running a finger over the bandage on my neck.

"Right as rain," Flynn says with a groan, hugging his ribs.

"Good. Now, I have a great deal of information to get through in this little team meeting, so I'll speak fast. Reviewing all the footage from a one-kilometer area surrounding the restaurant could take days, even with a team working around the clock. We are, unfortunately, no closer to determining the Producer's whereabouts than we were twenty-four hours ago, and the youngest Halverson brother, Aksel, is no longer present and accounted for on the family compound. Forensics is still working on biomarkers from the explosion. I have been out of coffee since four in the morning, and—are you sitting down?"

Oh lovely, the eyelid twitch is back. "Should I be?"

"What's going on, Gail?" Flynn says, almost harsh, a bruise slightly visible under his beard.

Gail pops her lips against the receiver. "In roughly six hours, you will be getting a knock at your hotel door. It'll be a hair stylist and a wardrobe stylist. They'll make you look presentable for this afternoon, Max. For the museum gala. An exhibit for modern Summerlandian art is opening just outside of Positano. The prime minister has promised her attendance, so you'll have to—"

"Wait a second," I cut in, blinking furiously at the phone, as Flynn rises from the couch, clocking something that I've clearly yet to understand. "*Sofia's* supposed to do the state affairs."

"That was true," Gail says briskly. "Until around seven minutes ago, when we learned that Prime Minister Christiansen has disappeared."

My heart stops. "What do you mean she's disappeared?"

"Synonyms include *gone, vanished, missing*. She isn't at the safe house, or with her security, or with her chief of staff, or anywhere we can reasonably find her."

Flynn jumps in before I can fully process that, white T-shirt falling over his shoulders like water. "Any signs of forced entry at the safe house?"

Gail's quick. "None. I *am* beginning to doubt the effectiveness of this security team, alongside the Italian police, considering that Max's roommate also disappeared before his flight. The man called Calvin was last seen buying a souvenir lollipop before entering the bathroom at Rome Fiumicino International Airport. His handlers lost track of him."

I pinch the bridge of my nose, hard enough to see stars. My brain doesn't know what to address first: turtle man or Sofia? I'll go with the world leader. "Do you think she went to the hospital, after the attack? Maybe she's at the hospital."

"Or maybe she's at the bottom of the Tyrrhenian Sea," Gail offers sharply, "duct-taped to a pool chair. Without more intel, everything is speculation. We've checked over a hundred hospitals, all across Italy, a few in Slovenia—even some back in Summerland. She might've sought private medical treatment somewhere, but I doubt it. Something tells me she isn't holed up in a shed with a Reiki master."

"What about the head of her special protection group?" I offer. "Could he be involved somehow? Or is there . . . There's no chance that she just walked away? Maybe with Roderick?" I ask this, hopefully, deliriously, like I'm questioning if Sparky really did go to the farm. At the same time, I text Calvin with my American phone: **Where are you???** "Or maybe she just got tired after a lifetime in politics with her family, wanted a break, thought she'd like . . . Thailand? Coconut mojitos? Bingo?"

"Are you having a stroke?" Gail asks, and I can almost hear the furious flick of her eyelashes. "I sincerely hope not. Our main goal now is to avoid international panic. Personally, I don't believe that the prime minister walked away, or that she's dead. Crime families like public spectacles. This is too quiet."

"What if the Halversons aren't behind it?" Flynn pushes. The phone's on the dining room table, and he's leaning forward, palms flat on the wood, just like last night. His forearms are tense cords of muscle. "You're assuming a lot there."

"Could her brother be a suspect?" I venture, stiff. "They seem like they have a terrible relationship, and if he's in the government, too, maybe he wants to push her out of power?"

"Jakob Christiansen," Gail says, "has been calling Hotel Giorgio every nine minutes since before dawn, demanding that Sofia look over a draft of a finance proposal. Unless his acting skills are impeccably crafted, he doesn't have her, and he didn't hire anyone to take her."

Flynn absorbs this. "Max is right, though. Maybe this isn't an 'easily' foiled assassination plot from the obvious suspects."

"Maybe so," Gail admits as I cross my arms close to my chest, suddenly cold. All the things that could've happened to Sofia dart through my mind. "Either way, we still need your services, Max."

"She can't protect a woman who's already missing," Flynn argues.

"She can protect that woman's *country*," Gail bats back, irritable. "If word gets out that the prime minister is missing and no one has a clue what happened to her, stock markets will collapse. Say goodbye to the Summerlandian economy. I wouldn't be surprised if the weapons trade picked up again. Civil unrest. The threat is higher than ever. Until we conduct a thorough investigation and find Prime Minister Christiansen, Max, you will maintain the status quo and take over her bureaucratic duties for the rest of this holiday."

The room tilts to the side. "You want me to do what?"

"Act as the prime minister," Gail repeats. "A touch more formally."

"You're joking," Flynn says, color leaching from his face.

"I rarely joke," Gail says, drying out my throat. "I'd suggest black."

"Black?" I parrot, losing her.

"Your dress for the museum gala; it's classic," Gail says, and on that note, hangs up the phone.

18

The museum sits on top of a winding hill, overlooking the afternoon sea. I've been to some truly beautiful places in my life—the peak of Cadillac Mountain in Acadia National Park, a boat trip off the coast of Nova Scotia—but nothing like this. The building is massive and all white, floor-to-ceiling windows wrapped around the front, ocean views at the back; the garden's full of ripening lemons, dropping into lush, exceptionally manicured grass. Doves sweep overhead, unaware that they're crashing an event—that rows and rows of photographers are poised in front of the red carpet, cameras at the ready, waiting for me to step out of the Range Rover.

"I've been thinking," I tell Flynn from the back seat, eyes almost watering at the corners. "If someone did get to the PM, what're they going to think when my face is splashed all over the papers? That I'm the decoy, or she's the decoy?"

In the rearview mirror, Flynn's eyes skate over my face, stopping at the base of my collarbone, where the necklace-microphone rests. "I've been wondering the same thing," he says, forehead furrowing; he's removed the butterfly suture, left himself with a healing cut that his eyebrow partially obscures. "I'm wondering if that confusion could be useful in any way. Draw out the suspects. See who makes moves. Of course, if they think they've gotten the wrong Sofia . . ."

"Right," I say, catching his drift. *They'll still come after me.* I thumb my earpiece, securing it one final time, knowing that if I don't leave the car now, Flynn might drive me straight to the airport, shoving me on a plane back to America himself. "Okay, let's keep up appearances."

Flynn brushes a hand over his freshly shaven face; I didn't think it was possible for him to look any sexier, and yet— "Let's keep up appearances," he repeats, tweaking his bow tie.

I think we're trying to settle back into our old dynamic—him the suave handler; me the only-in-it-for-the-mission asset—but the pieces don't quite fit anymore.

After the line went dead with Gail, Flynn made it clear that this plan was *absolute bullshit.* So I was supposed to wade into the waters of international politics in *six hours?* Well then, *we better get started.* For five of those, he quizzed me on who'll be at the gala: important donors (including, possibly, Roderick), Summerlandian expats, trade partners, and dignitaries, and how I might react to them. With the laryngitis lie in place, it boils down to body language; as the prime minister, I need to appear gracious, interested in all topics of conversation—but noncommittal.

It isn't drastically different from sitting on a beach. I'll just be . . . standing in my heels. In a museum. Surrounded by people in power, dressed to the nines like me.

The stylists arrived with a perky knock at the suite door, cocooning me in a swarm of satin and silk. On the bed, they splayed out a choice of six different gowns, all black and fairly identical. The Sofia I met at the restaurant probably would've preferred a pantsuit—or, I don't know, chain mail—but the sixth dress had the fewest sequins. Seemed like a safe choice. They zipped me up before working on my hair, applying hot curlers, and telling me discreetly, *Don't worry, we'll leave it down*—to cover the swipe on the side of my neck. What did they think that was from?

"That is some dress," Flynn said, more awed than I expected, when I stepped into the foyer with my hair styled, my dress falling over my thighs in a liquid sweep. He was standing there in a jet-black tuxedo, hands debonairly in his pockets, the fabric accentuating the lean lines of his body. I didn't gape at him, although . . . in a suit like that? Hard not to.

It's *still* hard not to, as he shifts in the front seat of the Range Rover, exiting the vehicle and gently opening my door, a wave of afternoon heat hitting my chest. It's a wall I move through, thick and heady, the sun uncomfortably high in the sky. The perfect time for gelato, for whipped cream, for anything but the flash of fifty cameras, tracking my every move toward the red carpet. *Not just me*, I think. *Flynn, too.* I'm not *absolutely* sure what they're snapping, but instinctively, I know that the two of us make a pretty picture. The young prime minister in her silk dress, hair soft at her shoulders, and the handler turned bodyguard, close to her side in his secret-agent attire, looking like an advertisement for Tom Ford cologne. Alone, we're striking, but together? We're full Hollywood glamour, the political power couple that the newspapers are crossing their fingers for.

I wonder if I should put more distance between us. Skip ahead a few steps. Sofia, she wouldn't like this. She'd give me an earful. *See how he walks so close to you? Never let him walk that close to* me. But after last night and her disappearance this morning, it isn't a *bad* idea to keep my security close. Or . . . is it? I know I can trust Flynn, but the others? Lars and his crew circle like hawks, out of the photographers' shots but near enough to swoop in if someone—anyone—makes a single wrong move.

"Prime Minister Christiansen! Prime Minister, this way!" The photographers, they're already shouting in my direction. The carpet gives under my heels as I step on it, maintaining my balance and my poise. Shoulders back. Think *tall*. The afternoon sun catches the black sheen of my dress, and I'm aglow like a river, careful not to let my hair fall a certain way, careful to keep the side of my neck hidden. As confidently as possible, I readjust a few locks and pause in front of the head-high poster promoting the brand-new exhibit: bold block prints of . . . what are those? Potatoes? Colorful, oil-painted potatoes.

Ah, modern art.

Cameras snap as I do my best—my very best—imitation of Sofia, throwing them a tight-lipped but warm (non-American!) smile and holding up a hand, barely a wave. *Keep moving*, I tell myself. *Just get inside.* But there's a bottleneck at the door. An elderly couple, maneuvering their walkers up a few crowded steps, and traffic has paused for the moment. Not for too long—although just long enough for me to hear it: members of the press, speculating, over the swarm of people; they're speaking loud enough to catch my attention. On purpose? Are they hoping I'll turn in their direction, give them a better shot?

Here's what drops my stomach.

There's a ripple through the crowd, a question from someone in the fray: *Is that a bruise on the prime minister's face?*

The light must've hit my cheekbone just right. Must've cut right through the cover-up that Flynn applied before we left, dabbing on an extra two layers of beige. My throat constricts as a few photographers click, and I cover my cheek a little, pretending to brush away a stray eyelash—but the position won't hold for long. It isn't raining. We don't have an umbrella. Or a newspaper, or a briefcase, or anything to realistically shield me from the snaps. Nothing that wouldn't arouse further suspicion (like, why is the prime minister sticking her head under the Slovenian ambassador to Italy's dress? Odd!).

A few feet behind me, Flynn is stiffening so hard, I can feel the tension radiating into my back; we both know that every photographer is probably zooming in on the bruise, giving themselves something to analyze later, to pick over in high definition. *How'd the prime minister get that? And why is the bone structure of her cheek slightly different than before?* I fell off the monkey bars once, in fifth grade, hitting my cheekbone on the tarmac; at some angles, you can see a fraction of an indent. Will anyone notice?

If my neck wasn't turning red before, when we stepped out of the Range Rover, it certainly is now. Pops of color crawl up my throat, itching, and that would be perfect. Hives would be the cherry on top. Flynn notices, masking a grimace; he's suddenly in front of me, seeing if there's any reasonable way through the crowd that doesn't involve barreling straight through several elderly patrons. (Nope, there isn't.) When he turns back, gaze catching mine, he's obviously debating something. His beard whiskers jump as his jaw tics. He's close enough that I catch the cold zing of his spearmint breath, his eyes tracing the lines of my face, flicking back and forth from me to the photographers, and it's a split-second decision. I know that. I can feel that: the quick, gentle hesitation before he closes the gap between us, the palm of his hand reaching to cup my cheekbone, shielding the bruise.

Those fingertips of his are steady and smooth, and despite everything, despite all the time that's passed and this weird, weird scenario, he still feels like Flynn.

Go with it, Starfish, his eyes seem to say.

That mouth of his tips up into a borderline mischievous grin.

It's for the cameras. In the background, I pick up the growing hush of the crowd—how everything, and everyone, has gotten just a touch quieter—as Flynn and I lock eyes. He might as well be whispering in my ear. I hear him. I understand him. If I'm going to make it out of this, my cover intact, no suspicions about the "gas explosion" raised, he's going to have to hide my face. We're going to have to create a distraction somehow, give the press a better story.

A "juicier" one, as Gail would say.

This might not be the only way—but, welp, it's the way we've got right now. And Flynn's already made the first move. We've already committed.

I guess we're doing this?

Heart thundering in my ears, I rise halfway onto my toes—the heels already help with the height—and slant my mouth over Flynn's. It's a familiar movement, like coming home, and . . . isn't this the plan? So why does it seem like I've surprised him? I feel this shocked little pulse at the base of his throat before he pulls me in closer, his eyelashes brushing my face, the snaps of a hundred cameras going off in our ears. People are shouting, lights are flashing, but everything has narrowed to the warm press of his lips, to the rough graze of his beard and the way his nose dips into the non-shielded part of my cheek. It's a classy kiss, how one black-and-white movie star might kiss another, perfectly restrained and elegant. I wouldn't be surprised if he dipped me back, his other hand curving above the crease in my hips.

Boy, he's good at this deception thing. Top-notch. Gifted.

They teach you this at the Farm?

I have to remind myself it's fake; it's all part of the cover-up, as artificial as the makeup on my face; even I'd be lying if I said I didn't notice the soft swell of his lips, how he tastes just the same. How a soft moan is rising at the back of my throat. I still wonder if I should muss my hands through that perfect, shiny hair. Sweep my tongue along the tip of his. Capture his bottom lip with my teeth. I'm sure it isn't noticeable to the cameras—no one else hears it above the hubbub—but it's like the air between us fizzes, snaps, and I wonder . . . if we might be, just a little bit, giving in to something.

What could've happened last night, on the dining room table.

What I might've wanted since I saw him in the foyer, back in Rome, standing there in those tight khaki pants, staring at me like he didn't just upend my whole damn life.

As soon as the camera flashes slow, he's the one to step back first, a gentle retreat, the rough pad of his thumb grazing the tip of my chin. I swear I do not gasp for breath.

"We can move now," he whispers to me, voice smooth as silk, back to his polished, professional self. He is all charm, as dashing as can be. On the inside, though, is he freaking out like I am? He *must* be. He's probably doing some quick internal calculations, already preparing himself for the cascade of phone calls he's about to field—the fiery hoops we're going to have to jump through to make this right. What's clear is, this is going to be the story. Flynn and Sofia, Flynn and I, we're the story. Not the hint of bruise that might just be a smudge. Not the subtle, subtle differences between me and the prime minister. Not the random "gas explosion" at a restaurant on the Amalfi Coast, kilometers from the PM's hotel.

Sex sells, and we've just sold it *hard*.

"That was the right move, wasn't it?" I whisper out loud to Flynn, filtering through the museum's main entrance. It's cavernous, concrete, with glass installations hanging in spirals from the ceiling. My voice catches in the microphone necklace, playing directly into his ear.

"We'll work it out," he assures me, not meeting my eye.

"Are we 'a couple' now?" I add, words echoing in the chamber, and one of the gala attendants perks at my voice. At the two of us, huddled so close to each other. How're Flynn and I going to play this for the rest of the event? Do we act like we're in love?

Holding up a finger to Lars, asking him and the rest of the security team to wait a second, I shove Flynn, covertly, into the coatroom.

Glancing around to make sure no one's in here, I yank out the makeup compact from my (very practical) dress pocket and dab on more concealer. Enough to blot out any purple, from any angle, even in the bright gallery lights. "Okay, what's the protocol here?"

Compared to the gala's main entrance, the coatroom is awash with silence. Flynn glances around surreptitiously, double-checking to make sure no one's hiding in the chiffon and silk. When he's satisfied that we're alone, he pins me with a look, half-apologetic and half . . . something unreadable. A gulp goes down his throat. "Here's the thing. I didn't think you were going to kiss me."

Come again?

"I was trying to cover your face," he says, fast. "Give the press something else to talk about, the story they were already leaning toward. But I didn't think you'd—"

I'm mortified. I feel like I've just gotten hit between the eyes with a baseball. "Oh my god."

"No, Max, it's—"

"This is *bad*, isn't it? Have I just seriously miscalculated here?"

Flynn grabs my shoulders. "No, look at me. You were smart. Quick thinking. I'm only saying that because the plan's evolving, and I need a few seconds to catch up." He clicks his tongue as his phone vibrates heavily in his pocket. "That'll be Gail, calling to ask us what's going on."

"Are you going to answer it?"

He double-checks the caller. "No."

"Good, I wouldn't."

"She told me she'd send a message if there are any updates on the prime minister. This is just a warning." Flynn skims his bottom lip with his teeth, and I have to physically drag my gaze away from his mouth. His mouth that I've just kissed, his tongue that I've just imagined clashing with mine. "We made a choice," Flynn says, running a hand through his hair. "So we stick with that choice for the gala. Nothing has to change; I'll still be right by your side, as planned. No one's going to be rude enough to ask if we're a couple. Not to our faces, anyway. I'm slightly more worried about the fact that you spoke out loud."

Know where my mind goes?

To the moan. I think I've moaned, while kissing Flynn, as the prime minister, in front of a sea of international photographers.

"In the lobby," Flynn clarifies, going a different direction, "a minute ago. If anyone heard you, word might get out that you've recovered from laryngitis."

I clutch a hand to my throat. "Maybe—maybe no one noticed."

"Possibly."

"Hopefully. Let's say that the kiss was distracting enough." I pause, letting out a big breath through my lips. "You're not going to receive any blowback, are you? Get into trouble?"

He pauses, too, eyeing me. "For . . . ?"

"For kissing me in public like that."

"If I do get into any trouble," Flynn says automatically, "they're fucking hypocrites. I don't know how much you've heard about the CIA's practices, but it wouldn't be the first time that an asset and a handler have . . . engaged in something like that."

"Ah, I see." Seduction. Illicit affairs. I suddenly regret asking. "To get assets to work with you."

His chest rises and falls in his tuxedo, the satin shimmering on his lapel. "To be brutally honest, yes, that's what we're encouraged to do, if it makes sense for the mission, but it's never been my style."

As soon as he says this, my brain goes rogue. Flynn's there in another hotel room, stripping off his shirt, hair mussed, mouth soft. Am I jealous? A dangerous curiosity pricks my skin. "Never?"

"Never," he assures me as we both hear laughter bubble up from beyond the coatroom. Italian, approaching quickly. Instinctively, both of us push in farther back, until we're cornered between two tall coatracks. It's stuffy in here, cloistered, private.

Reckless words fly out of me. "If you were trying to seduce me, I'm not sure I'd even know it." That's the truth, isn't it? I've always been obtuse when it comes to Flynn. After our summer together, I sincerely thought he'd show up for Thanksgiving. Nothing could've confused me more than that email.

He laughs kind of huskily at the back of his throat. "Trust me, Max, you'd figure it out."

I pass him a look, annoyed and unconvinced.

"You would," he insists, coatroom lights dusting the top of his eyelashes. "If I were really trying . . ." He hesitates for a moment, and I'm not immediately sure what he's pausing for. My core heats when I realize he's waiting on *me*, to give him permission. *Hey, Starfish. Can I pretend to seduce you?*

"Go ahead," I tell him, strangely confident. "Give it your best shot."

"You sure?"

"I'm sure."

"All right, then." He takes the bait—or maybe *I* take the bait—because suddenly, he's wrapped his hands around my waist, fingertips imprinting into the liquid silk of my dress, and he's spinning my almost-bare back against the wall. The cool plaster presses against my spine, and Flynn is mere inches from me. He brings his lips to my ear. "I'd probably start by telling you how fucking amazing you look in that dress."

It's not what he says—it's something about the *quality* of his voice. How uneven it is. It sounds like he's restraining himself.

He's barely touching me, hands traveling down my sides, fingers whisper-light against the fabric, but his tone says, *I want more.*

A flutter rises up from deep in my belly.

"I'd tell you how every person at this event won't be able to take their eyes off you," he breathes, the tip of his nose nuzzling my ear. I swallow, willing myself to stay composed, which is really hard to do when his lips drag against the edge of my cheek, and he speaks into my skin: "I'd tell you how, if anyone lays a finger on you, anyone but me . . ."

Sounds stir at the back of my throat. I run my tongue along my bottom lip, savoring those words. Because I like them. My body *likes* them. Outside the coatroom more raucous laughter and a band flare up, arctic flute and accordions, but inside it's just Flynn's breath and my breath, and—

Both of us seem to remember that we're in a coatroom, inches away from international scandal. A restrained kiss on the red carpet is one thing, but this? No. We can't do this. Whatever this is. Nostalgia? A game? Is he just trying to prove a point?

"Well, good," I say, clearing my throat as we both take a step back. "I know the move. I'll be . . . careful and on the lookout for that one."

"Good," Flynn says, mirroring my nonchalance, although his breathing is sort of labored, a flush creeping under his beard. His thumb hitches over his shoulder. "Should we . . . ?"

"Oh, absolutely." Let's leave. I can't stalk out of the coatroom quickly enough.

There's no way the rest of the museum will make my heart pound any faster than this.

19

Modern Summerlandian art, it turns out, is heavily fish-and-potato themed. Tiny felt potatoes and acrylic fishes, spiky fish crafted from aluminum and steel, abstract block prints mixed with two-story-high installations. "It's powerful," Flynn says into the microphone hidden in the collar of his tuxedo. He stuffs his hands deep in his pockets, keeping an appropriate distance from me: close enough to smell the spritz of perfume on my wrists, far enough that it isn't obvious—to anyone—that we've just felt each other up in the coatroom. "Does it make me sound uncultured if I have no idea what it is?"

Shoulder to shoulder, we're staring at the same installation, which appears to be . . . a gilded potato? With . . . swordfish emerging from both ends? *If you are, then I am*, I tell Flynn, silently tipping my head, my body still thrumming from his contact. I force myself to redact any sexual thoughts about him, like lines in a classified CIA case report, until all that's left are long black bars.

Respectfully, we move along, past a mural with reflective glass, and it messes with my mind, how I truly believe—at first, just for a split second—that I'm seeing Sofia in the mirror. She stares back at me in a hundred shattered pieces, her eyebrows crunched together, like she's about to ask me tough questions: *Do you know what happened to me, Max? And* you're *the one holding it all together?*

"Madame Prime Minister," Lars says, bringing over the first guest. I unclench my teeth, shaking out my hands, and so it begins. People filter through my security, offering introductions. I field several ambassadors, an Italian cultural attaché, and a handful of the museum's donors. Word of my miraculous recovery from laryngitis doesn't seem to have traveled far—thank goodness—so I'm able to get by with simple nods, tempered smiles. I'm gracious. I listen.

The cultural attaché tells me that the Italian arts community is delighted by the early response to the exhibition (and that the swordfish potato *clearly* represents the historic struggle for dominance between Summerland's fishing and agricultural industries). The donors largely pass along stories about how they amassed their millions (oil and gas; a jewelry company; yacht manufacturing). The youngest ambassador talks about his cat, also named Giorgio. Cat Giorgio, apparently, has a rich history, rising from the streets of Sicily in a mob-like feral cat community. He attacks anything that moves, or breathes, or thinks about breathing (but in a fun, playful way, *ha-ha!*), and has an extensive social media following, including the president of Croatia and two Korean pop idols.

Unsurprisingly, it's my favorite conversation.

Least favorite is with another ambassador, who tries to grill me about Summerlandian-Belarusian relations. He reminds me of a toad with anger issues, spluttering so badly that I consider reaching for one of the glasses of prosecco floating around, taking a glug before my face can betray anything specific. (I don't. Flynn's warned me not to drink anything from open trays; dehydration is better than poisoning.) I excuse myself with a stilted smile, pretending that someone *really* needs to speak with me.

Turns out, that's true.

"*Ciao! Ciao!* I'm Vittoria Morelli!" A representative for the museum has been waiting in the wings, and as soon as I'm in earshot, she pounces. "Your team and I, we spoke over email?" Her voice is too eager, too excited, and an instinctual part of me says *Run*.

"She's been cleared," Flynn assures me in my earpiece, but that's not what I'm worried about. She's clutching a thick, light blue envelope, the color of baby's breath, and I have no clue what's in it.

"We are *honored* to have you here tonight, Prime Minister Christiansen," she says after a quick security check, swaying up to me. "And I am overjoyed to hear that your voice has returned."

Shit. Oh shit.

"Oh shit," whispers Flynn. He's been scoping out the installation next to me, and is now—quite obviously—trying to figure out a smooth way to barrel into the conversation.

"I know how disappointed you were," Vittoria continues in a burst, literally boxing out Flynn with her body, "not to be able to give the speech, especially for the art you love so much, but it seems you can now! I have it all printed. Your team sent a copy over email."

With this, she hands me the envelope.

Flynn shakes his head in the background. *No, no.*

But I . . . take it.

Why did you just take that envelope, Max? Politeness? Diplomacy? Tucking the speech promptly under my armpit, brain working overtime, I step back as Vittoria advances forward, practically herding me around the corner of a muralled wall.

Where there's a podium.

A podium and a growing crowd of people.

"*Signore e signori!*" Vittoria shouts with a startling lack of hesitation, strutting over to speak into the microphone. "*Senza ulteriori indugi, la prima ministra di Summerland, Sofia Christiansen!*"

A round of applause rises from the audience, every patron in the museum suddenly circling, setting down their glasses of prosecco to listen, and is that *Giorgio*? Not cat Giorgio. Human Giorgio. He's whistling between his fingers and clapping, the sound of accordions rising up to offer a cheery, Summerlandian-polka-themed introduction.

An actual assassin wouldn't be entirely unwelcome right now.

Flynn can't yank me offstage without arousing suspicion, but his voice is loud and clear through the earpiece. "Max, get away from that podium." I've frozen, deer-like, body pelted with the stringent bleat of accordions. Ah, and here's the arctic flute, along with my eye twitch. How bad would I look—how bad would *Sofia* look—if I pulled out at the last second? "Max, just wave a hand, greet the audience, and turn around."

I could do that.

I could back away in my heels.

But this seems like one of those pivotal moments where I need to make a choice: Do I skulk away as the body double, or do I give myself the opportunity to excel in this role, for the sake of Summerland? Signs on the wall are clear: No filming inside the gallery. No cameras to capture the speech if I severely tank. The risk is moderately low. I can . . . read the speech cold, can't I? If I gargle my voice, tell everyone I'm recovering from an illness, maybe the accent will be passable?

In every spare moment, every bit of downtime, I've been practicing the roundness of her vowels, the slight rolling of her *r*, the soft way her voice lilts. She clearly enunciates her consonants, singsongs her sentences. Ideally, I could use another couple of days to hammer it down, but maybe—*maybe*—what I've done is enough?

"Good afternoon," I say strongly into the microphone, as soon as the polka music halts. Feedback squeals through the gallery, the undercurrent of Flynn's groan rumbling through my earpiece. *How'd the* good afternoon *sound?* Only two words. Passable. I blink steadily as I open the envelope, tugging out the speech and unfolding the paper to find . . .

Norwegian.

Norwegian?

You've got to be *kidding* me.

I mean, objectively, it makes sense. Many people in the crowd are Summerlandian expats, and Summerlandians speak Norwegian just as frequently as English. Even so, my fingers curl, gripping both sides of the podium, suppressing the tremor in my hands. The words on the page are soupy, the first sentence slapping me like an insult: *Velkommen, venner av landet vårt, og tusen takk for at dere er her i dag for denne store og lovende anledningen.* Beyond *Velkommen*, I'm stumped.

Tusen? Lovende? Anledningen?

Those could be different types of potato, for all I know. They could be species of fish.

"Max?" Flynn tries again. "You've got to make a move here."

Right. Moves. *What are the moves?* Gazing out over the hush of the crowd, I realize I have three options. None of them are good. Option one: sound out the words, in a language I've rarely heard spoken aloud, and hope that no one questions—like Gail did—if I'm having a stroke. Option two: flee the stage in as calm a manner as possible, as Flynn instructed, and let the prime minister's team develop a reasonable retroactive excuse. Food poisoning? Security threat?

Or . . .

The third option dangles itself, tantalizingly, frighteningly, in front of me. Call it stubborn grit. Call it a bone-deep desire to get something right, but I go for it, snatching it, diving headfirst into a speech that I'll create—in English—on the fly.

"Good afternoon," I say again to the crowded hall, thinking, *Actually maybe I should've gone for option two?* Flynn's shuffled to the side of my vision, visibly pacing, wiping a palm across his clean-shaven face, and I don't know what's more comforting: to catch his eye, have him support me through this, or ignore him entirely. "Thank you all for being here today for this auspicious occasion."

Is it just me, or does my Summerlandian accent sound . . . so-so? I'm channeling Nana Frida, the way she spoke after all those years in Summerland as a girl. How she used to explain recipes over her kitchen table, pointing out the ingredients in old books, her fingers tracing the letters. Words flow from my mouth, no longer the parody of a Norwegian sweater salesman. I'm using my most authoritative voice, like I'm in my own restaurant kitchen, calling out orders during the dinner rush.

"You'll have to excuse my voice," I say, adding extra scratch. "I lost it for a little while, but I couldn't miss this exhibit, showcasing the talent of Summerland's artists. We, as a country, are thrilled to be here, in Italy—building a bridge—through the arts, between our two great nations."

Flynn's perked up slightly in the background, like, *Not bad, Starfish. Not bad.*

I tell myself to keep going.

"Now, I had an entirely different speech prepared, but walking around this museum, I was reminded of my grandmother." According to Sofia's biographical information, she was close to her grandmother, too—so this'll stick. "She had photographs of Summerland's coastline in every room around her house, and I used to stare at them for *hours,* hours and hours and hours, hearing the water in those pictures. That's something that art can make us do—feel as if we're there, our feet on the rocks, and I'm very . . . I'm very proud to have that heritage. I'm proud to witness the next generation of artists, who'll reach out, grip our hearts, and put the sound of the sea in our ears."

Is this speech too airy? Does that matter? Nana Frida's the strongest tie I have to Summerland; she'd grind almonds for prince cake and tell me about her parents' gray-shingled house, how it blended into the rocky silver landscape. She'd wake up at dawn to fish, cold pebbles under her toes.

No one's looking at me like I've gone too far down an unbeaten path. In the corner of my eye, I see Flynn pause his pacing.

Gripping the sides of the podium harder, I say, before I can think better of it, "A long time ago, someone gave me a book of poetry by the American author Mary Oliver, who asked *what is it you plan to do with your one wild and precious life?*" Flynn. That person was Flynn. On a Sunday road trip to Bar Harbor, when we ducked into a little indie book shop to dodge the rain; he'd underlined the passage in black ink and written in the margin, *Restaurant?* "Artists, Summerland's artists, have answered that question, answered that call, and they've made beautiful, beautiful things. This afternoon, this evening, we celebrate them."

That's it. That's enough.

I'll quit while I'm ahead.

Flynn's staring at me, expression unreadable, as I pick up the discarded Norwegian speech, tapping the papers commandingly on the podium, like Sofia always does. "Thank you."

20

It's a near-silent drive on the way back to the hotel, just Flynn and me in the Range Rover. He's propped his elbow underneath the tinted window, hand on his chin, as we speed idly through evening traffic, headlights flashing, flags flapping at the windows.

"Any updates on the prime minister?" I ask, nervous, smoothing out the wrinkles in my dress to give my hands something to do. It's been, what, eleven hours since she went missing?

Flynn shakes his head, unreadable; I've been trying to pick apart his expression since the speech. "You were great back there," he says finally. "Just as likable as Sofia. Equally strong." He hesitates, eyes flitting from the road to the back seat. "That line you quoted, from Mary Oliver. Did I give you that book?"

"Bar Harbor," I remind him, quiet.

"You wanted to try out that popover stand," he says after a moment, swallowing. "We got caught in the rain. Yeah, I remember."

The past hovers between us like fog. "I still have it, you know. The book." I tuck a piece of hair behind my ear. "I think it might be my favorite. That and *Wild Geese*."

"I have that one, too," Flynn says, just as quiet as I am. "On my shelf, in my apartment."

For some reason, this surprises me: an off-duty spy reading poetry. "Really?"

"Saw it at a secondhand shop in Buenos Aires." He clears his throat. "Made me think of you."

Even as we turn into the hotel, I'm stuck on that—Flynn, half a world away, picking up a used copy of *Wild Geese* because I was there, somehow, with him.

Gail snaps me back to the present.

"Do you have any idea the chaos that you two have unleashed?" Gail says, clipped voice flying into the room. The second we stepped into the suite, she called. "Did you panic, Agent Forester? When the cameras started flashing? What about you, Max? Did *you* panic? When I panic—not that I ever do—my lips don't just fall onto the nearest state representative! Next time, Agent Forester, when you want to cover the woman's face, whip off your jacket and throw it over her head. Barrel through the elderly people. That would be easier to explain than the kiss heard round the goddamn world."

Flynn's listening with his hands on his waist, elbows poking the air, and I press my lips together in a tight line. We're like two schoolchildren being scolded by the principal.

"That's not even the reason why I'm calling," Gail says. Her flat-soled shoes click against the floor, wherever she's walking; I can hear the angry echo, how she's pacing like a caged panther. "We caught the Producer."

My pulse staggers. "Where?"

"When?" Flynn jumps in, all business.

"Twenty-six minutes ago," Gail says, answering us both, "eating a panini, just outside of Siena. Tripe and tomato broth, which tells you everything you need to know about his personality. Traffic police flagged him for illegally parking his motorbike, and he gave them one of his aliases—which set off our alarm bells. We're interrogating him now."

Blood pounds in my ears. "Okay, what about Sofia?"

"This puts us one step closer to finding her. Early signs still point to the Halverson family." Gail lets out a sharp breath over the phone. "The only thing you can do, Max, is keep up appearances. Look as in love with Agent Forester as you can. Otherwise, the prime minister is the woman who's having an ill-advised Italian fling with her bodyguard. You'll sell the relationship, tastefully."

Tasteful, in relation to Flynn, gives me actual goose bumps.

"Tomorrow's your last day in Positano. This is now a couple's retreat. Seaside in the morning, then travel to Rome. You'll attend a simple event: a birthday celebration for the Italian president's grandson. Very secure, a family affair. Don't worry about the political element; no one will want to talk shop around clowns. We're canceling the prime minister's slot on *La Visione Italiana*. National TV isn't a risk we're willing to take, understandably. We'll speak again in Rome."

When the call ends, I scrunch up my face. "Did that feel right to you?"

"When she randomly mentioned clowns?" Flynn pinches the bridge of his nose. "Or the fact that a notoriously evasive assassin eluded Interpol, the CIA, and Austrian intelligence services, only to be caught coincidentally by barely trained traffic police, while chowing down on a sandwich?"

"So we're on the same page here."

"I mean, I was wrong about Calvin," he says, shaking his head, "and the Producer hasn't exactly been bringing his A game lately. But my gut's telling me they haven't gotten it right, *again*. I'm not sure that I can—" He bites down, hard, on his lower lip. Like he has to physically stop himself from what he was about to say. "Do you need anything else tonight?"

He's so abrupt, so impossibly toneless, that it gives me conversational whiplash.

I stare at him. "No, I guess not?"

"Good. Well . . . sleep tight." He starts strolling away from me, hands buried in the pockets of his tuxedo. Where does he think he's going to go? We're sharing a room, for goodness' sakes. He's sleeping two yards away from my face. "I'm going to stay up and wait for intel from the interrogation."

I do my best to blink away the confusion in my eyes, grabbing another pair of silk pajamas and treading into the bathroom. Why's he acting *this* strange all of a sudden? Is it just Gail's phone call? Was it our moment in the coatroom? Or my speech? Or—

Wow, this is stuck. It takes approximately six seconds to realize I have a minor problem: The stylists who fastened me into this tight-fitting dress aren't here to squeeze me out of it. Twisting and turning, I re-angle myself, fingers scrounging for the zipper, which—of course—will not budge. It's the Soviet Union during the 1939 peace talks.

"Everything okay in there?" comes Flynn's voice, hesitantly, through the bathroom door.

"Yep, fine!"

"Doesn't sound fine."

"Well, it is!"

I make three more desperate attempts at unzipping myself, jiving around the bathroom like a drunk uncle at a family barbecue, as I release a stream of delicate grunts.

"Okay, I'm coming in," Flynn says, shoulder clearly against the door.

I press the lock button on the handle. "No, you're not."

"You sound like you're getting chloroformed."

"If I was getting chloroformed," I bat back, "I'd be silent."

"Stop being stubborn," he says, without any sting.

"I'm not being stubborn."

"She says stubbornly."

With a sharp inhale, I swing open the barrier between us, gesturing to the highest point on my upper back. "Zipper's stuck."

Grasping my shoulders, hands light on my skin, Flynn spins me around, almost like he did in the coatroom, taking a gander at the situation. His fingers pinch the metal, tugging hard and then harder—but nope, no dice. No glide. "Shit, you're right."

"Told you."

He pauses, pensively. "You know what we actually could use right now?"

I'm thinking some CIA gadget, or a plain old pair of scissors. "What?"

"A bottle of Calvin's ranch dressing."

His delivery is so deadpan, so unexpected compared to his coolness a few moments ago, that a laugh crackles out of me. "You could just lube me up, and I'd slip right out. Wouldn't even need the zipper." *Lube me up* is, maybe, not how I should've phrased it.

Flynn clears his throat with an echo that reverberates across the tile. "Security hasn't stopped looking for him, by the way. Calvin. We've diverted ninety-nine percent of our resources to locating the prime minister, but . . . I'll try again, wiggle it a little." He's talking about the zipper. After a few seconds, the metal finally gives way with a ragged *zzzz*, gliding to the base of my tailbone, Flynn's fingers skating all the way down my back. Neither of us moves. We're suspended in this moment, his fingers resting softly against my skin, and I'm almost afraid to break the spell.

A question bubbles out of me before I can stop it. "What do you mean they haven't got it right *again*?"

His words crash softly into the back of my neck, both of us breathing at the same pace, quiet in the hush of the bathroom. "Max, I shouldn't have—"

"Does this have anything to do with you almost dying? In the hospital? Just tell me. Please. It's one less thing I'll have to wonder about. My head feels like a squashed cantaloupe right now."

Flynn pulls back his fingers, but I don't turn around. It's easier if we aren't facing each other, if we can't look each other in the eyes. "My last mission," he begins slowly, "I spent over two years cultivating an asset, on and off. Intelligent guy, funny, always had a smile on his face. I liked him a whole lot, not just because he was a useful asset, but because he was a good human being. He ended up passing the CIA a few pieces of information that led to the arrest of some truly terrible people. Guy was a hero, and it was my job to get him out of the country. I had an American passport for him, a helicopter waiting. The CIA said we were in the clear."

My stomach clenches. "Oh god, Flynn."

"Next thing I know, the world's tilting sideways." His voice cracks for a second. "We were ambushed on the way to the helipad, after operations *assured* me that no one was on our tail. I went down, and when I woke up, my asset was gone."

"Jesus," I whisper.

"So I'm highly aware that the CIA makes mistakes, and I'll be damned if I let them make a mistake with you." He pauses like he's trying to get ahold of himself. "When the prime minister came on the TV in the safe house, and I mentioned offhand that I knew someone, once, who looked just like her? You have no idea how many times I've wished I didn't say that. How many times I've thought about just . . . going back in time, and stopping those words from coming out of my mouth. That day, when my boss called me in and there was your picture up on the screen, I thought they'd found you from your driver's license. Run a scan for women around thirty with Summerlandian heritage. And it was just some fucked-up coincidence that I knew you. But then it hit me that I . . . I *did* this to you, Max."

My forehead crinkles, even though he can't see it. I run a thumb over the gold-and-silver necklace, resting on my collarbone. "You didn't do anything to me. You said you refused to recruit me, and when Gail showed up at my apartment, I didn't have to say yes."

"You *think* you didn't have to say yes," Flynn says, like his throat is closing. "But that's what the CIA does, Max. They offer you this carrot that makes you feel like it's your choice, that you can better your life, but really, they're taking it away. They're taking a piece of you away. And I'm not just part of that—it started with me. I'm the one who's supposed to be protecting you, and I—" His voice breaks again. "I've *put* you in danger in the first place. If anything happens to you, Max—*Jesus*. You think I could forgive myself?"

I choose this moment to spin around, slowly, air grazing the bare skin of my back. The dress strap slips down one shoulder, but it's hard to care. *Forgive* is one of my trigger words. I know a hell of a lot about guilt, how it feels to wake up every morning regretting the decisions you've made and the people you've hurt.

"I want you to listen to me very carefully, Flynn." His eyes latch on to mine as I drop my voice to a whisper. "You are not responsible for me."

"I am *directly* responsible for you," he says, a sad laugh caught in his throat. It echoes against the tile. "That is exactly my job description. I handle the assignment; I handle you as an asset. And I keep thinking about your family. They wouldn't want this for you. I can't imagine the type of father who'd want to see his daughter put her life on the line for cash. I haven't met your parents for years—and I can tell you that, straight up."

"It's not like that," I argue, shaking my head. "I'm giving them their life *back*."

"And I think they'd tell you to keep it. *I'm* trying to tell you to keep it—and I'm trying not to let you down, Max. You deserve a

professional, someone who's one hundred percent focused, not . . ."
He doesn't finish that. He doesn't finish his next words, either.
"When we were in the coatroom, I . . ."

"You what?" I gulp.

He looks down at me through the curve in his eyelashes. "I was remembering how it was before."

I let that wash over me, like warm water, heat coiling in my belly. "Is that a bad thing?"

Now it's his turn to gulp. "It's a dangerous thing." Even so, he takes a half step forward, the space between our bodies reducing to a sliver. He looks like he wants to reach out and mold his palms against the shape of my hips, but he's stopping himself. Holding back. "Look, it wasn't just the opportunity to travel. I couldn't convince my dad to enroll himself in any of the open trials for his pancreatic cancer, and when he died my junior year, the CIA took *me* at my lowest. I thought, here's a way I can handle things. Literally handle things. Keep people safe, just not the people I love. But I can't keep assets safe if I form emotional attachments, and . . . the risks are too high here, with you, if I lose focus. I told myself that was going to be a hard line, but the line is getting . . . harder."

The way he says it, with the hint of a growl, makes my thighs tingle. At the same time, I'm absorbing everything, all the emotional bombshells that he's just dropped.

"I don't know if I'm the only—" he adds.

I cut him off. "You aren't. You aren't the only one."

It's a risk. It's a calculated risk. I'm hoping that he was about to complete that sentence in the way *I'd* complete that sentence. *I don't know if I'm the only one who cares here.* Who still thinks about that time on the beach, after midnight, when his lips explored the curve of my breasts, and I thought, *He is perfect, he is perfect, there is nothing more perfect than this.*

Maybe he's just as afraid as I am to go there.

But *here*—my body very much wants to go *here*.

"You have no idea how badly I want to touch you," he says, in a way that's so gentle, so genuine, it threatens to split me in half. We each raise one of our hands at the same time, almost shivering, pressing our palms together. Our fingertips brush before they intertwine—and it takes a whole lot of strength not to immediately close the space between us, not to say, *You have no idea how badly I want you to touch me.* His eyes fall on my body, slowly sweeping from the naked plane of my shoulders to the lipsticked curve of my mouth. "I thought you couldn't get any more beautiful, Max. But when I saw you in Rome, you just . . . blew me away."

"Right back at you," I tell him, voice barely a whisper, and I'm definitely not misreading the signals this time. It isn't like on the red carpet. No one's going to burst in here with cameras. We aren't covering for anything, distracting anyone, and there's a need in Flynn's eyes that—I'm sure—matches my own. He reaches up with his other hand, stroking the side of my face. That does it. That little movement bridges the gap, pins us against each other. The sequins of my dress glide against the smooth fabric of his suit, and I can feel the hard lines of him, the lean muscle of his chest. His heart's beating so fast through his shirt that I wonder who's more nervous—him or me.

Because I *am* nervous. When he first stepped into my suite, I drew a line in the sand. No crossing here. Nothing personal between us. And now—even though I'm scared, even though I'm afraid he'll break my heart again, or I'll mess this up—all I want to do in this moment is full-on submerge.

"I meant it," he says, thumb moving slowly along my jawline. "What I said in the coatroom. No one could take their eyes off you."

"It's the sequins." My chest isn't moving in a rhythmic pattern. Nothing about my pulse is smooth, under control. "I'm like a disco ball."

Flynn's breath flutters against the crook of my neck. "You would've done it for me in a pantsuit." It's funny, and it's sweet, and I'm laughing as he plants a soft kiss on the side of my cheek, then again, right by my ear. I stop moving, closing my eyes and homing in on that movement, that feeling—how every place his lips press leaves a mark. Heat is pouring off his skin. He is summer itself, and I can't get enough of his light, my hands roving under his jacket as he slips it off, the fabric falling in a pile on the floor. All that's left is the thin white shirt, my fingers skimming the lines of him, and he's doing the same with me. Gentle touches, gentle brushes, like if he presses too hard, I'll startle. I'll slip away from him.

"Wait," he says, swallowing hard, pushing an inch back from me. "I want to—I want to explain. What happened, back then. We should talk about it. You were never just some summer thing to me, Max. I hope you know that."

Immediately, I think about us. That night. One of the last nights, both of our firsts, and he was so careful with me, protecting my first time like he's protecting me now. "Please don't take this the wrong way," I tell him honestly, soft enough that the words barely come out, "but I'm not sure I want to go there right now. I just want to . . . stay here. Unless you need to talk about it, and then we can—"

He shakes his head heavily, giving me whatever I want, and leans in again. When his eyelashes dust my face, I don't know why I ever tried to convince myself that it'd be easier, somehow, to leave him in the past. A little gasp emerges at the back of my throat, and he reads me, every shift of my body, every subtle cue, dragging his mouth to my lips—and tasting the sounds I'm making for him. Only for him. Both of my hands clasp around the back of his neck, pulling him closer, until the hard length of him presses into my stomach. He groans when I slip my tongue into his mouth, and he meets me there—pulsing heat, the tip of his own tongue, the taste of spearmint.

How many times have I imagined what it would be like to kiss him again? The two of us, unencumbered by rules and restrictions—not having to sneak around. Not having to worry about making too much noise, or getting caught. What we might do with each other—to each other—if we were ever alone again. How he might lick a path across my collarbone, bite my neck, show me just how unrestrained he can get.

It's scary how much I've missed this.

Missed him.

I don't want to tell him that, but also, I'm saying it with every whimper bursting from my lips. Our tongues clash; his hands roam along the curves of my dress, finding my bare back again, fingertips imprinting against my skin. Goose bumps erupt everywhere, all the way down to my thighs, the other strap of my dress slipping down. Every goose bump, every touch and every gasp, is a confession, and he's soaking it up—giving me the same energy I'm giving him. I could wrap my legs around his waist, and I know he'd hold me tight to him.

"Your skin is so soft," he breathes. "Am I allowed to say that?"

"I think so," I bat back. "I think you're allowed."

"You're not going to *pesto* me?" he teases, nipping at my lower lip.

"God, that sounds wrong in a sexual context."

He laughs, our foreheads pressing together as my hands spread underneath his shirt, palms against the solid heat of his skin. Maybe, after everything—all the chaos of the past few days— we're letting ourselves get carried away, forgetting about the consequences or how this might work or anything besides the frantic need for each other. My hands want to explore him, map him, feel the rigid curve above his hips, sink my thumbs into the line above his shoulder blades. His hand reaches down to cup my ass, lifting me slightly, and together we're spilling into the bedroom, clashing into each other, our movements suddenly a lot less gentle. He's grasping for me; I'm grasping for him. His tongue is running down the front of my neck, along my freckles and my throat, traveling downward, lower and—

I remember. I remember the heat of his mouth, the warmth of his tongue, and it's happening again—as he dips down to tug my dress, exposing my breast, his tongue flicking over the nipple before he sucks. Heat ripples everywhere, down my thighs, between my legs—and I'm not sure that either of us is truly breathing. It's more like we're gulping in air, desperate. "Beautiful," he tells me.

One of his hands palms my thigh through the silk before sliding all the way along my leg and hooking the slit in my dress. He pauses, chest rising and falling, a question in his eyes—and my answer is yes. Half crashing against the wall, he pins me, leans into me, our hips rolling, his fingers roaming until he finds the thin fabric of my underwear. His thumb settles in exactly the right spot, rubbing.

If this wall weren't half holding me up, my legs would be shaking so hard, I couldn't stand.

"I need to hear you say it," he rasps. At first, my head's so fuzzy, so warm, I'm not even sure how to condense the words. How to say that I want his shirt off, his suit off, his skin against my skin. I want to bite down on his shoulder as he fills me completely. Instead, he's restraining himself, bulging against his zipper, waiting, and I meet his eyes, imagining how easily his fingers would slip in, how I'd clench all around him, my own hands sinking below the triangle of his waistline, tugging the length of him free.

"You're the only one who's allowed to touch me," I pant into the crook of his neck, echoing his words from the coatroom. "Just you."

This undoes something in him. He hisses out a breath, one of his fingers sliding into me, every shift of my body met with one from him. When I arch my hips, he adds another finger, and I'm unzipping his pants, tension coiling in my belly, the heat and weight of him finally in my hands. He tilts his head back, closing his eyes for a second before gazing at me again, half-lidded, and it's *that* movement—the head tilt, the way he's desperate to go inside himself but also doesn't want to stop looking at me—that makes me realize we're not even going to make it to the bed.

"I've missed all the sounds you make," he tells me in a strangled voice as I grip him, thick between my fingers, pumping faster, and then he's stepping out of his pants and lifting me up. We're moving toward the couch, so in sync it's like the years have evaporated. He tells me he's clean, and I whisper that I'm on the pill, that he can have me just like this, if he wants. "Are you sure?"

"I'm sure."

"Because if you change your mind, I can always—"

"I know." And I do know. I believe that he'd stop, wait, pull back if I said *Slow down.*

We stumble back onto the couch, my thighs straddling him, his hands curving into the crease above my hips. I light up everywhere he touches, the silk of my dress hot against my skin as he lifts it above my head, and then there's nothing between us. He palms his cock before sliding into me with a slow, deep thrust.

I actually tremble. *"Flynn."* My mouth falls open against his, and we rock together, his hands plunging through my hair.

"I would've . . . given anything for this," he murmurs, and the way he says it? Kind of makes me feel like he has. I bite his bottom lip, and he returns in kind, pulling me down hard on top of him.

"I've never wanted anyone like I want you," I gasp, a full truth, shaking as he holds me tighter. Maybe I've said too much, but at this moment, it's hard to focus on anything else but the velvet of his skin under my fingers, how tight I am around him, the wave rising up inside me.

"I've got you," he says, low, into my ear. His fingers intertwine with mine. "I've got you."

That last whisper does it, pressure mounting until I let go with a moan. He follows me, forehead dipped into my shoulder, his pulse colliding with mine.

Afterward—after the first time, and the second time—we stay wrapped up in each other, the night unfolding outside the windows. "You know, you don't have to . . ." I gesture to the sofa beneath us. "I'm saying that the bed is, it's . . ."

"It's what?" he asks, raising one eyebrow, almost taunting me to finish.

"It's big enough for both of us." My gaze flicks across the diminutive width of the mattress. "Well, barely. How are Italians so small, with all the pastries and the pasta?"

"They smoke. They drink coffee. It's very healthy."

I snort out a laugh, thinking, *Have we skipped the awkward part?* I don't feel any second-guessing, any *Should we have done this?* It's Flynn. It's natural. It feels so completely right when he runs his thumb along the corner of my smile, when he carries me into bed, nuzzles into my neck. How is it possible that his lips are even softer than I remember? "You have a gentle mouth," I tell him, nose touching his. "Like . . . a golden retriever."

He laughs so deeply, the bed shakes. "I'm not sure if that's the best or the worst thing that anyone's ever said to me."

"Let's go with the best."

"Okay," he says, smiling at me in a way that makes my heart race all over again. "Okay, Starfish. Let's go with that."

21

"Statistically speaking," I ask Flynn around midnight, the sheets tangled around our hips, "do you think that everyone has an identical stranger out there?"

My chin's resting on his chest, and I hear him press his lips together. "Maybe." We're trying to stay in this cocoon, just the two of us, even though every buzz of his cell phone makes me lurch. No further updates as of yet. "That's kind of like the soul mate question, isn't it? Yeah, there might be someone out there who looks just like you, just like you might have a soul mate, but statistically they're long dead and halfway across the world. You're probably soul mates with someone who died in Australia in 1842."

I tsk. "Who knew you were so *romantic*?"

He playfully nips at my ear. "I can be. Seriously, though, I do believe in soul mates. Dogs. Every dog I've ever had is a soul mate. Plus family, friends . . . Are you and Jules still close?"

I shake my head against his chest, eyes stinging. "I'm happy you remember her, though."

"How could I not?" he says, laughter at the back of his throat. "She threatened to trap a fisher cat and let it loose in my bedroom if I didn't ask you out. I had to google what a fisher cat was."

It's the closest we've come to discussing our relationship. We're tiptoeing toward the inevitable. "Weasel on steroids. Very savage."

"What happened there?" Flynn asks. "You two don't talk anymore?"

My heart clenches at the memory of our last phone call. "I borrowed money from her, too," I say. "For Frida's. She cornered me with a cashier's check and told me that if I didn't take it, she'd never forgive me, because she couldn't get a lobster omelet anywhere else in town." A sad smile works its way to my face. "Anyway, a few months after that, she told me she was expecting a baby, and I—I knew that's where the money *should've* gone. I kept apologizing. She kept getting angry with me for apologizing, and I . . . I thought I was monopolizing too much of her time. I told myself I didn't deserve her."

I can feel the full weight of Flynn's frown, tensing all the way down his body. "Max, you know that's not true. You shouldn't tell yourself that you don't deserve good things."

"Yeah, well—"

"No, I mean it." He hugs me a little closer. "There are so many people who care about you. You have to let them."

What I have to do is change the topic before I start crying into Flynn's shoulder. "How are your siblings?"

He nods against the pillow. "Good. Brian's an accountant now. He has a golden retriever and a recently renovated farmhouse in Vermont. There's an apple orchard in his backyard. On the outside, he's one step away from a Norman Rockwell painting. But he's also heavily into Dungeons and Dragons."

"We're talking conferences?"

"We're talking he legally changed his middle name to 'Faerqiroth.'"

"I love that," I say genuinely. "And your sister?"

"High school science teacher. Three kids. They're visiting a bunch of national parks this summer."

"Awww, Uncle Flynn. I bet you're the fun uncle."

"Actually, I'm the uncle who's babyproofing the house and making sure there are no spare pennies in the cup holders, so no one chokes on them. Walter, the youngest one, *everything* goes in the mouth. Buttons. Dog biscuits."

"Calvin's like that," I say, wondering, once again, where the hell he is. "Do they know what you do for work?"

Now it's Flynn's turn to smile a bit sadly. "They think I'm a contractor for the Department of Agriculture."

"Ah. Hence, Iowa."

"Right." He licks the seam of his lips. "I have to say, you're not the only one with strained relationships because of your job. I'm gone way too much. I've missed family Christmas three years in a row. Whenever my college buddies ask about my life, I have to feed them a bunch of bullshit, and I hate it. Here I am telling you to let people in, and I can't even take my own advice. Disclosing my involvement with the CIA isn't allowed, but if it was, I still wouldn't want to worry the people I love. Or shock them."

"Same," I say, quietly. "Not that I'll ever tell anyone about this 'vacation,' but I'm not sure anyone would believe it if I did."

"It does sound slightly implausible."

"Just a little," I say.

Flynn peers down at me through his eyelashes. "Although . . ."

I glance up at him through mine. "Although what?"

"Please take this as a compliment, because it's meant as one. The girl I knew was always jumping at these random, interesting opportunities. Remember when you told me we had to drop everything and travel four hours for that rock oyster festival? Or that one Sunday when you got this itch to bike down Cadillac

Mountain? You were spontaneous, and fearless, and as much as I think you shouldn't be here, it doesn't surprise me as much as it could that adult Max heard 'Italy' and—"

Something flickers in the bedroom.

I don't mean in a sexy way. I don't mean, like, a flicker of heat, or a flicker of lust, or even a flicker of the lights. When my gaze tilts to the ceiling, I see that a bird—a real, live *bird*—is staring at us from the chandelier. It offers a startled coo, wings flapping, like *we're* the ones who are surprising. Flynn flinches, drawing back from me. "What was—?"

"Oh my *god*," I say, pulling the sheets over my face as the pigeon dive-bombs us. Apparently, we have wronged this bird in a past life; it has a vendetta, a score that it's looking to settle. He darts in with a vicious swoop, narrowly missing my head—like he's been trained to assassinate me. Flapping around the ceiling in a frenzied pattern, the bird releases a stream of gray poop onto the Oriental rug. In Italian culture, is this a really bad omen, or a really good one?

"Has a pigeon been in here the *entire* time?" I bleat out, scrambling to grab my pajamas. This bird's like a falcon with a kill, latching on to Flynn's shoulder for a second, talons fully out, before springing into the bouquet in the foyer. The vase topples to the side, water spilling all over the table.

I suppose Flynn and I *could* just go back to talking. Ignore the wild pigeon that's somehow swept into the suite, accept that he lives here now. He can make a nest. Whatever. But the bird has, just slightly, killed the mood, especially when he's obviously trying to escape—fluttering frantically around the room, beak pecking against the mirrors, like they're windows to the outdoors.

Flynn's gotten out of bed. His face is flushed, his hair's messy, and his eyes are roving around the suite with a new, focused intensity. "Did you go out onto the balcony today?" he asks, his voice taking on an ultra-deep tone, which seems like an extreme reaction to a pigeon.

"No, I didn't, I—"

It clicks. Why Flynn's so guarded, so suddenly agitated. All the wind blows out of me.

It's just a bird.

But who let the bird *in*?

After the bomb-sniffing dogs leave, after the additional security sweep, Lars shooing the pigeon back into the outdoors with nothing but a champagne bucket and a bed pillow, Flynn can't sit still. He doesn't believe that housekeeping is responsible for the bird, even after Giorgio says that he personally delivered a few more bars of goat soap that afternoon, opening the balcony doors to air out the room for a few minutes. The bird must've slipped in then. *Scusi!*

Security footage captured the whole incident—Giorgio going in, Giorgio going out, no one else accompanying him—but I can read Flynn like the books he used to give me. He's taking it as a sign. He let himself get unfocused. He dropped his guard.

"Flynn," I say, "sometimes a cigar is just a cigar, and a pigeon is just a pigeon."

"I know," he says, but I can tell he doesn't mean it. "Hey, you should get some sleep."

I cross my arms, hugging myself. "Are you sure? I can stay up with you. I've been thinking, it *is* possible that they caught the wrong guy, right? What if the Producer has a decoy?"

Flynn rubs his eyes. "I suppose anything's possible. I promise I won't leave any stone unturned." He leans forward and kisses me, briefly, on the forehead. It feels slightly robotic. "Go rest."

Rest does not come. The room's too hot. The sheets tangle with my legs. My ears keep perking, waiting for a light *rap* at the balcony door (although, I'm fairly sure that most assassins don't knock before they enter). The sound of rushing water wakes me up again, several hours later, just after dawn. The light's egg-yolk yellow as I open my eyes and see that Flynn must've tiptoed to the bathroom for a quick shower. My head throbs like I'm hungover, the stress of the last couple days catching up with me.

Coffee.

If I'm going to get through today, I'll need coffee.

Giorgio must've put an espresso machine in here. Something tiny and fancy. Sure enough, I spot one, half-hidden by another vase of flowers, and brew myself a foamy cup, sipping it in the startling quiet. No police walkie-talkies, no footsteps outside. Downstairs, servers must be setting up the early-morning breakfast buffet on the terrace, beach attendants stabbing umbrellas into the sand . . .

"Max."

I jump, spilling half of my drink.

Flynn rounds the corner suddenly, toweling off his hair. It's spiked in the front, and he ruffles the cotton through it. A second towel is wrapped around his waist, barely tied—and this is the type of thing that, day one, would've made blood rush to my face. "What're you doing?" he asks.

"Drinking . . . caffeine?" I manage. The liquid sloshes all the way down my wrist.

He takes the cup away from me gently, the clean scent of his soap trailing in my direction. His collarbone's glistening wet. "No one replaced the coffee grounds last night, I don't think. I can't guarantee that someone didn't poison your . . . What is this?"

"Mocha latte."

"Well, that looks damn delicious, and I'm sorry. I'll get you a fresh one later." On the nightstand, by my unmade bed, Flynn sets down the cup and puts his hands on his hips, letting out a short, sharp sigh. The brush of his fingertips against my thighs, as he leaned me against the wall last night, flashes fresh in my mind. He pinches the bridge of his nose. "Sorry. I don't mean to be . . . I'm just being cautious. I've been reading the transcripts of the Producer's interrogation."

My stomach swoops. "Okay, and?"

"You could be right." Flynn keeps toweling off his hair, even rougher now, scrubbing. "There's a chance we've got the wrong guy. Assassins might be completely psychopathic, but successful ones—usually—are whip-smart. This guy hasn't asked for a lawyer, hasn't put up any roadblocks, and maybe that's arrogance . . ."

"But you don't think so."

Flynn swipes a hand down his face, holding on to the towel around his waist with the other. "It could be paranoia, but something feels off. The CIA wants you in the field for the rest of the vacation. To them, you're just a placeholder to keep the peace. They think the danger's over for you. But if the real Producer is still out there, if we still don't know why the prime minister's missing, then—"

A rap really does come at the door now. Room service.

"Should we get that?" I ask.

"You're hearing me, right?" Flynn holds my gaze. "You need to go home, Max. Forget about the money."

"And should I just forget about Summerland?" I argue, pulse rising. "You heard Gail—"

Knocking comes, again.

"Gail doesn't have your best interest in mind," Flynn argues back. "She's only thinking about the CIA's bottom line."

A third knock.

"One of us is going to have to get that," I say.

"This isn't over," Flynn grunts, begrudgingly throwing on a

robe and answering the door. So the morning begins, a fast-paced blur. Breakfast. Paparazzi on the cliffs. Beach. Flynn, twitchy, looking out for danger around every corner. And me, trying to tamp down my own anxiety. Sofia's been missing for over twenty-two hours; I'm much more worried about her than I am about myself.

"Quiz me," I tell Flynn as I pack. "For the birthday celebration, I don't have the luxury of laryngitis anymore. I know Gail said no one will want to talk shop, but I should have some talking points prepared, just in case I'm cornered."

Across the room, Flynn's only half there, checking and rechecking his phone.

"Flynn, please."

He blinks, nods, and starts scrolling her recent interviews before asking, "Would you care to comment on the ongoing state of relations between Summerland, Estonia, and Russia, especially in light of the recently proposed treaty?"

I fold a pantsuit and shove it into my suitcase. "No? I wouldn't?"

Flynn tips his head from side to side. "Actually, seems like the correct answer. How about . . . Could you please expand upon your thoughts about the increasing use of nuclear power in Summerland's west territories, and the risks and benefits of this growth as it relates to climate change, energy costs, and the possible threat of global terrorism?"

My suitcase shuts with an exaggerated click. "You don't suppose I could get away with a 'no' for this one, too, do you?"

"No comment is always an option," Flynn says, toneless.

Publicly, all morning, we pretended to be a couple—he even rubbed sunscreen on my back, down at the beach—but alone, there's this tension between us that I can't shake.

We leave Hotel Giorgio in a haze of anxiety—Giorgio, obviously, waiting to say his goodbyes. You'd think we were cousins, or longtime best friends, the way an actual tear escapes his eye. He kisses me on both cheeks with an extended *mwaaa*, and asks me if I'll visit Positano again.

"Every year." I respond like Sofia would, adding a bit of Max into the mix. "Next time, I'll leave my first tennis serve at home."

Giorgio laughs, his whole face flushed. "Maybe that's a good idea, Signora Prime Minister. Maybe that's for the best. But I will be in Rome soon, too! If we run into each other there, I'll say hello."

"I'd like that," I tell him.

My entourage ushers me out, a flash of cameras at the gates, and then we're gone. I'm used to the Range Rover by now: the cool back seat and the smooth, stoic ride. Flags flap against the tinted windows, heralding my trip to Rome. It's a little over three hours by car, but Flynn skips the polka this time, opting for more traditional Italian music as small towns and countryside slip by— Capua then Cassino then Ferentino. "I've pulled in a favor," Flynn says, out of the blue, over halfway into the drive. "A buddy of mine's a pilot. He's added you to his flight manifest, right after the luncheon, leaving out of Rome. I have clothes for you in the back. The party will be incredibly secure, because of the president's involvement, but after that, I can't guarantee your safety."

His words hit me in the back seat. Once again, it isn't what he's saying. It's the tone. Like he's pulled all the emotion out of his voice. Why? Is it because he can't protect me well if his heart's involved? Or—*oh god*—does he regret last night? Are we back to strictly an asset-handler relationship?

He keeps his eyes on the road. "I said you always have a choice with me, and I meant it. You have the option to leave. I hope you take it."

When I don't respond right away, he says, softer, "Promise me you'll think about it?"

"Yeah," I tell him, a little dazed. "Yeah, I'll think about it."

More houses. Trees flitting by. Old streets. Gardens. Head spinning, I tap into the Range Rover's roaming hotspot, checking my American phone for new messages. Nothing from Dad, nothing from Calvin. Maybe I'm just not receiving their messages?

I text Calvin again: **Could you just tell me where you are?**

Is he in Rome? He's not planning on gate-crashing again, is he?

One of Calvin's texts, from two days ago, springs back in reply: **If you're not going to have the pizza outside your door, then I'm going to eat the pizza outside your door. Sorry!** I stuff my American phone, alongside my CIA phone, into my pocket.

Unfortunately, right outside of Rome, traffic slows; the police escort pushes us through, around cars parting to the side, but by the time we reach Trastevere, we're running around fifty minutes behind schedule—without time to drop by the hotel first. We go straight to the birthday luncheon, filtering through the criss-crossed streets, past an array of craft breweries, golden piazzas, and shops selling everything from ceramics to sandals.

"Do we have a gift?" I ask Flynn as the car slows.

"The prime minister's team sent one," he says, looking up at the restaurant, a bright orange building with ivy spilling from the windows. Very fancy. "Kid's turning eight. When I was eight, I had a bouncy castle and a water-balloon fight in the park."

This is slightly more elaborate than that. The place is crawling with security. Guards on top of guards on top of guards. Guests are filtering through them, dressed to the nines, carrying presents wrapped in glittering paper. Two bakers (after presenting IDs) totter along with a cake, the top tier nearly reaching the height of the doorframe. Rosettes of vanilla icing melt in the heat.

Inside, it's just as warm. The tub that used to be filled with ice is now a half-chunky swimming pool, bottles of limoncello sinking toward the bottom. Flynn bats a blue, translucent balloon away from his face, and I puff away a chunk of my bangs. We're hovering near the entrance, surveying the tables: In the middle, they're spilling over with gifts; crystal plates surround edges, alongside sharp, glimmering forks and ice cream spoons. A few clowns mill around the guests, wearing polka-dotted pants and making balloon animals. Flynn shivers, speaking to me out of the side of his mouth. "Can't stand clowns."

I cup a hand over my mouth, speaking back. "Do you think that Italian clowns can just blow up a straight balloon and call it spaghetti?"

"I don't know," he says, acknowledging my bad attempt at humor. "But I'm not asking them."

Like at the museum gala, my security starts vetting each guest who comes my way, offering introductions; it's a blur of Italian government officials, cultural attachés, and people close to the Italian president's family. My Summerlandian accent spills out. It's getting more natural now, the more I use it. I wonder if I'll have a sort of reverse culture shock, going home to Maine, if I'll start speaking with a Scandinavian lilt while Calvin and I are commenting on reality TV. *Hey, who's watching his turtle?* That thought strikes me, but not as much as the bleating sound of the accordion.

No matter where I go, I can't escape the polka.

Around us, partygoers bob to the beat. Elderly couples mingle with young fashionistas, designer handbags in the crooks of their arms. There's laughter and a bit of yelling and middle-aged men chiding each other about politics. The president himself has yet to make an appearance—he's been held up at work, go figure—but the birthday boy doesn't look too displeased. He's busying himself with a mound of candles and cake as people kiss the sides of his cheeks, wishing him *buon compleanno* and *tanti auguri!*

Air-conditioning is nonexistent. All the windows are open, flowing in a breeze, but I find myself tucking a hand under my linen shirt, wiping away a thin sheen of sweat. I suck discreetly on an ice cube, internal temperature rising, and maybe it's all the singing or the family or the brightness. Maybe it's the painting of Julius Caesar in the corner, a super fun reminder that Rome is a great place for assassinations. (Historic, even! Sixteen emperors over fifteen years, if memory serves.) Maybe it's the way I'm afraid to glance over at Flynn, afraid to see any shred of regret or worry on his face, but my temple starts to throb. I need water. Just a bit of cold water, splashed over my face.

"Are you okay?" Flynn asks me, fixing his gaze on my cheeks. I must be red. Or pale. Or a bit green. I also think I might've just seen Roderick, on the street outside, entering the building with a stack of baby blue gift boxes. Did I? How paranoid am I being? "You look a little . . ."

"Was that Roderick?"

Flynn's head whips around the room. "Where?"

"Outside. I might've just seen him, trying to come in."

"I'll send someone to check."

Instead of waiting for Roderick to arrive and strike up a conversation, I hook a thumb behind me, telling Flynn that I'm going to pop to the powder room. Historically, we haven't had much luck with Italian restaurant toilets, but there are *so* many notable figures roaming around—so much security—that the possibility of another explosive device in the bathroom seems very low to me.

"We'll clear it first," Flynn says, reading my mind. "Twice."

After a thorough security sweep, I'm allowed inside the bathroom. There are two sets of doors. The first leads into a small sitting room with a set of ornate couches, wooden hardware painted gold, and that's where Flynn pauses. "There's a window inside, but it's padlocked shut. I'll stop anyone else from entering this way. No rush."

Wordlessly, I slip through the second set of doors and immediately sidle up to one of the pedestal sinks, running the cool water over my hands, suddenly a bit out of breath. My fingertips are shaking, and I'm not entirely sure why. Because of last night? Because of the Producer? Because Sofia's still missing? Take your pick! In two days, this'll all be over, and I'm wondering—besides the money—if anything will have really changed. Sure, the money's a big change, but will I have actually helped the prime minister? And not that this matters in the scope of things, but what'll happen with Flynn? Will we keep in touch now that we've met each other again as adults? Everything just feels so *unfinished*, so cut open at the edges. How do I just go back to normal life after this?

I mean, seriously. How?

The bathroom is deathly quiet, insulated from the party by thick marble walls. I wish I'd shoved a tube of lipstick in my pocket, just to give myself an extra way to kill time. Something to steady my hands. Splashing a bit of water on the back of my neck, letting the coolness trickle down, I puff out a breath and look over at the statue in the corner. It reminds me of Giorgio's lobby angel: a Renaissance-style sculpture of a rather curvaceous man holding an apple. I want to crack a joke about Trader Joe's—how that could be Joe with his organic, moderately priced fruit—but I'm alone. No one here to make it to.

"Just you and me, buddy," I mumble into the emptiness of the bathroom.

And someone, from inside the *ceiling*, laughs.

22

She dive-bombs me like the pigeon in the hotel. Except, she comes complete with a rappelling rope, kicking out a ceiling tile and descending to the floor before I even have time to scream. What is it about assassins and *bathrooms*? Do they just . . . have an affinity for small spaces? Or potpourri?

Blood pounds in my ears as I dart for the exit, but she is (obviously) faster, throwing her body in front of the door. In a quick snatch, she closes her fist around my necklace, ripping it off, damaging the microphone before throwing the whole thing in the sink, where the water's still flowing, and—

In the movies, I've seen how this goes. The assassin grabs my hair and smashes my head into the bathroom mirror; I kick, keep kicking, struggle by the sinks, and suddenly (Somehow! With movie magic!) one of us has knocked the pipework loose. The bathroom's flooding. Water's slippery under our feet, in kind of a fun water-slide-y way (this is a kid's birthday party, after all).

And know what? That is almost exactly how it begins. Her hand, shooting out. Reaching for my hair. The rope's wrapped around her arm, ready to strangle me.

But I *really* don't feel like dying today.

"Oooh, you're a fast one," she says as I dodge her, dipping low like Flynn taught me.

"How are you *so* pretty?" I bleat out, panicked, my palms out in the air. Not the first thing I should've said, maybe, but she is stunningly beautiful, the type of woman who—if you saw her walk into a fountain—you'd assume she was a movie star, filming. Her hair's so glossy, it's like liquid silk, and—"SECURITY! *SECURITY!*"

"Don't yell, Prime Minister," she says calmly, very quietly, advancing again. The rope tightens in her hands. Her fingernails are painted bubble-gum pink. "Yelling will do you no good. These walls are solid marble blocks."

"FLYNN!"

She lunges, and I act on instinct, palm thrusting toward her nose. Her head bobs before I have the chance to connect. Her reflexes are catlike. Comparatively, mine are . . . what? Panda-like?

A cold sweat breaks out across my chest as I wonder if she's right about the thickness of the walls—and really wish I'd grabbed one of the cake-cutting knives. Not like I have the training to *use* it . . . Actually, I take that back. I do. Totally beside the point, but the tiniest part of me also wants to shout that I was *right*. A female assassin! Knew there'd be one.

"They will think that you ate something spicy," says the assassin, pushing me back, hard, against the wall. "That you are taking a little longer than usual."

She says it almost like a joke, like she's expecting me to laugh, but I'm a little distracted by the throbbing pain at the back of my skull, where my head's hit marble. I twist, writhe, break free of her grasp for a second as I think about how much time has passed since I walked through the door. A minute? A minute and a half? It'll be way longer before Flynn knocks, checking to see if I'm all right—and honestly, I'm not sure I want him to. Then *he'd* be in here with an assassin.

Can he seriously not hear me?

"Bye-bye!" says the assassin, wrapping her hands around my neck. I try to do the move. The one Flynn showed me. The thing! The elbow-slam thing! But it's harder in real life than it is in practice, and I realize as her thumbs start pressing against my windpipe that I'm not going to win this one unless I say—

"I'm the double!" It comes out as a barely-there rasp. My throat burns. "I'm the decoy!"

She relieves some of the pressure, loosening her grip. "Say that again?" Her accent is . . . not Italian? But she *looks* Italian, dark mascara playing on her thick eyelashes.

"The *decoy,*" I manage through the crush of my windpipe. "I'm not the real prime minister! I'm not Sofia. If you kill me, you're not . . . You don't have the right person."

The assassin fully releases my neck, eyeing me. I'm stiff still. "You *are* different than I thought you'd be," she says, finally, sliding out a knife from the sleeve of her powder blue pantsuit and turning it over in her hands. *Oh, goody. A switchblade.* The tip of the blade pinpricks her index finger, but when she speaks again, she points the knife in my direction, like it's an extension of her body. She seems a little too comfortable using it. "There's a slight differentiation in your bone structure. And your beauty mark, it just came off. I have a question for you."

Does she believe me about being the decoy? Does it matter?

I swallow down acid. "Go for it."

Her accent sounds a heck of a lot more Eastern European now. "When the prime minister did the shoot for British *Vogue,* do you know if they let her keep the shoes?"

Excuse me? I press my lips together, giving her a tight nod. "They . . . did."

I have no idea if they did or not. Or if I just gave the "right" answer.

The assassin nods pensively. "Lucky. Those were excellent shoes. I have tried to purchase the same shoes for myself, but they were out of stock at many retailers. Do you still have the shoes?"

"Not with me currently," I venture, imagining boots. Leather ones, with laces you could use to choke someone. Strong psychopath vibes, this one. Even so, if she believes me, if she hasn't killed me . . . "Mind if I ask who sent you?"

"You can ask."

The pause is long enough that I add, "Okay, who sent you?"

Her ponytail glistens as she cocks her head, like she's solving a math problem—and I'm the equation. "Who do you *think* sent me?"

A member of the crime family? Aksel, the Halverson brother who's missing? "No idea," I lie. The longer I keep her talking, the longer I stay alive.

"Oh, come on!" she chides, prodding the air with the knife. "You must have guesses. When you saw me, your first thought was—"

"You have great hair."

She preens. "I use a silk pillowcase and rinse with cold water. You can also rinse with apple cider vinegar for more shine." Flicking the knife closed, she shoves the switchblade between her breasts. "So I will not kill you. I don't make errors on the job, unlike some people I know. Men can be so sloppy. They cut corners. Besides, it's hot—I don't like to kill people in the heat—and, woman-to-woman, I did not want to kill you anyway. I'm rarely sent to take out women. You should know, though, that the others will not give you as much of a chance."

She's stepped back. I'm inching toward the door, every limb in my body shaking. "Others?"

The thought strikes me cold: Why hasn't Flynn checked in? Why isn't he speaking through the earpiece?

"I wouldn't go out that way," she says, before pointing toward the bathroom window and tossing me the key to the padlock.

"Climb onto the fire escape, go one window down, slide into the kitchen, and leave out the *other* fire escape into the alley. You can't trust your own people. So I'd move quickly."

My head's spinning. My throat's closing again.

"Go on," she says, shooing me with her fingertips. "Scoot."

Is this a trap? What does she mean by *your own people*? The prime minister's or mine? The CIA?

"If you don't leave in ten seconds," says the assassin, reapplying a slash of red lipstick in the mirror, "I really might have to kill you for being so *stupid*."

I don't trust her. Don't trust her at all. But considering that the knife's still within her reach, I rush toward the window, undoing the padlock, then prying it open with my fingertips, wood and glass straining, and immediately there are city noises, music and sirens and traffic, and my pantsuit's skimming the windowpane as I slide onto the fire escape, losing my earpiece in the process. *No, no, shit*. Summer heat pummels my face, light reflecting off the metal, as I watch it fall through the grate, to the streets of Trastevere below me. It bounces briefly on the pavement, locals whizzing past on bicycles, people bustling in and out of B and Bs, before it gets crushed under the wheels of an Alfa Romeo.

I've officially lost contact with Flynn.

Flynn, who's either waiting for me outside the door or—*please, please, don't let this be true*—detained by the "others," and I'm out here, back against the wall, my heels clattering against the grate; breathing deeply through my nose, I crawl along the fire escape, finding the second window into the kitchen.

It's open. They're letting the heat out.

Frantically, I climb inside with an "excuse me, *scusi*," the ashen pieces of Sofia's note reassembling in my mind, *You're in more danger than you were told*, and this is . . . perfectly normal. Very normal for a foreign leader to Spider-Man-scramble onto the countertop of an industrial kitchen in the middle of a child's birthday luncheon. Perfectly average for her to knock into one of the dessert stations, smearing the side of her pantsuit with raspberry sauce (which looks delicious, by the way) as her feet touch the floor. Yes, I'm out of the bathroom, I'm away from *that* assassin, but the danger level doesn't feel like it's gone down. It feels, if anything, like she's turned up the temperature on the gas. The sous chefs pause in bewilderment as I rush past, scanning the countertops for something to defend myself. Spoons. Why are there so many *spoons*? Large silver spoons with the smoothest edges possible, and sure, if I really worked for the CIA, I could MacGyver that. I'm sure I could take someone down with those mini prosciutto sandwiches. But I'm me. I'm a *chef*. My comfort zone's cooking in the kitchen, not . . .

Not this.

Not Roderick, spotting me through the circular windows of the dining room and busting through the doors with a "Sofia! Sofia, *there* you are!" His voice carries above the clash and clang of the kitchen, and I tap at my ear, where the earpiece was, feeling the ghost of it, like that'll do any good.

I'm trying not to make a spectacle. Trying not to cause a scene.

"Sofia!" Roderick shouts again, and I steal a glance back at him as he picks up his pace, trailing me. He's wearing what can be described only as a yachting outfit: blue tailored coat, bright white pants, a yellow ascot wrapped around his neck. His face gives away very little. Has he come to try and kiss me or kill me? Who knows! So fun! "Sofia, wait! Be reasonable! Let's just talk about this!"

He charges left as I dip right, until we're on opposite sides of the same station. Bisque bubbles in pristine silver pots. Just-boiled lobsters gleam from trays, and I'm panicking, a little delirious. Underneath Roderick's slick, faux charm is the undeniable hint of malice. I see the flicker of it, the edges of it, bursting into the corners of his eyes. Maybe he and Sofia did have a thing at one point, but now? Now, I'm picking up a meat mallet. It's hot in my hands. It's . . . oddly smooth.

I look down, realizing I haven't grabbed a meat mallet.

I've grabbed the fucking *lobster*. Roderick gives me a giggle like, *Oh, Sofia, so silly, you think you can defend yourself with that?*

He doesn't laugh so hard when I chuck it at him, claws first.

"What the *hell* was that?" Roderick yells, clutching the side of his face, but I'm already gone. Already spilling out the opposite door, like the assassin told me to do. God, would you listen to me? *Like the assassin told me to do.* Assassins! Notoriously reliable!

But my gut . . . believes her. She had plenty of reasons to lie to me, but not many to lie to me about not trusting my own people. Couple that with Sofia's early warning, with the words she never got to say to me in the powder room, and I'm whipping off my heels in the street, clutching them in my hands, my bare feet pounding the pavement. I'm on the other side of the restaurant, the back end, without Sofia's security. Shouldn't there be more security here? Did someone call them off?

It's nothing but locals and kitchen staff, a few people in white coats smoking tiny cigarettes, eyebrows squiggling as I jet by. Should I go around, back to the front entrance? Find Flynn? Jesus, is he *okay*? In one of my pockets is my CIA phone, my American phone in the other, and whom should I call? Gail? What if Gail's in on it, too? What is *it*?

Your own people.

Would it have killed that assassin to be a little more specific?

Just then, a man in a dark suit bursts from the restaurant, jaw clenched, tightly focused. When he spots me, he picks up the pace.

"Taxi!" I yell, rounding the corner. A piazza opens up on the other side of the street—flower stalls and vendors selling espresso. *"Taxi!"*

The white flash of a sedan stops for me on the curb. All I can think is *Away. Out.* Away from Roderick, and any other assassins, away from the people who want to harm Sofia. And me.

Head whipping around, checking to make sure the dark-suit man is far enough behind, I dip into the cab shouting, "Drive, drive, drive!" The driver gives me a distinct double take through the rearview mirror, and I return the look with a desperate shake of my head like, *Nope, not her, try again.* Why would a prime minister be traveling by herself in a random taxicab? This, he seems to think, is a good point, and he turns his attention back to the road, taking off before asking—in Italian, then in English—where I'd like to go.

Where would I like to go?

Where *can* I go?

Geographically, I'm not even sure which part of Rome we're in, or where's safe, or if I have enough spare euros in my coat pocket for the fare, but—"The Trevi Fountain," I say, picking a place at random, somewhere with a crowd I can slip into. "Do you have a pen?"

The cab picks up speed, cruising away from the piazza, gelaterias whizzing by, and the driver passes me a ballpoint pen with an odd look, eyes flicking between me and the road. I take out my CIA phone, flipping through the two contacts, writing both numbers on the palm of my hand, just in case I run out of battery. Flynn's, I call first.

"Pick up, pick up."

My stomach jerks to the side, along with the taxi; I imagine how his face must've dropped when he entered the bathroom to find it empty, assassin gone, decoy gone. I imagine him traipsing back through the birthday party, chest heaving, flitting out the doors, wondering where the hell I am and if I'm okay and why it seems like I've crawled out a fucking window.

The other alternative is, he's in worse straits than me.

And I will not allow myself to imagine that.

When I try to call a second time, the phone dies in my hands, and my American phone—naturally—has no roaming Wi-Fi to connect to.

The taxi charges across the river, afternoon traffic giving way to a rushing flow, and it's *all* a rushing blur. The party, the assassin one-on-one, the past couple of days. Last night. God, was it just *last night*? The way I pressed my cheek into Flynn's bare chest, the way he held me. It isn't . . . it isn't possible that the assassin was talking about *him*. He is my people. He is very much my people. The person sworn to protect the body double can't—in the same breath—be working with the opposition. That's too complicated. Too messed up.

After nineteen minutes and a hefty charge, the driver drops me off around the corner from the Trevi Fountain. I pay with the second-to-last bill in my pocket, getting a few coins quickly in return, and set off on foot. Where I'm going, no idea, but it feels important to keep moving. Keep moving and find a pay phone. Do those still exist?

Whipping off my jacket and taking down my bun, trying to make myself look a little less ministerial, I weave through the crowd, bare-shouldered, sunburned, watching my back to make sure that no one's following me with a knife. Not that I'd really *know* if anyone was following me. I'm not trained in countersurveillance. Is that even what it's called?

Pay phone.

I spot one by a pizzeria advertising a lunch special in English, the sharp tang of tomatoes hitting my nose before I enter the box, checking the numbers on my hand, punching in the coins, and dialing Flynn. The phone rings; the line crackles with static. I press the receiver closer to my face, fingertips clutching the side of the box to stay steady. "Please, please, please, please . . ."

By this point, I'm frantic, sick, half out of my mind with worry.

"Hello?" I try when the ringing stops, right before the phone line goes dead, nothing but blank air, the crush of silence. My heart drops. *No. No.* This can't be happening.

A sob strangles the back of my throat as I slam in another coin and dial Gail.

She picks up on the first ring, the sharp stick of her voice punching through the line. "Max?"

"Gail." I don't recognize the sound of my voice; I palm away a tear before it falls. "Gail, where's Flynn? Is he all right?"

"Of course he is," she says automatically, and I allow myself the tiniest breath of relief. "I see that the geolocational services are off on your cell. Just stay on the pay phone another minute, Max, and we'll locate you. Come retrieve you."

Cold sweeps into my veins. She doesn't sound threatening. She sounds concerned, actually. Flatly concerned in a disinterested, Gail sort of way. I remember the first time I met her, how afraid I was, how I fled to the parking lot to get away from her. Sofia's handwriting, scribbled on the note, mixes with the assassin's words in my head: *Don't. Trust. Anyone.*

"You're sure that Flynn's okay?" I push out. "He isn't hurt?"

"No, he's perfectly fine—I just spoke with him—but my, this is a mess," Gail says with a puff of air. "Did you really assault someone with a lobster, *as* the prime minister?"

I squeeze my eyes shut, thinking. *She spoke with Flynn? Why didn't he pick up for me?* "I might've."

"Well, that was an oopsie, wasn't it."

"Look, I know you're used to dealing with professionals," I say through gritted teeth. "Professionals who know exactly what they're doing, how to identify who's an assassin and who's not, and how to take down people calmly and cleanly, but I'm not them, Gail. I'm doing the best I can, okay?"

She nose-breathes into the phone. After a moment, she says simply, "Okay."

"Okay? That's it?"

"Okay is a very versatile word, Max. It signifies that I heard you, and I understand you, and perhaps we underestimated the breadth of this mission, and how prepared you and Agent Forester were for it. I've booked you both flights back to Maine and DC. Yours leaves—"

"Wait, wait, slow down." I grip the edge of the phone booth, afraid I'm about to pass out. "What did you just say?"

"I'll sum it up: Vacation's over."

My voice is hoarse. "Did you find Sofia?"

"No, but you can no longer be trusted to act as Sofia. Did you blow your cover to an assassin, Max? I'm guessing that's how you got away? Smart thinking to save your life, but as far as this operation goes, it's hardly staying under the radar. Add that to your kitchen stunt, and our goose is cooked. Jakob Christiansen's on his way to Rome right now for damage control; he thinks his sister might've suffered a traumatic brain injury, as there's no other logical reason for her behavior. Only thing we can do now is extract you. Agent Forester has agreed to step down, since he hasn't exactly handled you properly. He's in a car on his way to—"

"He's already leaving?" The phone booth spins, sweat starting to pool above my lip. "He's leaving Rome?"

"I'm sure he would've told you eventually."

"I . . . I don't believe you."

"You don't believe he would've told you eventually? Or you don't believe he's leaving?"

"Both?" I huff out, doubting myself. Why would Gail lie to me?

Isn't it more likely that the past is repeating itself? Summer ends; Flynn and I end.

"I'll take a picture with him at the airport. Ten more seconds, Max, and then we can—"

Trace you, she's about to say. Probably. I don't wait long enough to find out. My hands are shaking so badly, it's hard to slam down the receiver. I tighten the jacket wrapped around my waist, hoping the pressure on my stomach will keep me steady. Everything feels like it's about to just . . . fall out of me. Fall apart. If I'm interpreting Gail correctly, if what she's saying is true, it *has* fallen apart.

Sofia's been missing for over twenty-four hours. At least one assassin is on the loose. And *my* goose is cooked. *All that matters*, Gail once implied, *is that you stay undetected as the body double*.

That's the definition of success for this mission. The only way I'll get the money. The way I was supposed to fix my life, sew the broken pieces of myself—and my family—back together. I've . . . blown that, haven't I? First with the assassin and then with the lobster. I think about my dad, in that old fishing boat, wishing for a better life for me, giving his away—and me just tossing everything down the drain. Failing. Failing then, failing now.

And Flynn.

He's off the case.

He's in a car right now, traveling toward a plane right now, when I'm in the middle of it all, wondering whom the hell I'm supposed to trust.

I stumble out of the telephone booth, into the bright heat of an Italian summer, stranded without a passport and less than twelve euros in my pocket, my chest so tight I can barely breathe.

23

After Frida's closed, my body entered total shutdown mode, fever peaking at 102.8 degrees. Everything ached, from my muscles to my bones, and I spent almost a week wrapped in a summer quilt, alternating between hot flashes and ice-cube-style chills.

"Pumpkin? Pumpkin, you in there?" A few days in a row, my dad called out from the other side of my door, delivering hot soup (clam chowder, from the small grocery store around the corner), but I wouldn't let him into my apartment. No way was I *infecting* him, on top of everything else. I'd caused enough damage. The wholesalers were already stripping apart Frida's, piece by piece, and it wasn't nearly enough to cover my costs.

Soup in my lap, I tucked myself into Nana Frida's old chair, notebook open, half-delirious, scrawling down every idea I could think of to come up with the money—to pay people back, to set things right. What did I have that I could sell, besides my refrigerator and my knives and my stoves? My bike. I'd sell my bicycle, and my computer, and I'd start freelance catering alongside any new jobs. I wouldn't eat anything besides ramen noodles and boxed macaroni and cheese. I'd move. Find a new, cheaper apartment, maybe within walking distance to a new job—so I wouldn't have to pay for public transportation.

"You could always move in with us," my dad offered, and he meant it. I could've moved back to the town house on Whippoor-will Street that had my first-grade handprints in the concrete outside; it wouldn't take long, he reasoned, to clear away the piled-high boxes in my old bedroom, to sort through the sewing machines and the ski equipment and chuck it into the garage. But I said no, automatically. I couldn't ask my parents for another thing. If they'd offered me a glass of *water*, I would've been too ashamed to take it.

As soon as my fever dipped, I applied for work at dozens and dozens of restaurants in the Portland metro area. Not many openings for chefs. Just breakfast places, flipping pancakes, pouring coffee, and scrubbing dishes in the back. I don't mind grunt work. The problem is, grunt work in kitchens doesn't pay down high-interest loans—and without fail, each place I applied told me that I was *overqualified for the position*.

"We're sorry," one of the chefs said, shaking his head. The dark circles under his eyes made him seem about ten years older than he was, and he gave me this look of pity that I'll carry with me to my grave. "You're good, I ate at your restaurant—the shrimp, I remember I had the shrimp. But every chef and their mother is out of work right now, and we just can't . . . we just can't take on anyone else. Have you thought about an office job?"

I did. I had. But with no college degree on my résumé, getting callbacks was even tougher than in the restaurant industry. Eventually, Andy offered me a front-of-house position at his catering company, just for wedding season, just until I got back on my feet again—but what happens if you're *permanently* wobbly? What happens if you're just one of those people who messes things up?

I thought I'd messed things up with Flynn, too, back then.

Before he missed Thanksgiving, I must've said something that up-set him, that damaged us; I must've misremembered what we had somehow. But I just couldn't put the pieces together—what I'd gotten so wrong.

The second-to-last night we were together, his parents left for dinner at Lobster in the Rough, booking their favorite table and promising to order way too much wine. They were giggly, like they were just kids, living out the last bits of summer. Flynn and I, we were supposed to go to the movies; I can't even remember what film we'd booked tickets for. Some rom-com with a happy ending, that probably took place at the beach. But he suggested, sheepishly, as soon as his parents' taillights hit the end of the driveway, that maybe we could . . . stay home. Here. At their rental property.

A flutter rose up so fast in my belly, I actually clutched my stomach. I could feel heat traveling up my chest, over the neckline of my sundress, and I was hoping—no, *praying*—that he didn't see the speckled spots. I didn't want him to know how nervous he still made me feel, even after a whole summer of knowing him, touch-ing him, kissing him.

"We don't have to do anything," he added quickly, redness crawling up his own neck. I loved how the tips of his ears flushed when he got a little anxious. "That's . . . that's not what I meant at all. I just meant that I want to talk to you, and it's quiet here, and we could go for a walk, or make a pizza, or—whatever you want."

What I wanted was to see his bedroom.

Not even, necessarily, in a sexual way. I'd just never been up there, up that set of knotty pine stairs, on the second floor of their rental house. And I was running out of time to know him, every piece of him, the hints of what his bedroom might look like back home. He told me he'd packed only two suitcases for the whole summer, but when I opened the door to his room, stepping almost reverently inside, it still felt so *Flynn*. Those stacks of sheet music—the ones I'd gifted him, from the Bar Harbor bookstore, after he handed me the Mary Oliver book—were spread out by a guitar on the wide blue rug. Shirts were hung neatly in his closet. A surfboard rested in the corner, freshly waxed.

"I can't believe you're leaving," I said, like he'd always been there, and my voice felt small and pathetic, even to me.

"That doesn't mean we can't talk," Flynn said, eyebrows furrowing. "We're going to talk, right? I mean, unless you . . . unless you don't want to."

I let out a short laugh. "Of course I want to. I'm just afraid that you're going to go back to Texas and find another girl." The words came out before I had a chance to claw them back. How jealous could I *sound*? But Flynn just . . . he just crossed the room in his socks, shuffling on that blue rug, and took both of my hands in his.

"I can *promise* you, Max, that you are irreplaceable."

It was the closest I'd ever gotten to an *I love you*, and I kissed him right there, slanting my mouth across his, tasting the soft breath he gave me, my lungs feeling too small for my chest. His hands traveled to the sides of my face, pulling me closer, and I remember being so nervous to touch him—really *touch* him, the heat of him, slipping my hand down the waistline of his jeans. This was a new type of skin, velvety soft under my fingertips, and he whispered into my mouth that I didn't have to, we didn't have to, but I wanted everything to be with him.

Two mornings later, I said goodbye before he drove—with his parents—to the airport, and it was like he sucked all the air out of my little town. I remember bringing my hands to my knees, heaving in a breath, and then I waited for him to text me. He did. Everything felt the same between us, despite the distance.

Weeks later, the breakup email crashed into my inbox.

Outside the telephone booth, I'm shaking. My hands are shaking and my chest is shaking, and the breath won't quite reach my lungs. It's too hot. Everything is too hot and too bright, and there are too many people—strangers, glancing at me with odd looks—and I wonder how many tourists off the street would be able to spot a foreign prime minister, without her security team, without a gaggle of cameras following her around. Did the CIA manage to trace the phone number? If so, how long until they arrive? And should I stick around for them to get here?

I'll admit that I'm not thinking particularly clearly as I stagger through the crowd, back toward the Trevi Fountain, into a mobile phone shop, and purchase a SIM card. The battery on my American phone is dwindling, but Gail disabled location services on it, right? It's untraceable? I fork over the remainder of my cash for a bottle of water, taking lukewarm gulps on the curb as I pop out my old SIM card and install a new one, flicking through my numbers.

I have just enough battery left for one call. Maybe two.

It rings. And rings. And rings.

He isn't going to answer. Why *would* he answer?

"Max?" At the last possible moment, Calvin picks up the call, his effortlessly calm voice floating down the line. "Heeey, Max, how's it going?"

I almost laugh. Almost cry. My throat feels like it's caught in a choke hold. "It's . . . uh . . . it's not going so well. I know this is a long shot, maybe the world's longest long shot, but are you still in Rome?"

Miraculously, improbably, Calvin *is* still in Rome.

He arrives, less than twelve minutes later, on a lime green motorized scooter, no helmet, his curls flapping in the breeze. The

scooter brakes screech dramatically as he pulls up to the curb, offering me a plastic bag with a T-shirt to slip over my fancier
clothes. He actually did get a souvenir from Rome Fiumicino International Airport; on the tee, falling across my chest, is the slo-
gan CAUGHT IN A BAD ROME-ANCE. "Catchy," I tell him, stepping on
the back of his scooter, my heart in my stomach. Over the tinny
roar of the scooter's engine, he explains how he slipped the security team at the airport, hiding in one of the cleaning-crew carts
and getting wheeled out with the industrial rolls of toilet paper.

"I thought you might need me to stick around a little while,"
Calvin explains, half yelling, the wind whipping past our ears.
Surprisingly, he's a careful (scooter) driver. I hold on to his shoulders, fingers half-numb, as we bump over cobblestones. "Plus, I
was already *in* Rome, and I've never *seen* Rome, so I thought, *when
in Rome*, I should be in Rome. Why miss it?" He is full of surprises.
I must've said this last bit out loud, because he says, "Right back
at you! I've been really worried. Almost thought about going back
to your hotel in Positano. Then I saw that news conference—"

"What news conference?" I splutter.

"Oh, you probably haven't seen it yet."

"What news conference?" I repeat, gripping a little harder—
involuntarily—on to his shoulders.

"Don't worry, it'll be on YouTube. They're calling it Lobstergate. Don't forget the hashtag." Briefly, he lifts both hands from
the scooter, crossing his fingers into a hashtag symbol, and I . . .
I'm not sure I can process that right now. My brain can't stand
any other hiccups.

Turns out, Calvin doesn't have many questions. You'd *think*
he'd have questions, after receiving a 911 call from his semi-
estranged roommate, dressed as a Northern European prime
minister, waiting outside a mobile phone shop in Rome; the last
time we saw each other, he was handcuffed to a chair in a hotel

conference room. But that all seems to be . . . strangely in the past. And he's strangely in the loop, having put the pieces together himself. "You're the body double," he says, stopping the scooter outside a tangerine-colored B and B and producing a key from his brown leather jacket. It's brass, the shape of a bee, and reminds me of Giorgio. "You and the prime minister of Summerland, you look *exactly* alike. It's freaky. You were pretending to be her—even though you were pretending you won the lottery."

"That is . . . correct," I manage, following him into the lobby, my head throbbing. He walks at a jaunty pace, leading me to an elevator at the back. The B and B is much more modest than Hotel Giorgio—no angel statue, no impressive bouquets of hand-cut flowers. It does feel very Roman, though, with air that smells ancient (like dusty library shelves, like catacombs) mixed with the hint of oranges. Orange cleaner? Orange potpourri? It's quiet, too, as if you're stepping into a church and shouldn't raise your voice or laugh too loud—or else a nun will come out and hush you. But it's comfortable, and quaint, and no one's popped out yet to kill me, so I'd call that a solid five stars on Tripadvisor. Every once in a while, I glance over my shoulder, just to make sure we haven't been followed.

In Calvin's room—with its pumpkin-colored, '70s-themed decor and view of the *panetteria* across the street—he fires up his laptop and his VPN, searching YouTube for a clip posted less than an hour ago. In it, reporters thrust those fluffy gray microphones around Roderick Flaa, who spins a dramatic tale about how the prime minister of Summerland chucked a lobster at him at a children's birthday party. Near the end of the clip, a photo of me appears, blurred, racing through the kitchen, and the comments are already pouring in debating if Lobstergate is a hoax or a sign of the extreme stress world leaders are under in this increasingly hostile climate. "At least Obama stressed out gracefully," one com-menter says. "All he did was get gray hair."

"They really didn't have to bring Obama into this," I say, winc-ing; the injury under my ear is healing, but when I rub my hand over it now, it only adds to the ache. I stretch my neck, rolling it, trying to release even an ounce of tension—but no good. No use. I have failed so profoundly in this role, have let so many people down—Gail, Flynn, Sofia, my parents, Jules, myself, and actually, an entire *country*—that a few yoga stretches aren't going to cut it.

"Pizza?" Calvin suggests, shutting his laptop, like food will fix everything. He cups his hand to whisper out of the side of his mouth. "It won't be the frozen kind, but I've heard—through the grapevine—that they do good pizza here."

I summon a smile, but it's a weak one. I'm not too keen on leav-ing the hotel, wandering back into the streets, where anyone can spot me and pick me off (incredibly easy to assassinate someone in the open air, on a scooter—that's what bulletproof cars are for), so I stay back in the hotel, head cradled in my hands, letting the world spin as Calvin picks up a Neapolitan pizza. When house-keeping knocks, I double-chain the door and count my breaths un-til he's returned, steaming pie in hand.

Eating cross-legged on the floor, he passes me a slice. My stomach is so watery, the first bite is practically impossible; a tiny blob of tomato migrates from under the cheese, directly onto Cal-vin's brand-new airport tee, and I apologize profusely as he chews, shrugs, and tells me, "Half my clothes have sauce stains. You're just speeding up the process. Christening the shirt. Hey, can I ask you something?"

I lower the pizza slice, thinking, *Here it is*. The waterfall of questions I've been expecting.

Instead, he hits me with, "Is your leg all right?"

"My leg?" Startled, I glance down at where he's pointing, a thick streak of raspberry sauce clinging on from the kitchen. In the right light, it looks like I've split my femoral artery and I'm seconds away from requesting a crash cart. "Oh! Oh, that's from the restaurant. It's just raspberries. I made . . . kind of a quick exit."

"With the lobster-throwing?" he asks.

"With the lobster-throwing," I confirm, shifting uncomfortably on the floor. "I thought that guy, Roderick—I thought he was trying to attack the prime minister. I'm still not sure he wasn't, honestly."

Calvin chews thoughtfully, reaching behind him into his "suitcase." It's one of those bright blue IKEA bags with the strappy handles, tied up into a bow; he picks out a bottle of ranch dressing, presumably that he brought from America, and douses his pizza slice in a thick white gel. "Yeah, even on TV, Roderick doesn't have good vibes. If anything, though, I think the public will see that. Your poll numbers might even increase. I mean, not *yours*, but— what's her name, again?"

"Prime Minister Christiansen."

"Prime Minister Christiansen's," he says, swallowing another bite and running a hand through his curls. His fingers leave the tiniest shine of grease, which, in the dim light of the hotel room, looks fabulous and intentional. "Can I ask you *another* question?"

I stop chewing, stop shifting on the floor, because the expression on Calvin's face is suddenly serious. It's a look I've rarely seen from him, the corners of his eyes pinched, his pupils dilated but not *too* much. "Yeah, sure. Sure."

"What happened to that friend of yours? The one who interrogated me in the hotel room?" Calvin rips off another corner of pizza, blinking at me. "It seemed like you two were more than pretend. Then all the news articles started coming out, about you and him together, and I guess I'm just curious. You never mentioned anyone."

I pick at my pizza crust, my face hot, dough dissolving into crumbs under my fingers. "I'll be honest, Calvin. There's not a lot that's worth mentioning." Calvin throws me a glance that clearly states, *I don't believe that for a second*, and it pushes more out of me. "The two of us, we knew each other when we were young. Younger. He came up and spent a summer in Kennebunkport with his parents. We worked together at a restaurant, hung out all the time, so much that he kind of became my person, and then he . . . He ended it around the holidays. Said it'd be too hard if we couldn't see each other."

Calvin narrows his eyes at me, processing. "I think I'm missing something. How did you get back together now?"

Back together. It stings, and it shouldn't, but the memory of Flynn is like a piece of sea glass that I keep stepping on. "He's the one who alerted the CIA that I looked exactly like the prime minister of Summerland."

"*Shiiiiit*," says Calvin, leaning back against the bed, his pizza slice drooping over his knee. "That's some seriously complicated stuff, Maximus. Are you okay?"

No. No, I don't think so. Besides the fact that I'm currently passport-less, semi on the run, having potentially lost five million dollars in one lobster-throw, I'm stunned that—after all this, after the explosion and the museum gala and days pretending to be the prime minister—I'm back to where it all started. More than penniless. Without my family. Eating pizza with Calvin, on the floor, mulling over every poor decision I've made in my life. Every way that I've failed, tilted off-balance, felt like that wonky restaurant table that *never* has enough napkins. And I think about Flynn, way back in the tunnel, rushing from the front seat, sidling up next to me and telling me to breathe when I couldn't seem to force any air into my lungs. I'd gripped his hand. I'd gripped his hand, without even thinking about it, without even questioning it—because at one point, he used to be my anchor.

"Do you ever have those moments," I ask Calvin, squeezing my eyes shut to fight the tears, "where it just feels like nothing you do is right? Like you can't make an intelligent decision to save your life?"

Calvin frowns. "It seems like you *did* save your life, Max. I mean, you're alive, aren't you?"

Night seeps across the city, the sky turning from rose-colored to black. Calvin offers to hang out with me a bit longer, but I tell him to go see the city. *When in Rome*, remember? He leaves reluctantly, waggling his phone in my direction, saying that I can call him at the first sign of trouble. Or the tenth sign of trouble. Or whatever sign of trouble we're on now.

Closing the blinds to block out the city views—I'd like to pretend, just for an hour, that I'm nowhere—I crouch down on the floor again, TV remote in hand, flipping through the cable channels and trying to give myself any possible distraction. Limited options flicker past: children's programming, a movie about a couple falling in love on the back of a Vespa (at least, that's all I can piece together), and—of course—the news. My blurred face flashes across the screen; they're covering Lobstergate, and even without the subtitles, it's obvious that I do not come across well. Tomorrow night, Sofia was set to appear on Italian TV—*La Visione Italiana*, I think the program's called. The newscaster mentions it, probably saying that I'm neglecting my media appearances in favor of chucking lobsters at Summerlandian diplomats.

I switch off the TV, leaning back on the carpet, staring up at the plaster cracks in the ceiling. Outside, the sounds of Rome whiz by—beeping horns, people laughing, summer, life. Life that I'm not living. Life that I'm not in. Less than twenty-four hours ago, I was in Positano with Flynn, my head tucked under the crook of his chin, sheets falling over us. It's been a long time since I felt that safe, that balanced, and the entire time, what was *he* thinking? What was going through his mind as I told him, with my body, things like *I missed you* and *I've missed this*?

That book he gave me, it's in my closet, tucked in a memory box. I'm not usually a sentimental person. I don't collect things. I didn't even save any copies of the menu from my restaurant. But in the box are a few oyster shells from that summer, ones we found together on the beach, interiors swirling and pearled; a fake diamond ring he won me after playing Skee-Ball at the local arcade, plus some of the leftover tickets; and the book, dog-eared, underlined, *what is it you plan to do with your one wild and precious life?* In the margins, next to Flynn's *restaurant* suggestion, I'd written *Frida's* with the swirly penmanship of an eighteen-year-old. It felt inevitable, that I'd spend the rest of my life in restaurants; that I'd cook good food for good people; that Flynn and I would stay in each other's lives, one way or the other.

When my American phone buzzes in the corner, I'm so deep in the past, I have to swim out of it. I reach, grab the charging cord, and pull, dragging the screen toward me, wondering if it's another delayed message from Calvin—something about Kevin the turtle or getting on a plane to Italy. But it isn't. The screen flashes a new message from Dad. A response to my message from the first night in Positano, when I told him I was traveling, and that I hoped he and Mom were okay.

Good for you, Max-a-million, he's written me. **You deserve a little fun, after everything. Your mom's making pot roast for dinner, and I don't have the heart to tell her that 4 tablespoons of**

salt is too much!!! Immediately, I'm imagining him eating it, with my mom at their simply set table, my dad giving her a thumbs-up and a smile, like it's the tastiest thing he's ever eaten.

Storms of emotion bloom in my chest. Sweep in. Thunder and rain and—

I text him back immediately, knowing now that he won't get it for a while, **Save some for me.** 😊

I finally get it. Fully get it. I understand what Flynn told me, the night he unzipped my dress and whispered against the back of my neck that my parents wouldn't want this for me. In fact, I think they'd be horrified, picturing me with raspberry bloodstains on my suit, lying on the carpet of a random hotel, after signing away my life to the CIA. It was always a possibility that I'd die. God, did I think they wanted me to *die* for them? That a pile of cash would make up for everything I did in the past, and for all the family Christmases I'd miss in the future?

I think . . . I think they just want me to be happy.

They just want me to feel whole, stable, capable of survival. Capable of getting by, even in the trickiest situations. Even when things feel impossible.

More than that, I want that for *myself.* I want to trust myself.

That is what I want to do with my one wild life.

24

When Calvin returns closer to midnight, I've already been on his computer for hours. His password, predictably, is *Kevin*, and the internet connection is slow but reliable; my eyes snap up at him, wide like an owl on a nighttime hunt. "If someone said to you, 'You can't trust your own people,' who's the first person you'd think of?"

He plunks down his shopping bags, crusty bread and souvenirs spilling from the plastic. I spot a miniature replica of the Colosseum, shrouded in Bubble Wrap, and a bottle of olive oil in the shape of the wolf who reared Romulus and Remus. In true Calvin style, he doesn't question the intensity of my inquiry, but considers it with a slow, thoughtful pause. "My sister, Keeva."

My head rears back. "Your sister's name is Keeva?"

"Yeah, why?"

Calvin and Keeva and Kevin. Even in my mind, it's a tongue twister. "No reason," I mutter before moving swiftly on. "I've just been thinking, sure, the Halverson crime family could be after Sofia, since she shut down their illegal gambling rings and weapons trafficking routes, and there was chatter from their side that something would go down in Italy, but that's not 'her own people,' is it? Outside of messing them over, she isn't *close* to them. Who stands to gain the most if the prime minister of Summerland dies?"

"The Russians?" Calvin guesses.

I consider this. "Well—"

"Big business CEOs who want to increase their carbon emissions without paying hefty international fines?"

Actually, those are . . . extremely specific and exceptional guesses, but also not what I'm circling around. "Her brother, Jakob." I spin the computer in Calvin's direction, screen shining in the darkness of the room; Jakob's face flares back at us. In the picture, he's trailing Sofia through the halls of parliament, his lips pursed like he's just sucked on a (really tart) bottle of limoncello. He's about fifteen years her senior, with more salt than pepper hair and a face that says (in Norwegian!), *Hey, you kids, get off my lawn.* "He's the special advisor to the deputy prime minister, and according to Wikipedia—"

Calvin leans back on his heels. "*Love* Wikipedia."

"If the prime minister dies, then the deputy prime minister automatically rises to power. No election. No casting ballots. It's a simple succession. And as special advisor, Jakob could be pulling the strings." Then, everything else spills out. The details of the mission, exactly what Flynn—unwittingly—recruited me to do. The switch in the tunnel, Sofia's note of warning. I tell him about the Producer and the explosion in the restaurant powder room, the soot and the ash; the pretending on the beach and the speech in the gallery; the glistening-haired assassin, who said she'd kill me if I didn't run. The whole time, Jakob's gray-eyed gaze pierces us, unblinking, from the screen.

Calvin picks up his newly purchased Roman emperor snow globe, shaking it thoughtfully. "So, you're saying . . ."

"I'm saying that her brother could've hired the assassin."

"Assassin*s*," Calvin corrects, making it plural. "First was the Producer, at the hospital. Second one was at the restaurant; that one probably didn't do a good enough job, you barely got hurt, so they hired a woman to finish the mission. Only—"

"I broke my cover, and she let me go." I run both hands through my hair, head spinning. "The woman did say that the others cut corners. Still, that's a lot of assassins."

"Maybe Jakob had a coupon."

"And the Producer the CIA caught . . . maybe Jakob *did* hire a decoy, as a distraction."

"*Or*," Calvin says, clearly enthused, "the Producer hired his *own* decoy. Because he really wanted to make it to Rome and correct his mistake from the first go-around. Like a pride thing. I bet he'd have the money. Assassins must be loaded."

"True," I say, heart pounding. "The thing is, no one believed me that Jakob could be a suspect, partly because he kept calling the hotel. He clearly didn't know that Sofia was missing. But what if . . . And this is a big *if* . . . Sofia's disappearance is separate from the assassination attempts?"

"Oooh," Calvin says, then pauses. "I don't get it."

I chew my lip. "But *I* think I do."

I'm trying to trust my instincts. My gut. My read of the situation. Since the mission began, *everyone's* been telling me what to do. *Wear this, smile like this, don't drink that, walk like this and wave like that.* And I've let them. I've let them because I didn't trust myself in this role. I didn't trust myself to make *any* decisions for another person. How could I, if I couldn't even make the right choices for myself?

But that . . . has to change. It has to change for me, and it has to change for Summerland. If my instincts are even *close* to right, if I'm putting the pieces together in the correct order, then a very dangerous man is about to start pulling the strings in my grandmother's home country. Jakob can't just go around using violent means to secure power for himself.

Sofia shoulders a hell of a lot of responsibility—and now it's my turn.

"Calvin?" I say, steeling myself, fists clenching. "I'm going to need a new suit."

The plan assembles itself at a rapid pace. By seven o'clock in the morning, drawing back the curtains—seeing the sunrise over Rome, tangerine and cotton-candy colors—I've gone over each step at least a dozen times in my head. My eyes whip back and forth over the road, double-checking that no one's scoping out the B and B. Across the street at the *panetteria*, pigeons pick at last night's crumbs, but that's it. Everything is almost silent, although I still feel that buzz of *life*, pulsing straight through to my fingertips.

Admittedly, that could be the three espressos from the hotel's room service menu. It could be five dizzying hours on the computer, streaming recent episodes of *La Visione Italiana* with English subtitles on YouTube, paying special attention to the host's interview style. A world-renowned broadcaster, she's in favor of open questions, not pinning down her guests, letting them freely speak their minds. That's why Sofia must've agreed to the interview in the first place, before her team canceled it. That, and each interview takes place at a truly stunning location around the country—inside Florence's Uffizi Galleries, on the seaside cliffs of Cinque Terre, on the banks of Lake Como.

This afternoon's broadcast? Inside Orto Botanico di Roma. Five o'clock.

I rub my lower back, stiff. When I turned twenty-nine, my birthday present was chronic lower back pain, and it doesn't help that I've spent the night hunched over on the floor as Calvin snored on the bed beside me. A far cry from the hotel suite, with Flynn.

Don't think about him, I tell myself, even as an image flashes in my mind, unbidden: the way he was lounging on the couch in the suite, a sliver of skin bared under his cotton T-shirt. The ruffle of his bedhead and the golden trail of hair extending below his waistline. How he feels underneath my palms. And I'm so *angry* with him. Leaving like that, again, just disappearing. Ending us.

I bet he's back in the States by now. Is he sleeping off the jet lag in his apartment, or is he just as pried-awake as I am?

"You ready for today?" Calvin asks, yawning, stretching his arms above his head. He's slept on a souvenir keychain and now has a four-inch imprint of Trajan's Column on his cheek.

I nod, staring out at the city. "Ready as I'll ever be." My gaze slides to the computer, where I've also been poring over a litany of Sofia's speeches from the past seven years. "I think I can do her justice—but she's witty."

"You're witty," Calvin says, biting an almond biscotti with the side of his mouth.

"She's sharp."

"*You're* sharp," he says. "You predict who wins *The Bachelor* every year, right out of the limo."

"A crucial test for a world leader."

"Hey," Calvin says, holding up his hands. "I just call it like I see it. Gelato's on me tonight after this all goes down."

Outside, on his scooter, he lists the flavors he wants to try, voice slightly muffled in the wind. "The lemon one, and the coffee one, and the one with the little black dots . . ." Right at 8 a.m., in a thin side street around the corner from Piazza Venezia, he screeches to a halt, and I step off the back of the scooter, staring up at a sign for ABITI IMPECCABILI. Google translates this as *impeccable suits.* In the window, effortfully posed mannequins—decked in swaths of expensive fabric—show us just how snazzy we can be. A bell tings over the door as we waltz into the mildly ancient interior, mothballs melding with the scent of mint, Calvin in his new ROME STOLE A PIZZA MY HEART tee and me in the raspberry-stained outfit from yesterday. We look like an odd couple from an indie film, so out of place, I'd laugh if I wasn't singularly focused.

"*Posso aiutarla?*" comes a voice from the back. A shop owner toddles out, all five foot five of him, with gold-wire spectacles and a pouf of white hair that reminds me of Giorgio.

It's clear that he doesn't recognize me.

Or, rather, doesn't recognize Sofia.

"*In inglese, per favore?*" I try, having looked up the phrasing.

He gives me a quick once-over with his elderly gray eyes, and says in English, "My, my, we can do better than that." He leads us to an array of suits, as Calvin *ooh*s and *aah*s over the choices, thumbing the fabric and even sniffing some of it. For what? What could he possibly be sniffing for? Despite everything, the corner of my mouth turns up.

At first, I was reluctant to accept any help from Calvin. I figured that I could put most of the plan into motion myself. But as soon as Calvin clocked the full extent of the mission, he wasn't just eager to help—he was desperate. "*Please,*" he said to me, hands together. "This is just like a movie. Even better than the one where Sandra Bullock has to go onstage before she wins Miss Congeniality, and everyone rallies around her. This is that moment! Let me be those people! What's that movie called again?"

"*Miss Congeniality.*"

"Right. That one. Hold on, let me cash out some Bitcoin."

So in the buttery light of an Italian tailor, we're measured and fitted. Normally, the turnaround time for close-to-custom suits is four to six weeks. Calvin puts an ultra-rush on the order, and we make the store our base camp for a little over eight hours, scarfing paninis from the adjacent *paninoteca* while Calvin places phone calls and I hone my approach down to the last detail. In the end, we purchase a sateen pocket square, a vintage porkpie hat, and two new suits—a bright-cream-colored one for me, and a teal-and-mint floral one for Calvin; it makes him look vaguely like a young Elton John, and has probably increased our visibility by, oh, 2,000 percent, considering that he wears it directly out of the shop, an undeniable pep in his step. Add that to a lime green scooter, and we don't need diplomatic flags flying. We're a whole parade, all by ourselves.

"Time check?" I ask him.

Under the thin brim of his new hat, Calvin glances at his cell phone. Kevin the turtle is his background. "Seventeen minutes to get there."

Not much time. That's partly intentional. We're carving this down to the minute, giving as little space as possible for anyone to stop us. At precisely four thirty-one, less than half an hour before the TV slot, we jerk a hard left around the backside of a Greek Orthodox church, evading a small colony of feral cats (Cat Giorgio's cousins, maybe), and sidle up to the jet-black Range Rover that Calvin contracted, an almost perfect replica of Sofia's vehicle.

"You sure you want to go in with just the actors?" Calvin says, one foot off his scooter, idling in the back alley. "I could come in with you."

I eye the metallic threading of his jacket, gleaming silver in the sunlight. "I have a feeling that you might . . . stand out a little."

"Is it the suit?"

"It's the suit."

"I *knew* I should've gone with the cummerbund," he says, like that addition—on top of the porkpie hat and the pocket square—would make every bit of difference. "But you're right. Here, my phone." He thrusts his iPhone in my direction, waggling it until I accept. "I've just turned on Find My Friends, so I'll know where to meet you for gelato after, if something happens."

"But how will you check my location if you don't have your phone?" I ask him, pausing by the Range Rover door.

"I'll use my *other* phone," he tells me, like it's obvious, before scootering off.

The humidity in the air is getting thicker. My new suit sticks to my elbow creases as I slide into the back seat, the driver giving me a tight, diplomatic nod. He's no Lars; there's no polka. It's a tense, silent ride to Orto Botanico di Roma, the botanical gardens in central Rome. When I crane my neck, checking out the back window, two more SUVs are following us—the fake motorcade that Calvin hired.

Each step of the plan is going off without a hitch.

Things could still go spectacularly, spectacularly wrong.

Am I even an asset for the CIA anymore? Technically speaking, no. Immunity is out the window. Isn't impersonating a foreign leader a crime?

I exhale, slowly, through my nose.

You can do this, Max, I tell myself as we cross the Tiber River, garden in the distance, sweet gum trees rising up to kiss the sky.

Near the palm-lined entry, my driver lets me out, and I steady myself in the blazing sunlight, smoothing the front of my bright cream suit and tucking a stray piece of hair behind my ears. The air's sweet with the smells of flowers, perfume from the rose garden. My bangs ruffle in the breeze of my "security," rushing ahead of me—and behind me—toward the confused-looking crew of *La Visione Italiana*, blocking pedestrians from the closed set. One crew member with a clipboard twitches when he sees me, leaping up from his folding chair. I'm dramatically unexpected. I'm not supposed to be here. The prime minister's team, they canceled . . . right?

In the background, birds chirp; wind rushes through the palm fronds; city noises slice into the chaos.

"Where do you want me?" I ask in a cool Summerlandian accent, gesturing to the entry path, and soon, assistants and showrunners are springing from the woodwork, offering their profound apologies for the confusion. You have no *idea* how sorry they are! There must've been some misunderstanding on *their* part; something lost in translation. Of course they'll reopen my interview slot. Of course. They'll push back the replacement guest and alert the host, if I'd like to hop aboard this electric shuttle cart? And they'll drive me to hair and makeup? Not that I need much! Just a little touch-up for the cameras.

We speed through the garden on the open-air shuttle, past a grandiose fountain and a sea of greenery, ferns hiding where they can in the shade. Roses bloom in fat yellows, reds, and pinks. Signs flit by for the French greenhouse, the Mediterranean wood, THIS WAY TO THE GRAPEVINES.

Just outside the bamboo forest, I sit as casually as possible, as steadily as possible, at the pop-up makeup station. My foot jiggles before I calm it down. Someone applies powder to my nose and a dusting of blush to my cheeks, alongside a dab of neutral lipstick. In my head, I practice my words. Turn them over and over and over. This plan is a Hail Mary long shot, mildly unhinged, but I think it might work. *It will, won't it?* So far, everything is unfolding smoothly, exactly as I'd envisioned at two in the morning, with a literal lightbulb burning above my head. Five minutes before the live broadcast, when the time comes to approach the cameras, I excuse myself to the side with an authoritative *one moment* finger and dial Gail, heart in my throat.

"Who is it?" she asks flatly, picking up on the second ring. She sounds as if she's been up all night, too. "How'd you get this number?"

I toe the gravel underneath my shoes, swallowing any last drop of fear. "Gail, it's me."

"Max," she says, recognizing my voice. "Max, where are you." It isn't a question, really. It's more of an interrogation, the end of a polygraph test that she's already decided I've failed.

"The botanical gardens, in Rome," I say quickly, with resolve. "On the set of *La Visione Italiana*, four minutes from the air."

If I had supersonic hearing, I'm sure that I could pick up the furious flicking of Gail's eyelashes. "I'm sorry. I must've misheard you. I thought you said you were about to go on live, national television, on a show with almost a million nightly viewers."

That last drop of fear I've swallowed down? It's threatening to come right back up. "Correct."

"No, I *must* be mistaken."

I dig myself farther into the garden, ferns by my feet, covering my mouth with my hand so no one can hear me. Behind me, rows and rows of bamboo stalks act as a backdrop; mobile lights glisten and flicker, cameras swiveling to a central spot by the forest, where a dazzling host takes her seat. Another plump, green chair (to match the bamboo) waits for me. A literal hot seat.

"I don't think the Halversons are behind the assassination attempts," I tell Gail, speeding up. "Did Jakob Christiansen make it to Rome? Can you get eyes on him?"

"Yes . . ." Gail says, a kettle ready to explode.

"You should watch him closely over the next half hour. I think the assassination attempts were an inside job, that Sofia's own brother is trying to take her down. One of the last things she said to me was 'family is tricky,' the female assassin told me it's 'your own people,' and if you look at the news, you'll see that Jakob made a trip to the Czech Republic for work, right before the Producer showed up at the hospital. I don't know where the PM is, but if he's guilty, once her brother hears what I have to say, he'll start making big, noticeable moves."

"So you're trying to force a reaction," Gail says, flat.

"Yes."

"And if it isn't him?"

Acid burns a little at the back of my throat. "Then I guess I got this suit for nothing."

"*Due minuti!*" an assistant calls out. Two minutes and counting down.

"I'll find out where Jakob is, put a tail on him, and send backup to the botanical gardens just in case, but Max—" Gail says, attempting to reason with me in the final seconds. "Max, I would strongly urge you to reconsider. In fact, I'm *ordering* you to step down. Immediately . . . Max, are you still there? If you're still there, put Agent Forester on the line."

Hearing his name, it's like Gail is suddenly a thousand miles away, shouting at me via a boat offshore. Her voice barely makes it across the water. My mind barely hooks on what she's trying to say. "Why . . . why would you think that Flynn's with me?" The tone that comes out of me is foreign and strange, even to my own ears. "I thought you said that he was on a flight back to the States."

"I may've lied."

"Gail."

"Theoretically, he may've had a run-in with a second assassin, who was hired to handle the PM's bodyguard while the female assassin took you out in the bathroom."

"*Gail.*"

"And theoretically, the reason why he didn't contact you is he was at the hospital, but now we've lost track of him. He really isn't with you? You haven't seen him?"

"I . . . haven't seen him," I manage, suddenly finding it almost impossible to breathe. In the hospital? What was he in the hospital for? Where is he now?

How many assassins *are* there?

The garden's suddenly taking on a foggy quality, the sunlight too bright, the gravel unsteady under my feet. I feel like I'm going to be sick.

"*Mi dispiace*, Signora Prime Minister! But it's time." That voice, too, comes from exceedingly far away. The assistant doesn't quite touch me, more air-guides me by the elbow, off the path and onto the mobile stage, as I pocket Calvin's iPhone, Gail shouting from the other end, "Max, Max! Listen to me. Don't do what—"

Disoriented, I hang up the call, the assistant pinning a microphone on my lapel and handing me a small white earpiece, much like the one I lost on the streets of Trastevere. Shoving it into my ear, I feel my pulse climbing as possibilities roar through my mind. What if an assassin came to finish off Flynn in the hospital? What if he's roaming the streets, injured, uncontactable, and—

A countdown follows, in Italian. *Dieci* to *nove* to *otto*. As soon as the camerawoman hits *five*, she counts silently with her fingers in the air. I wiggle, panicked, repositioning. The green chair isn't so plush, once you actually sit in it. It hurts my back, sends a rod up my spine. I'm probably sitting too stiffly, not naturally enough, but the beat in my chest has turned to *Flynn, Flynn, where the hell are you, Flynn?*

"*Buonasera*," the host says, directly to the cameras.

We're live on the air.

25

Buonasera. We're broadcasting tonight from Orto Botanico di Roma, tucked within the hustle and bustle of the eternal city. Tonight's program is a very special one."

The host's tone snaps me back into the garden. Snaps me back to the mission. Inside, I might be losing my mind, but on the outside, I have to be as calm as the bamboo behind us. For this broadcast, *especially* this broadcast, I need to be a perfect prime minister, a perfect Sofia, not a single hiccup.

"Although we initially reported that our guest, Prime Minister Sofia Christiansen of Summerland, couldn't be with us this evening, we've had a change of plans, and now, we are honored to welcome her."

Focusing the best I can, I dip my chin politely as the host—a beautiful Italian woman in her fifties, with striking white hair—says that tonight we'll speak in English, for the viewers overseas; she runs down a list of the prime minister's accomplishments, the ways that Sofia has already made an indelible mark on Northern European society. I hold back my American "ballpark smile," as Sofia might call it, crossing my legs at my ankles and hanging on the host's every word; there's no list of prearranged questions. No guarantee that she'll ask me about a topic I know.

Flynn, my pulse beats, underneath it all. *Flynn, where are you?*

"Does it bother you," the host asks first, swiveling in her chair to face me fully, "that people seem so fixated on your age? On your gender? Half of the time I see a story about you in the news, that's at the forefront. How do you respond to that sexism, and ageism, from the press?"

Threading my hands in my lap, I answer without hesitation, paying particular attention to the length of my vowels. "I think it's best to confront it head-on. Ask questions like Jacinda Ardern, former prime minister of New Zealand, did. Can you think of a single instance where reporters asked John F. Kennedy how he felt about being a young male in power? If his maleness made him any less suited to a political life? So, to the press, and to you, why is a question about my age and gender *your* first question?"

The host blinks at me, white eyelashes flicking.

Have I misstepped? Made a political gaffe right off the bat, my first few minutes on international TV? As much as I'm trying to focus, I'm also picturing Flynn in a ripped suit, fighting off an attacker outside the bathroom. So that's why he didn't come rushing in when I screamed his name. He was ambushed while guarding me, protecting me from—

"You have quite the point," the host says, and I relax infinitesimally into the chair. As a follow-up, she asks me about my time in Italy; I tell her about some of the delectable meals I've eaten (minus the floor pizza with ranch dressing). She asks about the ongoing state of relations between Summerland, Estonia, and Russia, especially in light of the treaty proposed last week, and I give her a bland, noncommittal response, directly from Sofia's talking points, word for word what I memorized overnight.

The cameras track us back and forth, and while being live on air doesn't feel natural, it also—after twenty-two minutes—doesn't feel terrifying. *Is this working?* There's no flicker of doubt in the host's eyes, no crinkle at the corners that suggests: *You're a deep, deep fake, Prime Minister, aren't you?* All across Italy, viewers might be picking me apart, but I've come on this show for one reason and one reason only: to deliver a message. Thankfully, the program bypasses #Lobstergate. Before I know it, the interview's slowing down. The host's about to open the floor. And I'm going to stare straight at the middle camera, mouth pinched with resolve, hands clasped strongly in my lap. I'm going to—

Look at Flynn.

Flynn?

He's panting when he pulls up along the gravel path behind the cameras, beige jacket clinging to his shoulders, his shirt and trousers wrinkled like he pulled them, crumpled, out of a plastic bag. His left pant leg's slashed at the thigh, and is that . . . is that *blood*? Or, I don't know, wine? Definitely leaning toward dried blood, considering that a hospital bracelet's encircling his wrist.

I want to sob.

Obviously, I can't sob—as a world leader, on television—but if this weren't the most important interview of my life, I'd race offstage and throw my arms (gently) around his shoulders.

Flynn's alive! He's okay!

Well, he's *sort of* okay.

He's messy-haired, flushed; his eyes go even wider as he spots me, a swell of something like relief—and something like panic—evident in the rise and fall of his chest. He looks like he wants to run to me. He looks like he *did* run to me, maybe halfway across the city, in evening traffic. After being hit by a gelato truck. And a Vespa. And maybe even a scooter. I've never seen him so shattered, not even after the explosion. The crew must've let him past after he flashed his badge.

"Prime Minister?"

I blink, holding in an apology—and then, *oh, screw it,* giving one anyway. "I'm sorry," I say, swallowing the growing lump in my throat, my peripheral vision stuck on Flynn, "could you repeat the question?"

The host shifts in her seat, thrown that *I'm* thrown. "I asked if you'd like to say a few words to close us out."

Right. This. This is the part I've been waiting for. The reason I'm here.

I just didn't expect to have to speak, almost directly, to *Flynn.* He's breathing hard, hands on his hips, throwing me a questioning look. *What are you up to, Max? What's about to happen?* The concern that's pouring from him, pouring into me, lights my chest on fire.

The clock's ticking.

I wet the seam of my lips, straightening my back, and drag my eyes toward the middle camera. "I have always wanted to serve a greater good, a cause, and a country. This downtime in Italy has given me an opportunity to reflect on the future of Summerland, and the many threats it faces, outside and *inside.* I am actively taking steps to secure my country, and will be holding a press conference to expand upon the intelligence that I've gathered—my brother." I cough, like I have a hitch in my throat, like I've cut myself off at the beginning of the sentence, instead of at the end. "My brother, Jakob, and I have much to discuss—with you."

In the corner of my eye, I catch Flynn wiping a hand down his beard, the weight of what I've just said crashing over him like seawater. Flynn knows. He knows it's a thinly coded message for Jakob—*I know you're the one who sent the assassins, and soon, the whole world's going to know.* Unfortunately, the other code to that message is: *Come and get me before I expose you, you bastard!* Which is why I'm already taking out my earpiece and leaving my seat so quickly after the interview's over, shaking hands firmly with the host before skedaddling offstage, my fake security wrapping around me, alongside my real handler. He smells like sweat and cologne and summertime, and his breath's as uneven as mine.

"Is there really a press conference?" he asks out of the side of his mouth, grabbing my hand as we speed walk.

"No. Were you really in the hospital?"

"Yes."

"Should you still *be* at the hospital?"

"According to my doctors, yes, but I'm fine. The stab's not that deep."

"You were *stabbed*?" I hiss as Flynn leads me off the beaten path, toward the Japanese garden.

"Mildly," Flynn says.

"What, did he use a paper clip?" Every new piece of information he gives me hits with a jolt. I told myself I'd keep a relatively cool head, but—

"I've been *out of my mind*, Max," he says thickly, refusing to drop the pace. Bushes whip by us. Flynn's speaking to me like I've given him a heart attack, and he's just learning to breathe again. "Gail said that you'd decided to leave, that you'd finally caught a flight back to the States. Then she retracted her previous statement and said you were MIA." He gazes at me desperately from a foot away. "When I saw you on TV, I ran. I ran here."

He sprinted out of the hospital. Across the city. With a stab wound to the leg. For me.

"Don't you *ever* do that again," I manage, bordering on teary-eyed, as if this scenario is likely to happen twice.

"I'd do it again in a heartbeat. Go left."

Curving around a cluster of date palms, I hear it—suddenly. A heart-stopping *bang*. Something whizzes past my ear, cracking the tree trunk by my head. *Was that—?*

"Go, go, go!" Flynn shouts, voice totally cold, my fake security team scattering for cover. Whatever Calvin's paid them, it is *not* enough for an active emergency.

Another bullet zings right next to my ear, and I shriek. "Jesus!"

Yep, no doubt about it. Someone's shooting at us. Shooting at me, and probably Flynn, and you'd think that an assassin could hit a moving target, but apparently not the kind that Jakob hires! Is it the Producer? Does he need glasses?

"Street's this way!" Flynn yells, hand on my shoulder, running, and I've already stepped out of my heels, bare feet pounding on grass, pulse like a siren in my ears. My first thought is, *I'm too old for this*—which, at the tender age of twenty-nine, is ridiculous. But I haven't stretched; I haven't warmed up my calf muscles. My lower back twinges as I lengthen my stride, and I'm increasingly thankful that I've worn pants. In the prime minister's black sequined dress, I'd have tripped ten times by now.

Another bullet, *zing*. Where are they even *coming* from?

I shout to Flynn as we dart from tree-cover to tree-cover, zig-zagging our way—ultrafast—out of the garden. "Here's the thing! I was imagining a delayed response!" In my mind, Jakob would take *at least* half an hour to send a team of professional hit men to trail me. By that time, I'd actually be at the airport, ready to board a plane back to America, where I'd enjoy the mini pretzels in coach and watch too many episodes of *MasterChef.*

But what if Jakob never got the memo that Sofia's team canceled in the first place? What if he'd *always* planned to assassinate her in the garden?

It's public. Poetic. Merciless.

"Left again!" Flynn says before we burst onto the road. The summer sky is starting to turn a dusky pink, and it's just too pretty for what's happening. My head whips around, checking for any sign of the fake security, because they have the keys to the

Range Rover. Taxi? Any taxis around? Nope. The street's been blocked off. Only a few people on bicycles are whipping by. Bicycles, and a sandwich delivery man, weaving through on a motorcycle.

"Excuse me!" I rush toward him, thinking fast—or barely thinking—Flynn on my heels. The motorcyclist stops for a prime minister in distress, his helmet lopsided on his head as he cocks it, obviously recognizing me. He's clutching a white paper bag of sandwiches in his hands, unstraddling the bike, and I—"I'm so sorry, really sorry, but I need to borrow this."

"Uh . . . really?" the man says, replying in English, the assassin probably reloading their weapon, and it's not motorcycle theft. It's motorcycle borrowing. The nation of Summerland is going to thank him. "Are you actually going to . . . ?"

"*Grazie!*" I throw back at him, swinging my leg over the two-seater saddle, a baffled but game Flynn settling in behind me. Now, the only question is, *How do you drive a motorcycle?* Does one even *drive* a motorcycle? Is that the right verb? Thick heat rushes up my throat as I channel every memory I have of my father's bike, back when I was a kid, before my mom insisted *You'll kill yourself on that thing, Richard*, and he sold it to our neighbor with the pug down the street.

Lever, clutched. Shifter into first gear. Twisting the throttle just so . . .

A bullet clips the handle, right by my fingers, and I *almost* feel bad for this assassin. Surely they are better at close-range kills. Poisonings. I don't know. Cucumbers in the salad. As soon as I think that, I wonder if the cucumbers back at Hotel Giorgio were intentional, if that was them, too, or—

Hold on, Flynn!

We're blasting forward, the motorcycle skittering and weaving, the front tire lifting ever so slightly off the ground before we curve around a line of parked cars. Two more shots ring out in the air, and Flynn yells into my ear, "Are you *okay*? You haven't been hit?"

"Are *you* okay?" I bat back, equally worried about him. I've just put him in a tremendous amount of danger for a broadcast that I assumed would be easy. Everything about this was supposed to be easy—the trip to the news station, the Italian "vacation" itself. And now look at us, zipping away from what's turning out to be a crime scene, my hair streaming into Flynn's face as he coughs it out.

And this is . . . not a fantastic motorcycle. It's coughing, too, engine spluttering like it has the motorcycle flu. At least it isn't a Vespa?

At least we've managed to lose the assassin.

In the rearview mirror, I see the blurry outline of a man in a plain blue shirt, disgruntled, regrouping by the building, before Flynn and I round the bed, bursting onto the main road. I integrate us into the traffic, thinking that my Roman holiday is turning out a *little* different from Audrey Hepburn's.

"I called for backup on the way over here!" Flynn shouts over the traffic. "Police, armed escort! They can track my location in the city, so they should meet up with us soon."

The words that he's saying should calm me, should make everything feel at ease. Jakob might've sent an assassin to the garden, but we escaped without a scratch. We'll tag up with Flynn's team—and with Calvin. We're away from danger now.

Aren't we?

Why does it feel like we are still *very much* in danger?

Wind cuts through my bangs as Flynn leans into my back, his fingers clutching the sides of my hips, and I'm so painfully aware of him, of his every movement, that I blurt out, "Why'd you do it?"

I sense his confusion, the way he shifts in the seat behind me.

"Leave the hospital? I told you, I saw you on TV. It's kind of hard to hear you back—"

"I meant why'd you break it off," I tell him, raising my voice above the hum of the motorcycle, not even sure where I'm going, and not entirely clear on the Roman rules of the road. "After that summer. After Thanksgiving. I got so used to talking to you, to you *being* there, and then all of a sudden you were just gone, and then you were *really* gone." A painful amount of emotion is welling up in my throat, and I can't quite believe I'm bringing this up *now*, in the speedy rush of traffic, Flynn's chin almost resting on my shoulder. If not now, though, when? Who knows what'll happen in two minutes, three minutes, four?

To Flynn's credit, he doesn't say anything like *We're really doing this? You're really asking me this on a speeding motorcycle?* His palms simply flatten on my hips, melting even more into me, like he's trying to memorize the shape of my body. "I know I was supposed to come see you at Thanksgiving," he finally gets out, over the engine roar, "but I couldn't—I couldn't afford the plane ticket. My dad's business took a nosedive, a big one, and after that summer, we lost everything. I'm talking *everything*. He built it up again, but back then, I was using email at the local library. I didn't want you to pity me, or worry about me, and you were such a free spirit, Max. I absolutely didn't want to send that letter, but I felt like I had to. I would've been such an asshole if I made you wait. Wait on someone who couldn't see you, touch you—"

"You could've at least given me the *option*," I say, blood rushing through my ears as we pull up to a stoplight. The newsstand to our left is coated with pictures of my face. And, *oh look*, Flynn's face. We tip our heads to the ultraconfused vendor, spilling his evening cappuccino, white foam on the tips of his mustache.

"I thought that I did," Flynn says at the stoplight, completely still behind me. Warmth radiates off him, a blaze at my back. "I thought that I was giving you a clear out, and if you wanted to make it work, you'd respond. When you didn't, I assumed that you'd . . . moved on." His voice cracks at the end. I hear the split of it, right by my ear.

"I hadn't moved on," I whisper.

And he curves his chin even farther over my shoulder. "What?"

"I hadn't moved on!" I shout, loud enough for him to hear me this time. What Flynn's just said has winded me. Knocked half the breath out of me, when I didn't have much left to start. I release the clutch, unable to determine if *I'm* shaking, or if it's just the vibrations from the motorcycle. "I thought you didn't feel the same way I did."

"Max," he says, more like breathes, his chest rising against my back. "I *loved* you."

Loved. He loved me. *He loved me?* The words are a shot of adrenaline into my bloodstream. They're everything I've been waiting to hear for eleven years. I'm thinking about how *angry* I was at him, how desperately I wanted him to say those words—and now? Now I'm wondering if he's hung on to any shred of that love, if he can feel how fast my heart is pounding, not just from adrenaline, but—

In the motorcycle's tiny rearview mirror, I spot the flicker of a black car. It looks . . . bulletproof, hard, out of place in a sea of Fiats and Smart cars.

"Someone's following us," I say, throat tight.

Flynn crowds against me even more, peering into the mirror. "Black car?"

"Black car."

"Gun it," he says, stoplight changing to green, and I do, night air slapping my face. As we speed ahead, I take one of the side streets at random, swerving around a restaurant with patio tables and accidently clipping one. Plates full of antipasti rattle. A glass of Aperol spritz topples, glass shattering in an orange bloom on the pavement.

"This may be a bad time to tell you!" I shout over my shoulder, terror streaming into my voice. "But I've never driven a motorcycle before!"

"You *think*?" Flynn bleats out, and it isn't harsh, isn't chiding. It's more like a gut reaction. I wonder if his pupils are as dilated as mine. "Make a left! Left, Max!"

"I'm trying!" I fire back, easing up on the throttle for a second at the next stoplight, biting the inside of my cheek before I just go. A symphony of horns blares around me. A man stops short in his dusty green Fiat, yelling out the window, *"Muoia, signora!"*

If you want to try to kill me, I think dryly, *you're going to have to get in line!*

My grip tightens on the motorcycle handlebars. "Are they still following us?"

Flynn gives a quick glance over his shoulder. "Three of them now."

Three? A peek at my mirrors reveals—yep. Two identical black cars now, and someone tailgating them on a Vespa.

"Any second," Flynn shouts over the traffic, "they're going to start shooting at us."

"Well . . . *shit!*" I say, the only thing I can get out. Flynn slips his hands tighter around my waist, gripping me closer, almost cradling me—and I'm focusing, trying not to crash into a porchetta stand by the Campo de' Fiori or lose control outside of the Piazza del Paradiso, toppling into a group of tourists who'll *click, click, click* their cameras.

Flynn's breath is warm in my ear. "Take the Via dei Baullari."

Thanks to the assassins, I'm a little agitated. "You say that like I know where that is!"

"On your right!"

"*When* on my right?" I bat back, weaving past a Lamborghini and a jewelry store.

"Now! Now!" Flynn says, leaning as I angle us—hard—into the turn, tires gripping the ancient road. It's obvious; Flynn is actively steadying his voice, attempting to be the cool and calm one in this scenario. Despite this, his throat gutters. "They're gaining on us. Our best chance is to make a sharp turn somewhere, pull off where they can't see. Confuse them. Let them pass us . . ."

"Where are the *police*?" I gasp. Did they get stuck in traffic, too? Is Flynn's backup coming? Gail's? "Where's the armed escort? They should be—"

"*There*," Flynn says, but he's talking about a gap between buildings.

I take a chance, jamming on the brakes, back tire skidding and pulse hammering in my ears as we slip into the alleyway. I cut the engine, listening for the sound of two armored cars, followed by a Vespa, *zzzz-zip*-ing by. Behind me, Flynn also seems to be holding his breath, not a muscle moving. As soon as the vehicles pass, he loosens a little, whispering, "Close call."

Gathering myself, the blood returning to the tips of my fingers, I unclench my fists from the handlebars. "What now?"

I'm asking Flynn, although my body already knows. I'm already swinging my leg off the bike, stamping the ground, traveling forward on foot. The fuel gauge on the motorcycle looks incredibly low—and we can't stay here. We can't wait for them to reach the main road again, figure out what we've done, and throw their cars in reverse.

I should make myself less recognizable, too. Better ditch the outfit I wore on TV. Shrugging off the cream blazer, satin lining sticky with sweat, I'm about to chuck it into the street, when—at the other end of the alleyway, no less than thirty feet ahead—someone appears. A shadowy silhouette in the dying sun, moving to block the exit.

My heart claws at my throat.

This person . . . there's a knife in their hand, and I can't immediately make them out. Just the glinting steel blade, the way it catches the half-light. Flynn told me once that assassins wouldn't attack at close range, that I'd never have to put those self-defense skills to the test. That hasn't exactly been true, has it?

"Max . . ." Flynn warns, throwing so much emotion just into my name, and I know—with every fiber of my being—that he's about to rush out in front of me. Sure enough, his hand meets my back, firm as he shoves me behind him. *Max, I loved you. I* loved *you.*

At the same time, I'm squinting. Registering the silhouette and the tailored lines of an impeccable suit. When the sun moves, revealing the man behind the shadow, I shout, "Calvin! I thought we were meeting closer to the river." Bypassing Flynn with a side step, I rush up to my roommate, glancing down at the blade in his hand. "Why're you holding that?"

"This?" Calvin raises the blade slightly. Flynn moves to yank me back again; he doesn't look like he's seen a ghost—he looks like he's seen a *hundred* ghosts, and they're all holding knives in an alleyway. Calvin, for his part, says, "Oh, no-no-no, sorry! It's a souvenir! It's for frosting cakes. See? It isn't even sharp! Before I started tracking you on my phone, I got a little bored while I was waiting and stumbled into a gift shop. I thought Max might like it."

"I do like it," I say, at the same time Flynn jumps in: "Would someone tell me what's going on?"

"It isn't too flashy?" Calvin asks, dead serious, about the gift. "The handle's got little Popemobiles on it, and teeny-tiny Pope hats. Maybe I should've gotten a baggie. Honestly, I've been getting some looks."

"I think that has to do more with you openly carrying a knife into an alleyway than the popes," I offer quickly, and Calvin gives me a tip of his head like, *Could be.* "Flynn, Calvin's been helping out. Calvin, assassins are chasing us. Both of you, I'll explain everything later, but we need to keep moving."

"You can't wear that," Flynn says, echoing my thoughts, as the three of us stalk down the alleyway. "If we're getting out of here on foot, they already have a clear image of you. We need to—" His phone dings, and he checks it in an instant. "Shit. *Shit.* The backup's been held up. An extraction team can meet us at the entrance to the Sant'Angelo bridge in thirteen minutes."

"How long does it take to get there on foot?" I ask, peeking out of the alley, gaze whipping side to side, checking for those black armored cars.

"Thirteen minutes."

My teeth grit. "Fantastic."

"Hey, you can swap with me," Calvin offers, gesturing to his suit. "They don't know I'm wearing this, do they? And they wouldn't expect you to be wearing this, would they?"

"It's actually not a bad idea," Flynn says, eyeing the teal-and-mint florals with a wince. "Hide in very plain sight."

That's how we end up emerging onto the street again, me in Calvin's suit, and him—rather tightly—in mine; he looks stately and elegant, dare I say ministerial. A double-decker sightseeing bus zips by, filled with people snapping photos of the architecture, and we duck our heads, curving onto the sidewalk. "No taxis," Flynn says, shoulder to my shoulder, setting the pace. His tone's more even now, but there's an undercurrent of panic. Like this is history repeating itself for him. Extracting an asset. Leaving the city. Making it out alive. "We don't know who's on the lookout for you. The only car you're getting in is a CIA vehicle. We cut through buildings where we can. Keep your stride steady but don't look like you're rushing. This is an urban escape, so we shouldn't slink; blend in with the crowd as best you can."

I roll up the sleeves of Calvin's suit. "I think I'd have better luck in a nun's habit."

"My aunt Eunice was a nun," says Calvin helpfully, and in the corner of my eye I catch Flynn peeling off his shirt, tiny scratches on his suntanned skin; if we are trying to be inconspicuous, he's missed the mark. He's half-naked on the streets of Rome, more than one person giving him a surprised—then, honestly, lustful—look. Still in motion, as we pass a souvenir stand, he rips down one of the Pantheon T-shirts from a hook, tossing the vendor about three times what it's worth in cash before slipping it over his head.

"Cut through the church," Flynn says, completely focused, like all of our hearts aren't in our throats. Well, maybe Calvin's isn't. He's lolling a few paces behind, mouth dropping open at the sights and sounds, but we're going a little faster now, slipping past a set of open doors—the stale church air a change from the warmth outside. It's loud, though. Voices. Murmurs. The sound of an evening service. Sixteenth-century religious murals glare down at us as we pass pew after pew, almost speed walking through a baptism. Someone snaps a photograph. Of me. And I just know, instinctively, at my core, that tomorrow's headlines are going to include the prime minister of Summerland, crashing yet another family gathering. The baby at the font coos, water passing over his teeny-tiny forehead, and I'm saying whatever comes to my mind to whoever catches my eye. "Many blessings. Cute baby. Beautiful family."

"Ten minutes," Flynn says, reminding us of the countdown, throwing open the door at the back of the church. More cars, flashing by. Bicycles. Honking horns and swooping pigeons. It takes me this long—yes, *this* long—to remember that I'm completely barefoot. It's like my feet aren't even my feet. I'm half-numb. All things considered, I'm coping well, but worry is like a wolf at my back.

How's Flynn's leg? What if those black SUVs round the corner again?

"Eight minutes," Flynn says, and we can't hear the river yet. Somewhere in the distance, the Castel Sant'Angelo looms heavy against the darkening skyline. I've seen pictures of the bridge, where we're going. Stone statues saying, *Enter here.* Saying, *Save yourself here.*

I'm just hoping this isn't like one of those spy movies where we have to jump into the river.

I know we're not supposed to clump ourselves together, not supposed to rush, but I grab Flynn's hand, our fingers intertwining, our strides almost syncing, and I realize that *I'd trust you with my life* isn't just a saying. I *am* trusting him with my life. And I suppose the corollary is true, too; he's trusting me with his. He knows that I'm capable—that together, we're a team.

"Five minutes," I say, keeping tabs on my own watch, my pulse picking up with every block, and it's truly a whirlwind tour. Handbag stores. Glassware winking at us from window displays. Palazzo after palazzo after palazzo. The three of us, we're blending in with the tourists, weaving gently around them. We don't want to be the only ones swimming upstream. We follow the pattern, follow the flow, and follow the main road, because we don't have time to zigzag through the side streets.

Every once in a while, I covertly peek behind me, see if they've discovered us. Caught up to us. Are they right at the edge of our backs? So far, we've gotten lucky. We've played it smart. And we reach the crosswalk near the Sant'Angelo bridge *exactly* on time, the moon half-visible in a soon-to-be-starry sky. It's gorgeous scenery. Breathtaking, even. And under normal circumstances, I'd gape like Calvin, taking in the bridge's stone archways, the slate blue rush of the Tiber River, the way the Castel Sant'Angelo rises up like a jigsaw piece, slotted against the sky. Instead, I'm noticing the trickle of traffic—the slow creep of commuter cars, no one glancing our way, no one stopping for us.

My gaze slips to Flynn. Even in the dying light, I can read his face perfectly.

The CIA is running late.

The extraction team hasn't arrived yet. Hasn't made it to the bridge to greet us. Which would be fine. Except that we're out in the open, near a busy crossroad, and . . . there's a black flicker around the bend, those armored cars popping into view. They're here? *How?* How did they find us? Police radio, maybe? An interception? Doesn't matter. Doesn't matter how. All that matters is we're exposed, under the bright lights by the bridge, and we *could* rush into the nearest store—but that's almost half a block back. It's too late. Someone's rolling down the window of the SUV, the man in the blue shirt—the one from the garden—leaning out of it. He's average-looking. About fifty years old. Dark hair.

And Flynn. Flynn's clocked everything. I know because I know *him*. I know because his lips brush a quick kiss against my cheekbone, *Goodbye, Starfish*, before he's running. Not running *away*. Running into the street. Left and right, cars jerk to a stop in the intersection. It's instant chaos, all around him. Horns, yelling, tires screeching. He climbs on top of one of the cars, a bright red Alfa Romeo, and yells with waving hands, "Over here! Over *here*!"

He's drawing away attention, giving me time to escape, time for the extraction team to catch up, and—

I think I love this man.

I think I've always loved this man.

There is absolutely no way that he's going to die for me.

I'm not even fully processing what I'm about to do before I do it: ripping off Calvin's jacket, wrapping it around my fist, and striding toward an empty parked car near the crossroad. I smash the passenger's side window with all of my might. Glass shatters in a rippled burst. The security alarm wails, sharp and ultraloud, cutting through the night noises.

Attention shifts. From Flynn to me.

And I see his whole face fall, his whole body stiffen, the SUV doors swinging open, at least one assassin getting out—and Calvin, in the background, purchasing a cone from a gelato truck. He thanks the vendor, nearly dropping it as *more* sirens pierce the night.

Police ones, this time.

And a helicopter, suddenly swooping overhead, over the bridge, the chopper blades kicking up wind, whipping up the stray strands of my hair. It's all happening so fast: The rush of backup, like a river undamming. The startled pedestrians. The assassins scattering. Flynn, shouting my name.

I step backward, onto the sidewalk.

I drop my guard for only a second.

A second is all it takes for a Vespa to round the corner, brakes screeching before it straight-up mows me down.

26

When my eyes blink open, the first thing I see is my face. I'm hovering above myself, my jaw clenched in mild concern. Light blue irises, narrowed pupils, a dusting of freckles on my cheekbones. The collar of my suit is impeccably ironed, my chestnut hair pulled into a sleek, meticulous bun.

"Am I dead?" I ask, out loud, only my lips don't move. *Why aren't my lips moving? What's wrong with them?* They're set in a solid line.

"I certainly hope you're not dead," I say above me, lips forming around the words this time. "If you're dead, that means I'm hallucinating, because you just spoke to me. Max, you're in the hospital. You've been in the hospital for over twenty-four hours, but you're going to be perfectly fine." The woman who looks exactly like me pauses, her gold-and-silver necklace winking under the bright white lights. "Well, you *have* been hit head-on by a Vespa, and one of your ribs has seen better days, but overall, you'll be good as new by . . . the press conference, let's say."

My head's spinning as I inch myself up in bed, pillow propped behind my back, and my mouth is so dry, it's like I've eaten a boxful of amaretti cookies without a sip of water. *Water. Desperately.*

Need it. I reach for the glass by my bedside, fingers surprisingly steady, and take a few glugs.

"I was run over by a *Vespa*?" I get out, wiping my mouth with the back of my hand; I can't believe it. The Vespa thing. It actually happened.

"Painfully Italian, isn't it?" Sofia says, realization hitting me in a thick burst. It's *Sofia.* She's here? She's okay? Her hands clasp at her waist, the demurest smile working its way into the corner of her mouth. "That's like saying you've been concussed by flying biscotti."

I have so many questions for her. Too many questions. They tangle and jumble in my brain, competing to get out of my mouth. "Where . . . where's Flynn?" I have a fuzzy image of him, climbing on top of that car, waving his arms, drawing attention to himself. A rush of love—and, honestly, pain medication—swells up in me.

"Ah, so you remember your handler," she says. "That's promising. He's completely fine. How's the rest of your memory? Who's the prime minister of Eswatini?"

"Is that supposed to be a question I'd know how to answer regularly?" I ask, shifting again in bed. The fuzziness in my peripheral vision is diminishing, and the room has stopped its funky tilt. Cream-colored walls come into focus. White curtains. Hospital machines. "Which assassin ran me over?"

"None of them."

"I thought you just said I was hit."

"I did," Sofia confirms, perching at the edge of my hospital bed. "Do you remember Giorgio? From Hotel Giorgio? He'd come up from Positano for a hotel conference, just around the corner from Orto Botanico di Roma, and saw you on *La Visione Italiana.* He dropped by the broadcast to say hello, witnessed the chase, and wanted to help. Ended up circling around the scene frantically, only to run you over. Accidentally, of course."

"That is so . . . *random*," I manage, running a hand over my broken rib.

"If it makes you feel better," Sofia says, "he feels just awful about it."

"Well, if it makes *him* feel any better," I say, cringing, "it's probably adequate payback for hitting him in the throat with a tennis ball." The lights flicker above us, and it strikes me—with a quick glance out the window—that it's dark outside. Maybe the middle of the night. It's registering more and more that Flynn isn't here, isn't with me. "Gail . . . you might not know her, but she lied to me before, about Flynn, so—just tell me. Please. My handler, has he visited?"

Sofia gives me a reasonably soft look, and it's still so strange—that her nose is my nose. That her eyebrows are my eyebrows. "Of course he has. Really, he's fine. Technically speaking, visiting hours are just over." She leaves it at that, diving into the details of the last twenty-four hours. How her brother was arrested by Italian police, outside of a private airport in Rome, after booking a one-way plane ticket to Colombia, less than a minute after I exposed him on live TV. Not exactly the action of an innocent person. Apparently, Sofia had her doubts about Jakob, which is why this mission was always more dangerous—a threat from the inside. She explains that she was reluctant to put me in harm's way, especially since she already had a plan in motion to stop Jakob: turning one of the assassins he'd commissioned.

"I was having rather good luck with the elderly Lithuanian duo," she says, frowning, "but then they went dark on me."

I guzzle more water. "The Lithuanian duo, too? How many assassins did he *hire*?"

"All of them, apparently. Jakob has always been, how do you Americans say it? 'Over the top'?"

"No kidding." I sit up farther in bed. "Where've you been, then? Here I was thinking that the crime family might've gotten you."

"Oh, they did," she says, unblinking. "Yes, the youngest brother, Aksel. He decided to use all his resources to kidnap me, so that we could talk things over. He was desperate for me to know that his family wasn't behind the assassination plot. Quite a gentleman, actually."

I don't . . . I don't even know what to say at this point.

"Little did I know," Sofia adds, not *entirely* unpleased, "you'd be playing me while I was gone. You threw a lobster at my blackmailer."

And the hits just keep on coming. "Roderick was blackmailing you?"

"He was trying," Sofia says. "He said he'd leak some *completely* falsified documents about an unsavory trade deal, if I didn't agree to go out with him again. I was planning on having him arrested for extortion after my holiday."

"What a way to win a woman's heart." I snort. "When he asked me to play tennis with him, he made it seem like you were in love."

Sofia scowls at me. "I have loved grocery store *pastas* more than I ever loved that man."

Over the next few minutes, she ties the last remaining threads of the investigation: how Jakob persuaded a low-ranking member of Sofia's security to plant the explosives at the restaurant; how the Producer *did* hire a decoy, in order to misdirect and evade capture; and how he was eventually caught after hurtling himself into the river outside of Castel Sant'Angelo.

"He was a bit soggy," Sofia says. "His name's Bruce, by the way. He very much looked like a Bruce. And that's that! Although . . . if I forget to say it later, I suppose I should be thanking you." She tucks a lock of stray hair behind her ear. "For saving my life, and *inhabiting* my life, and everything in between. The way you went about it, though, especially at the end, that was absolutely mad. It could've gone sideways so easily. Which leads me back to the lobster-throwing, and the kissing an agent of the CIA on the red carpet, and all the pictures currently circulating online of me, in the world's most outrageous suit, splayed out on the pavement, under the wheel of a Vespa."

My face bunches up. "Do we have to go back to that?"

She nods, tilting her head in my direction. "How soon could you be ready for a press conference?"

The carpet at the St. Anantara Hotel is a rich, velvety green. Alongside the far wall of the conference room is a table swathed in spotless white cloth, like a fancy restaurant buffet. A pitcher of sparkling water rests next to crystal clear glasses, and I'm running my finger nervously along the rims, two hours and fifteen minutes after my hospital discharge.

It turns out, one of the biggest challenges of my *simple job in beautiful Italy*—besides the assassins, besides pretending to be the prime minister of a foreign country—was stepping into a conference room as *me*, the true Max, with a hundred flashing cameras, reporters shouting my real name.

At first, I'd said no.

More specifically, I said, *"Absolutely* no way, Sofia." Why would she even want that? I thought the whole point was that I was supposed to be disguised, undetectable. "You told me, and I quote, 'What will my people think, mmm? If this ever gets out?'"

"I see you've been practicing the accent. Impressive." Almost pleading, she placed a hand over mine. "The truth is, it's already out. People are already speculating, and they love you. My poll numbers are up. And it's probably better for my nation to believe I was under threat of assassination, that I used a decoy at the utter behest of my intelligence services, than for them to believe I threw a lobster at a diplomat at a children's birthday party."

It was, admittedly, a fair point.

But as we rode up to the venue, just down the street from the hospital, my rib aching, the morning sun streaming through tinted windows, I started wishing that Flynn was there, in my earpiece, telling me, *Breathe.* I told myself the same thing. *Breathe. Breathe.* And I pictured that night, on the floor of Calvin's hotel room, when I stared up at the ceiling and asked, *What would make you feel like a survivor, Max? What would make you happy?* I might hate the spotlight, but I want to feel capable of impossible things.

"Reporter in the red dress, from *la Repubblica.*" In the conference room, the head of the prime minister's communications team sits between me and Sofia, calling on raised hands. "Please go ahead."

We rotate through the sea of them, questions flying about my background, where I'm from, if Summerland is giving me a medal for my service, if I've otherwise enjoyed my stay in Italy, how it's possible that I look so much like Sofia Christiansen. Are we related? Are you going to keep in touch after this? What's next, Max, for you?

I'm just about to answer the final question when the doors at the back of the conference hall hinge open. I can peek through the mass of reporters well enough to see them: my parents. *My parents?* Both of them, together, suitcases in hand, luggage tags clinging, fresh from the airport. My dad's in his best shirt, the blue polyester one that he wore to his brother's wedding, the look on his face a mask of pure relief when he sees me. I feel all his love from across the room. All his joy and all his worry. Same for my mom, who has a hand over her heart (and over her crocheted summer sweater). She reaches out for my dad as they glance my way, and it hits me—really, finally hits me—that despite every mistake I've made, they want the same happiness for me that I want for myself.

Calvin's chatting happily with my mom, while Flynn—he's leading them to a row of seats. Did he call my parents and relay the whole story? Did he pick them up from the airport? Is that where he was this morning? I stare at him intensely as he weaves through the crowd. The movement's drawing attention. Cameras start to flash when they recognize who he is, the guy who cupped the prime minister's cheek on the red carpet. The guy who seemed so in love with the body double.

The reporters' last question is still hanging in the air.

What's next, Max, for you?

I tap the microphone and lean forward, feeling brave. Blood pounds in my ears, my heart lifting as more cameras click. From across the room, I catch Flynn's gaze and hold it. His face looks exactly like home. "I'm going to take a simple vacation . . . and spend some time with my bodyguard."

Around fifty heads whip toward Flynn at the same time. He's running his teeth over his bottom lip, trying to contain his grin, but it's no use. We're beaming at each other.

"American," Sofia says, almost laughing. "American smiles."

This part of the trip—it actually is simple. Simple strolls through Positano with my parents, snapping photos and hiking up the Path of the Gods. Taking in the views by cliff and by sea. We hire a boat and sail around the coast, Flynn captaining, Calvin as a surprisingly handy first mate, the five of us snacking on pecorino, plump grapes, and fresh-baked crackers. I feel my sense of taste coming back. I hadn't entirely realized it was missing. But over risotto dinners and creamy desserts, I'm waking up. I'm remembering. I loved this once, and I can love this again.

At the very end of the vacation, we go back to Hotel Giorgio, at Giorgio's insistence. He books Flynn and me into a room overlooking the water; in the evenings especially, it's like a watercolor painting: cerulean at sunset.

"I've been thinking," Flynn says on the terrace, taking my hand, kissing the middle of my palm, "about going for a swim."

This time, there's no beach umbrella, no book. No other tourists. We slip down to the water under the cover of darkness, speckles of moonlight on Flynn's skin. He peels off his shirt at the edge of the water, not even bothering with the buttons, and I'm already stripping down to my bathing suit. We touch fingertips as we wade into the water, splashing, warm, and even though this is a city that never sleeps, it does feel—just a bit—like we are the only two people in the world. We're on a much more secluded part of the beach. It's rockier. The sea is quiet. No sounds except for the lapping of the water, and the waves we're making as we breaststroke out, beyond where our feet can touch. Pausing at the same time, Flynn and I face each other, treading water. Tiny droplets shimmer on his face, catching the edges of his beard—which is regrowing, after the gala.

Close, so close to him, I run my hand over his jawline, feeling the bristles. "I never told you how much I like this."

"I like everything about you," he says, so earnest that it makes me blush.

"Everything?" I joke back, brushing up against him, my bare stomach to his. "No pet peeves?"

"Unless you actually start baking sleepy chicken," he jokes back, a smile playing in the corner of his mouth, "I think we're good."

I flick a speck of water at him, treading backward as he follows me. I can't imagine it—leaving him again. Returning stateside and us going our separate ways. But I'll be damned if we hash this out over an email. "So what happens now?" I ask, tucking a wet strand of hair behind my ear. Sofia's tight bun is gone. I'm free-flowing. "After the vacation? Where are you going to be stationed next? Am I even allowed to know that, or come visit you? Are you allowed to come visit me? How does this work if—"

"I quit," he says lightly.

I blink at him, beads of water on my lashes. "You'd be willing to do that?"

"Not just willing," he says, tracing my lips with his thumb. "I already did. The CIA kept putting you in dangerous situation after dangerous situation, and I'd been thinking about quitting for a while. I didn't want to be in some station house in Belarus while you were thousands of miles away." The outline of his Adam's apple bobs up and down, his neck shiny and wet in the moonlight. "I'm yours, Max. If you'll have me, I'm yours."

I puff out a breath. "Well, when you put it that way . . ."

He laughs, my arms wrapping around him, his mouth catching mine. We're keeping each other afloat, suspended there, kissing. His lips taste like limoncello and sea salt, his tongue warm as it meets mine, and I want to be kissed like this forever: tenderly, like he's been waiting for years and years. I guess, in a way, he has.

My legs wrap around his waist for a second as the sea lifts us up, the thin lining of my bathing suit meeting his belly. He growls a little under his breath. "You have no idea what that does to me."

"Oh, I think I do," I tease.

He snickers. "What about the ground rules, then? No touching?"

My hand slips along the wet silk of his back. "Broken."

"No reminiscing?"

"Forget that one, too."

His teeth nip at my bottom lip. "And the code word?"

"Now, that's a keeper," I tell him, coy. "I think that could come in handy if we're, say, exploring things in the bedroom?" I'm saying it like a joke, but the mischievous spark in my eye—and the fire in his—tells a different story.

"You're just full of surprises, aren't you, Starfish?" he says, voice like velvet.

"Nicknames," I say, directly into his mouth. "I'll allow it."

Half of me wants to be completely reckless, to map his body right there in the water, but our faces are still splashed all over the papers; no matter how secluded this beach is, you never know where paparazzi are hiding. Add to that, we have late-night dinner reservations—at a cliffside restaurant that Flynn selected, a short walk from the hotel.

Reluctantly, with a groan at the back of his throat, he says, "Okay, come on," and we dry ourselves with plush cotton towels, wringing out our hair onto the sand. We get dressed, cold bathing suits falling to the floor; I apply a swipe of mascara, a slash of tangerine lipstick, and then we're out the door, rushing to catch the reservation.

It's just after ten o'clock. Lamplight dusts the street.

I think the restaurant's going to be quiet, too, a few evening diners and us, but two minutes later, when we round the corner by the cliffside, a small cache of photographers is waiting on the patio. One of them shouts to the others, *"Sono là! Seguiteli!"* Loosely, this must translate to something like *chase them*—because all of a sudden, the mob's coming for us. Fast.

"Run for it?" Flynn says, as I say, "Go!"

By now, we're experts. We dodge them, dipping back into Hotel Giorgio, crashing into the elevator, barely making it back to our room before our hands are finding each other.

"I actually wasn't that hungry," I say, pawing at his shirt.

"Food's overrated," Flynn says, unzipping my dress.

"I wouldn't go *that* far." He hoists me over his shoulder, and I yelp, laughing, as we travel toward the bed. "But I wouldn't mind room service? Staying in for the night?"

"Staying in sounds very, very appealing," he says, laying me down on top of the sheets, planting soft kisses on my neck. "In fact, I can't think of anything I'd like to do more."

"Scuba diving?" I venture. "A tour of the herb garden? I hear this place has an exceptional piano bar, if you're into that type of—"

He tsks playfully, stopping my mouth with a kiss. Our bodies connect, hips pressing against each other, warmth growing in my belly. We're picking up where we left off in the water, stripping off our clothes; he unclasps my bra, one-handed, and I quick-trace my fingers down the slope of his shoulders, winding my way to his belt. I fiddle with it, half-frantic in the heat of the room, until the buckle breaks free and I have him in my hand, stroking up and down. This makes him only kiss me harder, our mouths colliding. "Good god, Max," he manages, gruff.

"You're—not so bad yourself," I pant as his fingers glide against me, trailing down my stomach, settling between my thighs. And those are all the words I can get out for now. Everything else is just movement. Gasps. Him rocking against me and me rocking against him. The thick groan in the back of his throat when he slips inside me. How I bite down gently on his shoulder as he hits all the right spots. Again. And again.

When we're both close to the edge, I echo the words he told me in the water. "If you're mine," I whisper, "then I'm yours."

"I've *always* been yours," he says, cupping my face, as a wave arches up inside me; I ride it, trembling, until we're collapsing into the sheets.

In the morning, the sun rises over Positano.

And I feel brand-new.

EPILOGUE

PORTSMOUTH, NEW HAMPSHIRE
Two years later

I was never going to reopen Frida's—not in the same way. Not in the same building, with the same light, memories clinging to every corner. But when Flynn suggested that I take a look at a commercial space in Portsmouth, less than ten minutes from the bed-and-breakfast his parents used to own, I agreed.

"It just . . . feels like you," he said, driving me with the windows down. No more bulletproof Range Rover. We're a Subaru couple now, complete with bumper stickers from all the places we've traveled together: Montenegro, Sequoia National Park in California, the rocky beaches of Summerland where my nana grew up.

And Flynn was right. We pulled up to the bank of the Piscataqua River, blue-gray water rushing under a summer sky. As soon as I stepped into the converted dock house, historic floorboards creaking underfoot, herb garden overflowing beyond the plate glass windows, my bones knew I was home.

"Yeah?" Flynn said, looping his arm around my shoulders.

"Yeah," I whispered back, in the kitchen, all the broken pieces falling into place. I called the real estate agent from the property's love-worn dock, a late-June breeze whistling through my hair, and purchased the building on the spot.

Alongside a surprise reward from the Summerlandian govern-ment (for "going above and beyond the call of duty"), the CIA ended up making good on their five-million-dollar offer—extending another offer to boot. "We're always on the lookout for talented field officers who can handle themselves under pressure," Gail said over the phone, "even if they come from, let's call it, unique backgrounds and circumstances. Have you ever thought about joining the CIA?"

"Please don't take this the wrong way," I told her, laughing. "But hell no."

She laughed, too, the first one I'd ever heard from her. A short, raucous chuckle. "I can't tempt you with a healthy insurance pack-age? The possibility of lukewarm coffee in a nondescript bunker?"

"See, if you'd have offered me *bagels* . . ."

Gail's smirk was audible. "Very good. Fair enough. Money will be in your account on Monday."

After I paid back my parents, enough for both of them to re-tire, I drove down to York Beach, where Jules lives with her fam-ily, knocking on the door just after dinnertime. She answered in a bright orange dress, curls piled on top of her head, her face changing from shock to glee in a millisecond. Porch lights poured on my head as I held up a stack of enormous cue cards. I'd given this apology a lot of thought; I was going full-on *Love Actually*.

SAY IT'S YOUR BEST FRIEND, the first cue card read. (IF YOU'LL STILL HAVE ME.)

Jules paused, then called back over her shoulder into the house, "It's my best friend!"

Softly smiling, relieved, I wiped away a tear with the back of my hand and told her—through black-marker script—that my mended heart will always love her, and that to me, she's perfect.

"Finally seeing some sense," she said, joking, batting away a tear of her own, before inviting me in for dessert. We talked over wild-blueberry pie in her backyard, citronella candles burning low, until we'd hashed out everything. It was never about the money—but with the Summerlandian reward, Jules is putting a large injection of cash into her daughter's college fund. "She'll never *believe* how she got that."

"Bah," I said, with a wave of my hand. "We'll just show her the YouTube."

By the end of the month, I still had some money left, but I wanted to be frugal about it. Flynn and I did most of the restaurant renovations ourselves: revamping the exterior paintwork, refinishing hardwood in the dining space, and lugging secondhand kitchen equipment through the tiny, tiny back door. Turns out, Flynn's pretty handy with a hammer. He salvaged boards from the local lumberyard, building us a picnic table for the herb garden—and when the renovations were complete, we sat on the top with a case of craft root beer, clinking bottles, and it felt like the culmination of something thirteen years in the making. The two of us, perched on a picnic table outside of a restaurant—*our* restaurant—side by side.

"This is all you, you know," he said, gesturing around us. "Our life. Us together. You built this."

Playfully, I nuzzled into his neck. "So you're saying it was a *good* idea that I accepted that bonkers job offer?"

He snorted, the corner of his mouth tipping up.

"Because I can always do it again," I said. "Word on the street's that I look a lot like the prime minister of Liechtenstein, and the CIA's willing to give me a pony and a packet of mints if I—"

Fully chuckling, Flynn palmed my face and kissed me, root-beer sweetness on his lips. "You might have a *hundred* twin strangers out there—"

"Doubt it."

"But there will never," he said seriously, "ever be another you."

In the evenings leading up to the grand opening, Flynn curled in bed with me as I honed the menu, opting for sea-to-table favorites, garnished with herbs that we could grow ourselves. He'd rest his head in the crook of my shoulder and say, "If you ever want to add some *awesomely* cooked eggs to the menu, you know where to find me."

My fingers lolled through the silk of his hair. "I'll keep that in mind. You can be honorary sous chef, in between sailing trips."

After everything that went down in Italy, Flynn did hand in his resignation at the CIA; instead of spending his early mornings with assets, he's handling sails—watching the sunrise over Piscataqua River. "I'd like that," he said, leaning up to kiss the tip of my nose. "Although, don't let me anywhere *near* your kitchen."

Now it's the friends-and-family test run before opening night. I thought I'd be nervous, but the dining room's crowded with happy people, everyone laughing and scraping their plates—and Flynn's acting as busboy, for old times' sake, white towel slung over his shoulder. When I peek out from the kitchen, he's shaking my dad's hand, heartily, before pulling him into a full embrace.

I no longer feel like that wonky restaurant table, the one that's perpetually tilted. Tonight, here, with Flynn and our people, in my element, in my home, I am steady. I am balanced. And I am . . . being pulled from the kitchen by Calvin and Jules. Each of them has grabbed one of my elbows, and they're leading me enthusiastically—and also a little conspiratorially—into the center of the dining room. People are standing: Flynn's family, my family, our friends.

Flynn raises a glass of homemade wine, beaming. "I'd like to make a toast, to the best person I've ever known." With the other hand, he reaches out, interlocking his fingers with mine. "To Max!"

"To Max!" everyone says, so proud of me, and know what? I'm proud of me, too.

"You did good, Starfish," Flynn says, near the end of the night, as our closest guests linger, and the dining room turns into a makeshift dance floor. He brushes a stray bang from my eyes with a single finger, tucking it behind my ear, as Calvin fires up a playlist on the sound system.

The startling bleat of Summerlandian polka greets my ears.

I burst out laughing, turning to Flynn. "Was this your doing?"

He shrugs innocently, like *maybe*.

"You know this is my favorite song," I say. We've had a running joke about it for two years.

"Did *you* know," he asks, grabbing my hand and gently pulling me toward him, my eyelashes brushing against his cheek, "that there's an official dance that goes with this particular song?"

Laughter's still quiet in my throat. "*No.*"

"*Yes.*"

"I'm intrigued."

"It's a little bit of this," he says, dipping me back, "and a little bit of that, and finally—"

He's spun me, briefly letting go of my hand, and when I turn around to face him again, he's getting down on one knee, pulling a small velvet box from the pocket of his jeans.

"Oh, that was so smooth," I say, breathless.

"Max," he says, a bit breathless himself. "I've loved you for almost half my life, and I want the rest of it. Every second. Every year. I want us to be that old couple still going on date nights, and holding hands over dinner, and laughing at the same jokes. You aren't just a piece of my heart, you're all of it. Getting a second chance with you has been the biggest blessing of my life. Will you—?"

"Are you *proposing*?" says Calvin, hand to his mouth before bursting into tears. Jules swats him before shoving a cloth napkin in his palm.

Flynn chuckles, running a hand over the back of his neck. "Yep. Yep, Calvin, that's what I'm trying to do."

"Go on," Calvin says, blowing his nose into the napkin. "Don't mind me. You just—"

Just say *yes*. In the middle of the restaurant, I crouch down to meet Flynn, my pulse beating faster than the polka, the two of us in our own world. "Yes. A million times yes."

And I'm sure, more than I've ever been sure of anything, that what Flynn said is right. This engagement isn't the finish line. We're going to be that middle-aged couple, raising our kids in this restaurant—having big family dinners with plates of delicious food. We're going to be that elderly couple, taking walks in Prescott Park, stopping for tiny espressos and chatting about our lives. And one day, maybe we'll return to Italy, where we fell in love all over again.

Next time around, we'll skip the assassins.

ACKNOWLEDGMENTS

I wrote this novel largely in the second and third trimesters of my pregnancy and started editing it three months postpartum, so I feel compelled to insert a corny pun here: *Code Word Romance* was a labor of love.

To my son, Leo: Holding you while editing this book is now one of my most cherished memories. I love you completely, and I can't wait to watch you write the story of your life. (It's going to be a good one.)

To my editors, Kerry Donovan at Berkley and Sanah Ahmed at Orion, who were immensely kind about extending my deadlines and giving me the time and space I needed to finish this book— thank you. Your enthusiasm for the characters and insight into the story are so, so appreciated. I'm glad we could chuckle about Calvin together.

My agents, Claire Wilson and Peter Knapp, always know the right things to say; I feel entirely supported by you both. This is another book that never would've existed without your guidance. Major thanks as well to Safae El-Ouahabi, Stuti Telidevara, and everyone at RCW and Park & Fine. You all are the best in the business.

Mom, always my first reader—you are a born storyteller. You teach me how to be a better writer and a better person (and when to keep key, hilarious characters). Dad, who inspired the father in this book—thank you for encouraging me to follow my passions. You two know why this book is for you.

My husband, Jago, is a great source for story tidbits, like how to evade someone in an urban setting; I'm thankful for our walks (with Dany! Good girl!) where we smooth out rough patches in my plot. We've had a pretty eventful year, haven't we? I love our family dinners, and the life that we've created together.

To everyone who offered a kind word during a wonderful but challenging time—including Ellen Locke, the Bunco ladies, Erin Cotter, Kim Holloway, the Good Mews crew, all my neighbors (especially the Beavers) and writing friends: You kept me afloat. Shout-out to my doulas at North Atlanta Birth Services, Hannah and Rachel, for your strength and compassion, and to Amanda for helping me find my footing. The nurses at Wellstar Kennestone Hospital are angels.

And finally, to all the new parents out there—I know it's 2 a.m. and you're beyond exhausted. Your baby loves you. You're doing a great job.

Don't miss Carlie Walker's

THE TAKEDOWN

Available now!
Keep reading for a preview.

1

can't just approach him and ask to cut in. That would look suspicious. Instead, I've placed myself at the edge of the dance floor, and I'm sipping a glass of champagne so slowly that I'm hardly tasting it. What matters is my mouth. He should be looking at my mouth. On my lips is a thick coat of crimson lipstick. The color perfectly matches my dress: a strapless, thigh-slit gown that says, *I am* your Christmas present.

Every once in a while, Alexei spins his partner and cocks his head my way. It's subtle. But I notice things. Noticing things is my job. His gaze tracks from my ankle all the way up the bare skin of my thigh, and finally to my mouth. Automatically, I part my lips; my eyes capture his, sparkling for a calculated two seconds, before dipping shyly down.

I'm not shy.

I'm just smart. And well trained.

Also, itchy. Fingertips gripping the champagne glass, I ignore the prickle that's creeping its way under my wig. Maybe it goes without saying, but I prefer my own hair: a dirty-blonde bob that almost dusts my shoulders. Unluckily for me, Alexei "The Bulgarian" Borovkov—my target—has a thing for brunettes. It's in the file. All four of his girlfriends (four *simultaneous* girlfriends) have long, dark waves. So tonight, that's what I have.

I take another ludicrously slow sip of champagne—and wait.

Half of this job is waiting, keeping your cool under pressure.

Swishing the alcohol through my teeth, I survey the ballroom for the sixteenth time. Strings of fairy lights dangle from the ceiling, sprigs of greenery crest the snow-flecked windows, and a massive cut-glass chandelier shouts, *Fancy!* It's the kind of place I couldn't imagine myself in as a kid. Christmas bingo night at the Moose Lodge, maybe; a winter ball with tickets double the price of my first car, never.

There are two clear exit routes. Several bodyguards, milling around, attempting to look inconspicuous. And a man in the corner wearing an earpiece. Not one of our guys. One of Alexei's. At the far end of the room, a string quartet plays *"När det lider mot jul,"* a Swedish carol that's heavy on the violin, and my stilettos tap until the end of the song. Everyone applauds the violinist—then it's go time.

I don't even need to steel myself.

It's habit, muscle memory, my mind and body in sync.

Alexei takes another step back from his partner, bows, and shoots a look straight at me. For a second, it's like we're the only two people in the ballroom.

Now, all that's left is to reel Alexei in.

A slow lip bite should do it, like I'm thinking about how he might taste—but I stop mid-bite. I've caught myself. I'm so innocent! Alexei sees this and immediately struts over in his white tie and coattails, exactly like I knew he would.

"You are beautiful," Alexei says. He speaks in heavily accented English and extends his white-gloved hand, confident that I'll take it. My fingers slip gently into his, like I'm this fragile little bird—not, say, a deceptively strong CIA case officer who could incapacitate him swiftly and silently. Beneath the dress, I'm all power and muscular curves. A handler once described me as "more striking than beautiful." Emphasis on the *strike.*

Alexei pulls me to the center of the dance floor as the quartet revs up again. A slower song this time, with more cello.

"You're Bulgarian?" I ask in English, affecting a Swedish accent. The ballroom is in Uppsala, a half-hour train ride from Stockholm, so a Swedish alias makes the most sense.

Alexei grins, drawing my chest to his chest, and I make sure I don't stiffen. Make sure I'm breathing smoothly, normally. His neck smells like blood oranges, with a hint of leather, and his custard-blond hair is slicked behind his ears. In heels, I'm only two inches shorter than him. We match up. "Smart girl," he says after a click of his tongue. "You recognize my accent, then? You speak Bulgarian?"

"I speak six languages," I say honestly. It's the first and only truth I'll tell him all night. "But my Bulgarian isn't so good."

"My Swedish isn't so good." Alexei's lips quirk. "I bet there is a lot we could teach each other . . . ?" He leaves the question open, waiting for my name.

"Annalisa," I lie.

Annalisa Andersson. A socialite from Gothenburg. She's a Virgo. A horseback rider. Likes gin and Dubonnet with a slice of lemon.

It's funny how much you can know about a person who doesn't exist.

And how little you can know about a person who does.

Alexei's fingers intertwine with mine in a way that—years ago—would've sent a chilled spike down my back. "You are here all alone, Annalisa? It is no good to be alone at Christmas."

Alone at Christmas.

In my line of work, people hunt for vulnerabilities. What Alexei doesn't know is, he's tiptoeing uncomfortably close to mine. My family briefly flashes in front of my eyes—Calla, Grandma Ruby, Sweetie Pie, even Dad—before I blink and they're gone. They can't be here right now. Alexei is not what you'd call "a good guy." For the last three months, he's been financing arms deals against NATO allies. Give him anything less than total concentration, and I'll be flying back to the States in a body bag.

Reaching up, I trace the sharp ridge of Alexei's jaw and whisper directly into his ear, "I'm not alone anymore, am I?"

I can feel his heartbeat quicken through his shirt. His throat bobs in a discreet gulp, and I've got him. I know I've got him.

Ninety-five percent of the time, my work for the CIA isn't like this. Usually, I'm given a very specific set of instructions: Recruit foreign spies. That's it. That's what I do. I identify them, study them, and ally them with the US government. I've been posted all over Northern Europe and the former Eastern Bloc. Long, cold months of meeting assets in back rooms and bars—and then, sometimes, assignments come out of nowhere. *Son of a Bulgarian billionaire, touring Europe, attending a charity ball in Uppsala. Someone's persuaded him into handing over his father's money to buy missile components. Audio and satellite surveillance so far unsuccessful. Need to find out who he's meeting later tonight.* Suddenly, I'm trading in my cargo pants for a government-funded gown. I'm dancing, song after song, before slipping my hands under Alexei's suit jacket, tracing the slope of his chest. My fingers are nimble, delicate, skilled.

Alexei is practically purring. "You know," he murmurs, "you look like that American . . ."

I'm careful to avoid any tension in my shoulders.

". . . actress," he finishes, which is very preferable to *American spy*. "What is her name? The one with the face. The round face. Dark eyebrows, hair of blonde."

"Round face . . ." I pretend to think, distracting him more, my fingers roaming the sides of his body, and—*there*. I stick the miniature audio recorder into the lining of his jacket.

"Ah!" Alexei says, as if he's been stung by a baby wasp, and my muscles ready themselves to block an attack. Internally, I relax as he bleats out, "Ah, I cannot remember her name. You are such a good dancer, my mind is gone."

With a flick of my eyelashes, I thank him.

We don't get wins like this very often: a mission that goes so freakishly smooth, it's like a training exercise. Alexei might as well have been a Farm instructor acting the part of a billionaire. It irks me: the suspicion that the assignment might've gone a little too well. But I was as diligent as possible—and I'll be just as watchful on the way home. When the tech team finally pings my earpiece to confirm that, yep, they can hear everything through Alexei's bug, I deploy a blunt, evergreen excuse.

Need to pee! Goodbye.

Bypassing the bathroom door, I duck down the opposite hallway and slip into the coatroom unnoticed. Everything's choreographed, methodical. I double-check that I'm alone—then I absolutely blitz through the next part. Wig off. Black parka on. High heels off. Rubber ankle boots on. I yank a well-worn pair of cargo pants over my dress, tucking the silken fabric into my waistline. Twenty seconds, that's all it takes, and I'm street ready. Swiping my rucksack from the corner cupboard, I walk slowly but purposefully out of the coatroom—and into downtown Uppsala.

Cold wind and snowflakes nip past my ears, reminding me of Maine: snowshoeing in December; toes freezing before a campfire; that first lick of winter. I yank up the hood on my parka, obscuring the sharp angle of my hair; if anyone starts to trail me, all they'll see is the shape of a person: sleek, possibly athletic, relatively tall.

Luckily, no one follows me to the train station. No one suspicious boards my carriage. No one looks over my shoulder while I pretend to read *Plaza Kvinna* magazine. In the train bathroom, I puff out a tired breath and run my wrists under the tap, scrubbing, until the makeup disintegrates and the black outline of my crescent-moon tattoo becomes visible again. Sometimes this tiny, tiny tattoo feels like the only true marker of who I was.

Splashing a palmful of warm water onto my face, I gaze into the mirror and drag a paper towel over my sticky red lips. Do I look happy?

Maybe that's the wrong question. This job was never supposed to make me happy.

This job was supposed to make me . . . what? Untouchable?

Back in Stockholm, I stop at the first open convenience store and buy a loaf of Swedish cinnamon bread, devouring a third of it on my walk home. Not *home*, exactly. The Stockholm Riverside Hotel has just been someplace to crash for the last two days. It's fine. Way better than the station house in Macedonia, or that hostel in the Balkans. The vending machine makes a decent espresso (if you only care about the caffeine level; *so-caffeinated-that-I-can-predict-the-future* is about the right dosage for me). The hotel carpets are IKEA blue, paintings of extra-furry cows line the halls, and no one really asks any questions besides the occasional "How are you finding your stay?"

Which is good. Obviously.

In the wood-paneled lobby, I shift the grocery bag into the crook of my arm, press the elevator button to 3, and step in at the *ping*. My ankle boots stomp down the hallway, leaving a trail of snowy powder, and when I reach my room (306, by the caffeine delivery machine), I wrench off a mitten, searching deep in my parka for the key.

What's my family doing right now, six days before Christmas, at home in Maine? I can't help thinking about them.

Also . . . I hear something. *Someone.* Right now, in my hotel room.

The noise hits me like a dart to the neck. There has *never* been anyone in my hotel room before. Never, never. Definitely not after a mission.

I knew the assignment went too smoothly! Did someone see me plant audio surveillance equipment on Alexei? Have I been compromised? *Who the hell is in my room?* Bracing myself, I set down the bread, unshoulder my backpack, and reach for my gun. On the other side of the door is a female-sounding voice—and the blare of the television. The intruder is watching something. A game show, maybe? Can that be right? Every few seconds, a bell goes off, like *Ding, ding, ding, you've won a prize!* And the person inside my room lets out a loud, raucous laugh, like Miss Piggy in the Muppets.

This has every hallmark of a trap. And not even a particularly good trap. Shouldn't she, at the very least, be hiding in a closet, ready to spring out and knife me?

Even so, I can't stand out here forever. There's two months' worth of intel in that room, and it's not like I can abandon it. My handler would kill me. If the person in my room doesn't try to kill me first . . .

Suddenly, the television stops.

Then the voice calls out, "That you, Sydney? In here, please."

Her accent is American. Midwestern, by the sound of it. Another trick? My training kicks in like a reflex. Two deep breaths. Compartmentalizing any fear. Grabbing the pistol in my waistband, I sidestep the cinnamon bread and beep the door unlocked. I crack it open, peek inside. Blue carpets, blue walls. A pair of well-worn running shoes, placed by the door, exactly where I left them. Immediately, though, I'm met with the unmistakable scent of meatballs. In a . . . nutmeg-y cream sauce? Which is something that I did not order and have never brought into this room. I round the corner, past the entryway, into—

"Oh, good. You're here."

The woman in my room barely looks at me. She turns her head vaguely in my direction, just enough for me to see the harsh line of her profile. Short, chestnut-colored hair falls around her face. Everything about her says *windswept*, even though she's comfortably seated at the dining table by the TV. She must be about forty years old. Forty-two? Forty-three?

More importantly, I have no idea who the heck she is.

Or why she's ordered so many meatballs. The table's crowded with a platter of smoked salmon, a bowl of spaghetti, and what appears to be venison. Or reindeer?

"I was a bit hungry, so I just ordered everything." The woman shrugs, snapping a room service menu shut and fully looking at me now. Her eyes are hawkish, bright, and might scare the average person. "You eat meat, yes? Should've ordered double, but I didn't know when to expect you back, exactly. Orange juice? There's more food coming. Keep your ears pricked for a knock at the door . . . Aren't you going to sit?"

She gestures at the other dining chair.

"I'm sorry," I say, not sorry at all. Sarcasm bleeds through my voice. "Who are you, exactly?"

"You're not going to shoot me, are you?"

My gun stays in position, pointed at her head, but the slight fear-taste dissipates from my mouth. "Not unless you try to shoot me first."

"Good," she says with a wave of her hand. "That would be very messy. Too much paperwork, and it would probably make the news if you couldn't find somewhere to stash my body quick enough. Not many dumpsters in this city. You'd have to drop me in the river. But then, of course, the river is frozen, so you'd have to drill a hole. Quite time consuming." Grabbing the remote, she changes the channel, watches for roughly twelve seconds, then flicks a finger toward the TV. "What do you think is going on here?"

Nothing as weird as what's happening in here, I think. On-screen, a domestic scene unfolds. It's some sort of Swedish soap opera. Never taking my eyes off the woman with the meatballs, I listen for a short while, as Helga—I think her name's Helga—learns that her lifelong love, Sven, has cheated on her. On their wedding day. With her sister.

"Family drama," I say evenly. A muscle in my jaw feathers. Every few seconds, my eyes flick toward the closet, waiting for an assailant (Alexei? Alexei's contact?) to burst from my winter gear.

"Ah." The woman sniffs and rubs her nose. "I know all about family dramas. I'm supposed to be in Finland right now." She tilts her head toward the neighboring room, as if Finland were just next door. "Skiing holiday. I hate skiing. Too much snow. My son sprained both his wrists on the first day. Would you believe that? *Both* wrists."

"That's . . . awful," I say with just enough empathy, moderating my words. *If you even have a son.* Is she lying to me? Her body language is casual, unassuming; she seems truthful, but those things can be faked. Learned. My mind turns over her vowels, wondering if I can pick any holes in her American accent. Maybe she's putting it on. Is she FSB? Covert ops? At the same time, I wonder if my laptop is still locked in the dresser drawer.

"Yeah, well, it'll give him something to complain about. My son does love to complain . . . Seriously, though, drop the gun. I'm unarmed, see?" She pats down her woolen sweater, which looks so Finnish, it's like a gift shop souvenir. There are lingonberries on it. "Nothing under the table, either, see? Check the closet if you want. Check under the bed. There's no one here. Just you and me and some meatballs, hmm? We're on the same side."

I huff, a wedge of blonde hair falling over my eye. "I'm not just going to trust that you're—"

"Sydney Swift," she says, leaning back in her chair. Her hands fold neatly in her lap, like a school librarian. "Twenty-six years old. Case officer for the CIA. Excellent with languages. Currently turning a defected Albanian criminologist into a workable asset— and just getting back from a Christmas party. Billionaire's son, I believe? Something about missiles? You attended high school in Cape Hathaway, Maine, where you . . . let me see if I remember this right . . . played the flute in the marching band and won the All-State Debate Championship two years in a row. May I show you a picture?"

My mouth dries. *How . . . How in the . . . ?*

Slowly, from underneath the meatball dish, she produces a photograph, sliding it with two fingers across the table. The image shows a sixteen-year-old girl with sun-kissed hair, strong eyebrows, and a mouth full of braces. Her intelligent eyes flick, catlike, toward the camera.

She's clutching a debate trophy.

She's *me*.

"Studied international relations at Bowdoin," the woman plows on, "then Georgetown. Graduated with honors. Your mother passed away when your little sister was a baby—car crash, very sudden—so you were raised by a grandmother and a single father. At The Farm, you scored the third highest in your class in asset recruitment and the second highest in defensive driving. On your personal phone, you have more pictures of a dog named 'Sweetie

Pie' than you do of human beings. No current romantic relationship. In fact, very single. How am I doing so far?"

She's nailed everything. Absolutely everything. My last boy-
friend and I broke up at 2 a.m. in the Langley parking lot, after he
told me it was too difficult dating a spy. And he *was* a spy.

I grind my teeth.

"Fairly well?" the woman says. "I know. Time to sit down."

Her name is Gail Jarvis. Supposedly. Supposedly she is *the* Gail
Jarvis, an associate deputy director at the FBI. From her pocket,
she slowly produces her badge along with a prerecorded video
message from my handler, who doesn't *look* like he's under any du-
ress. (Although admittedly, it's hard to tell; Sandeep is a notoriously upbeat person.) Five minutes into our talk, I return my gun
to my waistband, moderately confident that Gail isn't about to
strangle me with chicken wire. At least, not imminently. Outside
the room, partygoers stamp by, yelling in Swedish about office
party drinks, and room service knocks on the door, delivering two
bowls of yellow pea soup. Gail tips the server and, without making any sudden moves, totters back to the table.

"Oh yes," she says, taking a few sips with a spoon. "That really
is good. Rich. The Swedes do know how to make a nice soup, I'll
give them that." Then she gets back to business. "So I've laid out
the beginning of it. Essentially, I need you to come work for me."

"Temporarily," I recap, hand under my chin. My fingers drum
against my cheekbone. We're in a chess match, Gail and I. Her
move.

"Temporarily," she says.

"As a sort of interagency transfer?"

"Correct."

I give her a look like *Gail, you know that none of this makes sense.*

It involves one squinted eye and a slight mouth tilt. When she doesn't seem to read the expression, I come out and say it, blunt as always. "This doesn't make sense."

Gail stabs a meatball with her fork. "Which parts specifically?"

Should I let her keep the fork? It doesn't pose much of a threat, although theoretically I could take down someone with less. "Let's say you are who you say you are," I begin, threading my hands together and resting them on the table. I've never been in this exact position before, so I'm leaning on my confidence. "Say you really did just happen to be in Finland 'on vacation.'" I use air quotes here. "Which is one heck of a coincidence . . . Why break into my hotel room? Why me? You haven't even told me what the assignment is. Why not select one of your own agents?"

"Can't." She twirls the meatball in cream sauce, making me hungry again. "Things are coming into the FBI and they're not *staying* in. Even the smallest detail of this case is too important to leak. I have suspicions about people in my department."

A too-long pause follows. The FBI doesn't half beat around the bush. "And?" I press. I like to get to the point. "Why do you need me?"

Gail bites through a meatball and swallows thoughtfully. "Well, first of all, you're a woman. I trust women. Not all women, of course, but whenever I'm voting, I vote women, straight down the ballot." She makes a sharp hand motion, like she's slicing through butter.

"That's not an effective way to vote." Even so, one corner of my mouth curves into a reluctant smile. There are so few women in upper-level intelligence roles, they might as well have their own secret handshake.

Gail shrugs. "Works for me. And I did not, as you claim, 'break' into your hotel room. No damage. Just a stolen key from that mess of a lobby. Now, I would say I want you for the job because you're the best. But that would start our relationship on a lie. You know that the CIA and the FBI fight like parakeets, so you aren't my first choice. I have no idea if you're the best. Your file says you're competent in the field, but really, I need you because you're the only one who can reasonably do the job."

In my stomach, mild dread mixes with curiosity, forming a sort of frothy cocktail. This always happens right before my handler doles out an assignment. It's like standing at the open edge of an aircraft, parachute strapped to your back. The ground ripples in a patchwork beneath you, and your breath catches in your throat. "The job is . . . ?"

"See these bags?" Gail responds by way of answer. One of her fingers tugs on the skin below her eyes. It's bluish and papery. "All this case. This *one* case. It feels like I've been following this family for half of my career. First the grandfather, then the father, and now the son. Johnny. Johnny Jones. Ring any bells?"

It does. Organized crime. A family out of Boston. "Should it?"

Gail sucks her teeth. "Oh boy."

"Oh boy, what?"

"I was hoping you knew."

"Knew what?" I ask, irritated.

"You should probably take a deep breath."

"I am breathing."

"Yes, but you aren't breathing *deeply.*"

Okay, my patience has expired. I'm blunt again. "Just say it."

To her credit, Gail does begin to spit it out. "The Jones family is harder to crack than the Italian Mafia. They used to be real broad-spectrum criminals. Gambling, auto theft, racketeering, corruption of public officials, you name it. Started by running everything through a chain of coffeehouses. The grandfather? They called him the Coffee King." She pauses for what seems like dramatic effect. "The last year and a half, though—silence. Everyone thought they'd gone completely underground. Until I started putting the pieces together. Connecting crimes throughout the country, across the Eastern and Western Seaboards and parts of Canada. *Heists.* The family is running heists now."

"Jewelry stores?" I ask, all business, pushing her along.

"Jewelry stores, museums, banks, private residences—millions and millions of dollars. You remember the art museum robbery in St. Louis three months ago? The one where two civilians were shot? *That's* them. I've spent nearly eight years trying to infiltrate their network. I was beginning to think that it couldn't be done, at least not in my lifetime. And then, last week, Johnny Jones—the son—announced he was engaged."

A trickle of panic slopes down my back. "Okay . . ."

"To your sister."

What she's said doesn't make sense at first. Her words don't sound like *words.* I think the television has short-circuited, but nope, it's just my vision. There's a definite blurriness at the edges. "No," I say automatically.

Gail lifts her eyebrows like, *Well, it's true.*

The tips of my fingers go numb, and memories bubble up like acid: Calla and me in elementary school, with our matching lobster-shaped lunch boxes. Calla sticks the tip of her tongue out at me, then says, "Race you to the swings!" Little sister. Best sister.

"That's . . . that's impossible," I tell Gail, unable to keep the tremor from my voice. Which is something that never happens to me. "You're joking."

"Do I look like the type of person who'd pull a rubber chicken from my pocket?"

"No," I repeat, less to her and more to myself. I see Calla and me, on vacation with Grandma Ruby in Acadia National Park. Calla and me, collecting dust bunnies from the attic and calling them pets. The two of us, curled under a quilt after Dad left, me whispering that I'd never let anything bad happen to her ever again. A wave of nausea crashes against my ribs. "No, Calla would *never*—"

"Calla *has,*" Gail interrupts. "I'm sorry she didn't tell you. But the fact remains, your sister is set to marry into one of the most evasive crime families that America has ever produced. And you're going to gather intel on them."

My chin dips, leveling Gail with a stare. "Are you asking me to spy on my sister?"

"See, there we go. Just as your file says. You *are* smart."

Her condescension is like a push into the ice-cold river, and this . . . all of this . . . it's pulling me under. "No. No, I'm not going to do that. You can't ask me to do that."

Gail frowns in a deep line. "Of course I can. I just did."

"She's my *sister*—"

"Who's marrying a suspected felon," Gail supplies. "Yes, I'm well aware. And you may believe that Calla's innocent, completely ignorant of the circumstances—and that's fine. Let yourself believe that. But here are the facts, Sydney. The last heist the Joneses pulled off, a man in his eighties was shoved so hard to the ground, he cracked his skull in three places. He's been in a medically induced coma for over a month, might never wake up, and his dog misses him. Should I show you a picture of his dog?"

My stomach gutters. I know what she's doing. "Stop."

Gail doesn't stop. "His name is Puffin. He's a chocolate Lab, very sad eyes. And another woman in her thirties, she was hit with a stray bullet. Still in the hospital. *Could* survive it, but there's a chance her two kids are going to wake up on Christmas morning without a mother."

A searing ache crawls into my throat. "Gail."

"There's a pattern," Gail plows on. "Every heist is bigger, more dangerous. Each time, casualties increase. Now, we've heard two pieces of chatter in the last forty-eight hours. First, that the Joneses' next heist is on New Year's Eve. And second, it seems that someone in their organization has purchased fifty pounds of C4 on the black market."

Fifty *pounds*? That's . . . enough to blow up a whole series of banks. A whole street. And on New Year's Eve, with the crowds? "Jesus," I whisper.

"This is much bigger than your family," Gail underlines. "With that much C4, *thousands* of people could get hurt. What's the target? What are the Joneses' plans? How can we stop them before they pull off their worst attack yet? Calla's bringing Johnny home to meet your grandmother for the holidays, so you'll have an opportunity to find out. Goody, goody, family time! Pack your bags for Maine."

Carlie Walker attended the University of North Carolina at Chapel Hill, where she first majored in Peace, War, and Defense, a feeder program for intelligence services—before realizing that she is way too anxious to be a spy. Having gone on to study at Oxford University and at City, University of London, she worked briefly in publishing before becoming the bestselling author of eight books for children and young adults. She has a registered 250-pound dead lift, volunteers at a cat shelter, and used to spend her Saturdays practicing martial arts. She lives in Marietta, Georgia, with her husband, young son, and their American dingo.

Ready to find
your next great read?

Let us help.

Visit prh.com/nextread

Penguin
Random
House